Praise for *Artifact Space*

'Now I've read *Artifact Space* I know what it's really going to be like serving aboard an armed interstellar merchant ship, with a smart lead character as my companion. Can't wait for part two'
Peter F. Hamilton

'Take an extremely likeable hero, throw in a clever and engaging re-mapping of real-world naval aviation procedures onto a detailed futuristic canvas, then wrap the whole thing up in a satisfyingly mysterious universe with some intriguing aliens, and you have a winner!'
Alastair Reynolds

'A superb military science fiction adventure, in a fascinating universe'
Garth Nix

'With all the thrills and intrigue of classic Space Opera served with a very modern heart, *Artifact Space* is a wild and hugely entertaining story'
Edward Cox, author of *THE RELIC GUILD*

'An excellent military space opera that serves up the feel of an old-school galactic adventure in a refreshing and cutting-edge style that's fiendishly addictive to read'
Jeremy Szal, author of *Stormblood*

By Miles Cameron from Gollancz

Masters and Mages trilogy

Cold Iron
Dark Forge
Bright Steel

Traitor Son Cycle

The Red Knight
The Fell Sword
The Dread Wyrm
The Plague of Swords
The Fall of Dragons

ARTIFACT SPACE

Miles Cameron

*A tale from the
Arcana Imperii Universe*

This edition first published in Great Britain in 2022 by Gollancz

First published in Great Britain in 2021 by Gollancz
an imprint of The Orion Publishing Group Ltd
Carmelite House, 50 Victoria Embankment
London EC4Y ODZ

An Hachette UK Company

3 5 7 9 10 8 6 4 2

Copyright © Miles Cameron 2021

A CIP catalogue record for this book is
available from the British Library.

ISBN (Mass Market Paperback) 978 1 473 23261 7

Typeset at The Spartan Press Ltd,
Lymington, Hants

Printed and bound in Great Britain by Clays Ltd,
Elcograf S.p.A.

www.gollancz.co.uk

Cross section

500 meters Amidships

0-3
0-2
0-1

Computers and life support

Launch tubes

Fuel

Fuel

Hangar Decks

Hangar Decks

1st Deck
2nd Deck
3rd Deck
4th Deck
5th Deck
6th Deck
7th Deck

500 meters

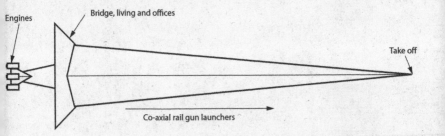

Engines

Bridge, living and offices

Take off

Co-axial rail gun launchers

Stern

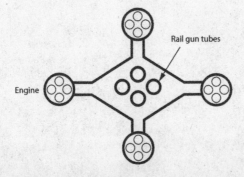

Rail gun tubes

Engine

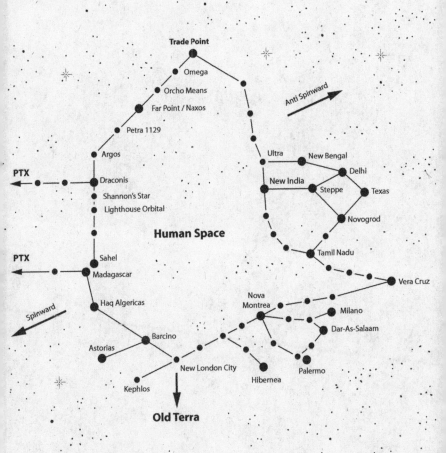

Trade Point

Omega

Orcho Means

Far Point / Naxos

Petra 1129

Argos

PTX

Draconis

Shannon's Star

Lighthouse Orbital

Human Space

Ultra

New Bengal

Delhi

New India

Steppe

Texas

Novogrod

PTX

Sahel

Madagascar

Tamil Nadu

Spinward

Haq Algericas

Vera Cruz

Nova
Montrea

Milano

Barcino

Dar-As-Salaam

Astorias

New London City

Palermo

Hibernea

Kephlos

Old Terra

Anti Spinward

I

'Someone's birthright,' the pawnshop's owner said. He didn't say it with any particular tone of judgement or moral responsibility. He just said it, and rubbed the top of his head. 'It's real?'

Marca Nbaro tried to force herself not to snarl. 'Yes.'

'Like I can trust a junkie,' the man said, but with no more tone than before. He had terrible cerisus and what little hair he had was lank; a failed rejuv.

Nbaro hadn't realised that her stolen 'social assistance' clothing was so bad.

The man pressed a tab in the little statuette. It was of a winged lion, in gold and enamel. A holographic coat of arms sprang into existence.

'Well, well,' he said. 'I guess I could loan you two thousand. Or I'd buy it for three, right now, in cash.' He nodded, coolly, but a faint note of emotion had crept into his tone for the first time, and the emotion was *greed*. 'Someone would kill for this.'

No shit, Nbaro thought.

'Pawn only. I'll be back.'

He shrugged. 'Suit yourself. Not a lot of junkies with patrician patents, eh?'

She held out her tab – a cheap thing, but the best she could afford that wasn't controlled.

'Pawn,' she said.

He shrugged. 'Retinal scan. Or half the amount in cash.'

Retinal scan would leave a real trace. On the other hand, if she'd been tracked as far as the pawn shop, Nbaro was fucked anyway.

'Retinal scan,' she said.

The hacker was next. A former classmate ... Sarah flashed to mind and Nbaro swallowed, hard.

A former classmate had found her the hacker. *A former classmate who'd been sold to a brothel, and wasn't broken. Yet.*

Nbaro walked briskly among the Gothic pillars of the restored *palazzo* under the xenoglas dome. It was the most beautiful place in the world, or at least in her world, which was City, the greatest orbital in Human Space. She was terribly out of place here in her trashy recycle clothes – the kind of clothes that were given away at the care centres, by Social Care and Assistance, to non-citizens, and mendicant citizens, who everyone called SCAMs. She walked quickly and with purpose, because that was her only defence.

If I'm a mendicant, I'll look like a busy one.

Nbaro passed under a light, with its embedded PTZ cameras and an audio link. She put the hood of her recycle jacket up and wondered if every mendicant she'd ever seen was on the run from someone.

If the Dominus is already looking for me, I'm going to show up on every camera in the City.

She might as well have worn her uniform. It was in the disposable spacer's helmet bag she carried. Her Orphanage uniform. It was really the 'Academy of the Hospital for Wards of the State,' but everyone called it the 'Orphanage.' It was supposed to be a finishing school for children orphaned by their parents, dedicated service to the DHC.

In fact, it was hell.

Maybe I'm a fool, Nbaro thought.

But if she was in Orphanage whites, she'd stand out even more.

A Security officer glanced at her and then turned for a better look. He wore dark blue, a flightsuit not unlike those worn by Service, and he had a winged-lion badge.

He waved a hand casually and stepped towards her, and she stopped.

He smiled. 'No begging here, OK?' His voice was pleasant and low.

Nbaro nodded.

'Need me to walk you somewhere?' he asked.

She wasn't taken in by his appearance of friendliness and she ducked her head, shook it, and walked away. She didn't look back, and he didn't follow her.

And there, at the end of the piazza, was her man. He was short, and somehow looked too old and too ... dumb ... to be a famous criminal hacker. But he was at the right table and he had the Old Catholic Bible next to his coffee.

He looked up as Nbaro sat down.

'Hells, kid, you stick out like a fucking starliner in a navy dock.' He looked around. 'I should just leave.'

'I have the money.'

He held up his tab.

Nbaro thumbed hers and the money was transferred. Just like that – two thousand ducats.

Her tab beeped, and he was up.

He glanced at her. 'I did it inside the shore establishment,' he said. 'That ship has a fucking AI. A little advice? Don't fuck with the AIs, sister. A ship AI will protect its own like a mother with a missing child. If that thing gets on to you, you're fucking

3

dead. So I didn't touch the ship. *Katalaveno?*' he asked in Greek. 'Got me?'

'I understand.' *Something else to fear.*

'Good. This is a favour for your friend. The favour is done. *Ciao.*'

Favour my ass. I paid you for this.

Shore Establishment?

That worried her. The Service had a gigantic headquarters, a small orbital of its own, near the New London shipyards. How...?

He turned and walked away into the vast crowd.

In happier times, Nbaro and Sarah had sat here in their uniforms and watched the crowds. Patricians. Spacers. Service. All kinds of people, shopping and chatting, flirting...

Before the Dominus sold Sarah to a brothel.

Before...

Fuck.

Nbaro saw the two men emerge from the web of lifts and alleys behind the facade of ancient Venice across the square. She knew them both. They were part of the Orphanage 'Security', the thugs who roamed the corridors and did as they pleased.

Was it bad luck? Or had they followed her from the pawn shop?

Nbaro dropped her tab on the ground and got down to retrieve it, but instead of standing, she started crawling between the tables towards the arcade of pillars. A tourist noticed her and grabbed her fashionable little backpack away, afraid that the SCAMer would take it; another, a 'gyne from the stations, put their hand on their tab.

Nbaro kept crawling.

I'm so fucking close.

If the hacker had done his job...

4

It was all insane. The risks were insane, but... *No one is taking this away from me. I'll die fighting for it.*

Nbaro needed to get to the main drum of the Old City – to the space-side end. It was a single long lift ride away. That's the way she'd planned it. And she could change in the lift car.

But those two bastards were between her and the lifts.

The dome that held the square of San Marco, as well as most of the original buildings that had surrounded it, sat in its own xenoglas bubble on the outer walls of the cylinder that was the Old City, where it got the full benefit of spin gravity back in the old days before large-scale artificial gravity came in. Every lift and train from the two docksides at the ends of the cylinder ran to San Marco, because that's where every spacer and tourist wanted to be. Underside, with its seedy bars, brothels, and nightlife, was almost directly under their feet, ready to relieve them of their digital ducats in a variety of ways.

Nbaro reached the arcade of pillars and stood up behind one. No security, no thugs. A couple of interested tourists. And the cameras, of course.

She walked along the arcade, head down, trying to blend in. She glanced sidelong at the two Orphanage officers, and kept moving.

They began to scan the piazza. So... they didn't have a tracker on her and they weren't watching her on remotes or using the cameras.

Still in the game.

Nbaro changed her plan. She could go all the way along the arcaded walk to the far end, and then take a tourist lift downstation to Underside. She could catch a lift for Dockside from there, and leave them...

Shit.

They both saw her at almost the same time, and they both smiled.

Nbaro knew what those smiles meant.

This isn't how I want to die.

She dropped caution, and ran.

She was running along the arcaded shopfronts and coffee houses towards the ancient cathedral itself, its strange domes silhouetted by floodlights against the darkness of space. The planet beneath them was just coming into view, the reflected sunlight almost dazzling after the artificial light. The square to her right was full of people, and now she was running *away* from the lifts.

Marca Nbaro was long-legged, and fast, and neither of the Dominus's bruisers was particularly gifted at running. But in three steps, she saw one on his tab, and she knew that her options were narrowing.

I have to try for Dockside, she thought. *Now or never. They can get fifty friends on me in Underside.*

Nbaro put a pillar between herself and her pursuers and turned into a service corridor marked Emergency Personnel Only. She got through the door and already felt she'd made the wrong decision; the door was taking too long to close. And she was taking an absurd risk: she was guessing that there were service corridors behind the shopfront facade.

I'm an idiot.

Nbaro ran. She was behind the row of shops that catered to spacers and tourists in the square, and heads turned, but she ran until she reached a cross-corridor, and then she turned, again, functioning on some innate understanding of how the station was constructed and that there must be some access to the spaces between compartments ...

A ladder, and a lift down. A woman coming out of the lift.

Nbaro leapt past her and pressed the stud and the mesh doors hissed shut. She could hear pounding footsteps, and Bruks, the terror of the hallways back at the Orphanage, appeared around the last corner.

'Nbaro, stop. We can talk this out.' He had a tab in one hand... and a small sub-lethal in the other.

'Talk this out' meant he beat the crap out of her, or he and his partner raped her. Both, probably. Nbaro knew the drill.

The big woman frowned and pressed her override button. The lift sank away into the floor.

For absolutely no reason, the big woman by the lift had just saved her life.

As Nbaro sank away, she heard the woman say, 'You got some ID, buddy?'

The lift had only two stops – up and down – and it sank into the main cylinder of the Old City. For a moment she passed through the old armour plating – massive plates of cerocrete and steel. Then the lift burst into brilliant light and stopped, and the door opened.

A cargo elevator. From an internal loading dock on one of the City's magnificent vacuum canals. Nbaro stepped out onto the loading dock and someone shouted on the dock, but she just kept moving, out through the open hatch and...

'Hells!' she spat.

Nbaro was a long way up in the drum, and from here, with the artificial gravity, the 'sky' was now below her. Which meant that her loading dock was now upside down, and ten thousand metres down.

There was a space skiff, a little hob boat with a simple hydrofus engine sitting against the airlock, dogged in, and being unloaded – recycle crates marked for shops. Nbaro was tempted to steal the boat; she suspected she could.

But that way madness lay. The canal control AI could shut her down in seconds.

This is insane.

Instead of stealing the boat, Nbaro crossed the airlock-bridge and walked out into a street in Underside. When she let the hatch close behind her, the artificial sunlight of the main drum vanished, to be replaced by brilliant LED lighting, and the mixed smells of urine and food.

Back in Underside. The last place she wanted to be.

Nbaro blinked. Her stomach growled, despite everything. But it wasn't a time to hesitate.

She crossed two passages without incident, and she was one short alley from the Underside square when the blow took her in the side of the head.

It hit her hard. Pain flared, and anger with it, and Nbaro rolled as she'd been taught even as a hard hand clenched on her collar.

She went limp. She was, at best, semi-conscious, and it wasn't hard to play to worse. She knew they'd want her alive. *He* would want her alive.

'I got her,' the man said into his tab.

Nbaro rammed her shiv into his groin and ripped up, avoiding his body armour, and severing the artery where the leg joins the trunk. Blood seemed to explode over her outstretched hand, and the man died against her. Nbaro breathed in the exhalation of his last breath; they were close as lovers.

Karlo. Now that's…

No heads turned.

…satisfying…

Nbaro let him fall off her. She was covered in his blood, slick with it. Hands sticky.

I killed him.

I killed him…

No time for that shit now.

Nbaro was behind a restaurant, or a taverna; it was an alley she'd used as a short cut to the square before, and the litter of

8

condoms and other toys suggested that other people used it for various other purposes, too. But the taverna had a kitchen, and the kitchen door was open so the cook could smoke something.

By luck, he stepped out. He glanced her way ... and then deliberately turned his back on her and lit something.

Nbaro was tempted to cross herself. Instead, she slipped past him and inside – kitchen, washroom. It was tiny, and filthy, and she didn't have time to be careful.

The dirty little washroom didn't have a camera. That much she checked before she stripped and pulled on the Service Blue coveralls of the very lowest ranking officer. A midshipper. She washed her face as fast as she could, attempted to dry it with a recycle towel that did nothing to take water away. She got her feet into the regulation boots she'd bought on the black market. They were too big.

The little stall had a mirror, and she looked in it. There was blood beside her mouth, and three spots like caste marks on her forehead, and she cleaned it again.

No time. No time. Once they find the body...

There was blood under her nails.

Nbaro pulled on her Orphanage gloves, which were white, and correct with the coverall.

'Midshipper Marca Nbaro,' said the woman in the mirror. 'Reporting aboard.'

She sounded good. She was surprised at herself; ninety seconds ago, she'd ripped the life out of a man she hated.

'Reporting aboard,' she said again.

Nbaro walked right out the front of the restaurant, and her Service Blue was suddenly like armour; Security didn't even look at her. Spacers smiled, or frowned, but they got out of her way.

She walked two shabby blocks to Underside Square, pushed through the crowd, and boarded a lift.

Should have worn this from the start.

9

I over-thought it. As fucking usual.

In ten minutes, Nbaro collected the rest of her baggage at a locker in Space Side – a duffel and a longer, non-regulation bag – and then, without letting herself think about it, she was at Dockside. She saluted the Shore Patrol station and was passed without an ID check; the Marine on duty saluted.

That stung, somehow.

All her bags had to go through sniffers and scans, and the sailor at the security scanner grinned.

'Nice swords, miz,' she said.

Nbaro tried to smile back, but the fear was too much. She heard the lift doors open behind her, and she made herself collect her bags, nod to the sailor, and moved to the nearest brow in near zero *g*, a long umbilical of reinforced plastic running through the vast open space of the Docks to the matt black of the ship that hung above her by a hundred such connections.

'Officers' brow, miz,' the sailor on the security sensor said. 'That's for enlisted.'

Nbaro could barely see the greatship; the thick plastic umbilical hadn't been built for tourists. And she had a moment of panic, because this wasn't in any sim, and she didn't know which brow to take.

Another spacer in a bright yellow harness for moving cargo raised an eyebrow.

'First time, miz?' he asked. 'That one.'

Nbaro gave him a grateful, distracted nod.

Christ.

She couldn't stop herself from looking back at the lifts.

No one she knew. But three men, heavy…

Keep going.

Nbaro entered the access tunnel and it seemed to run forever, rising above her in the very low gravity. She climbed hand over hand, keeping one hand for the ship at all times as she'd been taught remorselessly. Her duffel bobbed along with her, accelerating when she moved too fast and then tugging at the short tether that held it to her like a faithful pet in a holo performance. Her sword bag looked as if it might hold a musical instrument – broad like the bell of a trumpet at one end, tapering away to narrow enough for the neck of a guitar.

It was surprisingly cold in the plastic tunnel. Simulations never seemed to match reality; in the sims...

My experience in sims is going to be the death of me.

Nbaro had expected everything to be... cleaner. Neater. And warmer, to say the least.

At least there was air. Very cold air.

She looked back down the long tunnel to the Dockside. She half-expected pursuit, or arrest, or an announcement...

Maybe, just this once, something worked.

Nbaro smiled nervously, and continued to tug herself along. She was alone in the brow; it was a routine dockside day, and the vast cargo ship wasn't even loading for its next run yet. Most of the crew would still be in City with their families.

She'd timed it that way. Sort of.

The spin of City was imparted to all of the habitable portions, but the greatships docked at the non-spin ends. Nbaro had grown up watching them from the Orphanage; they were so large that they were visible from almost anywhere, extending for kilometres past the City's docks and drum. And they were distinctive. Greatships were shaped like sword blades, needle-sharp at the bow where their railgun tubes opened, and tapering to broad hilts to support the massive engines. They weren't aerodynamic, precisely, but they were built to support enormous velocities – up to 0.3c – when even interstellar particles and monatomic hydrogen needed to be brushed aside. They were so big that at sub-light speeds they had drag, and needed to be shaped accordingly. City might have hundreds, even thousands, of ships in its merchant and military fleets, but there were only nine greatships, and she knew all of them: *Dubai* and *Athens*, *New York* and *Venice*, *Hong Kong* and *Tokyo*, *London* and *Samarkand* and *Tyre*.

And now Marca Nbaro was going to serve on one.

Imposter.

She looked back again. She was going to make it.

Maybe.

At last, Nbaro got to the end of the tether and linked her feet to the little platform. Despite the presence of atmosphere in the long plasteel tunnel, there was an airlock. Of course. She felt foolish for not imagining an airlock. But there wasn't a sim for *boarding*. She had to play this by ear. Her one ride on a Service warship had been completely different, and she'd gone aboard while it was hard-docked to station.

She put a hand on the amber plate beside the lock. It was cold, right through her uniform gloves, but the chip in her palm was read by the device, and the airlock hissed open. Her big duffel coasted past her from some motion of her shoulders, and then fell to the airlock deck with a thud.

Artificial gravity. The boundary felt funny as she crossed the line from the brow to the deck.

And then Marca Nbaro was aboard the *Athens*.

She couldn't budge the grin from her face, despite the conflict between delight and anxiety. The lock closed behind her and she glanced up at a beautiful tell-all, a baroque brass or bronze instrument that looked handmade, and was fitted with a cut crystal screen. The instrument, and the inner hatch, radiated age and craftsmanship. And careful maintenance.

I'm here.

The telltale went from red to amber to green, and as it passed into green Nbaro put her gloved hand on the inner plate and was rewarded with a deep, musical sound like a bell.

The inner hatch, etched on every brazen blade with a pattern of acanthus leaves like something from a museum, irised open, the blades sliding over each other almost instantly. It took Nbaro's breath away, and with it what remained of her composure, so that she eventually went through the inner airlock like a startled rat, clumsily dragging her duffel.

Training and constant repetition saved her, and she faced aft automatically and snapped a crisp salute, despite the fact that she couldn't see anything like the banner of the DHC floating in the hard vacuum of space. That salute was a ceremony older than space, and she knew it.

Nbaro relished it, just a little.

I'm doing this.

Salute complete, she turned to face the officer of the deck, who stood casually in a shipboard uniform of midnight-blue coveralls just like hers, except with two thin gold lines at each cuff.

'Midshipper...' Nbaro's voice came out like a pen nib scratching paper, and she cleared her throat. 'Midshipper Marca Nbaro reporting aboard,' she said.

Here we go.

The officer's mouth twitched – not quite a smile, and yet quite friendly, in a military way.

'Welcome aboard, Ms Nbaro,' he said. 'You're very early.'

He was a first lieutenant, and thus far enough above her that she had to be careful.

'Yes, sir,' she said.

Nbaro was tempted to say, '*Sir, I overthink everything and I'm not always the best with people and a lot of what you're about to read is a lie and I may be pursued so I thought I'd come aboard all by myself, and you know, the Orphanage is a wretched place and I've waited my whole life to be here...*'

She was distracted and missed what he was saying. Her brown skin flushed.

I am an idiot. This isn't going to work. This is insane.

The lieutenant smiled. 'He'll be here in a moment. First time aboard the *Athens*?' he asked, as if she was a person.

'Yes, sir,' she said.

He's going to see through me.

'Tab, please,' he said.

Nbaro fought down her terror.

What can they do to me if they catch me? Throw me out? To the hells with them all if they try.

She stripped off her uniform glove and saw there was still blood under her nails, but it was too late. She reached into her coverall pocket and produced her tab – the smallest and cheapest authorised by the Service: no AI; barely capable of reading all the required systems. Far more expensive than she could afford. And it carried the big lie. The hacker's lie.

Poverty, pawnbroker's records, a tab ducat balance of minus 6. And a criminal hack job.

Why?

Oh, right: no choice.

Nbaro waited for some little dig about her cheap tab, or for his keen eyes to take in the dried blood, but he took the tab and looked it over.

'Codes, please,' he said.

Same as the Orphanage; not that she'd ever owned such a device as an orphan. A few others had.

The ones who co-operated.

Nbaro typed in the code.

He ran the screen across some sort of reader. He made a face. She could smell her own sweat.

'You're not in the system,' he said. 'AI says …' He raised an eyebrow. 'Ah.'

Nbaro couldn't breathe.

Oh. Fuck.

'Ah, I see. Morosini just updated from the Shore Establishment and there you are.'

He shrugged, as if this sort of thing happened every day, and handed the tab back.

'Now you're in the system. Your tab has your codes, your stateroom location, your workspace, your battle station, and a whole lot of SOP that I recommend you read as soon as you have a chance.'

Nbaro nodded. Incredulous.

'Yes, sir.'

That's all? It worked? Some two-bit hacker in Castello made it work?

'We've downloaded your retinal scan, fingerprints and palm print. Any door that ought to open to you will. If it doesn't, it shouldn't. You can no doubt find your own way to your stateroom on O-3, but I'm getting you a guide. *Athens* is a lovely ship, but she's had several hundred years to become a labyrinth.'

Now her brain was starting to function, and so Nbaro began to take in the formal quarterdeck: the magnificent bronze statue of Athena, an ancient Terran goddess; the dark blue velvet that covered the protective matting that lined every bulkhead and every corridor on any City ship; the crisp bronze edging, sometimes intricately decorated with acanthus leaves; the oil paintings of past Masters of the *Athens*, more than twenty of them. At some point in the testing for her assignment she'd memorised all their names, but they were gone now, learnt and dumped like a lot of celestial navigation and a whole pile of mathematics.

It was all *old*. And unbelievable.

I'm here.

The officer of the deck was smiling broadly.

'We're so glad you like our ship,' he said.

'It's incredible,' Nbaro said. 'Sir.'

'You don't know the half of it,' he said. 'It really *is* incredible. I've been aboard four years and I'm not sure I've seen her stem to stern.'

She was looking at the paintings. One of Elena Svaro was quite old, done in an impressionist style no one would use any more, and she had been painted in powered combat armour, faceplate open, the hump of her armoured air tank rising over her left shoulder like a wing. Nbaro thought Svaro had been the second captain; certainly the Svaros were one of the most powerful patrician clans. Ancient, too. Powered armour had gone out when EMP beams came in.

'My ancestor.' The officer offered her his hand to clasp. 'I'm Anthony.' Nbaro flinched, and then took it. 'Anthony Svaro,' he added. 'You may call me Anthony off duty.'

She nodded, overwhelmed. 'Sir.'

She glanced at the sixth captain.

Ricardo Nbaro. My own ancestor.

His blue-black African face held an open friendliness that carried across the centuries and accused her of being too closed, too reticent.

Guilty, ancestor, but also here to make changes. I can do this. Let me try.

The aft compartment hatch chimed, its crystal tell-all flashing through the cycle, and a small man in a tight jumpsuit came through, his sleeves rolled up to reveal intricate tattoos, some of which moved, and all of which defined muscles that spoke of constant training in high *g*.

'Petty Officer Locran, if you'd be so kind as to take Midshipper...?'

'Nbaro, sir,' she said.

He really was treating her like a person. Nbaro wasn't used to it and she was suspicious. What did he want?

'Just so ... Midshipper Nbaro to her stateroom, please.' He paused.

Here it comes.

'Where's the rest of your kit, Miz Nbaro?'

I have no kit. I have sixteen demerits and I'm not even a cadet any more. If they catch me, I won't be disciplined, I'll be sold. Or killed. Stop that.

'I'll bring it aboard when I settle in,' she said. 'Sir.'

The duty officer nodded. 'Carry on, Miz Nbaro.'

The rating smiled affably. 'Come with me, Miz Nbaro.'

She hefted her duffel, which was *much* harder to move in artificial gravity. Weight and mass – they were not the same thing at all. She got it on her shoulder with the other bag, which was strapped to her back. Naturally, it caught in the hatchway.

'I can take one of those, miz,' Petty Officer Locran offered.

Nbaro bent over enough to get the tapered end of the bag through the hatch and also managed to get her legs *over* the knee-knocker. Every compartment was airtight, and the bulkheads that held the hatches rose as much as twenty centimetres above the deck; she heard the hatch iris close behind her, and the flash of light reflecting from it threw a brilliant spray of colour over the bulkheads, which were themselves covered in decoration.

'I've got it,' she said.

Locran said nothing; just led her along a series of passageways. The tiles and carpeting changed under her feet, and the straps of her luggage and the management of it kept her from seeing much else, so she watched as the green and white parquetry tiles gave way to black and white, and then dark blue and gold.

Locran paused in the hatch, which was dogged-open, an old sea-cant phrase that meant the iris was locked wide, only the knife edges of the xenoglas gleaming in the golden light of the overhead lamps.

'Blue-tile,' he said quietly, with something that sounded like reverence.

Marca Nbaro had passed every examination they could throw at her, done every simulation available, but she didn't know what 'blue-tile' meant, beyond that it was the most luxurious combination so far. Even the ducts running along this passageway were brightly polished; old alloys of copper and brass that pre-dated the xenoglas tubes that glowed overhead. Scenes from ancient Terran mythology were painted along the bulkheads as murals, the florid style somehow at peace with the polished brass and copper. Right in front of her, a fire hose access port, polished like a beer tap in a very expensive taverna, emerged from a Satyr's loins, and she grinned at the visual joke.

Nbaro considered asking about it, but Locran hurried along. The opulent passageway wasn't wide, by any means, and every frame of the ship had its own dogged-open iris and its own bronze battle lantern, perfectly polished and throwing the same golden light as the modern xenoglas.

'Shit,' Locran whispered. 'Brace!'

That was one command one heard all too often at the Orphanage. Nbaro turned and stood at attention against the muraled bulkhead, shoulders pressed in between two fauns.

Three officers came through a dark bronze hatch. Two of them were commanders – beings so senior to Nbaro as to be both perilous and alien – and the third was a captain, the highest rank in the DHC Service. They were all tall, all dark-haired; one strongly male, one androgyne, and one female. The woman had been speaking, and was caught in mid-sentence.

'...nothing if we go back in the green,' said the lighter voice.

'Nah,' the 'gyne said, navigating the knee-knocker.

They stopped.

'Locran?'

'Sir?' her guide responded.

'And who's this?' the softer-voiced androgyne asked. They had wide shoulders, a hint of breasts, narrow hips. And long legs and torso. Most 'gynes came from orbitals.

'New midshipper, tir.'

Locran spoke over her, using the respectful 'tir' for the non-gendered, thus relieving Nbaro of making any hasty decisions.

The tall man didn't even glance at her.

'Locran, is it? You know the regulations for using the Blue-tile, do you not?'

Nbaro knew that pompous tone. She'd heard it all her life.

The tallest of the three officers was the 'gyne. They gave an eye roll.

'XO, do you have to play the game? We're in port and Locran's actually working.' They winked.

Nbaro got that one. The XO was the Executive Officer; the second in command of the ship. She knew who he was from her studies; Captain Rajiv Aadavan.

The man addressed as XO grunted. He returned to conversation with the other officers and shrugged.

'I expect I'll be downing a pint before anyone has to make the decision. Why do these things happen on my watch?'

'You're a goose,' the woman replied and Nbaro saw the captain flush, as if the teasing comment actually insulted him. And then they were gone at the next intersection, a cross-corridor that ran from the starboard side main passageway to the port-side main passageway.

'Lucky,' Locran breathed, and they passed the intersection themselves, the androgyne's voice carrying until they were through another iris valve and into another green and white chequerboard passageway.

Locran breathed out a long sigh, and flashed her a smile.

'My apologies, miz,' he said. 'I thought, as we was on shore watch only, that we could…' He shrugged. 'Cut through Blue-tile.'

'Blue-tile, Petty Officer Locran?' she asked.

He seemed nice enough that Nbaro could risk revealing this small piece of ignorance, and she was determined not to be afraid of everything. Determined. Besides, his shoulder flash said Intel and she was Flight. She'd probably never see him again; there were ten thousand people in the crew of a greatship.

'Blue-tile, miz.' He looked both ways, as if imparting a secret. 'Master's command spaces, miz.'

Almighty, what else didn't they teach me? she wondered.

'Thanks,' she said. 'Forbidden?'

'Well,' Locran said with a slight smile, 'restricted. Master's pretty lenient if you have a compelling reason.' He shrugged. 'And that was Mister Aadavan. He's the XO and he can make your life…' The petty officer smiled. 'Interesting.'

Nbaro nodded. No one in her life at the Orphanage had ever used the word *lenient*. But *interesting* sounded normal – and bad.

'Cheers, miz,' he said. 'Come on, let me carry that.'

She flushed. 'Thank you, Petty Officer Locran, but I have them.'

He nodded, as if dismissing their moment of intimate communication.

'Very well, miz. This way.'

They took a cross-corridor towards the spine of the ship. The *Athens* – she'd memorised the ship's vitals as part of her examinations – was more than nine kilometres long, and had her own gravity system. Her decks were stacked like planet-side buildings, bow to stern on the enormous ship, instead of being stacked like a wedding cake, the way smaller ships had to be to take on a simulation of gravity when under thrust. She had sixteen main decks, six above her main flight tubes and massive cargo bays, numbered O-1 to O-7 as you went 'higher', and ten decks below called First Deck through Tenth Deck, the tenth being 'lowest' in the realm of artificial gravity, except that everything below fifth deck was a warren of giant holds, some without artificial gravity, some without air, all the realm of the Cargo office. Most of the decks had engineering spaces towards the stern, where the four giant power plants and the enormous subordinate reactors were a kilometre deep on almost every deck and level.

Each deck except the open cargo/flight deck had two main passageways, one on either side of her spine and the massive railguns that ran the whole length of the ship. The cross-corridors went either over or under the railgun tubes. Subsidiary passageways, some so narrow that two crewers couldn't pass abreast, ran off the main passageways and sometimes off the cross-corridors, although the enormous electromagnets of the railguns and the super-cooled quantum computers at the heart of the ship's function filled most of the spaces on the centreline. The overhead of the cross-corridor had straps running along the walls and the overhead.

'Petty Officer Locran, does the ship ever operate without artificial gravity?' she asked.

Locran nodded. 'Combat. Battle drills. Some station man-oeuvres.' He nodded at the straps. 'Have you been in the Black, miz?'

Nbaro nodded. 'Yes,' she said. 'While training. I've been to Tooler and Kephlos.'

That was actually true. She knew they were both small pota-toes: Tooler was the massive orbital yard over New London, the major inhabited planet in the same system as City; Kephlos was the extensively mined gas giant a single jump away. That experience was real, too. Her only live experience of the Service.

'Been out?' he asked. He meant *out* of the environment, in a suit.

She hitched her bags again. 'Yes.'

'Like it, miz?'

In truth, her shakedown cruise to Kephlos had been made a living hell by two young men determined to bed her by whatever means they could, and equally determined to make it a competition in which she was a prize, not a participant. They were both patricians and both bigger than her, so she'd had to be very careful indeed. One of her more successful tactics had been volunteering for every single Extra-Vehicular Activity that was available.

'I have my pin,' she said.

The air-bottle pin meant the wearer was fully qualified for EVA.

He flashed a grin. 'Outstanding.' He sounded as if he meant it.

'And I like it,' she admitted.

EVA was humbling, in a way that she imagined staring straight into the eyes of one of the ancient gods might be humbling, but she liked it.

'Ever used a drop-shaft?' he asked.

'No,' she said sheepishly.

Drop-shaft? How many details hadn't she learnt? How much would she have to pretend to know, and learn on the fly? How in twenty freezing hells had she missed a detail like this?

'We can climb a ladder or even take an elevator up to O-3, but you might as well learn to use the zero-g shafts now.' He looked back at her. 'They're fun,' he said, sounding less than professional. 'And we only have them on greatships. The moment you step off, you're in zero g. It's important to swing off onto a handhold and be sure you have a good anchor. Then you can kick off or use the rungs. Don't just float into the shaft – they're big enough that you can float around for a while, and people will mock the shit out of you.'

No doubt they will anyway, Nbaro thought bitterly. Mockery was the social currency of the Orphanage, the punishment for every infraction.

She watched him lean out, grab a rung beside the entrance, and then swing over into zero *g*. In a moment he had gone from vertical to horizontal, his feet facing her. It was odd, but she understood the concept. She stepped after him and grabbed the other rung, and her duffel slammed into her head. She almost lost her grip and fought down panic, embarrassment – all the usual things.

'Fuck,' she squeaked.

'Miz, I could take that duffel now,' he said.

Nbaro was sure he was trying to help her.

'No thanks,' she said.

This time his smile was more *suit yourself* than *yes, miz*.

He kicked off with the ease of long experience. Almost any born and bred citizen of City had used zero *g* since adolescence, but Locran was truly expert. He passed through the shaft like a porpoise swimming in Old Terra's seas.

Nbaro started down the rungs of the ladder set into the sides of the shaft, moving far more carefully. She kept one hand for the ship and thus moved slowly, while Petty Officer Locran made it to his target platform with one kick and a balletic landing, rotating in the middle like an acrobat.

She managed in minutes what took him seconds.

'Watch when you step through, miz, there's gravity,' he said.

He went through and Nbaro watched as his uniform flightsuit changed in gravity, the billowing of the legs and midsection suddenly gone as the fabric fell.

She stepped through and managed to misjudge her luggage once again, and it fell far enough to unbalance her.

Locran's arm shot out, caught one of her luggage straps and hauled her onto the O-3 level.

'Officer country,' he said, as if he hadn't just saved her from floating back out into the drop-shaft.

Without asking again, he snaked the duffel off her shoulder and threw it over his own.

Nbaro flushed with embarrassment. One of the absolute rules of the Orphanage was to never, ever make anyone do menial labour to serve you. She hadn't been aboard an hour and here was a senior rating carrying one of her bags. She felt she'd failed a test.

Locran seemed unbothered as he headed along the cross-corridor to the main passageway, after a hundred metres of green and red tile.

'O-3 level, Port Side main passageway, Section 5, frame 0333 aft,' he said. 'That's you. So, this is the—'

'The Port Side Aft main passageway,' Nbaro said in a rush, to prove that she understood what he was saying. 'Five kilometres from the bow, frames counted from forward to aft.'

'Yes, miz.' He pointed forward. 'The Space Operations Centre and the Combat Information Centre are on this passageway because we're directly below the Tower. Further forward, you'll find all the flight ready rooms on O-2 and O-3. You'll basically live on this passageway.' He grinned. 'After all, it's ten klicks long.'

He led the way, and they irised through two hatches and past the next cross-corridor; Nbaro read a few of the plaques on side-hatches: Onboard Logistics; Main Cargo; Small Cargo . . .

She wasn't a Cargo officer but she knew they were very important. They controlled the load and the unload, and they bought and sold with full authority from the DHC; in some instances, they outranked the Master. Her cabin was on the same corridor as the Cargo offices. So noted.

Locran pointed at a side hatch. It was painted green and had a blank brass plaque and an elaborate floral decoration cast into

24

the airtight door. A personal cabin didn't rate an iris. She put her still-gloved hand to the touch plate and a bell rang, indicating that she had permission to enter. The heavy, airtight metal door pivoted beautifully on its hinges; it was incredibly old-fashioned, and so was the stateroom beyond.

'Miz, you must have won some sort of lottery,' Locran said. He was still standing in the passageway. 'A two-rack? For a midshipper?' He smiled to show that he meant no offence.

Nbaro shook her head in awe. 'I've never...'

She was used to sharing her bunk room with twenty-four other orphans, all wards of the DHC. On her shakedown cruises, the six-acceleration-couch staterooms had seemed lonely. This was unthinkable luxury.

She looked into the cabin, with two acceleration couches – often called crash-couches or racks. They sat one atop the other like old-fashioned bunks, in a frame of bronze, steel and carbon laminate that allowed both couches to rotate through every axis. The couches themselves were made of a respondent gel, and they were equipped with straps and injectors for high-g survival. They looked like baroque torture devices and their elaborate outer decoration, while beautiful in a clockwork, rococo way, gave Nbaro a moment's unease.

The stateroom was completed by two fold-down desks, and one fold-out chair as well as one that moved. It seemed difficult to believe that half of all this space was just for her.

Nbaro turned back.

'Oh, please come in, Petty Officer Locran.'

He smiled without mirth. 'No, thanks, miz. No enlisted in an officer's private space. Double that for opposite sex, miz.'

'Oh.' Nbaro flushed again and felt foolish. 'I'm sorry...'

He shook his head. 'When you been in the Deep Black three months with nothing to do but watch-standing,' he said, 'all the rules will make more sense. Miz.'

Three months. She was aboard the Athens, *and they would travel. For two years. Or more.*

'Thanks, Petty Officer Locran,' Nbaro said formally. She was still taking in the … the … richness. There was a beautifully framed *wooden* panel between the upper and lower crash-couches, and another decorative panel over the desk that proved to be a small hatch.

The only jarring note was that one desk was open and on its polished metal surface sat a stack of rather incongruous recyclable boxes marked in katakana. The Japanese script was familiar enough throughout the Human Sphere; she could even read some. These were screens.

Locran followed her glance.

'We're installing new screens ship-wide,' he admitted. 'Sometimes the old equipment isn't …'

He shrugged, unwilling to say anything against his ship. Greatship sailors were famous for their loyalty to their vast hulks.

Nbaro went to the far bulkhead. The decoration and the bronze edging had fooled her; there was supposed to be a screen here – a surprisingly large one for the amount of wall space available. The edges would cover a handful of pipes, one of which was surprisingly warm to the touch. The other was shielded by xenoglas protective fibre and was still cool.

The bulkhead itself was covered with the remains of a decorative fresco – a scene of some ancient god waving a sword. But that was obviously meant to be concealed behind the screen.

She looked at the boxes. Good screens weren't cheap, and the ones stacked on the desk looked expensive.

She threw her bags on the upper acceleration couch, automatically assuming that she would be junior to anyone entering the cabin with her – bunk, or in this case, crash-couch location being a sign of social status everywhere she'd ever been, and 'Midshipper, Orphanage-trained' being the lowest life form of which she was aware. New London and City Academy gradu-ated their officers the same day, staggered by grade-point average so that each new midshipper had their starting seniority based on their performance. The Orphanage graduated a full day after, ensuring every single Orphanage graduate was outranked by any graduate from the academies.

Which is a technicality anyway, since I didn't graduate.

Nbaro turned back to Locran.

'I'm sorry to keep you, Petty Officer Locran, but is there a... workshop? Where I can get my screens cut?'

Locran gave his slightly patronising smile. 'You think you can install your own screens?' he asked.

Nbaro shrugged. 'Yes?' She was annoyed at the uncertain rise at the end of the word.

Locran didn't lose the smile. He looked at her for quite some time, and she flushed.

'Miz, if I could... arrange for them to be cut –' he glanced over his shoulder – 'in exchange for a favour.'

Well, that was familiar ground.

'No sex,' she snapped.

He looked shocked. 'Miz!' he protested. 'I was thinking pie. Officers get pie and cake, in their mess.'

Nbaro deflated, and her hand, reaching for her shiv, fell away. She was shaking with adrenaline, ready to go. To fight.

'Sorry, miz,' he said. He looked as if he might say more.

She blinked, focused, pushed away all the bad thoughts. She'd promised herself a new start; promised herself she would be less afraid. Be an officer.

'Pie and cake can be managed,' she said.

Smile. Make them like you. This is it, you have one shot.

'Then let's see what we can do,' he said. 'Come with me, miz.'

Nbaro followed him out, clicking her beautiful hatch closed, and hearing the closed-and-locked chime sound softly. She almost wanted to go back inside, to touch everything again.

He walked her forward along the passageway, which seemed to stretch on forever past the Cargo offices and the Logistics office again, and then some unmarked hatchways that looked like more staterooms and storage.

Left at a cross-corridor, towards the outer hull. They were near frame 120, well forward; she couldn't exactly leave breadcrumbs, but she was trying to follow along in her mental picture of the ship.

Locran stopped.

'There's your ready room. You'll be there all the time. And this is EVA Rigging – all the spacesuits and anything you'll need for space operations are in this shop.'

They took a turn to the right into a very narrow corridor, like one of the alleys in the seedier inner parts of the City, and through a dogged-open hatch; inside, the space extended up into the level above, forming a high loft for storage. EVA suits hung in near-infinite rows – at least six high above her – all on some sort of rail system so that any suit could be dialled up and summoned.

'Hey,' Locran called.

A young woman, not much older than Nbaro, came around a counter.

'Spacer Chu,' Locran said formally. 'Midshipper Nbaro.'

Chu frowned. 'Miz?' she asked.

'Midshipper Nbaro wants to install her own screens,' Locran said.

'Got the measurements?' Chu asked, all business.

Nbaro felt foolish. 'I can get them.'

Chu shrugged. 'Then sure, miz. I got nothin' else goin'. It's shore watch.'

'Slice o' pie?' Locran asked.

Chu looked pained.

'For a new spacer? I'll hook Ms Nbaro up, *hakuna matata*.' She made a shooing motion. 'Get the measurements, miz. I'll warm up the table.'

Nbaro was aware that a spacer, who was vastly inferior in rank, was giving her orders. On the other hand, the woman was most definitely doing her a favour.

'I'm on it.'

'And bring the screens,' Chu said.

Nbaro considered a variety of responses to that, and settled for '*Hakuna matata*.'

'I'll leave you to it, then,' Locran said.

Nbaro waited until they reached the main corridor junction, then said, 'I appreciate your time.'

'Know your way back and forth?' Locran asked.

'Yes, Petty Officer Locran,' she said.

He nodded. 'Good. Welcome aboard, miz. One more word? *Athens* is old. There's ... things here. And places you don't go. At least, not alone. Not until you have your space legs. Right? Mister Svaro assigned me to you. Hit the call button on your intro app and I'll report to your stateroom.'

'Oh,' Nbaro said. 'Is this bad duty?'

He made a face. 'Not so bad, miz.'

She nodded in what she hoped was a crisp and officer-like manner.

'Very well,' she said. 'Thanks, Petty Officer Locran.'

'*Hakuna matata*, miz,' he said with a smile.

Nbaro walked back to her new quarters with a thrill to have her own space, and find it exactly where she expected it. She had a tape measure in her bag, along with a cheap multi-tool manufactured on New London. It was based on originals made in far-off India, on Old Terra, from far superior metal. The steel of her multi-tool was soft, but sufficient for unscrewing the latten edging meant to hold the nanoscreens; after the decorative edging was removed, she measured the inside tracks, and even worked out where one screen would need to be flexed to get past the pipes.

Nbaro noted it all on her new tab, picked up the stack of screen boxes and carried them down the passageway, meeting no one. She turned at the correct corner, seeing every frame had a little sign indicating its number and location, like street signs in City. It was a simple thing, but she felt another little thrill of accomplishment getting to the workshop. Just the stroll from her stateroom to the workshop reminded her that the ship was *vast*.

The hatch was still dogged-open, but this time she caught a glimpse of the door-plate.

'EVA Rigger' it said.

The interior of the shop was as elaborate as the rest of the ship; one full wall was dominated by a screen, which was playing a popular drama with second-rate swordplay, but the rows of EVA suits hung on elaborate trifold bronze hooks that were themselves affixed to the bulkhead on rails of blue molybdenum steel; a glance up confirmed that EVA suits could be accessed in three dimensions, running on those rails.

'Petty Officer Chu?'

'Spacer Chu,' the woman said. She'd been sitting at a very old-fashioned sewing machine. 'Might test for petty officer next year. Let's see what you got.'

With the kind of technical competence that Nbaro most admired, the other woman stripped the protective coating off the screens and then fitted them together on a big nanotable that dominated the centre of the shop. She put the measurements into the table from Nbaro's tab.

'Looks right,' she said. 'You sure?'

'Yes,' Nbaro said, forcing back her instinct to go and measure again. She'd measured twice.

The rigger-tech nodded, took a xenoglas knife, and made six cuts, including the notch to fit the pipes. Then she picked up a nanoreader of some sort, turned it on, and ran it along all the outer edges. Nanoreaders really had no nano-tech at all. They were powerful laser cutters that also carried the electronic signatures to 'open' and 'close' nano material couplers, but everyone called them 'nanoreaders'. Another mystery of the DHC.

'Let's go install it,' she said, and the two of them went back down the passageway to her stateroom.

'You're an EVA rigger?' Nbaro asked.

'I'm striking for it. I'll get there eventually. I'm good at the craft – my ma's a rigger. But I have trouble with all the maths.' She shrugged.

'Oh, gods above, maths,' Nbaro said in genuine sympathy. Functions still gave her a headache.

'Yes, miz. And you're Flight?'

'Yes,' Nbaro said. 'So I may actually get an EVA suit.'

'Got your bottle pin, miz?'

'I do.'

The rigger shot her a smile. 'Me too. Here we are.'

Nbaro opened her hatch. 'Can you come in?'

'Not supposed,' the rigger said. 'But we're working, and we're both female. The sky won't fall.'

She stepped over the knee-knocker with grace and began pressing the cut panels into place, while Nbaro used her multitool to put the very low-tech, pedestrian and effective screws back into the decorative edging to mount them.

'Nah,' the spacer said. 'Hold it, miz.'

Nbaro did as she was told.

The rigger fed the screens into the clips until it was all up.

'Good fit. But I have to join the panels into one screen, right?'

Nbaro felt foolish, but the rigger didn't seem annoyed. She turned on the reader, checked its feed, and then pulled on black gloves and took a small black rebreather out of her waist-pack.

'Best stand outside, miz,' she said.

It was probably more than a hundred years since there'd been an accident with nanotech, but the Service had safety procedures and Chu clearly believed in them.

Nbaro stepped out, and in less than a minute, Chu waved her back. She was already packing her tools.

'Nice. I'll report this as completed. It's not on my work list, but the spacers in Habitat will be happy to get a freebie,' she said. 'I'm on "in-port" duty, miz. So why don't you give me your jumpsuits and uniform jackets and I'll put your patches on.'

'Oh!' Nbaro said with unmixed pleasure. 'You'd do that?'

Chu didn't seem like the kind of sly operator to be taking advantage of her. Which was weird, all by itself.

Chu shrugged. 'You're Ship now. Might as well wear it.' She paused. 'Miz.'

Nbaro managed a smile – forced one, in fact. She went to her duffel and pulled out her shipboard jumpsuits, her flightsuits, and her EVA underall, as well as her quarterdeck uniform jacket.

'Might as well give me *all* your suits,' Chu said, taking the pile.

'That is all I have,' Nbaro said.

Damn. Shouldn't have said that.

'Almighty, miz. Two flightsuits? I have six.'

I'm too fucking poor to buy more than the minimum, and even that had consequences. There's a pawnbroker in Below who's already owed my first month's pay.

Nbaro knew perfectly well that midshippers and above had to *buy* their own, and that ratings like Chu were *issued* their own. Six. Of each.

'Orphanage,' she said quietly.

'Oh,' Chu said. 'Sorry, miz. I wasn't making some . . .' She shrugged. 'Anyway, you'll look sharp tomorrow!'

She nodded. It was a little like a salute; Nbaro nodded back. 'Thanks, Spacer Chu.'

Chu left her alone with her massive cabin, which was almost a two-metre cube. Nbaro spent fifteen minutes putting all the screen edges back into their clips, and then she ordered it on.

And it cycled, and came on. Another thrill of happiness.

Six channels of entertainment; another six of education, most of it for Able-Spacers and above reading for their next promotion. She unfolded a holomenu and ran her hands through the options, amazed by the selection; almost every non-classified course in the Service. The officer courses were mostly concerned with watch-standing, and she was a little chagrined to see that there were watch-positions for which she was not only not qualified, but whose requirements she didn't understand. There were layers and layers of things she'd never heard of. Blue-tile was not going to be the sum of her ignorance.

I'm good at sims, though.

'*Athens,*' she said.

And only then thought of the hacker's comment about shipboard AIs.

'*Welcome aboard, Ms Nbaro. I'm Morosini. Is your stateroom comfortable?*' The AI was polite, the voice male and deep, almost husky.

'It's . . . beautiful, *Athens.*'

She was telling the truth. Could it read her?

'*Why, thank you, Ms Nbaro. I see that you have screens in your cabin – a very spacer-like job. It appears to me that you have not connected your cameras – they are located in the decorative edging. Shall I show you the installation manual?*'

Nbaro was annoyed.

I forgot the cameras.

33

'Not at this minute,' she said.

'Very well. How can I help you?'

'Athens, can you read me the sections of the Standard Operating Procedures of this ship while I stow my gear?'

'Delighted, miz,' the AI said. *'I prefer to be addressed as "Morosini".'*

She smiled. The Orphanage didn't have an AI; indeed, they weren't common. Talking to one gave her a thrill. 'Of course, Morosini,' she said.

The AI began.

This SOP promulgated initial date—

'Skip all that,' she said, reaching for her duffel.

'Right,' Morosini said. *'Directorate of Human Corporations Military and Space Services, hereafter notated as DHC MASS; Standard Operating Procedures, DHCS Athens; References. Ref A, DHC MASS Standard Operating Procedures; Ref B, DHC MASS Space-based Operating procedures; Ref C—'*

'Skip to the actual procedures.'

'Three point one point one. Life Support Systems, one point one point one oh. In every case, the first consideration of every shipmate should be the effect of any action on Life Support . . .'

Nbaro listened attentively while she stowed her few personal belongings in the upper crash-couch's drawers and in the inward-positioned desk, which, due to its light controls, appeared to go with the upper crash-couch. She had curtains for her bunk; the dimensions had been in the Welcome packet and she'd made them in her required sewing classes at the Orphanage.

She had an odd feeling as she attached their tabs to the sliders in the overhead; she'd daydreamed of this moment for more than a year, stitching away at the lightproof curtains that would give her crash-couch privacy. She'd worked on them in Sewing and again in Embroidery, and the central panel had her family coat of arms in all its ancient splendour – her father's sable lion superimposed on her mother's Zeno arms of blue and white bars. Their coats of arms were almost all she had of them.

Nbaro thought of her father's dress sword on the Warden's desk, and she fought the urge to anger. To tears. She shook her head and *put it away*. One chance.

One chance.

She stood back and looked at the privacy curtains, and was amazed at how well they went with the space; her painstaking and inexpert embroidery was at least bold, and the blue, white and gold matched the cabin.

'Well,' she said.

'Ref. A DHC MASS one five zero zero dot five, DHC MASS Small Spacecraft manual, ref. B DHC MASS five four five zero dot three DHC MASS Spacecraft Operations in near-planetary orbit manual...'

'Skip to the procedures themselves,' she said again.

'Yes, miz.'

'Stop. Download that last manual. Show me the cover? Damn.'

She stood looking at the screen. It went black, faintly shiny; a dark mirror except where a picture of a yellow cover with a simulated wire binding appeared, with a picture of an ancient spacecraft in a low orbit indicated by a spiral of black trailing from its impractical rocket fins.

'I don't have that manual,' she said.

After another moment, the cover vanished. The screen was black, and she could see herself reflected.

'Mirror,' she said.

'Miz Nbaro? You didn't hook up the leads to the screen interactive phase-cameras. Here is a diagram indicating their location.'

Nbaro laughed mirthlessly and followed the instructions to connect them. Naturally she had to disassemble almost everything: remove all the housing screws, unclip sections of the flexible screen, find the leads that were cunningly hidden inside the clips and attach them. It took a surprising amount of time.

I am, as usual, an idiot.

Just for a moment, it all overwhelmed her, and Nbaro sat suddenly on the fold-out seat, tears welling up in her eyes. She fought them down.

This will never work. I can't get away with this.

Morosini spoke to me, and that means the AI accepted my Ident. Gods.

This time, and perhaps with less hubris, she said, 'Mirror', and the screen functioned, showing her an adolescent woman with brown skin and almost perfectly matching brown hair; when blood rushed to her face, as she was aware that it did far too often, her hair and face were almost exactly the same colour. She had been teased about it since she was old enough to hate teasing.

Her fellow Orphans had called her 'Brown'. Only her eyes weren't brown – they were a shockingly bright green, and they were large enough that people, most of them men, repeatedly mistook her for someone who was 'innocent'. And, perhaps, for a victim.

Her uniform jumper had no badges, no decoration at all beyond one very small gold pip at the collar. That pip represented the culmination of everything Nbaro had ever done or attempted since she was old enough to understand what being an Orphan meant.

And it's fake.

She looked back at her bed hangings.

'Here I am,' she said aloud.

'*True statement,*' Morosini said. '*Should you be in Privacy mode?*'

'No,' she said.

After life in an Orphanage, Nbaro was mostly in favour of round-the-clock surveillance by the cameras now engaged in the wall screen. Of course, they hadn't been on when Spacer Chu had been in her stateroom, which was probably better for everyone. And now that she thought of it, Chu hadn't told her how to engage them.

She listened to the SOP for more than an hour, past four bells, and then the door chimed and she opened it to find Chu.

'Your kit,' she said. 'I accessed your personal record and got you an EVA suit – here's the number.'

'You are amazing,' Nbaro said.

It was a phrase she'd learnt from a popular teacher who used it too often, but it had effect.

Chu grinned. 'It's good to be amazing, miz. You're in Flight 6, mostly Small Cargo shuttles – torpedoes, though. Combat capable. Good outfit, if you ask me, miz. Skipper Truekner is great. Here you go.'

'Thanks again.'

'Skipper Truekner, commander of Flight 6, is on board and in his ready room,' Chu said. 'Passed him on the way here. Just sayin'.' Chu pointed her tab at Nbaro's where it lay on the desk, and the laser flashed. 'There you go – it's your duty station too.'

'I owe you,' Nbaro said past an armload of flightsuits.

'Chocolate cake is nice,' Chu said. 'But I did this for fun. You know you're on the flightsuit authorised list? You don't have to wear a jumpsuit or bridge uniform unless someone orders you to.'

'Is everyone on this ship as nice as you and Locran?' Nbaro asked.

Chu shrugged. 'Good shipmates help the time pass, or so my ma always said. *Ciao*, miz.'

'*Ciao!*' Nbaro replied.

She tried to imagine a world where everyone was so pleasant and co-operative.

She closed the hatch and changed into one of her two flightsuits.

It was close-fitting, intended to be worn under either armour or an EVA. A real flightsuit had a few stents built in so that an EVA suit, or a crash-couch, could connect directly to the bloodstream. That's why they were expensive.

And now both of her dark navy-blue flightsuits had a set of embroidered patches – an *Athens* patch showing the goddess half-turned away, with the aegis on her shoulders and a heavy spear, and under it a Flight 6 patch with a winged horse.

Nbaro felt like a queen. She wanted to go back to the Orphanage and...

I will never go back.

I can never go back.

Very carefully, she blocked the thoughts that threatened to come pouring out, irised shut that hatch in her mind and shook her head. She made herself smile and watched the way it changed her face.

Smile.

Do it. Face the new boss. Find out what kind of arsehat you have to deal with.

Nbaro went out into the passageway and was surprised to find that her tab prompted her down an access ladder 'down' to the O-2 level that ran in a very slight curve along the outer hull, outboard of her stateroom. She noted that in between decks there was a hatch; she flashed the hash code with her tab and saw it was a close-in weapon system turret access hatch. She logged it for future reference and went down to the next level, noting the handholds that made the access ladder as useful in zero *g* as in artificial gravity. She followed her prompts all the way across to the starboard side, and then forward and back up a long ladder to the Flight 6 ready room.

Nbaro stopped and tabbed through her route and found that a cleaner bot was at work in the main passageway, and she'd been routed around it. Problem solved; another thing she'd not been taught. Cleaning bots. None of those at the Orphanage.

There was a small cubbyhole by the hatch – probably where an admin petty officer sat during flight operations. Across the narrow corridor was a larger office space with a blackboard; she smiled to see something so ancient. There was even chalk.

There was a non-airtight door between the office space and the ready room, and it was open, so Nbaro went in. There were rows of crash-couches inside – twenty-four, in four rows, facing a large screen that filled the starboard side of the room, floor to ceiling. On the screen, a beautiful and somewhat exotic-looking long-haired dog was cavorting, bouncing around what appeared to be a planetary environment with distant horizons and blue sky and free-growing plants.

Nbaro had touched a dog once; they were lovely.

A middle-aged man sat alone in the front row, watching the dog.

'Pause,' he said.

He was relaxed, legs crossed, leant far back. Some hair loss, bright eyes, dark skin; she couldn't decide how old he was. Rejuv made such calls very difficult, and promotion in the DHC MASS was glacial, especially at higher ranks.

His flightsuit name patch said 'Truekner'.

'Midshipper Nbaro reporting aboard, sir,' she said, standing at attention.

His lips twitched. 'You have the 6 patch,' he said.

Nbaro wondered if she'd done something wrong.

'Yes, sir,' she said.

'You put up your patch before you even reported,' he said sharply.

Well, there was no denying it.

'Yes, sir.'

Gods, what have I done? Did Chu sabotage me?

'That's some team spirit,' he said, cracking a smile. 'Welcome aboard, Nbaro. I'm Dick Truekner. I promise that despite our ageing spaceframes, Flight 6 is not a bad way to go. We're mostly Small Cargo, but we have some teeth, too. Flight ticket?'

'Small Craft, pinnace, and low atmosphere,' she said. *In sims. Never for real.* 'The SOP says you fly XC-3Cs, and I've never even ... seen one.'

He seemed easy to talk to and there she was, already admitting weakness.

'Low atmosphere?' He rose to his feet and took her hand. 'Interesting,' he said, with some reserve. He pointed at her left breast. 'Eh?' he grunted.

Nbaro flinched. And then realised he was pointing at her EVA badge, which was represented by a small embroidered patch.

'I got my EVA ticket on my cruise,' she said.

'Not bad,' he said. 'Nbaro?' he asked the AI.

Her entire life appeared on the screen behind her, including a terrible photo of her in her Orphanage uniform.

Nbaro flinched. She could *see* the hacker's alteration. The slight typeface change, and the zeros that didn't have a cross through them ...

'High marks across the board,' he said. 'Heh. Sixteen demerits. Kill someone?'

Almost. Oh, fuck, he left the demerits in.

Over already.

'I made a serious mistake,' she said. Her voice shook.

And now it all comes apart.

'Heh,' he said. 'But your cruise officer rated you "ship immediately".' He glanced at her. 'You really do not have to stand at attention, Nbaro. Maybe, in the next two years, you'll stand at attention ten times. Maybe.'

She nodded and didn't relax much. The truth was that she

40

liked standing at attention because it was harder for authority to find fault with you at attention.

In my last moments in the Service.

He was looking at the wall. He sat again, throwing himself back into the crash-couch, which caught and enfolded him, the active gel cushioning his impact so that his backwards dive had no consequence.

'What'd you do to earn sixteen demerits?' he asked.

The file is closed and I cannot be required to discuss it.

Nbaro knew that was a bad answer, even though it was true and legal.

No lie came to her.

Fuck it.

'I brought a lover into the Orphanage,' she said.

'And got caught,' he said.

She almost smiled. 'Yes, sir.'

'Pretty stupid,' he said.

'Yes, sir,' she said.

He nodded. 'Well, don't try that shit here.' His eyes bored into hers. He was serious. 'On the *Athens,* it's no one's business but yours who you do, as long as it's not someone in your chain, up or down or sideways.

I don't ever plan to have sex again, actually.

'Yes, sir.'

That's it? For sixteen demerits?

'I'm sorry, Midder, but as you have a near record number of demerits, I feel required to make sure you understand. That means no one in Space Ops, no one in Small Cargo, no one in Flight 6, and no one on the command decks, all the way up to the Master. Clear?'

'Absolutely, sir.'

Do men get this lecture, too, or does he save it for women?

41

'That leaves about eight thousand potential partners.' He shrugged. It was almost endearing.

Nbaro wanted to tell him his speech wasn't necessary, but she was aware that he was doing this for her, and not to her. Probably.

He smiled.

She tried to meet his eye. Tried to smile back, but anger and fear made her lips tremble.

'Anything you'd like to tell me?' he asked.

The fucking Dominus didn't graduate me? I'm under house arrest? He'll throw me out? Right now the Orphanage is hunting for me?

'No, sir,' she said.

'Nbaro is a patrician family. But you're Orphanage.'

'My parents died. In Service.'

That was true, and worth something.

He nodded, as if he'd expected that. 'That sucks. Very well, Nbaro. My door is quite literally always open. You'll be the most junior pilot in my squadron, and the only new pilot this cruise. I'm going to fly you as a co-pilot *a lot* before you have your own stick. Your tactics scores are excellent – you like games?'

'Yes, sir,' she said.

Also true. I'm the queen of sims.

'Hmm,' he said. 'Want to be Assistant Tactics Officer? There's paperwork, and Suleimani can use the help.' He pointed his tab at the screen, flicking through information. 'Personal. Quals.' He looked at her. 'I'll need you to get a Space Operations qual.'

'Yes, sir.'

'Do it as soon as you can. One of my little rules – all my officers are Space Ops watch-standers. Then we always know what's happening in Space Ops. Eh?'

She smiled. 'I'll get it done.'

'Excellent. Anything else, Nbaro?'

'No, sir.'

'We're going out to Kephlos to fuel up with scoops. We'll do it with half crew – be gone a week. If you want leave, I can make it happen.'

She considered. 'Can I request to remain aboard?' she asked.

Forever?

He nodded. 'It's like that, eh? Sure. You can fly with me. Good times.' He chuckled. 'I'm only in here watching my dog because I can't get to New London again. My leave's done.'

'You have a dog?'

It was as if someone told her they owned a palazzo in City. 'I do,' he said.

Nbaro departed, deeply impressed and almost light-headed with relief. He'd believed her.

I'll work like a dog. I'll do anything. I'll take every shitty duty. I'm still in the game.

Nbaro played a game with herself, finding her way back to her stateroom without looking at her tab or the overhead signs with the frame numbers, and she used the drop-shaft while there was no one around. She leapt from O-3 to O-2 a little too hard, missed, and found herself glancing around, which became a kind of game. She leapt back and forth, up and down; she took a long plunge all the way 'down' to Sixth Deck, and then back up to her own O-2.

There, despite one wrong turning, Nbaro found herself at her already familiar door. She saw a pair of spacers coming in the passageway, opened her hatch and stepped through.

She turned to close the hatch and found herself face to face with a strange petty officer and a tall midshipper – female, pale-skinned, freckled.

'0333 Port Side aft,' the midshipper said. 'I'm Thea—'

The petty officer stood at attention. For the first time in her life, Nbaro said, 'At ease,' and the man relaxed and smiled.

'Midshipper Drake,' she corrected. 'I shouldn't have said Thea! Too informal. So we have a fucking two-man? We are the luckiest girls afloat.'

She offered Nbaro her hand.

Drake. One of the oldest names in City and in the DHC. One of the most powerful families – there were at least two Drakes on the Board – and they had all the skinny, tall good looks that came with money and time in zero *g*.

Nbaro reached out her hand and pasted a smile on her face.

'Almighty God,' Drake said. 'You took the upper bunk?' She shook her head. 'You were here first.'

'You're senior,' Nbaro said.

Here we go – rich girl.

Drake was looking at the screen.

'I can't believe we've got a two-man,' she said.

'Two-person,' the rating said. 'Ms Drake.'

'I stand corrected.' She nodded to the rating. 'Thanks for the walk, Petty Officer Itto.'

'Any time, miz,' the sailor said. 'You have my tab data. I'm assigned to you, don't hesitate to ask for directions – it's easy to get lost.'

'Sure it is,' Drake said.

She closed the hatch with a deft toe; in one glance Nbaro saw that her ship's jumpsuit was tailored, made of a fine and fireproof fabric with xenoglas woven into the fibres, and that she had soft, handmade jump-boots, a little worn.

The taller woman turned to her and dropped her bags on the lower bunk.

'Assigned to me. Sweet heavens. So …' She glanced around. 'I don't know you, so you ain't City Academy. New London?'

'No, ma'am,' Nbaro said carefully.

'Midders don't call each other sir or ma'am,' Drake said. 'Christ, you ain't Orphanage?'

'Yes, ma'am,' Nbaro said with icy formality.

If Drake noticed, she didn't change expression.

'I've never even *met* an Orphanage grad.'

'Yes, ma'am.'

'Almighty, stop with the ma'am already,' Drake said. 'I'm Thea and you are ...?'

Midshipper Nbaro. It was so tempting.

New person. Not afraid. Not angry. Not terrified at being discovered.

'Marca Nbaro,' she said.

Drake leant forward. 'Yeah, you totally look Nbaro,' she said. 'So ... what's a Nbaro girl doing at Orphanage?'

'My parents died in Service,' she said bitterly. 'Along with all my aunts and uncles and cousins.'

Drake nodded. 'OK. You don't want to discuss it. Word taken. You don't have to take the upper bunk.'

Nbaro was so disarmed that she felt suddenly shy.

'I'm fine.'

'Really? I'm a younger sister – I'm used to being in uppers.' Drake looked at her.

Nbaro let herself thaw a little. 'I've already moved in,' she said.

Drake nodded. 'I came on board ten hours early to get a lower bunk,' she admitted. 'So there's some serious irony that you're here first and you're *giving* me the lower bunk.'

'Still time to go back ashore and get a beer,' Nbaro said.

Drake smiled. 'There is at that, but as I've waited my whole life to be here ...'

Nbaro returned the smile. Took a long plunge towards sociability.

'Me too,' she said.

'I vote food,' Drake said. 'Been to the mess yet?' She looked at Nbaro's flightsuit as if just seeing it. 'You're Flight?'

'Yes, Thea.'

45

'Hey, we've moved past *ma'am*. Score. I'm Cargo.'

'Small Cargo or Main Cargo?'

'Small Cargo,' Drake said. 'The family insisted. I'm watching family investments this run.' She opened the hatch and stepped over the knee-knocker. 'Tab says section seven frame 720 – that's almost all the way aft … Damn, should've known that.'

They walked aft along the passageway.

'That means our mess is more than three klicks away,' Nbaro said.

'It'll keep me skinny,' Drake said.

She moved through the hatches with a sinuous grace. Nbaro was shorter so the knee-knockers required more of a stretch to get through. She started leaping through them just to keep up with Drake.

As they went further aft, they began to meet up with other people – mostly ratings but, as they approached the mess, an increasing number of officers. Nbaro might have braced herself against the bulkhead and waited for them to pass, except that Drake didn't, and the taller woman seemed to know many of them.

'Drake!' called one – a senior lieutenant with pilot wings and two cruise marks on his flightsuit cuff. 'Your brother still alive?'

'Yes, sir,' Drake said. 'I'm sure he'd tell me to say something insulting.'

'He would, too. Luckily I outrank you. Send him my regards.'

'Yes, sir.'

Drake's smile came off as easily as it went on.

Nbaro watched her.

This is how aristocrats act. Good to know. So stay close, be her friend, do what she does.

And again. 'Now, Allah be praised, Ms Drake. Does your presence here mean I've aged so much that you've graduated from the Academy?'

'It does, Mister Ahmad.'

Drake's smile was much less automatic with this one.

The junior lieutenant grinned at Nbaro and shook his head.

'Where was I? Oh, yes, on cruise. Perhaps this is the relativity that people talk about so often.'

Drake smiled back at Nbaro. 'Ahmad is one of the good ones. He was a Senior when I was a Newb.'

'Oh,' Nbaro said.

'He's funny. Anyway…' She looked around. They were entering the mess, which had wide double doors – non-airtight. Made, in fact, of wood.

The entire O-3 level officer's mess, not by any means the most formal, was panelled in wood.

Nbaro couldn't stop herself. She reached out and touched it. The chapel at the Orphanage had some wood panels and a wooden chair; she already knew how it felt.

This was dark and rich – very plain, as if its own luxury was enough. The tables were simple, designed to be folded, and made of milled aluminum or some similar alloy; the chairs were ancient and had seen better days, but nothing could distract her from the sheer luxury of the wood panelling. On a spaceship.

Across one whole bulkhead, a dozen paces long, was a xenoglas display that held some weapons, and some items of silver.

'No table service in port,' an officer said to Drake, who'd taken a seat. The woman was a commander, yet the words were said in a helpful, non-authoritative tone. 'You two new?'

'Yes, ma'am,' Nbaro said.

The commander was in a flightsuit, and the name on the zipped pocket said 'Lee'. Her fair skin and epicanthic fold suggested she could have been any kind of Lee from Old Terra – Asian or Southern Virginian, or both of them combined.

'We're at minimum manning for port-side, so no mess waiters. Go to the kitchen and get a tray.'

'Mess waiters?' Nbaro asked.

But Commander Lee was already eating, as if in a tremendous hurry, and Drake gave a somewhat theatrical sigh and stood.

They got food easily; there were only two dozen people eating in a room that seated hundreds. Nbaro had to restrain herself the moment she smelt the mushroom stew – and there was *bread*. She poked it with her finger...

'Is it... real bread?'

'Shit, I hope so,' Drake said. 'We're in port. I suppose we'll eat some bioengineered crap out in the Black, but here, we should be getting the real thing.' She paused. 'Nbaro,' she said gently.

Nbaro was sitting with her elbows out, arms stretched around her food, protecting it from predators. She'd already eaten more than half of her mushroom stew and all her bread.

'Barbarous,' Drake said. 'Incredible, really.'

'What?' Nbaro asked through an inhaled spoonful of stew.

Drake ate a spoonful, made a face, and ate more.

Nbaro finished hers.

Drake shook her head. 'You'll go far,' she said. 'Where'd you learn to eat that fast?'

Nbaro stood. 'Do you think I can have a little more?' she asked.

Drake looked at her, and her smooth forehead wrinkled.

'Honey, we're *officers*. I mean, no one expects us to know *shit* yet. But we're not kids any more. You can eat ten bowls of stew. The cooks will just give it to you.'

Nbaro looked at Drake as if she'd grown a second head.

'Orphanage sounds rough,' Drake said casually. 'Go get more food.' And then, leaning forward, 'I better teach you how to eat, though.'

That stung.

When Nbaro came back, she had another bowl of stew and two pieces of chocolate cake. She sat back down, noting that

Lieutenant Ahmad was sitting across from Thea Drake. They both fell silent as soon as she sat, which made her uncomfortable.

Ahmad leant back. 'Thea says you're Flight,' he said.

Nbaro nodded, already eating.

'You made a cruise?'

'Destroyer,' she said around her cake. '*Isis*, New London to Kephlos and back. Sir.'

Ahmad nodded. 'You served with Lieutenant Umbers.'

Nbaro brightened. 'I did!' she said.

Her EVA instructor.

Ahmad nodded. 'Friend of mine. He mentioned you.' Ahmad smiled; the smile had a little hesitation. 'Some people gave you a rough time?'

Nbaro met his eye, as mild as she could manage.

'Nothing I couldn't deal with, sir.'

Could he know that she'd been dis-enrolled?

Ahmad looked at Drake, who shrugged.

'OK, we're talking about you. How many middies did Orphanage graduate this year?' she asked.

Nbaro looked down at the remaining slice of cake and swallowed the lump in her throat.

'Nine,' she said. *Or maybe eight.*

'Nine,' Ahmad said. 'I see.'

'There's four hundred in my Academy class,' Drake said.

Nbaro rose to her feet.

'Excuse me, sir.'

There was nowhere this could go but bad. It was all insane. What if they looked up the graduates? Her hacker couldn't have closed every loop.

Drake nodded, and she walked away, carrying the cake.

Behind her, Drake said, 'That was my fault. She feels ganged up on. Probably an Orphanage thing. I'll apologise.'

Nbaro didn't need an apology.

Does he know? He didn't act like he knew.

Nbaro just didn't want to talk to other people for a while, so she moved briskly through the double doors. No one stopped her; she had no idea what the SOP said about taking food out of the dining area or mess hall, and she had a debt to repay, so she just kept walking forward, all the way to the riggers' shop.

By the miracle of port watch rotation, Chu was still sitting at the desk.

'Chocolate cake,' Nbaro said.

'Damn, miz Nbaro,' Chu said. 'You're OK!'

Later, Nbaro lay in her rack, listening to the sounds that a 400-year-old ship made when in port. The movement of fluid through the pipes in her stateroom; Thea's delicate snores; the hum of various machines, far away aft, and the occasional, inexpressible pings of metal changing pressure; the slight, discordant ringing of the xenoglas conductor in the overhead, and the almost imperceptible high-pitched sound of the screen on the wall of the cabin.

It was a gentle cacophony, and it kept her awake and thinking for a long time.

This is all I want. Please, let me keep it.

2

'My stateroom-mate grew up in hell, has her own collection of swords, and eats like five middies,' Thea Drake said theatrically. 'Five barbarous middies. Aside from that, she's perfectly normal. Except she *volunteered for refuelling*.'

Drake was lying on her crash-couch in her expensive, custom underclothes. Nbaro thought her bras might actually be silk. She was depressingly attractive and had clear skin. And hair that apparently brushed itself.

'Thea,' Nbaro said. 'I don't have a house or family. I'm not trying to tell you I escaped from hell. I'm just—'

'Happy. Perfectly happy to do fuel dives on a gas giant for two whole weeks when you could be leading one of my brothers astray or buying food stores for the cruise or … I don't know … maybe reading the SOP?'

Nbaro knew herself pretty well, and she knew that she was a sucker for people who liked her. Drake seemed to fit that bill.

You cannot tell this girl the truth.

Nbaro was putting her precious flightsuits in a laundry bag. She would be in a shipboard jumpsuit all day, working in admin, preparing for her Space Operations qualification and meeting with Lieutenant Suleimani.

Zeynep Suleimani, she thought. *Learn everyone's names.*

But the two flightsuits were the most expensive things she owned.

'So do you really mind the swords?' she asked.

Thea shrugged. 'Not really. I've just never seen anything but a boarding sword or a dress sword before.' She made a motion. 'They look barbarous.'

Marca tried not to bridle. *Barbarous* seemed to be a cant-word from the Academy for anything outlandish or unacceptable; Thea used it a great deal.

'Don't mind me,' Thea said. 'I'll get used to the headsman's swords.'

'They're not—'

'Whatever.'

Nbaro had put up all three of her swords, neatly fitted in between pipes and fittings and an air duct: her mother's officer's sword, which had only been preserved because it had been in a shop for cleaning and sharpening; a long, slim two-handed sword with a complex hilt; and another, very like it but with dull edges, for sparring, both of which had been her father's. She'd almost sold them. Almost.

But not her father's dress sword. The bastard still had that.

'I may read the SOP anyway,' Nbaro said, changing the subject.

She knew that she amused and puzzled Drake, but she also knew she could have done a lot worse than a rich girl with good manners and a sense of humour.

Drake rolled her eyes. 'By the way, where'd you get the curtains on your bunk?'

'I made them,' Nbaro said. 'Patterns are in the Welcome Guide.'

'You *made* them? I suppose you embroidered them too?'

'I did,' Nbaro said.

'Oh, God, make me feel more like a useless societal parasite. You *made* them.' Thea sighed. 'I did see the patterns in the

Welcome Guide. I *did* read the Welcome Guide.' She shook her head. 'Really, you made them?'

'I did.'

Drake sat up. 'Make me a set. I'll get you something nice.'

Nbaro was perfectly willing to trade some service for the other girl's regard. It worked in the Orphanage, and she didn't really expect Drake to do anything 'nice'. Nice was a code word for 'something, whenever I remember' with the rich and powerful.

'Sure,' she said. A little slaving for the popular was useful.

Smile.

Drake was looking at a portion of the screen she'd mirrored.

'Do you know that back in the Age of Chaos, women wore paint to make themselves more sexually desirable?'

Nbaro smiled without force. 'Yes?'

Drake shrugged. 'I always wonder what it would look like. And why they did it.'

Nbaro shrugged. 'An Age of Scarcity thing. Maybe there was intense competition for partners?'

'Maybe the capitalists put a price on everything, and women wanted to command the highest price?'

Nbaro sat back. 'We're merchants. We put a price on everything.'

Drake nodded, staring at herself. 'Yesss. Well, I'm told that we're not really dirty capitalists. We have rules. Right? That's what the DHC is all about, or so my brothers tell me. Labour relations, corporate responsibility, fair trade, fair wages … right?'

Nbaro nodded. 'I should read up—'

'You are the readingest room-mate on this ship. Would I look good in paint, do you think?'

'You'd probably look good. Maybe you can experiment in the next two weeks?' Nbaro asked.

You always look good. Damn you.

Drake smiled. 'Enjoy your gas giant, Marca.'

'Enjoy misleading men, Thea.'

'Oh, I will. You know you're missing the Service Ball, right? And there isn't another we can attend for four years.'

Nbaro smiled. 'I'll survive.'

'Suit yourself. Want me to buy you anything?'

Everything.

'I'm set,' she said.

'One to launch,' Nbaro said into her helmet mic, repeating her memorised script from the sims. 'Alpha Foxtrot 6–0–7.'

The spacecraft was older than she was, some of the matt black surfaces showing radiation damage and fuzzing, and the whole cockpit smelt ... old. Burnt electrics, old plastics, a strange resin smell and a human scent: sweat, and something sharper, organic and nasty.

They were pretty, though – atmosphere capable, so stream-lined; full of avionics and even radars and other sensors, so the nose was rounded, but with a complex fractal look that suggested that the whole frame was radar-resistant. The outer skin was a carbon laminate that all but glowed black, and the atmospheric wings retracted; the multiple nozzles of her manoeuvring thrusters retracted invisibly, as did most of the sensor arrays. They were incredibly complex, baroque spacecraft, which were essentially just glorified cargo shuttles.

'Alpha Foxtrot 6–0–7, I copy one to launch. Syncing ... Got you. I read your mass at 21765 kilos. Over.'

Nbaro read down the utterly unfamiliar display until Truekner's hand reached over to her side of the cockpit and pointed at a digital display.

'Roger, Tower. We're at 21765 kilos.'

'You're on the sched as number nine to launch, Alpha Foxtrot 6–0–7, but there's some folks behind the power curve so I can move you up. Copy that? You could be number one to launch, that's number one to launch, as soon as I warm up the magnets.'

Truekner turned his helmeted head. 'Your first catapult launch?'

'Yes, sir,' she said.

For real. My first time that it's real.

He hit his own mic. 'Tower, this is Alpha Foxtrot 6–o–7 and we're fine to move up to number one.'

'Roger.'

'Lock your harness,' he said to Nbaro. 'We'll be at six gees all the way down the railgun tube.' He nodded.

I know. I've done this in simulators a hundred times.

But now I'm so nervous I can't breathe.

'Yes, sir.'

Nbaro tapped her harness buckle and saw the 'lock' symbol come up on her helmet display.

She was *ridiculously* nervous.

Truekner either didn't notice or didn't care.

'We'll be at our orbital insertion speed when we come off the rails,' he said. 'Saves reaction mass.' He looked at her. 'Welcome to an XC-3C, Ms Nbaro.' He smiled.

He's really trying to put me at ease.

'I guess I imagined that it would all be ... newer,' she said.

Truekner laughed. 'We have brand new avionics and all kinds of new toys – ask the sensor operators. But the spaceframes are older than I am. Trust me – old is good. Old is strong and airtight. Old will bring you home.'

Nbaro understood that. She knew that spaceframes didn't really age, and that the DHC just re-rigged them. She also knew how refuelling worked on a smaller ship. She knew that most ships just opened big sail-shaped fuel scoops and took in the hydrogen needed for reaction mass by diving through an appropriate gas giant atmosphere, but the *Athens* was too

55

big and too heavy for such operations, so all her shuttles and operational craft had fuel scoops, and they refuelled her like bees feeding a queen.

'Yes, sir,' she said.

'You know our flight profile?'

'Yes, sir,' she said.

'Alpha Foxtrot 6–o–7, you are now one to launch,'Tower said.

Nbaro looked to the left, where a sailor sat behind an armoured window on the other side of the launch tube. The space between them was vacuum, and he seemed very far away.

The whole vehicle moved forward very slowly, and electromagnetic couplers snapped into place.

The skipper ran the power up to max.

The whole craft quivered like a predator eager to jump. Nbaro could imagine a feral cat in the alleys behind the Orphanage…

This is real, Nbaro thought, as Truekner snapped his salute and the sailor fired the railgun.

Their atmosphere-capable shuttle slammed her back in her seat and made her tongue sink back against her teeth and her eyeballs feel as if they were squashed into her skull, and she didn't breathe for several seconds.

The entire length of the *Athens* hurtled past her, and then, 5.7 seconds after the railgun fired, her spacecraft left the brightly lit blur of the launch tube and shot out into the star-studded velvet black of space. Kephlos filled her cockpit bubble to starboard – a blindingly white-orange gas giant with livid scarlet spots. Truekner's hand on the yoke guided them with nudges from their manoeuvring thrusters.

He brought up a targeting computer, lined up a point in the atmosphere, and tapped it to send it to her screen.

'Take us there,' he said. 'I'll have a nap.'

You bastard.

'Yes, sir,' she said. 'I assume you mean by hand, and not on auto?'

He grinned. 'At the Academy, I was always told that the word "assume" makes an ass out of you and me.'

Nbaro hated that she could feel her face flushing.

'However, just this once I'll say – yes, your assumption is correct. I want to see you fly.'

'Roger that, skipper,' she said. Indeed, there was no other possible answer. 'Permission to ask a stupid question, sir?'

He'd laid his head back and now was using the power in the acceleration couch to run it back to flat, like a very narrow bed.

'No stupid questions, Midder,' he said. 'Only the stupid people who ask them.'

Nbaro felt the blood rush to her face. And remained silent.

'I'm just being an ass, Midder. Ask away.'

'What are the two seats behind us for?'

The XC-3C had four acceleration couches, two in front and two behind. The two behind were empty.

'If we ever get in a fight, you'll see,' he said. 'We have sensor and weapons specialists for combat, who are stationed there.'

'Roger ... Sir.'

Nbaro had spent the last four days running sims of her new spaceframe in her empty cabin. She'd thought she had a feel for the XC-3C, but now she'd have the real yoke in her hands.

Her shaking hands. Because she'd only ever flown a spacecraft in sims.

Truekner had already started the manoeuvre and handed over to her with the fuel calculation done. Nbaro ran his numbers in her head and they looked solid, and she didn't think he was out to get her, which was a little surprising.

But then she thought of the fuel scoop.

'Sir?'

'I'm asleep, Midder,' he said. 'Not available for questions.'

Fuck.

It was a trick question.

Or was it? Am I overthinking it? I always do. I overthink everything. What if he's done all the work and all I have to do is coast down his timeline?

What if he's deliberately set me up to fail?

Fuck fuck fuck.

OK, steady down. Let's peek at the fuel scoop stats . . . there. And . . . No, we're not within margins. So I need a shallower angle of attack and different course – assuming the launch vector was correct . . .

Nbaro had the numbers in her head *and* on her screen. She didn't run them again.

She executed, her fingers typing, her index finger moving across the screen. She'd lied to Chu; she was good at maths, as long it was calculating numbers. Conic sections, on the other hand . . .

The thrusters fired a series of staccato puffs like an automatic weapon firing in the distance, and the plane shuddered a little and the nose went down.

Truekner didn't open an eye or move.

Nbaro took the yoke.

'I have the plane,' she said formally.

He actually appeared to be asleep.

I could eject. That would show him.

She smiled at the image of destroying her fake career merely to surprise her skipper.

They touched the outer wisps of atmosphere and the lifting body under her began to vibrate.

Nbaro felt the manoeuvre in her gut as the plane steepened its descent. Her hands were on the yoke, and she pushed the plane through a steeper dive, following the green line on the head-up display, then hauled back on the yoke as they settled deeper into the atmosphere and began to pull out of the dive.

Gravity had them, and they were accelerating. Now she realised her mistake; under the influence of gravity, they were now too fast for the optimal performance of the fuel scoops.

Fuck. I'm an idiot.

Why isn't this working?

It wasn't that hard to solve; it was just an adjustment to her elegant solution. Nbaro used her flaps, and climbed to dump velocity. Then, and only then, did she allow the nose back down.

'Ready to deploy the scoops,' she said.

'Put 'em out,' Truekner said.

Nbaro found and tapped the icon on her main display and felt the fuel scoop come out. The whole craft began to hum. Outside the view screen bubble, the atmosphere was blindingly white and her visor was having trouble compensating.

'What's your velocity?' Truekner asked suddenly.

'A little under 300 kph,' she said.

'Pressure on the scoop?'

Nbaro looked around, found the number reading out by the scoop indicator. She didn't even understand what she was looking at, but it was in green.

'Green and…'

'Those are millibars,' he said. 'And the tanks are filling, and we're…' He paused. 'About six kilometres off my chosen position.'

Uh oh.

'Satisfactory, if not exactly right.'

She took that in.

'Taking the controls,' he said.

'You have the plane,' she said.

Nothing changed.

'Tell me about the Orphanage,' he said.

Nbaro reached up to the visor control stud and fiddled with it, but the white-orange atmosphere continued to strobe. It was annoying and very distracting.

'Not much to tell,' she said. 'Sir.'

'Try me. Tell me something. Tell me how bad the food was.'

She tried raising the visor, but the atmosphere was too bright. 'Sorry, sir, my visor is malfunctioning and I'm all but blind.'

He reached over to the comm cord that hardwired her helmet and suit to the cockpit and her tab. He unplugged it and re-plugged it.

Her visor flashed and then settled to a dark green.

'Oh!' she said.

'It shouldn't work,' he said. 'But it does. When in doubt, turn it off and back on again. Humans have been in space for six hundred years and that has *not* changed.'

'Thanks, sir,' she said.

'Thank me by telling me about the Orphanage.'

'The food was ... bland,' she lied.

'It was terrible,' the skipper said. 'The very cheapest that the Dominus could purchase and avoid prosecution by the Board.'

Nbaro writhed. 'Yes,' she agreed, her voice very small.

'I read an article about it last night,' he said. 'And an opinion piece with twenty-two million likes. On Hermes.'

Hermes was the juried information service that most citizens subscribed to; there were others. Hermes had an Ultra bias, but as it was juried, it was difficult to propagandise.

She sank down a little in her crash-couch.

'It sounds ... much worse than the Academy. And the Academy is no picnic, Ms Nbaro.'

'I wouldn't know, sir,' she said.

'You know what's fun?' Truekner asked.

Nbaro almost laughed aloud.

No, I'm not much good at fun right now.

'Flying is fun, and flying in a gas giant's atmosphere is the

60

best. See that tower of cloud? See the frothing stuff like steamed milk?'

'Yes, sir?'

'We can use it as a deck and practise flying low levels.'

She knew what a low level was, technically, but her experience of *really* low atmospheric flying was minimal.

Almighty, my experience of almost everything is minimal. Except in sims.

He'd turned the plane towards the massive tower of scarlet cloud.

'Tanks almost full,' he said. 'So ...'

Uh-oh.

'Were you the whistle-blower? At the Orphanage?' he asked.

Oh God.

Her chest was frozen. A sort of sound emerged – not a sob, quite.

'I'm going to take that as a yes. I've only known you about ten days, but I don't think you are someone to fuck with, mmm?'

'I tried to do what was right,' she said. 'Sir.'

'So you reported the Dominus to the Board,' he said.

'Yes, sir.'

'You, an uncommissioned Orphan, took on a senior patrician from the most powerful family.'

'Yes, sir,' she agreed.

'And he logged sixteen demerits against you,' the skipper said.

'Yes, sir.'

Here it comes.

'Want to fly?' he asked.

Now? For the rest of my life?

'Yes,' she said.

'Take the yoke,' he said.

'I have the plane,' she said.

'Fly as if the red cloud and the frothy yellow are hard decks. Get as close to them as you dare.'

'As I dare?' she snapped.

Nbaro turned the plane, banked into a shallow dive.

She had a few seconds in hand, so she checked the fuel and the scoop.

'Tanks are full,' she said.

'Close the scoops, then,' the skipper said.

'Closing the scoops, aye, aye. Scoops are closed.'

Nbaro remembered where the scoops were and where the telltale to mark them open or closed was. Fuel scoops didn't exist in the simulator.

The faint hum was gone and the plane handled much better, so she steepened the dive and then side-slipped right on the frothy cloud deck, skimming perhaps five metres above the 'surface'.

Nbaro added power as they appeared to hurtle along. Gravity fought power and lift; she could feel them through her hands and in her gut, could feel the fifteen thousand kilos of reaction mass that were now almost doubling the mass of her craft.

The massive tower of scarlet was now almost dead ahead, and she turned into it, rising in a corkscrew spiral, the port-side wing tip *almost* in the scarlet fog. Wind reached out for her; there was a strong Coriolis force, which she'd expected, but it was stronger than she'd anticipated, and she slammed the throttle all the way forward and shot off her spiral.

'Sorry, sir,' she said.

'So you reported corruption ...' She was coming in again, this time at a flatter angle '...and he tried to kill your career before you'd even started.'

Nbaro got the wing tip at the edge of the scarlet, and she had the winds this time, but it was still very dangerous, especially with this much fuel on board; any change in the spiralling winds around them and she could plough right into the scarlet storm.

He did kill my career.

'Was it faked?' her skipper asked.

Oh gods

'What?' she asked.

'The surveillance footage of you. Was it faked?'

'No,' she said. 'It was genuine, and I was an idiot.'

The words came out before Nbaro thought of it. Her whole mind was concentrated on flying.

'And he still has that camera footage?'

'Oh, yes,' she said, the bitterness unhidden.

'Embarrassing enough that he's blackmailing you?' he asked.

She began to suspect that he knew everything.

Nbaro was going to top out the cloud. She was well up into the planet's stratosphere; that was a 12,000-metre cloud tower. She edged away, because the winds coming off the tower were weakening.

Not yet. But he will if he ever learns what I've done. Or he'll just burn me. He will if he figures out that I'm aboard a starship, pretending to be an officer.

She came up over the top of the scarlet cloud and began to set up a course to match orbits with the *Athens*.

'Will he?' the skipper asked again. 'Blackmail you?'

They were just at the edge of space now; above them, the black velvet began to spread like night falling. The sun of Kephlos was bright and white and very distant, and still by far the brightest point in the sky.

'Probably,' she said.

Her skipper turned and looked at her. 'Well, we won't be back for two years. Do you think anyone will still remember by then?'

'Sir, with respect, I have to believe that footage of me having

63

sex in the Orphanage chapel will haunt me for the rest of my fucking life.'

...I should not have said that.

'Isolating the flaps and going to manoeuvring thrusters,' she said.

'Alpha Foxtrot 6–o–7, this is the mission commander, do you hear me?' Skipper Truekner was speaking carefully, the way you did when you wanted the AI to hear you.

The somewhat tinny voice of the plane's AI came on.

'Yes, sir.'

'Alpha Foxtrot 6–o–7, erase all cockpit recordings from this mission at mission termination and destroy all audio,' he said. 'My authorisation.'

'Aye, aye, sir,' said the plane.

Truekner glanced at her. 'I begin to see how you got sixteen demerits.'

'Yes, sir,' she said.

He laughed. 'Sorry. Sorry, I'm wrong to laugh. But...' He shook his head. 'In the chapel?'

'We were promised there were no recording devices in chapel,' she said. 'The Free Spirituals go to confession. As do Old Catholics.'

He stopped laughing. 'But this dickhead put a recording device there? That's grotesque. Listen, Nbaro, your Orphanage sounds bad. Was it so bad that you can't be an officer in my Service?'

Nbaro wanted to be calm, and in control, but even her *lips* were trembling.

'I want... I hope...' She was surprised to find that her hands on the yoke were steady, despite her lips and lungs. 'No, sir. I can handle it.'

'Good,' Truekner said. 'Understand I needed to know this.

64

I need to know who you are. If this dickwad comes at you again, I want to know. Understand?'

'Yes, sir.'

No, sir. Fuck, if only I could trust you.

'Good. Want to fly the landing?'

She thought that through.

'I don't think I'm ready,' she said. 'I've only done it in simulator. Never even seen it.'

'It's easy enough. And the simulator is exactly like the real thing. Keep control.'

'Sir,' she said.

Nbaro had the ship coming up over the horizon now, and she had the AI match the orbits. She thought she could *probably* fly the orbits by hand, but she wanted to review landing procedures first. She brought them up on her HUD and nodded along, Orphanage temporarily forgotten.

'Mother Lioness, this is Alpha Foxtrot 6–0–7 on approach,' Truekner said, taking the role

'6–0–7 I have you on ladar and good for orbit. Be advised 6–0–2 is matching orbits behind you.'

Nbaro glanced at her screen, updated by the feed from the much more powerful detection systems on the approaching greatship. Suddenly her screen synced and she could see the entire solar system: a freighter decelerating from jump, and another outbound; a dozen small craft scooping in the lower atmosphere; fifty more service shuttles working in the atmosphere of the gas giant, most of them industrial craft. She split her cockpit screen to show a real-time 3D from her perspective and another top-down flat display with the *Athens* at the centre.

Her HUD flashed a code indicating that she was within one minute of completing the automatic piloting sequence that had been matching orbits with the *Athens*. Another ship from her

Flight, 6–0–2, was 10,000 kilometres 'behind' her and not yet in her orbit – lots of time.

It was surprisingly like the simulators, except that this was real, and if she failed, they'd both die ... and in that moment, Nbaro realised that she was happy. It made no sense, but her horrible, dirty secret was partway out and she was still about to land a military shuttle on a greatship. For fucking real.

Try taking that away, you bastards.

'I have you at a thousand kilometres,' the *Athens* said. 'Call the ball, 6–0–7.'

'Roger, ball,' she said. 'I have a landing mass of 38176 kilos, over.'

Almighty, it even felt good to say.

'Roger, 6–0–7. I have the magnets set for 38176 kilos. And I have lock.'

'Roger, lock.'

A bright green light went on over her head, high on the windscreen.

As Nbaro approached, she couldn't see much of her ship except the stern, with four enormous engine nozzles for the main drives, each with its own magnetic bottle and hydrogen fusion plant and backup reactor, and in the centre of them, like the stamen in a flower, the four tubes of the railguns. One of the four tubes was lit and strobing, indicating to any pilot which tube was the correct one for approach.

She was going to land at her orbital velocity, hitting a moving needle with her fast-moving thread, because a nine kilometre-long tunnel lined with electromagnets could slow her at the same 6 *g* she'd left. Nbaro was aware that she was going almost six metres per second faster than the *Athens*, but she watched the green light and the data stream and the Landing Officer had accepted her path and her velocity and her mass ...

She flexed her hands on the yoke.

Orbits are very slight curves, but the gravity well handles the perfection of the curve like a set of rails, as long as your ship meets the parameters for a given orbit exactly.

Nbaro scanned her instruments, looking for anything that might indicate trouble.

'Lock your harness,' Truekner said quietly.

I'm an idiot.

She was hurtling at the ship, and had a desperate impulse to *slow way down.*

'6–0–7, I have you in the slot,' said the Landing Officer.

'Slot aye. Green and go,' she said, for the first time ever.

Green and go . . .

'Dirty up,' she added, toggling a button.

On the hull, her electromagnetic couplers deployed, sixteen heavy metal struts emerging from the body of her spacecraft ready to interact with the railgun magnets.

Almighty, she thought. So fast. Reckless. Stupid.

Truekner wasn't saying anything.

The stern of the *Athens* rushed at her. Without meaning to, her eyes flicked to the green landing light.

Still on.

Everything was exactly right, and Nbaro killed the over-whelming temptation to change anything.

A pulse of darkness . . . flash of LIGHT.

BAMMMMMMMM.

She slammed into her harness, but before she could count to three, the weight was off her chest and knees and eyeballs and she was at rest.

'6–0–7 that was dead centre and OK.'

Truekner tapped his mic. 'Landing, that was Midshipper Nbaro, pilot.'

The Landing Officer chuckled, the first crack in her perfect professional demeanour.

67

'Nbaro, dead centre and OK.' Pause. 'Welcome aboard, Midder.'

'Thank you, ma'am,' Nbaro said, and her voice cracked. She wanted to cry. She'd heard about tears of joy, and suddenly, her eyes were full.

I did that.

The magnets that held them began to pass the shuttle along, so that they moved slowly, as if on invisible rails, down the length of the ship. The electromagnets clamped them to a purple compartment labelled 'Fuels' in a corrosive yellow.

Truekner walked her through the discharge of their cargo of hydrogen – a process that was slightly more complicated than she'd expected.

'Everything about fuels is complicated,' he said wearily. 'The consortium that owns all the hydrogen doesn't want us to use anything but their software. They don't seem to realise that we have to refuel in other places, too.'

'So it's a workaround?' she asked.

'Yep.' He was silent until a faint metallic gurgle rolled through the cabin. 'That's the good sound.' Truekner had adjusted something. 'Now we're cooking with gas.'

'We are?' she asked.

'It's an expression,' he said. 'Apparently, once upon a time, cooking with gas was very . . .' His eyes met hers. 'Honestly, I don't know. Half our jargon is from the old United States Navy and the other half is from the ancient British Royal Navy, and there's a bunch from early spaceflight operations and some even from Old Terran trucking. Navies are the most conservative linguists anywhere – we preserve even the meaningless terms for hundreds of years.'

Nbaro smiled. 'Like by and large.'

His eyes kindled, a fellow enthusiast. 'Exactly.'

When the fuel had been offloaded, they were moved along to

a hangar bay and the magnets slid them into a slot between two other identical shuttles, each bearing the Pegasus on the tail fin. The pilots didn't even have to choose a parking place.

The plane clicked to a stop as the magnets matched with receptors in the deck and locked.

'You know what's fun about refuelling ops?' Truekner asked her.

The interrogation? she wondered. *The confession?*

'Cloud deck flying?' she asked.

'Sure, that. But you always finish fully fuelled.'

Truekner unclipped and swung his legs up and over the central console. The whole Hangar Deck was at zero *g*, and he kicked out of his seat, a sort of writhing kick that spoke of years in XC-3Cs. He swam back along the tunnel to the lower hatch.

'Hard vac check,' he said.

Nbaro ran the checklist, making sure her helmet was on and cycled, air flowing.

'Check.'

'Opening the aft hatch,' he said.

There was a clear sound as the internal atmosphere of the shuttle was sucked back into vacuum bottles for reuse. Something felt different in her inner ear.

Nbaro got out of her crash-couch with about a dozen little kicks and after bouncing her helmet off the backrest. She grabbed handholds and pulled herself to the tunnel and down to the open hatch.

The skipper had already locked his boots to the decking and was looking at the shuttle's engines. Even from here she could see the heat.

'Pretty hot, Skipper,' she said.

He nodded and stepped back.

'Too damn hot,' he said. 'Engines have been off four minutes in hard vac. Mark it, will you?'

'Aye aye, skipper.'

Nbaro pulled her tab from her thigh pocket and typed a note to maintenance, gloved fingers clumsy.

She followed him across the deck, her boots clipping down to the steel deck with every step, crossing the hangar bay into a little workout before they climbed an exterior ladder. Truekner just leant out and leapt, and Nbaro followed his lead with a little more caution.

They airlocked into the maintenance section, where she downloaded her tab into the maintenance mainframe. Chances were they already had it all directly from the plane, but her version had her notes and the skipper's. A junior rating who looked as young as Nbaro handed both of them bulbs of coffee, which she took with enormous gratitude.

'Ready room,' the skipper said.

Nbaro followed him, carrying her helmet awkwardly, her boots no longer set to grip the deck, so merely heavy and clumping along.

There was an elevator straight up to the ready room, and the skipper smiled at her.

'Not bad,' he said. 'I think I lost a year off my life landing at six metres per second, but hell, it was exciting.'

She flushed. 'Oh, sir . . .'

He laughed. 'Powers, miz, you make me feel old.'

She tried to meet his eye, but the elevator doors opened.

'Should I have matched velocity?' she asked.

'Well,' he said, 'most folks do. Means you make a smaller ding if you fuck up.' He slapped her back. 'Don't sweat it. Landing gave you an OK and now every pilot on the ship knows you aren't afraid of shit.'

Guess again. I'm afraid of everything.

'Yes, sir.'

'And your first trap was a nice start,' he said. 'Go get a wafer or two and then meet me to brief. We're on again at 0730.'

'Almighty,' she said.

It was already 0630. She'd done more in two hours...

'Refuelling ops are almost as hard as combat,' he said. 'Almost as hard as full-on Cargo Ops. Did you eat breakfast?'

'No, Sir.'

'Go and eat. That's an order, Nbaro.'

'Aye, aye, sir.'

Nbaro ate, flew again, landed for a second time, flung herself on her crash-couch and listened to SOPs. In the late afternoon she had a third flight; this time, the skipper flew but she had to do everything else, including fuels. Just before midnight, ship-time, she landed her fourth of the day.

'How's your Space Operations qualification going?' the skipper asked, with what had to be an evil glint in his eye.

'Oh,' she muttered.

'Best get on that,' he said. 'We're event one, 0645 Ship Time. See you then.'

Nbaro dragged her weary body into the EVA riggers' space, got out of her flight harness and saw it stowed, even cleaning it with a disinfectant cloth. There were two sailors there; neither was Chu.

'Ms Nbaro,' one said. 'I'm PR-1 Carlson and this is Able Spacer Po.'

She nodded.

'Spacer Chu mentioned you,' Carlson said. 'Everything good, miz?'

'Visor problems, but Skipper says they're normal,' she said.

Carlson made a face. 'Worth buying a better helmet, miz,' he said. 'This is made by Copex on New London. Pretty crappy.' He shrugged. 'Dowland makes the best – Old Terra. Mugali is also excellent, although different – on Sahel. We'll be going there...'

71

This was all I could afford and it's a miracle I got a loan shark to float me, she thought.

'I'll take that under advisement,' Nbaro said.

'Want me to look around for you?' Carlson asked.

She took a moment to consider this from various angles.

'Look around?' she asked.

'Sometimes there's old helmets around. No scams,' he said, raising his hands in a way that indicated there were, indeed, some scams.

'Around?' she asked. 'As in, sometimes people leave five-hundred-ducat helmets sitting around?'

Behind her, a silken voice. 'Well, yes,' they said.

Nbaro turned to find a Flight 6 pilot she didn't know; their smooth face and ageless eyes suggested an androgyne.

'Tir?' she asked.

'Jan,' they said, offering a firm handshake. 'Most people call me Smoke.'

Jan's pocket flash read 'Mpono.'

They were so tall that Nbaro wondered if they fitted in a cockpit. But lots of zero-*g*-born – Floaters – were androgyne. And very tall.

'The very rich do sometimes – the patricians,' Mpono said. 'They're required to do a cruise, by law. So they buy excellent equipment and then leave it for others to pick up when they leave. There's a thriving black market. And Carlson will definitely know where to find that market.'

'Tir is very hard on me, miz,' Carlson said. 'I'm only interested in what's best for the ship.'

'I love you like a brother, PR-1,' Mpono said. 'I just want our new girl to know what a shark you are.'

'I'm hurt, tir,' Carlson said.

'To be fair, since you're Flight, Carlson will only screw you a little, and you can probably get a better helm, cheaper, from him than anyone else.'

'Now, fair's fair,' Carlson said.

'Just count your fingers after you shake on the deal,' Mpono said. 'You going to chow, girlie?'

Nbaro had last been addressed as girlie by a non-friend at the Orphanage. On the other hand, the Floater pilot's tone was obviously meant to be friendly. Obviously.

Right?

Smile.

'As soon as my visor's clean, tir.'

Mpono nodded, handed their kit over the big nanotable and leant their long body against the forward bulkhead.

'Is that pornography I see on your screen?' Mpono asked Carlson.

Carlson blinked. 'Yes, tir.'

'Skipper would fry you,' Mpono said.

'Yes, tir.'

'I might fry you myself. Get that shit off my ship.'

Nbaro had to admire Mpono's tone – firm, but almost impersonal. Almost.

Nbaro's ears were burning, but she got her kit onto its beautiful bronze hook, gave her EVA suit a tug so that it hung free to dry, and slipped back to the table.

'Ready?' Mpono asked her.

'Yes, tir.'

'Smoke. Seriously. Call me Smoke.'

Smoke surprised her by turning right instead of left out of EVA Riggers, and going to the outer hull. Then they turned right again, walking *away* from the mess, to two hatches leading to a pair of matt silver-steel doors.

They thumbed a button, and the doors opened.

'Mess,' she said as the doors closed.

'There's a lift?' Nbaro asked.

Mpono looked at her, wide-eyed, and a deep pink flush came to their dark cheeks, and then she roared a laugh.

'Gods, you know, you hear about newbs doing things, but you have to see it?'

Nbaro waited, stony faced.

'There's a lift!' Mpono said. 'Ladybird, there's a lift at the end of every cross-corridor. They run along the skin.'

I should have known that.

Why didn't I know that?

'It's all right, girlie,' the pilot said. 'I probably did ten things just as stupid when I came aboard. Which was so long ago that we still ate dinosaur meat in the mess.'

Nbaro breathed in and out.

'Hey, Nbaro, word to the wise – don't show that much anger. Ever. Never let 'em see you sweat. Never. No one teases a tough target.'

'Yes, tir,' Nbaro said.

Mpono smiled. 'Honey, I was a midder once. All two point five metres of me and the wrong sexual orientation. Eh?'

'Yes, tir.' Nbaro, who'd heard this advice fifty times in her life, sighed. 'I know.'

Mpono nodded. 'If you know, then do it. You know why they call me Smoke?' they asked.

'No, tir.'

Smoke smiled. 'I've ejected from not fewer than *three* multi-million ducat spaceframes.' They shrugged. 'All accidents and malfunctions. But I've destroyed more craft than enemy action. So they call me Smoke.'

The elevator doors opened and they emerged into the mess. The wood panels still got her – and she was wrestling with what Mpono had said.

'Commander Mpono,' said a voice, and there was a *captain.*

It was a little like unexpectedly meeting God. Four broad gold lace stripes on each cuff, a Sun-in-Splendour on one collar and the Lion on the other. A *captain*.

Also, Mpono is a fucking commander, so they are the Operations Officer.

'Captain,' Mpono said. 'May I introduce Midshipper Nbaro?'

Nbaro desperately wanted to salute, but no one saluted unless they had a hat on, and no one saluted in the mess anyway.

'Sir,' she managed.

'Ms Nbaro,' the captain said.

He was pale, short and hairy, and his hair was red. He had a beard, a very rare affectation, and unlike most of the crew during the refuelling operations, he was in full uniform.

'Captain Fraser is the Astrophysics Officer,' Mpono said.

'However hard to believe you find that,' Fraser quipped.

It was obvious the two of them knew each other quite well, but that was fine; she could sit with them and not interrupt. Nbaro went and fetched food and came back to find them gone, but Mpono's flight jacket was on a chair, so she sat next to it. The jacket was carbon armour and xenoglas fibre – expensive. Amazing. Three months' pay, easily.

The captain returned first, and Nbaro almost couldn't eat. Almost.

He smiled at her and ate some greens.

'How do you like the *Athens*?' he asked.

'I love her,' Nbaro said.

He grinned. 'That's the spirit,' he said, as Mpono sat down. Mpono was so tall that they seemed more to fold than to sit.

'You Nbaro?' asked another officer, leaning over her. He was in a flightsuit, tailored like Thea's, with the same expensive boots.

'Yes, sir,' she said.

'Names in the mess, Nbaro,' Mpono said. 'This ne'er-do-well is Ko.'

'Lance Ko,' the pilot said. He had a Flight 5 patch – a five of spades from a Classical deck of cards. 'I saw your shit-hot landing. Six point two metres per second all the way into the tube!' He laughed. 'You made my day.'

Mpono rolled their eyes. 'Now he's got to land faster than six point two,' they said. 'Mister Ko, do you know what the max landing speed for your crap-arsed Gunslinger is?'

'Eighteen point seven,' he said. 'And let's face it, that's probably got an order of magnitude built in for safety.'

Mpono gestured with their bulb of tea. 'This, girlie, is what's called a *fighter pilot*.'

Nbaro met Mpono's eyes. She made herself smile.

'Smoke?' she asked. 'I'd really prefer not to be known as "Girlie".'

There was an awkward silence.

Fuck. My big mouth.

Fraser leant forward, but Mpono shook their head.

'Bingo, Nbaro. I'm sorry.'

Nbaro was stunned to silence by the apology.

Ko leant over as if nothing untoward had been said.

'What other "frames" have you flown?'

Nbaro shook her head. 'In sims?' she asked.

'Actually flown.'

Nbaro was trying to catch Mpono's eye to smile at them.

'I've only flown in sims,' she said. 'Before today.'

Ko rocked back.

Nbaro was still busy protecting her food, but as she was almost finished she got to her feet and offered her hand.

'Hi.'

Ko shook her hand. Another pilot came up behind him – another male, shorter, darker, also Flight 5. He inserted himself smoothly between Ko and Nbaro.

'Well met, miz. Welcome aboard. Though I'm not in your

chain of command, I wanted to say I like your style.' He smiled. 'I'm Jesus Cortez,' he added, and walked away.

'Oooh,' Mpono said, and laughed. 'A come-fuck-me line. Ignore him, Nbaro. He's actually an excellent pilot.'

Ko rolled his eyes. 'Cortez doesn't have any other kind of line.'

I can take you both.

Her hand was on her shiv.

Don't think that way.

Her reaction must have been visible, because Ko winced and retreated with a backward glance. She saw him punch Cortez ungently in the shoulder, and Cortez barked a laugh.

Nbaro calmed her breathing and realised that she hadn't practised in a week. No fencing, no martial arts at all.

'Is there a dojo aboard?' Nbaro asked Captain Fraser as the two pilots walked away.

'Yes. O-1 level, all the way forward and known, by ancient tradition, as the Chain Locker.'

He flicked open his tab, pointed it at her until she lifted her own, and thumb-typed rapidly.

'What do you do?' he asked her.

'Swords,' she said.

He smiled. 'Ever fight in zero *g*?'

Nbaro shook her head.

'Armour?' he asked.

'No, sir,' she said. 'I'd love to learn, though.'

Fraser's eyes bored into hers as if this was a very important issue.

'Ha, hmm,' he said. 'What sword?'

'One or two hand,' she said. 'Sabre. A little kendo, some Iai-do, and some duelling.'

'Olympic Two Hand?' he asked.

'Yes, sir,' she said.

77

'Ha, hmm.' He smiled. 'We may get to know each other better, then. Right – back to work. Mpono?'

'Fraser?' Mpono asked. Both were smiling with an easy familiarity.

They're lovers. Wow, I'm slow.

Flight and Astrophysics. Totally allowed.

Oh. I'll bet they're ... married.

I'm an idiot.

Her observation skills had entirely failed her; they wore identical wedding rings. And she thought, *Is this what my mother and father were like, when shipboard? This familiar formality? It's ... nice.*

It was also clear that Mpono – *Smoke* – bore her no ill will at all.

Nbaro walked back down the spine of the ship after consuming a huge slice of cake, mostly because she could, and went to sleep in her flightsuit.

She awoke to her whole screen flashing red.

'Alert! Battle Stations. Battle Stations. Alert!'

She was standing on the deck of her stateroom, and nothing made sense, including the flashing red light.

'Alert! Battle Stations. Alert!'

The roar of the siren seemed to pierce her body, the primate urge to panic made it difficult to focus, and *nothing* made sense.

Battle Stations.

Almighty.

She got it now.

Nbaro was still in her flightsuit; she put her bare feet in her issue boots and got out of her stateroom. Thea was still ashore, at the Service Ball. Right.

We're at Battle Stations? In refuelling orbit at Kephlos?

Must be a drill.

The corridor was the busiest she'd seen it, and Nbaro considered the newly discovered elevators momentarily and then elected to run. She started forward, hurdling the knee-knockers unless there was a crowd, and using her small size to slip through whenever she could.

All the lights were flashing and red.

'Zero *g* in five minutes,' a huge voice said. 'Prepare for Shipboard Integrity.'

She knew what that meant. It meant all the hatches would close.

'This is not a drill,' said the voice. 'Five minutes and I'm locking the doors.'

Almighty. Not a drill.

Nbaro was past the riggers; she brushed past a Flight 5 pilot in her full flight kit waiting for the Flight Deck elevator, and slid into the Flight 6 ready room.

Truekner glanced at her. He had the screens up: views of the space ahead of the bow; the launch tubes; some statistics she didn't recognise.

There were a dozen officers and flight-qualified enlisted already in the ready room. She'd only met Mpono, who nodded to her.

As Nbaro listened, the godlike voice of Space Operations came into the ready room. It was as if it was all in a different language. She understood the words, but none of the directives made any sense.

'Launch the Alert 5 screen,' the voice said.

'Upgrade the Alert 10 screen to Alert 5.'

Nbaro felt the ship shake. A ship almost ten kilometres long.

We launched something.

They'd launched a ship. That was the Alert 5 – a Gunslinger. Maybe Ko or Cortez.

Right? The alerts are some sort of interceptors, ready to go on short notice . . .

'Now launch the Alert 5 Screen,' the voice said. 'Master to the Combat Bridge.'

Truekner winced.

Mpono shook her head. 'Upgraded 10 to 5 to launch in forty-five seconds,' she said. 'I hope they were ready for the cat.'

'Flight 6,' another voice said. 'This is Space Operations, setting a Space Control Alert 20.'

Mpono looked at Truekner.

'6–0–2, ready in the hangar. Fuelled. No load out.'

'Space Ops, can you have Weps put torpedoes in 6–0–2?'

'Roger, Flight 6. 6–0–2.'

The ship shuddered again.

'Get kitted up,' Mpono said to Nbaro. Then, leaning closer to their tab, they said, 'Space Ops, this is Flight 6. Let's put 6–0–3 on deck with torps.'

'I like the way you think, Flight 6. Roger. Weapons is on it. Crew 'em.'

The skipper looked at his tab.

'Nbaro, we walk in four minutes.'

Another pilot looked up. 'Skipper? What the fuck is happening?'

Truekner shrugged. 'No idea,' he said. 'Didier? You're on fuels?'

'Yessir.'

'Smoke, check if we're ditching all the refuelling runs? I bet we don't.'

Mpono didn't look up. 'I bet the same, which is why you and Nbaro, me and Guille are taking these dusters. Combat crews?'

'If we fly torps we fly the back end,' the skipper said, as if in code.

Nbaro had absolutely no idea what was going on. She didn't know what a duster was, and she was still working out that 'Alerts' were emergency launch events.

Mpono glanced at Nbaro.

'You good to go, Nbaro?' they asked. 'You were toast last night.'

'Good to go,' she said.

Though her tab told her last night was only three hours ago, ship-time. Nbaro was sorry she'd looked.

She went into the riggers' shop, where Chu already had her kit on the table alongside three other flight kits. Another Flight 6 officer was getting into her harness – Guille, her pocket flash read – and there were two others she'd seen in the ready room: Petty Officer Eyre, a man as young as she was, and Petty Officer Indra, a young woman from City.

'Hi, ma'am,' Nbaro said, making herself smile. 'I'm the new midder.'

'Hey, Nbaro!' Guille was a small woman; Nbaro towered over her and she thought Guille might only be the minimum height requirement. 'Nice landing, midder.'

Nbaro blinked.

She shrugged into a lightweight EVA suit; if she punched out, it would keep her alive for maybe an hour before she froze. She dogged her flight helmet down to the collar of her EVA suit and felt the needles plug in through the stents to her flesh – creepy, but she was getting used to it.

She dropped her tab into a thigh pocket and scooped up her helmet bag.

'Something in there for you, miz,' Chu said. 'You could share,' she added.

Guille was out the door ahead of her.

Nbaro flashed a smile at Chu and trotted to the elevator. Somehow, Truekner had beaten her there, and was holding the button.

'You met our partners in crime?' he asked, pointing at the two petty officers.

They grinned.

'Hangar,' he said.

81

'Zero *g* in ten seconds,' said a voice.

'Is that the Master?' she asked.

Her commander nodded. 'Yes. Visor down. Hangar won't have pressure.'

She closed the main visor and clicked her tongue to acknowledge the lock symbol.

'I'm good,' she said.

'As am I,' her skipper said.

The gravity just … cut out.

He hit a button. The elevator read all four of them as buttoned up and opened the doors.

'6–0–3,' Truekner said.

An indicator flashed on his tab.

'Already moving to the tube,' he said. 'Let's go.' He reorientated himself and then *dropped* through the elevators, treating them as if they were down. Eyre followed the skipper with the grace of an athlete, Nbaro emulated his leap and then Indra jumped. They passed through maintenance, handhold to handhold, the crew all in their couches or strapped in at action stations, and then cycled through the airlock and dropped through zero *g* to the Hangar Deck. Space Ops held their empty craft as they clunked up to it and swung through the open hatch.

Nbaro grabbed the overhead handhold and swung into her crash-couch.

'APU on,' she said, thumbing the switch.

The auxiliary power unit gave them light and heat and computers before the engines started. Same as sims, thank God.

Both of the petty officers climbed into the back. Nbaro had never flown with the spacecraft full, and she wasn't really aware of what they did back there. In the sims, the co-pilot did it all from her armrest…

But green lights came up on her board.

'Roger,' Truekner said.

Indra spoke up. 'Closing aft hatch... Closed. Locked. Green light for atmosphere.'

Nbaro started on her own checklist. 'I have a computer.'

'I have a system,' came another voice; that must be Indra. 'System is go.'

Nbaro was rattling through her checklist as if she knew what she was doing, and she was just a little proud of herself – which warred with her fear that she was doing something wrong.

Indra and Eyre exchanged checklist items that she'd never heard before, even in the simulator. But it was immediately obvious what they did.

'Remote sensors?' Indra asked.

'Green, twenty-four in the pipes.'

'Torpedoes?'

'I have four, all green, and they are real, repeat – real.'

The spacecraft, which had been moving softly on the magnetic rails, came to a stop with a soft click.

'That was fast,' Truekner said.

Nbaro looked out to see they were on the launch tubes already. The railgun was a long, brightly lit tube stretching to a tiny black dot almost eight kilometres away – open space.

'Ready for engine start,' she said.

Truekner pressed buttons.

'Fuel. Hydraulics. Magnetics. Navigation. I am go.'

'I am go,' Nbaro said, reading the same things he was, and hoping she was reading them correctly. This had all been fine in the simulator.

Indra said, 'Weps and Sensors are go.'

'Engine start in five. Four, three, two, one. Engines lit. Lioness, I have engines on and I'm on the rails. One for launch.'

She was remembering the whole litany—

'That's Tower, not Lioness,' Truekner said with incredible calm. 'That's Tower.'

'I'm sorry!' she blurted. 'Tower! This is Alpha Foxtrot 6–o–3 ready to launch.'

'Roger, 6–o–3, I have you ready and hot, four torps loaded.'

Indeed. Nbaro looked down at her screen and there, on it, were four torpedoes, small spacecraft tipped with nuclear warheads.

As if delivering a lesson, Truekner said, 'Lioness is actually a different person in Space Ops.'

'Yes, sir.'

'Lock your harness,' he said.

She did, feeling her usual chagrin.

'Since this is real, just let me do it,' Truekner said. 'If I want you to act, I'll tell you, OK?'

'Roger that, sir.'

'Good.'

'Alpha Foxtrot 6–o–3, you are next to launch.'

'Ready to launch.'

'Copy. Mission…'

There was a pause. Seconds ticked by.

'We're on hold, Alpha Foxtrot 6–o–3.'

'Roger. Hold.'

The tube lights flashed and something hurtled past them.

'Sir, what is our mission?'

Truekner didn't take his eyes off the screens.

'If there's a ship out there and it's shooting at us, the kids in back find it for us and we put our fish in it,' he said.

Nbaro took that in.

'At Kephlos?' she asked. 'What's our enemy?'

He didn't reply.

'Sir, is an "Alert" a spacecraft tasked with being ready to launch in a set number of minutes?'

He turned his head and his gold visor reflected the cockpit and the lights of the controls.

'Exactly,' he said, without judgement.

The lights flashed again and the ship shook.

'Alpha Foxtrot 6–0–3. Mission update coming in now. Ready to launch?'

'Roger, Tower.'

They clicked forward into the launch position and by now, Nbaro knew the drill. She felt the magnets lock to their struts.

Truekner flashed his salute.

Bang.

They were away, the weight of five or six Nbaros pushing her deep into the reactive nanogel of her acceleration couch while the bright lights of the tube dimmed; a flash of red . . .

And the ship was falling away behind and below them. They were already turning under Truekner's hands – turning and rising out of the gravity well as he fed power to manoeuvring thrusters.

Nbaro leant forward as soon as the acceleration stopped and brought up the ship's 4D space display as a holograph. Every contact in the system was tagged and there was a colour code for the age of the information.

She asked for a filter on hostiles, and got nothing.

'No hostiles marked, sir,' she said.

Truekner was decelerating, gradually matching the *Athens* but in a much higher orbit.

Her HUD flashed.

'General Message. General Message,' it said. 'Now hear this.'

Nbaro was looking at Chairman Sagoyewatha. The chairman of the Directorate of Human Corporations. The Doje.

'Citizens,' he said. 'This is a DHC-wide full alert. The greatship *New York* has been destroyed by unknown agency.' The chairman of the DHC's board of directors looked calm, and prepared for anything. 'Until we have more information, we ask all ships to remain at full alert.'

'Almighty,' Nbaro muttered.

Truekner was staring straight ahead.

The New York. *Nine thousand crew. A trillion ducats in cargo —*
an irreplaceable asset.

What the veritable fuck?

'Nbaro, take the plane?' Truekner's voice sounded strange.

'I have the plane,' she said, putting her hands on the yoke.

'Good atmosphere,' the skipper said, and opened his visor.

He was crying. And his tears were stuck to his face and visor in zero *g*, forming a bubble of liquid against his face, surface tension glittering.

Nbaro had the plane, but she was fighting an urge to wake herself up. The *New York* was destroyed? Her indestructible skipper was weeping, and her heart was racing, and she felt as if she was choking…

Nine thousand spacers.

Truekner produced a wipe from his helmet bag and proceeded to ruthlessly clear his eyes and visor. Nbaro watched the screens, only slightly less shocked by her skipper's tears than she was by the idea that a greatship could be destroyed. None of them had ever been lost.

Ever.

It was the longest flight of Nbaro's brief career; they were still space-borne eleven hours later, circling the planet while refuelling operations continued. She learnt the miserable intimacy of having to pee in the cramped conditions of the cockpit; there was, Petty Officer Indra told her, just room for a little privacy between the two upper nuclear torpedoes. Everyone was taught in training that you could pee inside your vac suit; everyone knew that in reality it left you wet and uncomfortable for hours.

Otherwise, Nbaro had nothing to do but watch as small craft left the *Athens* and dived into the soup, gathered hydrogen and climbed back into orbit to feed the greatship.

She was a little weak on her astrophysics, but she knew the

signal virtue of greatships was that they could jump further than any smaller ships, with their huge Tanaka drives, and their equally vast computing power. Their AIs were fully sentient and *engaged*, allowing them to find the ideal pinprick in the infinite M-brane and then navigate it. She'd taken a course on Thruspace travel, as professionals called it, and thought she understood the concept until the professor told her class that the M-brane was an allegory and that it was entirely possible that the universe the jump-drive capable ships re-entered wasn't the same one they left.

Nbaro had started to lose interest then. Multi/Infinite universe theory smacked of religion and piety and belief. Even quantum entanglement left her uninterested.

Speaking of which...

She looked at the date-time stamp on the chairman's communication. It was eighty hours old. Out of curiosity, she used the ship's system-wide display to locate the messenger drone that had entered the system and checked its travel log.

The *Athens* had gone to Battle Stations within four minutes of the drone's system arrival. Probably exactly the time to send, and receive, and decode.

Truekner wasn't talking, and Nbaro wished she knew more. She wished that someone he liked, who knew him, was aboard, He'd lost someone on the *New York*.

She felt useless.

She couldn't ask.

Other fighters landed and took off, but Space Ops left them out, with Mpono somewhere above them.

'You know why Smoke has vanished?' the skipper asked suddenly.

'No, sir,' she said.

'She's taking this seriously. Best way to get a torpedo into an enemy ship is to fly silent, no power, no emissions, and get really close using manoeuvring thrusters. They're very hard to pick up, even on ladar.' He checked the screen again. 'She's already dark.'

'Yes, sir,' she said.

'We're going dark too. Button up.'

The four of them closed their visors and went on canned air, and Truekner cut the internal power back until all they got was heat into their suits and mission-critical screens.

They sat in the dark for another five hours.

Nbaro went back to her figuring; her tab wasn't going to give off enough heat to register to a probe.

At some point, the skipper said, 'Could be worse. You could be in a crash-couch on shipboard with *ten* people watching you pee.'

Nbaro glanced at him. His helmet gave nothing away. His visor was lined in gold foil against radiation, and reflected her against the very soft red lights of the cockpit systems still on.

'You OK, sir?' she asked. And felt like an ass.

He was silent for too long.

'Yes, I am,' he said. 'Thanks for asking, Midder. Hit me hard, at first.'

Some reply was called for, right?

'Yes, sir.'

'My sister's on the *New York*. And my ex-wife.'

Almighty.

Nbaro couldn't think of anything to say.

Truekner turned his head. 'They should have been inbound,' he said. 'I knew they were overdue at Medulla Station. But homeward-bound is almost always late because the Starfish have no sense of time.'

Starfish. The non-bipedal aliens at the end of the run. Nbaro had seen pictures of them. Like two squid bolted together at the top and turned sideways, with a racing bike tyre in between.

The makers of xenoglas. The original *Xenos*.

88

Makers? Growers? Caretakers?

No one knew. No one had ever communicated directly with a Starfish.

Nbaro tried to wrap her head around it. She knew the trade route as well as any other citizen: eleven stops, each of the last a huge jump into the barely known, so that the last jump was way the hell and gone out into spinward space, almost to the edge of the Orion Spur. Parsecs beyond the so-called Human Sphere, which was itself more like a reaching hand than a sphere.

She doodled with her light pen.

Medulla Station was almost a subjective *year* away, never mind the distance or the light-years that you skipped by threading the M-brane quilt with your ship's needle.

So the news was a year old. A year and eighty hours.

'Sir? May I ask who's outbound now?'

The DHC sent a greatship every year. On a few famous occasions they'd sent two. Most Xeno Runs were at least three years long – a little less than sixteen months outbound, with six ports of call, and then the long run home with five more ports. And Trade Point, of course.

One ship inbound every year, bringing the cargo of xenoglas that Human Space craved – the ultimate trade material. The outbound route was all about collecting the cargo that the Starfish wanted, so that the greatship could return with a hold full of xenoglas. Glas, as most people called it now.

And most of the City's industry ran on glas, and by-products. Even on New London, glas was king; glas, and a thousand laboratories studying it and trying to reproduce it.

The skipper turned his helmeted head.

'The *Hong Kong* should be on her run home. The *Dubai* should be docking at New Catalonia Far Point in a month or two. Hard to measure their progress in our time bubble, but...'

Nbaro played with the numbers, but however she played it, the *New York* had died a year or more ago.

When she was done tinkering, she remembered that Chu had told her that she had a surprise in her helmet bag. When she looked, she found a dozen oatmeal-raisin cookies wrapped in recycle.

Nbaro handed the skipper half the cookies.

'Damn,' he said, and popped his faceplate.

'Atmosphere isn't running!' she said.

'Residual is good enough to eat cookies,' he said. 'And I'm hungry enough.'

Nbaro popped her faceplate, against the advice of her suit. She could feel that the air was old and thin, and cold as hell, but she enjoyed the cookies nonetheless, passing half of hers back, where Indra and Eyre murmured their thanks. They were still subdued – even shocked.

She closed her visor and got the tip of her nose warm again.

Another hour.

Then another.

Nbaro was asleep when Lioness called their sign.

'Roger, Lioness,' the skipper said.

'Bring it in, 6–0–3.'

'Roger, Lioness, copy come home.'

The skipper landed them, matching orbits by hand with a minimum of fuel expenditure and at a low relative speed.

It took half an hour to make their way back to the ready room through a ship at full Battle Stations, with every airtight door or hatch fully cycled closed. It was even harder to get food. She ate with Truekner in relative silence. While they were eating, taking food through bulbs and sealed recycle packets, Smoke and Guille joined them.

'Sorry, skipper,' Mpono said.

He nodded. 'I liked your silent running,' he said, without a hint of sorrow. 'We went dark as soon as I got my head together.'

Smoke shrugged. 'I can't get my head around someone attacking a greatship,' they said. 'Much less killing one.'

'Sabotage?' Guille asked. 'One bastard in Engineering...?'

Truekner glanced at the small pilot.

'I don't think that kind of speculation is going to be very useful,' he said.

Guille looked down.

Truekner got up. 'Excuse me, folks,' he said, and walked off with his tray.

Smoke watched him go.

'Pirates,' they said softly. They drank something brown from a bulb and made a face. 'I hate eating in zero *g*. Everything tastes like recycle.'

Nbaro looked at them.

Guille looked shocked. 'Pirates can't take on a greatship.'

'Someone did, though,' Mpono said.

It was extremely disconcerting to see that Mpono was as rattled as the skipper. That everyone was. Nbaro could see it on every face in the mess – not panic, but fear. Real fear. And anger.

3

Nbaro used the buttoned-up run home from Kephlos to learn everything she could about Space Operations. She read the test manual, passed Level 1 and Level 2, and requested and received permission to begin watch-standing in Space Ops as an observer.

Space Operations was fascinating, not least because they had the kind of command centre that entertainments and holos usually portrayed as tension-filled rooms full of drama. The Space Ops area was a little more than ten metres square and the overhead was quite low, and almost every square centimetre of bulkhead and overhead space was covered in screens, redundant and hardened communications, and data technology support equipment. The deck underfoot was like a nest of snakes, with hundreds of coils of electrical cable, fibre-optic cable, nano-tubing. The systems installed in Space Operations represented four hundred years of installations and removals, technological changes, obsolescence and innovation, and she could see that the command centre had an archaeological past: new screens in ancient housings, and a barely visible mural on the aft bulkhead that was hidden under a relatively recent layer of duplicated repeaters for other stations on the ship.

There was very little drama in Space Operations. In fact, every station projected an elaborate aura of calm, as if they were competing to be dry and emotionless. No one swore, no one spat, no one was angry or afraid.

Nbaro loved it.

At the same time, she was a little surprised to see how much Space Operations *did not do*. They were responsible for all EVAs and flight operations – in effect, for anything leaving the ship. But EVAs were processed through Engineering, mostly because Engineering deployed all the EVAs. Spaceflight operations involved all the various flight sections as well as a host of so-called minors, meaning minor commands – small ships carried in the belly of the *Athens*, including four escort frigates and two pinnaces, which were the smallest craft capable of interstellar travel with a Tanaka drive. Almost unarmed, they were like tiny wasps in a fight. One of the two was a Messenger: the fastest ships in the Human Sphere, with a massive engine and a single human pilot, capable of running far ahead of the greatship. Each of the six minors had a rep in Space Ops; so did most of the flights. Flight 8 was the largest section, with two dozen unarmed cargo lighters, and while they were directed by Space Ops, they seemed to feel that they really worked for Cargo.

Space Ops was one of the multiple and distributed command centres on the ship. It was a form of auxiliary bridge – if needed, the ship could be entirely operated from the Space Ops command deck. Or from the Combat Information Centre, or from the Bridge, or even from Navigation. The command and control functions had been distributed and repeated by the designers as if to duplicate the checks and balances of DHC government in a ship.

Nbaro liked being able to watch everything. From Space Ops, not only did she know who was flying and with what to where, but she also could see the navigational track the ship was on: she could hear the Con steering the ship; hear Astro report on everything from solar radiation to asteroids; watch the ship move to Insertion and emerge into real space.

When she was in Space Ops, she felt as if she was actually *in space*.

The time passed quickly. Almost everyone in Space Ops was a pilot, and they all seemed to know her. On her third time in the centre, Smoke was the Space Ops Watch Officer – the voice of Lioness, and the officer responsible for all operations outside the hull. Smoke listened to the off-going watch officer for ten minutes, and then let him unbelt and unclip from the command seat; the ship was still at Battle Stations.

Mpono climbed into the command couch, strapped in, and winked at Nbaro.

'Skipper has you doing the qualification?' they asked.

'Yes, tir.'

Smoke waved at someone at a station.

'Cruz, let Ms Nbaro share your couch.'

'Aye aye, tir.'

Mpono waved. 'Go learn how ladar works,' they said.

Sharing a crash-couch with the ladar tech was slightly embarrassing, although the man was perfectly polite and gave her a solid four centimetres of space. Most command space couches had room for two fit people; crews had to be able to turn over, report and change.

Petty Officer Cruz worked his lasers like a master, reaching out with coherent light to detect and track objects throughout the solar system at the speed of light; and he explained his various information strategies to her. Nbaro couldn't pretend that she fully understood, but at the end of an eight-hour watch, she'd seen what the ship could 'see' with active emissions. And developed a new appreciation for the difference between projected paths and real paths and the passage of time.

She sat in Space Ops for the whole docking procedure, as the greatship was mated to City. She got to see City from space. She'd seen it on holos, of course, but approaching from above the plane of the New London system was ... breathtaking.

City was a habitat built long ago in Old Terra's orbit, but it had bloomed in the first xenoglas boom. The technologies that had allowed the Human Sphere to explode outwards had been brand new when the keel of City was being laid down, and City was the last major habitat produced in the yards above Old Terra – or at least, her foundations were built there, and then built upon in the Belt and nudged through a pinhole to New London by pioneers in astrogation. City was born in a time of enormous change, when the environment of Old Terra was collapsing into chaos alongside the first major moves out to the stars.

City was beautiful, even from the outside. Unlike, say, Tooler – the vast yards that orbited New London and were also a city – City was built to be admired: a wide ring, itself a fractal tracery of branching substations, and massive arms linking to the central hub, all white and blue and gold and black glass as seen from space, and studded with ships. The greatships only docked at the ends of the central cylinder, or Old City; but hundreds of other ships, most of them privately owned or corporate ships, docked along the ring, on both the outside and inside. Three and a half million people lived on City; a million of them were citizens.

Nbaro found herself crying. She hadn't ever imagined herself homesick, much less patriotic; she thought that the Orphanage's empty prating had erased all that, and here she was moved to tears by the mere *sight* of City.

And as they got closer, she made herself count the greatships docked at the ends. Four. Four in port, three on missions, and the *Athens*.

As they heard Bridge begin docking operations, they finally came off Battle Stations. All over the ship, irises opened and hatches undogged; sailors rose from crash-couches and stretched, trying to force cramped muscles into action.

Her tab cycled, and cycled again, making little pinging and buzzing and gear cog noises.

The same noises were coming from every tab in Space Ops.

Nbaro suddenly realised that she'd been foolish, and she had a great deal to fear in docking. Like her truths being revealed. The death of the *New York* and the excitement of Space Operations had fooled her into believing...

She was afraid to look at her tab.

The Landing Officer was Cortez from Flight 5. He smiled at her over his screen.

'Messages from home. Someone loves me.'

'No one loves you, Cortez,' said another pilot.

'My mother loves me,' Cortez said, in a hurt voice.

Most of the ratings were laughing. And then...

'Oh, god!' someone said.

'Prophet Mohammed,' another said.

'*Kutte ke tattem*,' spat a third.

Nbaro realised that she was back in a world... a world where a man who hated her was going to put her stupidest life moment on the Net for her shipmates to see. And kill her career. And discover where she was, and end the dream.

I wasn't afraid enough.

She closed her eyes.

Waiting to hear her name.

'Bastards,' someone said, and Nbaro opened her eyes, leaning out from her couch to look at a tech's screen.

On his screen she could see a greatship dying, pounded by... nothing.

'Oh, Almighty God,' she said.

The *New York* – it had to be the *New York* – was hit four times. Each hit did enormous damage; gas vented, and secondary

96

explosions rippled out from the initial flashes. At the third strike, a piece broke off the ship about a third of the way back from the bow.

The fourth strike broke the remaining hulk into two parts which began to spiral away from each other in real space.

'Oh, God,' she said again.

A talking head appeared to explain that the footage had been shot by a drone launched by the stricken ship and retrieved by DHCS *Illyria*, a system merchant ship.

Where? she wondered.

The drone must have been jump-capable; if normal warships could get to Ultra Star, they wouldn't need greatships.

Nbaro knew enough.

She went back to her own tab. The terrible death of the great-ship was at the top of every queue; it was as if the DHC wanted to make sure everyone saw it.

But she had other messages. A reminder from the pawnbroker that her debt came due in twelve hours. A demand for a 'contribution' from her service pay to the Orphanage.

And there was a message from someone called Hakon Thornberg.

What?

Her mind filled with the Dominus's door plate, an oiled voice saying *Dr Thornberg will see you now.* Her hands trembled.

You have made some very odd accusations that speak to a lack of mental fitness, he'd said. *While your lack of moral fitness is amply demonstrated in these disgusting videos. I am disrating you from the Service. It's really a terrible shame to see the last Nbaro choose to become a menial, a sex worker.*

All that, just seeing his name. Nbaro wanted to retch.

Instead she pressed *play*. She was incapable of not pressing *play*.

'Ms Nbaro,' that hated voice said. 'It is with a strange mix of pleasure and concern that I see you have been promoted to the Directorate's elite, despite your many failings. I must congratulate myself for having prepared you so brilliantly that, despite sixteen well-deserved demerits, you were still *somehow* accepted for duty.'

Fuck you, you bastard.

'But I am concerned that when the nature of those demerits comes to light, as it inevitably will, your poor character will reflect on us. We should meet, to see if we can chart a path. Don't be foolish, Nbaro. Contact me immediately.'

She fought an urge to throw her tab across the command deck.

A holo-image leapt up out of her tab.

'Hi, Marca! It's Thea. It's terrible about the *New York*. I wish I was aboard – everyone's talking about it and I want to fucking scream. So I'm screaming at you. My mum wants to meet you, so take some liberty and get your ass down here for some real City food before we're off into the heavens. I need someone sane to talk to!'

Pause.

'And did you make me some privacy hangings? Because I got you a present!'

That was unexpected.

I was a little busy.

Ping.

Nbaro blinked. This one was a live message, from an onboard tag. She activated it, and saw Mpono.

'Midder, want to earn your Ops Officer's undying gratitude?'

'Yes, tir,' she said.

'Take my Space Ops watch. You can do in-port. I'll hold your hand through the shuttle launches, they'll lock down the tube, and it's all entirely symbolic.'

No way.

98

'Yes, tir.'

'That's my girlie. I'm on in fifteen.'

'I'm already there,' she said. *Girlie again. Sigh.*

First, Commander Piers, commanding officer of the frigate *Newton*, had to sign off on her 'Watch-standing/In-port' qualification, which he did while reading the freshly spooled in-port flight sched and waving at a tech who was waiting to do some service installations. He didn't even ask her a question.

Then Mpono arrived, looked at the imprint, and laughed.

'Good. Block checked. OK, Jehan, I've got the chair.'

'Master's skiff is going ashore in forty-five minutes,' he said. 'Otherwise, I see four, maybe five launches, all Cargo, and then shut down the magnets for maintenance.'

Mpono looked at Nbaro.

'Once the maintenance bots start into the tunnel, you only have to be on call. That means you're in uniform of the day and reachable on board.' They gave her a serious look. 'On board means you absolutely have to be on board. Got that?'

'Yes, tir.'

'Great. I owe you. Now …' They looked at the list. 'The Master's skiff pre-empts everything else, so he gets a cat to himself. Let's make that Cat 1. 3 and 4 get all the cargo, so Cat 2 can be shut down immediately.'

They made motions with a light pen.

'Cargo, this is Space.'

'Copy, Space.'

'Cargo, I have you down for three shuttles. Then I'm shutting the magnets off for –' they looked down – 'seven hours twelve minutes.'

'Roger, Space. Three shuttles. Alpha Hotel 1–6 is good to go. Alpha Hotel 2–2 ready in ten. Alpha Hotel 0–6 is at hold.'

'Roger.' Mpono pointed with their light pen. 'OK, Space Ops. What should we do?'

Nbaro nodded. 'Um ...' She looked at the light board. 'Hold Cat 1 open for the Master's skiff. Launch 8–1–6 as soon as possible from Cat 3 and cycle it for 8–0–6. Launch 8–2–2 from Cat 4 and shut it down for maintenance.'

'That's satisfactory.'

Smoke drew arrows on the board and pointed at a tech, who gave them a thumb's up and the main board showed the events as written.

'Bingo,' Smoke said. 'Tower, you are clear to launch Alpha Hotel 8–1–6.'

'Roger, Lioness,' Tower said.

Tower was sitting off to the right, with his own screens. He gave a wave. Nbaro had sat with Tower a watch; in her opinion it was the hardest job, launching and recovering the missions.

She looked at her own in-port duty roster, noted that she was down for ready room admin in two days, and thumbprinted for twelve hours of liberty at the end of her Space Ops watch. Nbaro noted with enormous satisfaction the nearly 3000 DHC ducats deposited to her account as of system entry; a little over 1800 was Midshipper base pay, and an incredible 1200 ducats was flight pay. She noted that the Corporation paid a bonus per mission flown, which she hadn't known, and there was a critical performance bonus for good landings.

She'd never had so much money in her life. Sadly, she'd already spent most of it, at least in her head.

Fucking Thornberg was going to ruin her.

Nbaro ran her fingers through her hair and wondered if she could just kill him. Duelling was illegal, but it was *almost* socially acceptable, at least in his class.

He'd never fight her, but she daydreamed about killing him all the same ...

'Hey,' Mpono said. They pointed at the main board.

8–1–6 had launched and the big cargo shuttle was already inbound, dropping away towards the west ring.

'Doubtless getting beads and trinkets,' Mpono said. 'You going ashore?'

'As soon as this watch ends,' Nbaro said.

'There's 8–2–2 ready to move now. Enjoy liberty and don't be late back aboard – a little bird tells me we may get outbound early.' Smoke watched the board, put a hand to their earbud, and nodded crisply. 'The Master's walking to his skiff.' They glanced at Nbaro. 'You heard me? Don't be late.'

'Yes, tir.'

'Good. I'm out of here. You can launch the Master and 8–2–2 all by yourself.'

'Not qualified,' she squeaked.

Smoke made a face and pointed silently at the board.

'Yes, tir,' she said.

Mpono smiled and handed her a pair of tiny wireless earbuds. 'You can do it, and I'm already late.'

They gave Nbaro a pat in thanks, grabbed their flight jacket and were out the hatch.

'Lioness,' came a voice in her ear.

She blinked.

I'm Lioness.

'Archon, ready to launch.'

Archon was the Master's call sign. The commander of the mighty *Athens.*

'Roger, Archon. I have you good for launch.'

Shit, did I say 'good'? Should I have said 'Number one?'

'Roger, Lioness.'

Archon switched to Tower and Nbaro looked at the board, terrified that she'd forgotten something. She heard Tower launch the skiff and then he gave her a hand wave.

'Do you have 8–2–2 up yet?'

Nbaro scanned the screen. 'They reported ready but they're not on the board yet, Tower.'

'Roger.'

Her heartbeat steadied as, before her eyes, Alpha Hotel 8–2–2 appeared, moving to the cat.

'Alpha Hotel 8–2–2, I read you as moving to the rails, over?' she asked.

'Roger, Lioness. Lost signal at the hangar bay. I marked it.'

'Roger, copy. Break break. Tower, this is Lioness, 8–2–2 is on the rails, over.'

'Roger, Lioness.'

Tower gave her a wave. He was only seated four metres away. Nbaro called Cargo.

'Cargo, this is Lioness with a reminder that we're shutting down the magnets.'

'Roger, Lioness. We're shutting down here. No one inbound or outbound for eight hours.'

'Outstanding, Cargo. Thanks.'

Nbaro looked back at her screens to see 8–2–2 launch in a blur and shoot away into the Black, turning sharply for the upper east ring. She saw it again on her launch camera.

'Tube, I see 8–2–2 out the door, over?'

'Lioness, this is Tube. All clear.'

'Can I close the deck?' she asked.

'Roger, Lioness.'

Nbaro looked back at the ladar tech. Then she thumbed the private link to Tower.

'Tower? How do I shut down?'

Tower was a thin, pale man with jet-black hair – Lieutenant Commander Musashi of Flight 5. He got up from his crash-couch and walked over to her.

'Smoke abandoned you?' he asked.

'Yes, sir,' she said.

He laughed. 'Call main Engineering and tell them you're good to go. Then call Bridge and tell them you are closing out Space.' He ran a finger down the arm of her couch. 'Here's Engineering, and here's Bridge.'

'Thanks, sir.'

He smiled down at here. 'Technically, right now, you are the Chair and I'm Tower,' he said. 'So I call you ma'am.'

Nbaro rolled her eyes. He was a lieutenant commander, and she was a midder.

Not even really a midder.

He shrugged. 'It happens,' he said, and went back to Tower.

Nbaro called Engineering.

'Sure,' an engineer said. 'We'll shut down as soon as we've checked a few things. Tweaking. Thanks for the call.'

'Yes, ma'am,' she said. Then called Bridge.

'Bridge, this is Lioness.'

'Roger, Lioness. Go ahead.'

'Shutting down Space Ops, Bridge. 8–2–2 was our last event. The magnets are going down for inspection.'

'Roger, Lioness, copy all.'

Pause.

'Who is this?'

'Midshipper Nbaro, sir.'

'So noted. Bridge out.'

Musashi was already out of his chair.

'See? Now you're immortal – your name's in the log,' he said.

Nbaro shivered. She didn't want immortality. She wanted to be invisible, and enjoy the ambition of her life.

She stood up. 'Do I declare Space Ops closed?'

Lieutenant Commander Musashi shrugged. 'When Mpono does it, they say *Pull the plug*.'

She looked at her techs.

'Pull the plug, folks.'

All the techs gave her a thumbs up, and one by one the main screens went dark, or silver, depending on their manufacturer.

Nbaro had all their comms. In her best command voice, she said, 'Space is now on call. No one leaves the ship, understood?'

'Yes, ma'am,' came a dozen answers.

Musashi smiled. 'Nicely done,' he said.

It all felt very satisfying, as if she knew what she was doing. Nbaro took a moment to breathe in her triumph. Routine to others. For her...

Nirvana.

Nbaro spent a few hours in EVA Rigging on the sewing machine, making curtains for Thea. Then she went to her cabin, hung them, and fetched a nanoreader to alter the screens slightly, making a single cut and then using her cheap multi-tool to put the decorative edging back so that the whole crash-couch looked shipshape and professional. And then she took a nap. She woke in time to have a shower, put on a clean shore-jumpsuit uniform – as she owned almost nothing that wasn't her uniform – and went back to Space Ops. Most of her people were already in their seats.

Nbaro brought up her feeds, perused a really badly written and highly speculative article about the death of the *New York*, and leafed through the juried newsfeed: fashion; sports; a very interesting article on new ship design, that suggested that there were changes coming in insertion systems; and a somewhat hysterical claim that the Anti-spinward worlds were in contact with another alien race and hiding their expansion from the DHC.

Nbaro read that one. The Anti-spinward worlds weren't a government or a coalition or even a corporation – just the fastest spreading frontier of the Human Sphere as it expanded outward. They weren't fond of DHC tariffs or oversight, and places like Novogorod and New Texas were almost big enough to matter in the slowly moving world of interstellar politics. But the 'new aliens' accusation was a bugbear raised by conservatives every time they wanted to brush back the Outers' influence.

Nbaro looked up in time to see Guille, who looked a little frayed around the edges. She was in correct uniform of the day and she looked capable of some rational thought, so Nbaro smiled and gave her the Lioness chair.

'Nothing to report,' she said.

Guille waved. 'I've got it. Go have some fun. I did.'

Nbaro dropped down the brow towards Old City Dockside with a little more skill than she'd climbed up, although her gloved hands were just as cold. There were a dozen other sailors in the tube, and she arrived dockside to find two spacers already caged by shore patrol and a long line waiting to be checked against the shore-going list. Nbaro waited her turn, only to get a laugh from the shore patrol officer.

'You're an officer, Mid,' he said. 'You don't need my permission to go ashore. While you're down there, please do all the things I can't.'

Nbaro smiled. The whole smile thing was getting easier. She bounced along the zero g dockside, feeling a different person from the one who'd come across this dock three weeks before.

There was no gravity dockside, being at one end of the massive City station where there was no spin. So Nbaro bounced to a handhold and then made her way fairly quickly up to a lift, or a train, depending on the orientation. She paid for a seat with a flash of her tab, feeling ridiculously rich.

Belted in with two ratings, both a little older.

'Off to see the city, miz?' the man asked.

Nbaro smiled. 'No,' she said. 'I was born here.'

They nodded. New Londoners.

As soon as weight came on with the movement of the transit car,

Nbaro felt the tug of her jumpsuit and discovered to her chagrin that she had her multi-tool and her nanoreader in one of the zip-pockets of her shore-going rig. She'd picked them up by habit.

I am an idiot.

Too late to take them back now.

Taking the nanoreader was a pretty serious infraction, as its function was both classified and industrial proprietary. Nbaro was tempted to go back, but time was short.

Idiot. I'm the same person after all – the self-destruction expert.

Then her attention was seized by the City's greatest view.

Because of the low gravity of the giant orbital, the transit cars could roll in three dimensions as the tubes passed between decks, where a gifted architect had designed the great Square: a re-creation of old Venice's Piazza San Marco with the *original* Doge's palace and the great cathedral. It was a magnificent open space, the largest open space on any orbital in the Human Sphere.

The Transit ran above the great square, and for a moment the passenger was upside down, looking through the roof of the car at the people moving around the square far below. The fountains with free water, the gilded bronze horses, two thousand years old, were from yet another of Old Terra's cities.

People caught her eye, dressed in the kinds of clothes she'd never owned: patrician men and women in their elaborate long-coats and tight-fitting undersuits, a few wearing daggers or swords of rank. They were modelled on the ship jumpsuits and flightsuits, but made of richer fabrics and lacking the practical pockets and stents. A few wore deliberately impractical clothes – breeches and boots, or shoes with heels – but those were rare. City's patricians were still ship owners and merchants, and most of them were careful to ensure they could drop the long-coats and put on a vac suit.

Nbaro had seen it all before, on infrequent school trips and on illegal escapes from the Orphanage. It never got old – the panorama of old buildings, the modern gold-tinted xenoglas structures, the plumage of the wealthy.

The transit car, secure in its own gravity, hurtled across the sky and then down and around, like an amusement park ride, to stop at the station hidden inside the spinward facade of the square.

All the ratings disembarked at the Square. Nbaro felt the tug to join them; old things fascinated her and she wanted to walk in the cool darkness of the great cathedral and perhaps listen to the choral re-enactors who kept some of the ancient music alive. She'd gone in once with Sarah.

Or she could sit at one of the open-air cafes and watch people. *Best not think too much about that.*

And Nbaro wasn't sightseeing.

She allowed the doors on the maglev to close, and sat back as it dived again.

The station after Square was Underside.

Nbaro rose, held on to one of the standing poles, and waited for the doors to slide open. When they did, she smelt it immediately. Curry and marijuana and tobacco smoke and a sharp smell like hot metal and rotting garbage. She knew that smell so well…

The pawnbroker was in Underside. He wasn't very far from the Orphanage, either; Nbaro had made her arrangements with him through friends, because at the time she'd been restricted to quarters by the Dominus. Now, just walking into Underside felt bad. Her stomach flip-flopped harder than it had for her first launch from the *Athens*'s railguns. She could see the Free Believers' convent at the end of Underside Dock 1, which everyone called Orphan's Dock. Holotattoo parlours and chip surgeons and three brothels all along one short, slightly curved dock-front.

And right in the middle, the white marble and plasteel of the Orphanage.

It's just a facade, Nbaro thought bitterly. *Everything behind that marble is old and dingy and horrible.*

She turned anti-spinward and made her way along Dockside into Underside 2, known as Guns, a neighbourhood so bad it didn't rate a transit stop. When City had been built, there had been enormous railgun turrets along the top and bottom docksides, in between the big docking clamps. Most of them were now warehouse space and Underside Turret 4 was one of the few active turrets, used by the Orphanage as a training area – hence 'Guns' for the neighbourhood.

Nbaro turned right, off the dockside, and into a passageway so narrow it might have been on shipboard. Most of it was cheap residential buildings, but they were zoned for businesses: fly-by-night import-export businesses and pawnshops catering to spacers, interspersed with tavernas and drug shops of varying degrees of legality. A med clinic advertised a full system flush, which Marca assumed was for spacers who'd used all the other shops.

Nbaro turned right at the cross-corridor, crossing the canal of hard vacuum that City kept open for in-City travel by small craft; the arching bridge was well-maintained and decorated in much the same old style as the *Athens*. A small in-system shuttle passed under her, its propulsion nozzles secured and being moved along the vacuum tube by electromagnets. It was quite beautiful and she stopped to watch it. It was an antique, or perhaps a rich person's toy, with deliberate elements of old-style craft: visible rivets in alternating bronze and steel, the hull itself covered in engine turning and elaborate etching, so that light was refracted as if from thousands of jewels as it passed.

On the other side of the canal lay Underside Residential 2, which went by various uncomplimentary names, mostly sexual, because brothels and sex-related shops were its principal mercantile endeavour. Her pawnshop was at the next intersection. Now Nbaro was passing crowds of spacers, and she drew stares. In this section, any woman did. But her crisp dark blue Service jumpsuit deterred outright harassment, and those spacers who saw the officer's pips on her collar mostly got out of her way. A Service senior, worse for drink, cast her a sloppy salute out of habit.

Nbaro knocked on the outer hatch to the pawnshop. It wasn't airtight, but it was a heavy door with cameras and a buzzer, and she had to wait to be buzzed in.

The same man stood behind the counter, with the lank hair of a bad rejuv and enough tattoos for three or four spacers.

'Nbaro,' she said. 'Here to clear my debt. And retrieve my... item.'

For a panicked moment, she thought she'd lost her pawn ticket, but there it was on her cheap tab, and she thumbed it to life.

The old man nodded.

'Ms Nbaro,' he said, his voice flat, uninterested. 'You owe 2116. You have it?'

She frowned. 'Where'd the 116 come from?' she asked.

'Today's interest,' he said, bored.

'I don't owe interest for today. I have a contract.'

He stared at her. 'You can pay,' he said, 'or forfeit.'

Nbaro shook her head, suddenly stubborn. He thought he could bully her? Fear and anger combined to make her sharp.

'Bullshit,' she said. 'I know my rights. I have my contract, and it says two thousand by twenty-four hundred hours today. It's 1735.'

'Contract must be wrong.'

She shook her head. 'Nope. Your reminder, twelve hours ago, said two thousand.'

He shrugged. 'I recommend you pay. Otherwise…' He left the threat in the air.

Nbaro made a face. She had the money – thanks only to her flight pay. She *could* just pay. If she hadn't flown so much, she'd have been unable to meet the charge. And the item she'd left in pawn was perhaps the most valuable thing she owned. That anyone owned.

Another risk I took.

Nbaro thought about it.

'How often does this kind of shit work on your customers?'

He spread his hands.

Nbaro took out her tab and called Shore Patrol Post 1. In the forest of risks she was running, this seemed a small one.

'Who are you calling?'

'DHC MSS Shore Patrol,' Nbaro said. 'We'll get an auditor down here and straighten this out.'

He made a slight movement with his lips, barely visible, then snapped, 'Fine. Two thousand. And never come here again.'

She pointed her tab at him.

'Cash,' he said.

'Doesn't say so in the contract,' she said. 'Pay your taxes, man.'

He was angry now.

'Who the fuck are you?' he asked.

Nbaro smiled. 'I'm an officer of the DHC.' It felt good to say. Almost true. 'Show me your terminal. Thanks. Now I want a quit claim and a receipt, please.' She made herself sound relaxed, even languorous. 'And my item.'

He wrote them out and Nbaro stood at his counter and read them over. Then he went to the back and unlocked a DNA-coded safe; she saw him prick his finger on a pipette, and then wipe away the blood. He came back and slapped her 'item' on the scratched glass counter. It was her small lion, in gold and enamel.

The pawnbroker nodded at it. 'Take it away, and take some advice. That thing's real. The toffs will kill to keep them. I could have sold it, any day. So fuck you and your 116 ducats.'

Nbaro picked the beautiful thing up and dropped it into her pocket.

'A deal's a deal,' she said.

But then she realised that she was not following her new rules. She made herself smile.

'Thanks.' But as it struck her that she was actually going to be done with him, Nbaro felt... happy. She relented. 'Without your loan, I'd never have got my commission. So I'm sorry for being a knob.'

He blinked. Then a very small smile touched his lips.

'You drive a hard bargain, sister.'

But he scooped up the twenty-ducat piece Nbaro left on his counter. She'd never tipped anyone before in her life. But he nodded at her as she left. Respect? Or just greed?

She slipped out the door.

Tempting to visit the hacker and get the fonts corrected on her personnel record.

But he'd been paid in advance, eating most of her ready cash a month ago. And it had passed muster. No need to go back.

No. The die is cast, either way. What matters is Thornberg.

The corridor was crowded, and a dozen drunk or drugged spacers pushed past, almost slamming her back into the pawnshop. Two women were having an argument so loud and vehement that it flooded her with adrenaline as she watched them, prepared for violence, but they vanished in the direction of the outer docks.

Nbaro climbed the bridge back over the hard vacuum canal and stood at the top, looking through the plastiglas canopy at the city above her, and the narrow slice of the star-struck void off to her left.

She opened her tab and cycled her messages until she found the message from Patrician Thornberg.

She took a deep breath, as if the air was very thin.

She typed her reply.

Sir,
I'm available for a few minutes if you would care to meet.
Nbaro

Nbaro hit *send* before she could change her mind.

Then she found Thea's message and hit *live* in green.

'Wow, where are you?' Thea asked, answering almost instantly.

'The canal near the Orphanage,' Marca said.

'Looks terrible. Are people being killed behind you?'

Marca looked over her shoulder.

'Yes,' she said.

In fact, the two women were struggling inexpertly, and the others were betting on them.

'Perfect,' Thea said. 'We have to be back aboard in ... six hours, seven minutes. Come for dinner? How quickly can you get here?'

'I have an appointment first.'

'OK,' Thea said. 'Twenty hundred?'

'Should be good,' Marca said. 'I'm in a shore-going jumpsuit. Will your mother explode?'

'No, that's good!' Thea said. 'Don't be late. Mum will have food on the table. You know where we are?'

Marca shrugged. 'No.'

Her tab gave a little ratcheting buzz, making her stomach flip as she saw the Downside address.

'Palazzo Drake,' Thea said. 'Just come to the loggia and they'll let you in. I have your palm print in my scan.'

Palazzo Drake.

Nbaro smiled – a bitter, thin smile.

'I'll be there.'

Then she closed her tab and dropped it into her hip pocket and began to walk anti-spinward. She stayed in the narrow corridors of Off-Dockside from habit, and she kept one hand near her shiv all the time. But her dark blue jumpsuit was more of a charm than her white Orphanage jumpsuit had ever been, and spacers gave her room.

This area, the far side of Underside Dock 1, was for shady financial offices, private banks and tavernas, bars, street food, and more brothels, if of a slightly less criminal nature. A pair of DHC security officers in full body armour stood at the intersection of Calle and Stretto. They both saluted her.

Nbaro nodded, and turned back dockside, feeling very out of place and wishing for one of her swords. She didn't even have a crewer's knife, and she thought maybe she could afford a nice one.

Her stomach was rumbling.

I'm going to eat in a palace.

If I survive the next forty minutes or so.

Nbaro was cautious approaching the doctor's address now – another import/export business. She felt the trap closing... but she was curious all the same.

This is wrong, wrong, wrong.

She hit the buzzer on the door.

The door opened automatically, and inside was a good carpet and expensive office furniture. She could see a receptionist, so she stepped inside...

Nbaro took the blow on her shoulder instead of her head; she couldn't have said how she knew to dodge. The second blow was aimed at the side of her knee and meant to do permanent damage.

She caught the kick and threw her assailant, trapping his leg and kicking the man viciously between the legs. Then in the one-third *g* of spin, Nbaro pivoted on her hips, using the screaming man's body as a weapon. His head hit the bulkhead with a hollow thump, having taken another assailant down in a tangle of legs and arms.

A door by her left side opened on silent electrics. Nbaro glanced, saw stairs down.

Looking had been a mistake.

A shove, and she was falling down those stairs. Nbaro bounced twice in the low gravity, hit her hip with her nanoreader in the pocket, hard, and fell into a room at the base of the steps.

She looked up, and a man was pointing something at her.

He pulled the trigger and Nbaro felt the tingle of an EMP. Now her tab would be dead.

She scrambled to her feet and he pointed a slug-thrower at her instead.

'Stay there, bitch!' he shouted.

Before Nbaro could consider her options, a door between them clicked shut on silent runners and she was in imperfect darkness in a small room, with scuttling cockroaches and a basement smell. The only light came from a window high in the wall that let in the day-cycle lights from the corridor above them.

'Ms Nbaro.'

The voice came from the wall. Flat, disinterested, metallic – a disguised voice. Nbaro knew who it was anyway.

'You bastard.'

'In approximately six hours your ship will leave without you, and you will be recorded as a deserter,' the voice said. 'I have no idea how you convinced the Navy to take you, and I hope you have enjoyed your brief Service career. You are now headed for the career you deserve – perhaps a bond-girl for a mining colony. Goodnight, Ms Nbaro.'

She stood in silence.

I'm an idiot.

Why did I come here? He never plays fair. He's a liar and a thief. And I only think I'm smart.

I'm a fucking idiot.

Now her anger welled up. She pulled at, and then hammered on, the door and found it solid as concrete. She went to the window; it was too high to reach and too small even for her slight shoulders.

Nbaro blinked. Tears. Despair welled up. It wasn't her first bout of pure despair; she fell in, as if to a deep, horrid pool, and there she stayed.

Un-fucking-fair.

Nbaro wept. Later, she thought she'd screamed; her throat was swollen and raw. She didn't doubt his threat about a brothel on a mining colony. That was where he'd sent Sarah; she knew what he did. After all, she'd reported it all to the DHC and the Board.

And look where I am now.

Even as Nbaro let herself scream and sob, in case of cameras, she reviewed one of her many Service sims, about escape and evasion. A haunted-looking man laid it all out for them, having been captured by pirates, made a slave, and escaped only after terrible torments.

'You either escape in the first four hours, when they relax after they've caught you, or after a year. If it's a year, it'll be a bad year.'

First four hours, she thought. *Here we go. Time to be broken.*

Nbaro threw herself down in despair. She rolled against the door, and wept. It wasn't hard and it wasn't all acting, and even when her tears were spent, she continued sobbing and slowly taking stock of the tools at her disposal.

It was about 2200 hours, give or take, she guessed. Darkshift would begin any minute ... and sure enough, the ruddy light from the passageway diminished and then went out. The room wasn't pitch black, because there was a very low light up above, but it was dark.

Nbaro continued to sob and shake, reached into her pocket, and took out the nanoreader. It was a crime to have taken it off the ship, and it might not be hardened against EMP, but it was the first thing to try.

She shielded it with her hand and her whole body, curled into a shaking foetal ball.

I am small, and broken. You caught me, and you have nothing to fear from me.

Nbaro turned it on, and the telltale lit green.

She sobbed. It was a genuine sound.

It was more real than she wanted it to be.

Nbaro rolled over to huddle against the door, and she ran the nanoreader along the bottom, with no obvious result, and then against the side. She rose to her feet slowly, wiped her nose, went to use the sink and came back to lean against the door. She ran the reader along the handle edge, as if she was clawing at the door.

'Please let me out,' she said to the darkness. 'Please.'

Nothing from the speaker.

Be crazy. Be desperate.

Nbaro shouted, pounded on the door, and ran the reader along the top of the door while she screamed her rage.

What if the door wasn't made of nanofibre, which the reader could slice through?

What if it was uncuttable carbon or steel?

Nbaro ran the reader down the hinge side, around the dur-alumin hinges.

And she felt it give.

Nbaro remembered a line from an old, old novel she'd loved: 'These things must be done with immense planning or all at a single hazard.' With that in mind, she put her shoulder to the door and shoved with all her desperation and rage.

She was on the stairs. She couldn't plan, and she couldn't let herself hope. She went right up to the top and tried the door handle.

Open.

I'm not the only idiot, Nbaro thought with joy, and went right through into the expensive lobby. The receptionist was a detailed dummy, not an actual person, but there was someone in the shadows behind it.

She reached the main hatch faster than the man could come around the desk, and by the time he raised a slug-thrower and fired, she had put the airtight door between them. The slug ricocheted viciously around the small space, the sound so deafening he wondered if he'd fired a burst.

'I've got her,' said the man.

No you don't.

Nbaro was out and into the passageway's subdued lighting, and she ran towards the docks.

Her assailant fired the slug-thrower again.

It was very loud in the passageway, and the force of the slug turned her as it hit her hip, or something down there, but her entire will was on running and she was damned if being shot was going to stop her.

A man came out of a cross-passage and Nbaro was down, rolling, and then up, pain like a lightning strike through her. Her shiv was in her hand from long practice and she turned at bay, backing into the side-passage that was no wider than her shoulders.

I can die here. I joined the Service, landed my craft on the Athens *and I escaped your fucking hell.*

Nbaro screamed with the full force of her lungs as the man came around the corner cautiously. She planted her shiv in his forearm and pulled, ripping down his arm. No skill, all speed and rage and fear.

117

He lost his grip on his weapon and flinched and she stepped in – a rising knee into his stomach, a punch.

Another one stabbed her from behind and white-hot pain lanced into her.

A whistle. A long, high whistle – the sweetest sound. Station Security.

'Halt!' roared a voice.

'Finish her,' spat the man she'd put down.

'Contract says no killing!'

'Fucking finish her!'

The man who'd put a knife in her back had stepped away, imagining his job was done. Nbaro glided back, body still functioning, and got him in a foot trap – sort of – and punched him in the jaw with her right, and then she threw him atop his friend, hard. Her right foot lashed out on pure training, collapsing the fallen man's larynx with a burst of blood from his mouth.

The other one, with her shiv in his arm and his partner lying across him, managed to get his free hand on the fallen slug-thrower. All Nbaro could do was watch as he raised it from the deck and aimed at her. The big barrel pointed right for her, and when she threw herself to one side, it followed remorselessly.

Bang.

It took her a moment to realise that she was not dead.

Suddenly the cross-corridor was full of men and women in body armour, and the smell of cordite.

With the fight over, shock took her, and all Nbaro could think was *Why is Thea here?*

4

'Some people will do anything to avoid one of my mother's dinners,' Thea said, which was when Marca realised she was alive. And in a bed with sheets. Well... a crash-couch with a sort of sheet-bag strapped...

She was on a ship.

With Thea.

Nbaro had made it back to the *Athens*.

'You also very cleverly missed most of the City cargo load,' Thea said. 'It was fucking hard.'

Marca croaked, feeling terrible, and Thea handed her a bulb of water, which she sipped gratefully as a science tech came in and glanced at her.

'You can leave whenever you're ready, Ms Nbaro.'

Marca made a noise somewhere between a hungry cat and a dying wasp. She rubbed her head with her hand and found a spot of scar tissue she hadn't expected.

'Drink your nice water,' Thea said. 'I've worked about sixteen hours four rotations in a row, and all I want is sleep, but they made me come here to get you.

Marca blinked. Her legs worked. Her head sort of worked. The spot she'd found hurt.

'Can't believe they put you in the rehab clamshell,' Thea said, sounding impressed.

The tech reappeared with her shore-going jumpsuit and a number of items, including her nanoreader.

'I'm ST Yu,' he said with a disarming smile. Then he pointed at the dented nanoreader. 'That's really not supposed to leave the ship, Ms Nbaro,' he said. 'I didn't log it. But don't take it off ship again...'

Nbaro smiled weakly. 'Thanks.'

'You'll start to feel more yourself over the next hour or so. If you have any problems, come back here. You spent three days in full rehab, so your muscles are going to be a little weak. That's a long time.' Yu shrugged. 'At least, the manual says it's a long time.'

Nbaro raised her head and found she was naked. Panic flashed through her. She clamped down on it, and Thea squeezed her hand.

'Relax,' she said.

Yu came over and began pulling feeds out of her flesh. He did it with a casualness, as he talked.

'Sometimes fine motor co-ordination is bad for a day or so, so you can't fly until we give you an up-chit,' he said cheerfully. 'Come back here tomorrow for the test.'

'Lucky goose,' Thea said. 'Could you hit me in the head so I can get a day off?'

'Sorry, no. First do no harm...' the tech said. 'Anyway, we have actual science to do, Ms Drake. This *physical* medicine is really beneath us.'

'That's nice,' Thea said. 'And anyway, sleep is not harm.' She smiled at Marca. 'Come on.'

'I need to get dressed,' she said.

Nbaro didn't like being naked with a stranger, especially a man. *Orphanage thinking*, her rational side said. But she was a hurt animal, somewhere inside, and was grateful when Thea helped her pull her jumpsuit on, and zipped up.

'Better?'

'Yes.'

Thea half-carried her through the corridors and passageways of the ship. They were on Second Deck, below the railguns, and they had to navigate up a drop-shaft and across a passage, but the further they went, the better she was at moving. By the time the two reached their stateroom, she felt almost human.

Thea got the hatch open, and the bell rang, and Marca felt a rush of something like love.

I almost lost this.

Her swords. Her beautiful gem of a cabin, with the neat privacy curtains and the beautiful brass-bound desks and elegant chairs. The panel of wood between the upper crash-couch and the lower.

'Welcome home,' Thea said. 'And thanks ever so much for the curtains.'

Nbaro slid into the desk chair. The screen showed deep space, probably a view off the bow. Stars twinkled against a deep black – the deep black only really good screens could project.

Home. And we've launched. Two years of freedom. Paradise.

She fought her tears back, and won.

'You're quite welcome,' she said.

'I wanted you to come to dinner,' Thea went on, 'so I could give you some stuff. We have tons of it – all my brothers served.' She shrugged. 'After you no-showed and I had to find you, you've got whatever I pulled out, OK?' She smiled down at Marca. 'You too proud for some hand-me-downs? I'm not.'

Marca blinked.

'Here's Janna's flight helmet. Probably needs to be resized for you. Four non-regulation flightsuits – all small. Some other stuff. A kneeboard, a holster and sidearm – I took the best one for myself, I'm afraid…' She winked, and carried on sorting through an enormous pile on Marca's crash-couch. 'Some body armour. It's good stuff – Alexi's not much bigger than you, but it'll take a rigger to make it fit.'

Marca staggered up and threw her arms around Thea.

'Well,' Thea said. 'This is embarrassing.'

Marca didn't let go.

'I thought I'd lost all of this,' Marca said, suddenly. 'Everything.'

Thea held her a moment and then let go, and Marca retreated, stunned to have such a friend. And to have shown her feelings so obviously.

Thea laughed. 'And I thought you were such a hard case.'

Marca laughed. 'I'm about as hard as old recycle.'

'You killed those two gangsters.'

'Gangsters?' Marca asked, and it all came back to her. It wasn't that she'd forgotten – just that she hadn't thought about it. Now she did. All in a rush.

'There's a very threatening flimsy from Ship's Security,' Thea said. 'I didn't want to worry you, but…'

Marca's heart almost stopped. Flimsies were legal documents; anything else went digital.

She wanted to look at the astonishing wealth of stuff Thea had brought her. Instead, she took it.

It had black edges, which she'd never seen before. The text was simple and direct.

As soon as you are recovered from your injuries, please report to the Special Services office on Sixth Deck.

Marca looked at Thea. 'Special Services is most emphatically *not* Ship's Security.'

In fact, she hadn't even known that the Board's secret service had an office on board the greatships. But of course they did. There was no physical asset more important to the DHC than a greatship.

'Thank you for everything,' she said. 'I need to go and get this done.'

The end.

'Whenever you see danger, you run towards it,' Thea said. 'Don't you?'

'I used to run away,' Marca said. 'This is better.'

She felt calm. That was odd.

Thea smiled. 'Almighty. Good luck.'

Sixth Deck was a *long* way down. Nbaro went to her local drop-shaft and jumped a deck at a time, feeling too woozy to make the whole descent in a single pass. She jumped to O-1, where there was a chapel and a Ship's Store among other things, and then to Flight and Hangar, where there were vision panels into the operational space, so that she could see Space Operations at work. Even as she watched, a big cargo shuttle from Flight 8 launched in a blur of blue light and sparks.

Down to First Deck, passing a dozen spacers coming up, because it was near to shift change and they were headed for their duty stations, or to get food, or maybe to the Ship's Store for some treat before work.

Down past Second Deck – more spacers, main medbay and some enlisted berthing, taking up all of Second Deck and most of Third and Fourth with pockets even further 'below.'

Nbaro had no real idea what was on Fifth Deck. The volume of people moving through the shaft died away; below Fifth Deck were the engineering spaces and various mysterious work-shops and mostly, the cargo areas. Sixth and Seventh Decks were triples – each space being three times as high as the decks above – and scuttlebutt said that there were spaces in Seventh Deck where no one had been in a century.

Nbaro caught a handhold at Sixth Deck and swung back into gravity, which hurt her knees a little, but otherwise she felt almost fine, for a woman who felt sure that she had escaped capture and forced desertion, only to be suspended as soon as she was healed. She had been an idiot to take the nanoreader. Her mistake had saved her life. She steeled herself and continued walking aft, counting off frames and reading signs.

At the first corner, Nbaro had a visceral image of one of her attackers rounding the corner, of her shiv going into his arm, the precise feel of the shiv's point grating against the bones of his forearm.

She recoiled. Then stood there a moment and made herself walk past, happy that there wasn't anyone else nearby.

It was dark on Sixth Deck, and the overhead panels hadn't been fitted with xenoglas tubes, so the passageway was only lit at the frames, and because it was mostly cargo, there was only one passenger tube running fore and aft, and it was busy. Nbaro took her cheap toolkit out of her pocket and used it as a torch, and was almost sure she saw something *move* at the next knee-knocker. The bulkheads were beautifully decorated, just as they were above, but even more breathtaking because of their scale. These appeared to be battle scenes of men and women in exotic armour, covering the full six-metre height of the shadowy passageway.

Nbaro moved aft, walking quickly. She loved the frescoes and the beautiful bronze work, but she wanted to get this over with, and she didn't fully trust her own senses. She wondered if she had drugs in her system, left over from meds; or maybe this was the attachment trauma she'd read about.

And the Special Services ... Nbaro assumed it was about the

nanoreader. She'd brought it with her, ready to turn it in and take whatever came.

Section 8 Frame 936 Starboard was almost against the stern, it was so far back in the ship, past hundreds of airtight hatches and doors. Nbaro hadn't seen more than a dozen people, all junior ratings moving with purpose along the corridors. All of them gave her the same look, which amounted to a 'What is an officer doing down here?', followed by a fixed forward expression.

The Special Services office was marked with a bronze plaque embossed with the DHC's winged lion. It was perfectly direct; beneath the lion it read 'DHC Department of Special Services'.

Nbaro knocked, entered, and braced to attention.

'Midshipper Nbaro reporting as ordered,' she said.

There was a young man behind the single desk. He was perfectly ordinary looking and wore the standard shipboard blue jumpsuit. He had brown, or perhaps tanned, skin and large eyes and a moustache that was a poor choice for his narrow face.

'Ah,' he said. 'Ha-hmm.' He rose. 'Ms Nbaro. I'm ...' He seemed to be struggling for words. 'I'm Lieutenant Devid Smith.'

He seemed confused, which made no sense.

'Please have a seat,' he said – then, seeing there was no seat, 'Hmm.'

He went and got her a folding chair and placed it for her.

'Coffee?' he asked. 'Water? That's all I've got, I'm afraid.'

'I'd take coffee,' she admitted.

If his intention was to put her at ease, he was instantly successful.

Nobody gives you coffee before they arrest you.

He went to a very old wall-mounted unit, with more buttons than she would have imagined on a coffee machine.

'Cup or bulb, Ms Nbaro?'

'Cup, please,' she said.

The cup he brought her was *porcelain* and the coffee smelt magnificent.

'Thanks,' she said.

'Think nothing of it.' He sat. 'Now. How are you feeling?'

'All right, I guess,' she admitted.

He nodded. 'Gunshot wound, knife wound, severe laceration on the lower left leg, numerous abrasions.' He smiled. 'Can you explain, please, miz?'

Nbaro took a sip of coffee. 'I was attacked,' she said carefully.

'Yes,' he said. 'Two assailants, both now dead.'

She met his eyes. 'Yes?' she agreed. 'I killed one. Did Security kill the other? I really don't remember that part.'

He leant back. 'You killed a man. How do you feel about that?'

Nbaro thought about it and filtered it past her lifetime in the Orphanage.

'Fine,' she said. *Not even my first time.* 'They attacked me.'

'Why did they attack you?'

Nbaro looked around his office to cover her indecision. Special Services worked directly for the Board. The Board was controlled by the patricians. Thornberg was a patrician. QED.

'I don't know,' she said.

He nodded. 'That would be an excellent response in most situations,' he said.

She blinked.

'Listen, Nbaro. Those two who attacked you? Professionals. Very bad people, brought in from New London. Organised crime. It happens that we know a great deal about both of them because we'd ... Ha. Hmm. We've had contact with them before.'

She didn't allow a muscle on her face to move. He was the worst interrogator imaginable; how had he ever made the grade in Special Services? He was telling her more than she told him ... and then he nodded, as if he'd read her mind.

'So ...' he said slowly. 'I'm afraid I must insist you tell me what you know.'

She frowned. 'I don't know.'

Insist away, little man.

'Let me help,' he said. 'Seven weeks ago, as an Orphan-Cadet, you sent the Board a detailed account of the malfeasance of the Director of the State Orphanage – Messire Hakon Thornberg of the City Thornbergs.' He didn't smile or lean forward. He just raised one eyebrow fractionally. 'Sound familiar?'

Gods. They know everything. I'm fried.

God, then they know my record is faked and ...

Nbaro took a deep breath. 'Yes,' she said. 'That's true.'

She hated the sound of her voice. The weakness.

Don't whine.

Smith folded his hands. 'And now he's seeking revenge.'

She felt the blood leave her face like a tide going out. She made a small noise – very like the noise rats made when the feral cats got them.

Eek. My last sound. Damn it, I want to die on my feet, not squeaking.

Easier said than done.

'Yes,' she said in a very small voice.

He nodded. 'You see? That wasn't difficult.'

He reached up to press more buttons on his ancient coffee maker, and Nbaro saw that he had a very slim – and very black – weapon in a tight-fitting shoulder holster. She was more shocked than she'd expected to be.

He turned to face her.

'So ...'

He seemed like a bumbling but well-meaning teacher. She'd had one: Mrs Hardrede. One of her favourites, actually. She'd made the Orphanage's required Home Economics course something exciting and interesting: a tour of the City's justly famed cuisines;

instruction in the history of fashion and how to fake it on a low budget; a thousand bits of life advice. All from a woman with a personal turn-out that verged on slovenly, who always had spots of egg somewhere on her uniform blouse. Most courses at Orphanage had been sims, even when they were required by law to be live-taught, but Home Economics was always live.

Nbaro wasn't sure why she had connected the two. Except that, over a handful of classes, Mrs Hardrede had convinced her that she knew a thing or two. Smith had that quality. Her assumptions had been wrong. He was an expert interrogator. She was, as usual, an idiot.

'So ...' he said again. 'You turned him in to the Seventeen. He tried to kill you. Is that a fair summary?'

'Yes,' she said again.

Though it leaves out a few things.

'Why don't you tell me, in your own words, for the record.'

Nbaro took a deep breath. She was already committed. And there was no place to go.

'Let the record show,' she said, engaging the ship's recording devices as well as anything the Special Services had, 'Patrician Thornberg made our Orphanage a living hell. He attempted to manipulate the Orphans, especially those who were ... patrician-born. When I blew the whistle on it, passing evidence of his behaviour to the DHC, he abused his authority to learn my identity, and he punished me, attempted to destroy my career, and when I was ... *lucky* enough to be commissioned ... he arranged to have me kidnapped so that I would miss the *Athens*'s departure and be disrated as a deserter.'

Lucky. Lucky that I used money a friend gave me by selling her body to pay a hacker to cheat the codes so that it looked as if I'd been commissioned. Fuck you all.

Smith nodded as if he believed her.

'He swore he'd have me sent to a brothel. It's what he did with dissenters, as he called them. I know of two others.' Nbaro took a breath. 'When I escaped, his thugs tried to kill me. So to be honest, sir, I'm glad I killed one, and I'd kill him again if I had to.'

Smith nodded. His voice changed; it became calm, almost the voice of an AI.

'This statement contains assertions that reflect Ms Nbaro's bias and are not yet proven,' he added. Then he smiled at her. Then his voice returned to its warm, almost bumbling note. 'But by and large, I'd say it was accurate.'

For a moment she couldn't breathe.

'There's more,' she said. 'He has—'

'A video?' Smith asked. 'Of an embarrassing nature?' he added.

'You know everything,' she sighed.

Do you know everything?

'That's my job,' he said pleasantly. 'Our job.'

Why did I think he was a bumbling little man? He's a shark.

'I won't make promises we can't keep, but I will say that in our current … hmm … negotiations with the patrician, we'll attempt to ensure that he cannot use those videos against you.'

'You're negotiating with him?'

He looked at her. 'It's part of our mandate.' He pointed at the holographic projection behind his head, which said *Quis custodiet ipsos custodes* under the winged lion. 'We make sure the untouchable patricians are touchable,' he said. 'I'm sorry this happened, and I'm sorry that it happened to you, but your actions have revealed a … ha, hmm. A dedicated region of damage in the fabric of the Republic.'

A region of damage in the fabric of the Republic. I'm so sorry, Sarah, that your fabric was damaged.

'That sounds bad,' she said.

'I won't lie to you in this matter. It is bad, and it may still all blow back on you. But you've surprised us,' he admitted. 'We are not often surprised.'

She took that in. 'So what now?'

He opened a drawer and took out a tab, which he slid across the desk.

'Your new tab,' he said. 'It's a little better than your old one. Be aware that it's completely monitored – absolutely everything you say and do will be captured. I beg you, for your own safety, to use it exclusively. We need him to contact you. We need to monitor him. It is even possible, although I don't find it likely, that he will continue to attempt to destroy you on the *Athens*.'

'Almighty,' she said.

Nbaro felt her new freedom vanish. They would monitor her. *Were they actually on her side?*

She feared the ship's AI as much as this obviously dangerous man and his secrets. Orphanage rumour said that AIs were hyper-protective of their ships, and treated dangerous individuals the way white blood cells treated infection.

The AI will now know everything I do.

But I'm still here. No one has said anything about disrating or court martial.

Breathe.

She'd missed a few words, apparently about Thornberg.

He nodded. 'He's very powerful and very rich. But so is the DHC. So is the Service. And so is Special Services.' He nodded again. 'We'll see if we can't manage to keep you alive, eh?'

'I'd like that,' she agreed.

'Use the tab,' he said. 'I'm going to give you a code phrase – White Rain. If you say those words together, I'll be alerted and will immediately begin live monitoring your tab. Understood?'

'Yes, sir.'

Nbaro was confused, at least in part because he hadn't threatened her in any way.

'That's all?' She cursed that her voice carried all her fears.

'Good God, Midshipper, is there more?'

His bland face managed to convey that he didn't particularly relish the tangle she'd set him; perhaps didn't like her at all...

Nbaro rose, and paused. 'I have a nanoreader...'

He looked up, amused. 'Of course you do. Only reason you escaped. Probably best to return it to the EVA Rigger spaces before someone starts an investigation. Hmm?'

She nodded. 'Yes, sir.'

'Carry on, Ms Nbaro.'

She only began to breathe when she was in the corridor.

They still don't know.

Or they're using me as a stalking horse. They want Thornberg, and...

Fuck.

The next days were a blur. As soon as Nbaro had her up-chit from medical, she was back on duty; within three cycles, her attempted abduction was forgotten in the endless routine of a cargo load in the atmosphere of New London. Flight 6 craft had relatively low cargo capacity, even with cargo pods bolted under the atmospheric flight wings that made the XC-3Cs both dull and dangerous to fly; but they could transport high-value small cargoes up from multiple warehouses, and New London's population had surpassed Old Terra's a generation before. More than eighty major cities sprawled in a light haze across four big continents and twenty sizeable islands.

Nbaro flew with the skipper, with Mpono and Guille – always as co-pilot. She learnt a great deal about cargo stowage; she found that she had a low bonded-cargo rating thanks to her status as a penniless Orphanage graduate, meaning she could only fly with pilots who had high bond status, because small patrician or wealthy citizen-class businesses were often taking existential risks on their cargoes. On one trip they transported a magnificent pearl crown for some unnamed potentate on some distant star, all Old Terran pearls in black and rose; Smoke guessed the value at two million ducats.

'Don't drop it, honey,' they said.

'Almighty,' Nbaro muttered.

She had to hand-deliver the thing to Small Cargo to get their imprint, and she found Thea on duty in the Small Cargo office.

'A remarkable piece of vulgarity,' Thea said, popping the seals.

'Should you be opening that?' Marca asked, recoiling a little.

'That's my job,' Thea said. 'The insurers need to know that I personally examined anything worth more than a million ducats. And I did.' She ran a nanoreader over it. 'Looks like real pearls to me. If it's faked, it's faked better than it's my job to prove.' She tapped her ring against a code plate on the packaging. 'Received,' she said. 'And it's not even the gaudiest or stupidest thing I've received today.' She grinned at Nbaro and leant around her. 'Next!'

Marca flew round the clock. It was exciting, because despite having her atmospheric ticket, she did more flying in atmosphere every cycle than she'd done in her entire life to date. It was dull, because as co-pilot, she had to do all the signing and data collection and move all the cargo into appropriate bays and offices. Still, the four hectic days over New London gave her a deep sense of what was involved in filling the cargo spaces of a greatship; hundreds of sorties by the biggest cargo-haulers on the greatship didn't fill her holds.

Because Nbaro was much given to counting, she noted that her seventeen sorties alone were worth about a hundred million ducats. That put the total value of the cargo at billions.

Trillions.

And the whole xenoglas industry sat in near-paralysis because of the death of the *New York*. Her new tab, which was a hundred times more capable than her old tab, told her about the markets, which were about as intelligible to her as xenobiology. But the loss of the whole incoming xenoglas cargo caused the markets to tumble across three star systems, and despite many reassurances from the DHC Board of Directors that there were sufficient reserves to prevent wholesale unemployment, there were rotating strikes and worker demands across the industry as stock prices tumbled.

She read a juried article on the effects of instability on real wages. The Orphanage had many flaws, but the founders had intended that the orphaned children of DHC's service personnel get good educations, and part of that was a set of classes on the delicate balance between mercantile capitalism and state-directed socialism that made the DHC function. Lifestyle differentiations from the Age of Scarcity were unacceptable to a spacefaring civilisation, but some elements of status and class remained; some were even enshrined.

Her beloved Mrs Hardrede had once told her that it was all more practical than ideological.

Regardless, the article suggested that the instability would benefit the bigger corporate interests at the cost of the workers. The loss of the *New York* had, according to the article, engaged certain 'machineries of the state', which made her think of Devid Smith, who was – most certainly – the machinery of the state.

Nbaro lifted her eyes. She was sitting on, not in, her acceleration couch in the nose of her plane, legs crossed, reading from her tab, and when she glanced out the great xenoglas canopy, she could see longshorers loading her cargo pods with high-end pharmaceuticals.

Nbaro's tab buzzed. She had her feet up over the yoke in the co-pilot's seat and she was comfortable, munching an oatmeal-raisin biscuit. There were crumbs…

'Yes?'

'*Marca? This is Sabina.*'

Sabina was the name of her AI. The new tab was *much more capable.*

'Hi, Sabina.'

'*My operations processor says you are not, strictly speaking, busy.*'

'Too true, Sabina. What's up?'

'*My core says that I'm to watch developments in financial sectors controlled by the Thornberg Patriciate,*' Sabina said brightly.

'Are you, now?'

'*Oh, yes,*' Sabina answered. '*It is in my core.*' Pause. '*There, I checked again.*'

AIs could be very literal.

'So?' Nbaro asked.

'*So, Thornberg Heavy Industry owns the Milestone Group, which is, in effect, a holding company with sixty-two sub-companies. Do you want me to list them?*'

'Store,' Nbaro said.

'Roger,' her AI said. 'One of those sub-companies is Blitz-Beauty, a cosmetics and pharmaceutical company on New London.'

Marca looked out her windscreen, expecting to see Blitz-Beauty security attacking her plane.

'*BlitzBeauty has just purchased a controlling interest in Halcyon Glasworks,*' Sabina went on. '*This is an anomaly. The value of most of the glasworks had been artificially depressed since the death of the New York. But because humans are irrational actors when it comes to market values—*'

'Spare me,' Nbaro muttered.

'*Sure,*' Sabina said. '*The point is, this is an anomaly.*'

Feeling slightly guilty, Nbaro typed into the interface.

'Should you inform Lieutenant Smith about it?'

Sabina said, '*Already have.*'

'Sabina, *why* is it an anomaly?'

'*Well, a small but well-financed cosmetics company just purchased a large and very well-respected xenoglas processor.*'

'And that's weird because . . .'

'*Because the cosmetics industry doesn't use xenoglas.*'

'Huh. OK, Sabina, give me a heads-up when another Thornberg company buys another xenoglas processor.'

'*Of course. I would anyway.*'

'Of course you would. You are the smartest kid in the class, Sabina.' Nbaro smiled at her new AI.

Because Nbaro had learned at the Orphanage that no one should be included in a secret, and that included her flight, she used her override to scrub the plane's memory.

Yikes. I'm a spy.

For . . . Lieutenant Smith . . .

Yikes. Or they're spying on me.

Sabina became part of her everyday life. Nbaro had never owned a tame AI to do her thinking for her, and she found it annoying. She'd never had parents to parent her, so she resented the intrusive AI and its repeated commands to undertake tasks she'd already accomplished, like making up her crash-couch or updating her system reports. On the other hand, she was almost never late.

And . . . the AI was a massive support when Nbaro was in Space Ops, because it – *she* – interfaced perfectly with the ship's AI, Morosini. Morosini was one of the oldest AIs in the Human Sphere and was accounted both incredibly wise and a little mysterious; most of the spacers aboard called him the Oracle. Not everything that Morosini said was comprehensible to humans, but it was all comprehensible to Sabina, and she would pass the messages into Marca's ear unobtrusively, allowing her to function as if she knew what she was doing. She still wasn't a fully qualified watch-stander – that was months away – but she was attentive and she was learning Tower and several of the technical stations.

And that was all to the good, because Nbaro was terrified of Morosini. The AI could see through her hacker in a nanosecond, if he looked, or cared. And ultimately everything she said or did went through Morosini.

Morosini *was* the *Athens*. And Nbaro feared to be spat out.

But so far…

So far, she was still a midshipper, and she was keeping her head above water.

She had even sat at ship's weapons. In fact, she sat at Weps more and more often because, though there was a mirror station in Space Operations, it wasn't usually manned. Weps was run from the Combat Bridge.

Weps was full of surprises, the gist of which could be summarised as: the *Athens* was very well armed indeed, at least for a supposed merchant; she was more like a battleship with cargo holds. And Weps had an interface for a VR helmet; Nbaro liked the 3D interface for understanding locations, and she used one whenever it was available. The VR helmets also accessed simulations that gave her an even more thorough grounding in the greatship's combat abilities.

This lesson was learnt while most of the ship's gossip was about the possible causes for the death of the *New York*. In the aft officer's mess, where Nbaro usually ate; in the O-1 level formal mess, where she ate by invitation on the last day of the cargo load from New London; in Space Ops and in the flight ready room: officers and spacers discussed every possibility imaginable.

'Pirates' was the most popular conclusion.

'Sabotage' was a close second.

'Aliens' was an acceptable theory.

'No one knows what they say or do.' Mister Hanna, sometimes

known as Rick, was a New London academy grad, a junior lieutenant pretending to years in space he didn't really have yet, with bright red hair, freckles, and a cheerful disposition that he put down to having lots of sisters. 'No one knows what the fuck they do,' he said, carefully inserting the word 'fuck' several times in his sentences, the way the veteran spacers did. 'We can't speak their language...'

'They built half of Trade Point...' Thea put in.

'So? That was two hundred fucking years ago. Maybe they've had enough of our shit, and they blew the *New York* to tell us as much.'

'My brother says their ships are behind ours in development,' Thea said.

'Maybe they're stupid?' Hanna asked.

'Maybe there's other aliens and we picked the wrong friends,' Marca said.

'Oh, that's pretty fucking good,' Hanna said, laughing.

It was six hours until they were due to launch from Tooler, moving out to the latest insertion point and launch for Barcino, the first system on their long outbound voyage.

Sabina pinged.

'I have to walk,' Nbaro said, *walk* being ship-speak for going to her spacecraft to fly a mission. She got up, wondering anew that she had six people to sit with – a social miracle. Really, they were all Thea's friends, except for Yu, the scientist, who'd joined their group.

She kept her ears tuned for insults as she left. Orphanage habit. She made herself smile. New habit.

Nbaro dropped her tray in recycle and her tab chimed again, a different sound, this time an incoming call, and she was already headed forward towards the EVA riggers before she thumbed it open.

'Nbaro,' she said.

It was an automated call, requesting her presence at section I frame III on the O-1 level in about four hours, ship-time. She ran the address; it was the Chain Locker.

Nbaro remembered Captain Fraser saying something about martial arts and the Chain Locker and tabbed back, Accept.

She went into the riggers' shop, got into her flightsuit and harness, and found Spacer Chu.

'Can you guys refit some old body armour to fit me?' she asked.

Chu shrugged. 'I dunno, miz. Probably. I'd have to see it.'

'You on shift for a while?'

'I'll be here when you land, miz.'

Nbaro nodded. 'Thanks, Spacer. *Ciao!*'

She was flying with Smoke, and she took the lift down to the hangar bay to find that they had already done the walk-around and had Alpha Foxtrot 6–0–7 ready to launch. 6–0–7 was known throughout the flight as 'Double O Seven' and had a fancy slug-thrower painted on the side, and Nbaro didn't know why, but much of the ship's mythos was lost on her and she just accepted the name and moved on. Today, she pulled herself into her crash-couch, adjusted the angle to suit her, and locked her harness before turning on the auxiliaries and bringing up the craft's AI and systems.

There was a fault in the diagnostic.

'Reboot it,' Smoke said.

Nbaro dumped the system, trying to imagine what happened at a quantum level when she did so – an entire idea of the universe falling away into chaos. She restarted; this time the system came up cleanly.

'Faeries.' Smoke grinned.

'Why does Alpha Foxtrot 6–0–7 have a pistol on the side?' Nbaro asked.

Mpono just looked at her, faceplate open.

'You ask the oddest questions,' they said. 'How would I know?' Then they steepled their fingers as if they were about to address a spiritual leader. 'I believe it has to do with some ancient ancestor worship.'

Marca wondered if the 6–0–7 spaceframe was used for carrying the most valuable cargoes – hence 'Bond'.

I'll ask the skipper. He likes old words.

'System's good,' she said.

'Let's go for a little trip,' Mpono said. 'Tower has us three to launch – I'm putting us on the railgun.'

When they were launched and well down into the gravity well, Mpono handed her control.

'Captain Fraser call you?' she asked.

'Yes, tir,' Nbaro said. 'That is, Smoke.'

'Roger that. He's going to look you over to see if you're suitable for Shipboard Security and boarding parties.'

It was an exciting idea.

'I think I'd like that.'

'Nbaro, do you know what the acronym NAVY stands for?' Smoke asked.

'Never Again Volunteer Yourself,' Marca said, and they both laughed as she banked into the pattern over New Carlisle.

'Boarding parties are dangerous at the best of times,' Smoke said.

There speaks a spouse.

After a delay, Mpono spoke again. 'May I ask you a personal question?'

Shit. Here we go.

'Yes, tir.'

'Hey, I don't call you girlie, you don't call me tir. Deal?'

Nbaro nodded.

'Good. You killed a man last week,' Smoke said. 'I had to kill a man once – in a mining ... incident. Made me sick.'

Nbaro said nothing.

'Want to talk about it?' Mpono asked.

Nbaro thought about that. 'No.' She bit back on the 'tir'.

Mpono stared ahead and then scanned their instruments.

'You sure, Nbaro? It can be heavy lifting…'

Nbaro turned her head so she could meet the pilot's eye.

'He attacked me. I put him down. End of story.' After a pause she said, 'Tir.'

Mpono nodded slowly. 'Not your first?'

Nbaro thought, *Lie.*

But I like this person.

'No, tir.'

'Call me Smoke,' Mpono said.

Smoke let Nbaro land, only her second atmospheric landing with aerodynamic wings, and they talked to the New Manchester Tower. They landed in light rain at ground level, and that was so odd that Nbaro almost asked Smoke to take the craft back, but there was little wind and the rain on the windscreen did them no harm. She'd even had rain in sims. Just not the same…

They loaded high-fashion products, mostly Old Terran silk dresses so fine that they were stored in egg-shaped packages made of beautifully glazed recycle to avoid breaking the packaging laws.

The loading clerk took her signature and showed her the dresses with pride.

'Have one,' he said, glancing at her and picking one out. 'We sell 'em at a thousand ducats a throw. You make sure you get 'em into stowage and offloaded at Sahel and this one's for you. I'm sure you'll look quite smart in it.'

Nbaro smiled to hide a number of other reactions. 'I can't accept gifts.'

The clerk looked at her as if she had a third eye in the middle of her forehead.

'I tagged it and it's on the consignment.' He smiled. 'I'll just tuck it into the box. Your choice.'

She left it there, and related the whole tale to Smoke.

The androgyne laughed. 'You are such a midder,' they said. 'He named a contract – it's yours if you get the goods aboard and then delivered to Sahel. If you want to be a stickler, make sure the cargo gets delivered and send them a message to that effect. Then it's yours. Implied contract. Ask your AI.'

'We're Service!' Nbaro said.

'We're also merchants,' Smoke said. 'The Service is not an armed force, it's a socialist merchant class. Look it up! Besides, it's not a bribe if it's a contract. You told me. He told you. It's not a secret.' Smoke shrugged. 'I don't dress fem or I'd want it for myself. They have nice stuff.'

'I've never worn a dress,' Nbaro admitted. 'Never owned one.'

'Orphanage sounds really fun,' Smoke said. 'Checklist, now.'

Back on the *Athens* Nbaro raised Sabina and queried the AI, who seemed to think the dress was a routine reward. She put her tab away with a nod, as if she'd been talking to a person, and walked the consignment of silk dresses straight to Small Cargo and waited for Thea.

She finished with two others, another midder, from Flight 8, and a mid-grade commander who was negotiating on behalf of a dirtside merchant for more space.

That was fascinating. Nbaro hadn't known that cargo space on a greatship was auctioned years in advance and then traded as a futures commodity. Her burgeoning economics education, driven by Sabina, had included futures.

But the commander doing the negotiating was doing so on behalf of a merchant, for which he was being paid. He said so, in contract form. In fifteen minutes Nbaro had learnt more that the Orphanage had left out than she would have learnt in a day of reading.

But then, the Orphans hardly ever went to greatships. And apparently no one expected them to make any money. Ever.

The commander smiled at the end of his negotiation, shook hands with Thea, thumbed a contract and walked off.

'And *that's* why my brothers wanted me to be in Small Cargo,' Thea said. 'How can I help you, Ms Nbaro?' she asked formally, her eyes on Marca's consignment. Then she pounced like the leopard she secretly was. 'Suvaroff!' she said, naming the company.

'You've heard of them?'

'High-end fashion. No bling, very... athletic.' She grinned.

'What you like, then.'

'You might say.'

'So, they told me this one –' Nbaro touched it – 'was mine if I saw the consignment stowed personally and saw it to the destination.'

'Fair.' Thea ran a reader over the nanotag. 'Yeah, that one's coded as a shipping and handling cost.' She nodded. 'Lucky you.'

'This is legal?'

'We're merchants,' Thea said. 'Every spacer aboard has the right to ship any legal merchandise in the space under their crash-couch, right? And a cube of goods, dependent on status and ship size.'

Nbaro nodded. She knew that was a rule. She'd just never thought about what it meant.

'If you and I had the ability to buy at Trade Point, we could stuff our cabin with xenoglas and sleep in Ops, and make a couple million,' Thea said.

'We could?'

'Nah. We can't, but only because the Xenos will only trade

through Trade Point and that means with the Master, not with Midder Drake. But I plan to pick up some stuff as we go.'

'And you can bid on cabin space. I'll happily sell it to you.'

Drake nodded. 'Nice. You understand?'

'What I don't understand is how I ever managed to get on board the *Athens*. Weren't there other kids like you fighting for the positions, for the potential to make this kind of money?'

Drake looked at the hatchway, as if it might have ears.

'A longer conversation for another day,' she said with un-characteristic caution.

Marca went back to her stateroom and pushed all the shaped xenoglas panels and complex Kevlar webbing of the hand-me-down armour into her duffel. It was all dirty and smelled of male sweat. There was physical dirt on some of the panels.

She carried it all down to EVA, and finally, and gratefully, shucked off her EVA suit. Her jumpsuit was stuck to her body with sweat, and Chu pretended to hold her nose. Carlson looked at her bag with interest.

'I see you got a new helmet, miz,' he said.

'Ms Drake's brother gave it to me,' she said. 'Can you change the seals and the support pads to fit me?'

Carlson smiled. 'If you can get me pie,' he said. 'I don't like cake.'

'Done.'

He nodded. 'For apple pie, I'd make it look like it was new. Get me two, and I'll have nanotech put your device on it.'

Nbaro. In her case, the Nbaro lion rampant on a field striped blue and white.

'I guess I'll have to find you two pies, Petty Officer Carlson.'

'Glad to hear it, Ms Nbaro.'

She brought up the Nbaro coat of arms on her tab and shot it at him and he caught it on his own.

143

'Nice. Simple. That'll be a striking helmet, miz.' Carlson leant over. 'You're a real Nbaro, miz?'

Nbaro narrowed her eyes. 'Yep,' she snapped.

Carlson made a noise – disbelief? Amazement?

'Carry on, Carlson,' she said, using her skipper's tone.

Chu rifled through her bag for the armour and laid it out on the nanotable, building the suit quickly and efficiently: breast-plate, formed in a bulbous, unisex manner; waist plates that flexed; leg armour articulated like something from a thousand years before, except made of xenoglas panels and layered over stretch Kevlar leggings; arms the same.

There were four gauntlets, all remarkably intricate, and no helmet.

The next ten minutes passed in measuring Nbaro, with some cursing and some re-measurement.

'Yes, I can do it, miz,' Chu said. 'Any chance you'd tutor me in maths?'

She looked at Chu's tab.

'What's this for?'

'Testing for petty officer.' Chu was proud.

'Nice.' Nbaro had a look through it. 'I can hack all this – most of it's pretty straightforward. I'm not very good at Functions and Calculus. This stuff I can do in my head. *Which may mean I'd suck at teaching it.* She looked at Chu. 'Didn't you do this in school?'

Chu looked at her. 'No, miz.'

The tone had changed, and Nbaro realised with a snap that not everyone got to go to school. In some ways, at the Orphanage, she had been lucky. That was oddly disorientating.

'Sorry, Chu,' she said. 'I'll do it.'

'Thanks, miz. I'll have your armour … I dunno. Next week?'

'Great. I'll take the gauntlets that fit.'

'And the other pair?' Carlson asked. 'I can find them a home

144

if you want. Maybe replace the inner gloves and sell 'em. Give you a cut.'

'85–15 for me,' Nbaro said.

He looked at her coolly. 'No thanks.'

'OK,' she said. 'Does this change our other deal?'

'Of course not, miz. Strictly business.'

Nbaro went back to her stateroom and collected her practice sword and helmet, kept the gauntlets, and walked all the way forward to the Chain Locker: a big room with a slightly curved bulkhead and an overhead almost twice the height of her stateroom. There were forty men and women gathered, and mats on the deck for falling.

Captain Fraser spotted her and came over, wearing exactly the sort of armour she'd just handed in to get refitted, and carrying a long sword with a long handle and a complex guard.

'Ms Nbaro. Thanks for coming. You've fought before?'

'Never for real,' she said. 'With a sword. Sir.'

'A little bird tells me you killed a man in a fight in City.'

Nbaro took a deep breath. 'Yes, sir,' she admitted. 'Not with a sword.'

He smiled. 'Let's spar a little. Olympic rules.'

She nodded, relieved; not a metre away, two men were fighting with punches and throws in a way that was not the Olympic rules, and she had no armour.

They moved forward, and the bulkhead began to curve into the bow, making a space that was strangely non-linear.

'It's a busy night,' the captain said. 'Not everyone here volunteers for the boarding parties, but most do. If you want to join, just tell me, we're not choosy. We do a lot of dull boardings – in truth, anything risky is done by Marines. But we're not too bad...'

'My tab says I have to volunteer for boarding parties or damage control.'

Fraser smiled. 'And there's that.'

He flipped his visor down. He was in full combat armour; Nbaro was in a stretchy workout suit with armoured gloves more expensive than she'd ever be able to afford and a very old fencing helmet she'd 'liberated' from the Orphanage. It had once had a fencing program; there was a room full of equipment. Using it had started as a prank...

'Ready?' Captain Fraser called.

'Yes, sir,' she said.

He came forward cautiously, treating her with respect, his big sword point up, hilt close to his body. He wasn't a large man, but he moved with grace, and there was something snakelike about him; his sword flickered as it moved.

Nbaro stuck to what she knew, so when he came within reach, she snapped her sword down from her high garde and struck his a glancing blow, tossing it a few centimetres offline, then struck again, her thrust driving forward...

She hit him hard enough to drive his head back.

He laughed, stepped forward, slapped her hand.

'Nice. Fuck, you're *fast*.'

'Sorry, sir,' Nbaro said with genuine contrition. 'Too hard—'

'I'm in armour,' he said. 'Come on.'

At the second pass he came into her reach and cut hard, from a high garde, and she slapped a parry – only it was a feint, and his crisp and well-controlled blow would have cut off both her hands.

'Oh,' Nbaro said. But her new social skills taught her to go slap his hand and smile. 'Nice,' she said, when in truth, she was thinking, *Almighty, I'm bad. I used to be better than that.*

On their third pass she feinted but took too long, and he cut her arms.

Fourth pass, he raised his hands as a provocation and Nbaro stabbed him in the left wrist.

He laughed. His laugh turned every head on the deck.

People were starting to watch them.

They circled again, and he raised his hands, exactly as he had before, but the distance was fractionally too far, so Nbaro circled, and he circled, changed gardes, did the same thing again...

She stabbed him in the wrist.

'Loveack!' Fraser called.

'Right here, sir.'

'When is a provocation not a provocation?'

'When your midder is as fast as lightning, sir?'

Fraser shook his head. 'There's a lot we can teach you, Ms Nbaro – but your mastery of the basics and your speed make you a challenge right now.'

Nbaro had learned a great deal in the last five minutes. Fraser's body movements were refined and precise, like a ballet dancer's, and hers were, by contrast, broad and violent, like a street dancer's. He used very little energy, and he had... She struggled to describe it. He had a greater vocabulary?

'Thanks, sir. I'd be happy to learn.' She meant that.

'You're so fast,' the spacer named Loveack said. 'You're a blur.'

She grinned. 'People are always surprised at how fast I am.'

Nbaro spent the rest of the next two hours doing exercises, guided first by Loveack, and then when he went off to fight with a tall blond man who looked like a Holo cast fantasy creature, with a big dark woman, a spacer called Serina from Flight 1. She did the exercises over and over – forms that were different from what the old Phys-Studies teacher had taught at the Orphanage, but not so very different.

'Tomorrow we do zero g after the jump,' Fraser said. 'Can we count on you?'

'Yes, sir,' she said. 'I'm in.'

'Can you afford armour?' he asked.

'My room-mate gave me a suit. I won't have it for a week.'

He smiled. 'That's fine,' he said. And added, 'That's a good room-mate to have.'

Nbaro was coming to the same conclusion.

Later, when both Marca and Thea were strapped in to their crash-couches, needles pricking them to mild discomfort, ready for the M-brane insertion to Barcino system, Drake said, 'You know, it's not that I am very rich … but you are very poor.'

'Sure you're not,' Marca said, agreeably.

She heard Drake cough. 'No, really,' she said. 'My dad was Service and he died when I was a kid. My mum is patrician, and she kept us to it, but we've a plumbing system older than this ship and I always got hand-me-down clothes from boys.'

Marca lay in the upper bunk, watching the screen which showed the deep space ahead of the ship. Insertion points were mathematical constructs by quantum computers, not physical realities; they'd never see the 'gate'. Marca still loved to watch space.

I had four pairs of underwear and one bra, three uniform jumpsuits and one dress jumper, all heavily used and ill-fitting until I tailored them myself, with some help from Mrs Hardrede. At its worst, I only got one meal a day because the Herdys, the cool faction, took all the food in the cafeteria and sold it for favours. When Sarah said I could sell my body for a thousand ducats a throw, I almost did it.

Then I decided to kill the lead Herdy.

'Yeah,' she said.

You have a palace with twenty-six rooms; I know, I looked it up on Hermes. I had an upper bunk in a dorm with twenty-three other vicious predators, which was patrolled by rapists and murderers.

Nbaro felt a moment of hesitation – a moment in which her mind seemed slow, the way she'd seen cheap electronics behave in hard vacuum and low temperatures. Nothing around her made sense, and the very structures lacked meaning …

And then she was looking at a new star field – mostly just a subtle shift, but with a few major changes, not least of which was the very pretty blue and white marble in the upper right corner of the screen.

'Show the plot?' she asked.

'Cool!' Thea said. 'We're *above* the plane of the ecliptic. Nice.'

'So you were as poor as an orphan?' Marca said.

'Hey, don't be like that. I just mean that we're not rich.'

'No one ever admits getting too much sleep or having too much money.'

Thea laughed. 'Fair. But I mean it – we're not rich. I'm saying this badly. Because my *pater* died in service, and because we were poor, and because we're very old-fashioned, we all went to space. But there's not the demand for places you think, not from richer families who don't need it . . .' She frowned. 'If my mum was here, she'd say that the rot's set in. Lots of patricians evade their space service now. I'm guessing that the loss of the *New York* will accelerate that.'

'Yikes.'

'Notice how *few* of our officers are patricians?' Thea said. 'Anyway, I looked, honey. You're a Nbaro. You're not just patrician, you're Golden Book.'

'I'm an Orphan,' Marca said.

Thea's head popped up. Transit sickness affected everyone differently. Thea bounced up; Marca tended to lassitude for half an hour, although at least she was awake; some people took a lot longer. Officially, the science said there was no reason for anyone to be affected by transit.

Unofficially, ships were cautious and run by AIs for some time after transit because the people on board sometimes made very poor decisions afterwards.

Thea looked her in the eye. 'You know what, Marca? You're really tough – you've put up with some shit, right? But you aren't an Orphan any more. You're an officer in the Service, and I suspect you'll stick to it.' She smiled. 'Also, you can't be that poor. At the very least, all the Patrician houses have income from the DHC. I really don't get how you can be this poor.'

'I wasn't the only Patrician kid at the Orphanage,' Marca said. 'And we were all that poor.'

Thea made a face. 'Your Dominus – the one who you talk about in your sleep...'

'That bastard,' Marca spat.

'And to think that I used to believe you were cold and unemotional,' Thea said. 'He must be taking the money. And that would be a fair amount of money.'

Marca sat on her crash-couch, stunned that she'd never considered this apparently trivial motive.

'Except...' Thea shrugged. 'You're Service now. Service will collect every solido of your due and put it on your Earning Statement.'

Marca blinked.

Thea smiled. 'Time to let go, honey.'

Easy for you to say warred with *I tell myself that every hour.*

Marca sighed and made herself roll off her crash-couch.

'We're inbound to a new world!' she said. 'I'll try to lighten up.'

Thea nodded. 'Listen,' she said. 'I know you had it bad – you kinda mutter when you're asleep. But my life wasn't a bed of roses either, and I used to watch the Lexi girls or the Thornbergs with their endless money and their contempt for the law, and think how hard I had it.'

They were at eye level now.

'I hear you,' Marca said.

'But I'll bet there are seventeen-year-old women in City who'd fucking *kill* to be where we are.'

Marca thought of Sarah.

150

'Yes,' she said softly.

'OK. Pep talk over.'

Marca pointed at the big screen.

'Space Ops schedule, please?'

When ships passed through the M-brane, they couldn't absolutely predict where they'd come out; prediction improved with each level of computer improvement, of course, but a few million kilometres was a very small distance in terms of interstellar space, and a very large amount in human travel time. Space Ops couldn't plan all the operations in atmosphere on their next trade contact until they knew where they were and how long it would take to get there. Space pilots like Marca and Cargo officers like Thea shared a relative lack of work while in deep space.

There was a long pause, and then the screen showed a detailed spreadsheet.

'Sort for my duties,' Marca said. 'Tell my tab.'

Her tab made a *ding*.

'*I have your schedule*,' Sabina said in her ear.

'And how come you have a tab with a fucking AI?' Thea asked.

'I notice you swear a lot more now that you're in space,' Marca said with a grin. 'I shoplifted the tab, of course.'

Thea blinked. 'Nah,' she said, 'I don't believe you.'

But her tone was respectful.

Marca went to her first zero-*g* combat class. It was a lecture, and – as seemed to happen to her every day – she learned more in an hour than she'd learned in her whole life.

It turned out that almost nothing about space combat was as it seemed.

The instructor was a Marine major, a big, lanky, dark-skinned 'gyne who could have been Mpono's birth twin with an outlandish spacer name: Chastity Darkstar. Major Darkstar had muscles on their muscles, held their class in a zero-*g* space and refused to orientate their head with the rest of the heads in the classroom.

'EMP beams changed everything,' Darkstar said. 'A hundred years ago, everything had a chip and elaborate computer-enhancement – the sights on your rifle, the muscles in your power armour, everything.' Nbaro knew this, but Darkstar told it well. 'Then, in one of those annoying techie revolutions, it was all worthless. Worse, it was a disadvantage, because any two-bit insurgent or anti-government rebel could tinker up an EMP beamer in their workshop and bang, there you were, frozen in a million ducats' worth of useless powered armour.'

Major Darkstar went on to discuss the game 'stone, paper, scissors' which remained a historical artifact among spacers. Once everyone had grasped the concept, they said, 'That's how boarding actions work. Firearms are the scissors – all very well, but they don't work for very long in vacuum and they're just impact weapons against good xenoglas armour. They'll hurt you and knock you around. A well-placed shot can pluck you off a handhold and send you off spinning, out of the fight, or even lost forever, but at least from in front, it's hard to kill you with one. Armour is the rock that blunts the scissors. Paper is close combat – up close and personal, just like our ancestors. And it does less damage to a ship's systems than spraying a corridor with depleted uranium. The game is coming prepared for whatever your opponent does.'

They looked over the class.

'Those are the basics. There's also biological and chemical agents which can be released into ships or pumped aboard before the boarding ramps are fixed. There's deliberate venting of a target ship's atmosphere – a standard pirate tactic meant to kill everyone aboard. How long does it take to get into a vac suit?'

A hesitant spacer raised his hand.

'Twenty seconds?'

'Exactly,' they said. 'So if you get on an enemy hull and blow the air out of every part of the ship then – bang. Everyone decompresses and the ship is yours.' They smiled grimly. 'Only works on small ships.'

The major looked around.

'We are not a small ship. We're a gigantic battlefield, with variable terrains, and we invite you squids to learn to fight our way so that our ship cannot be overwhelmed by sheer numbers. In point of fact, with a thousand boarders, we can overwhelm the defences of most ships we'll ever meet with personpower alone.'

A spacer, a very big man with a holographic tattoo, raised his hand.

'Tir,' he said. 'Why train with swords? Why not ... hammers, or axes?'

'I've seen both,' the major said. 'But swords win because of their functionality. The point of a good sword can be used between plates, and the length gives it a wrestling advantage, and believe me, wrestling is part of the game. In zero *g*, a throw is not a fight-ender, unless you throw your opponent off the ship – unlikely in a corridor. But a dislocation lock or a break will probably break the bone right under their armour.' Major Darkstar nodded. 'But listen, spacer. If you finish the whole course and you still want an axe, we'll find you one.'

The spacer grinned. 'Thank you, tir!'

After class, Nbaro went down to the hangar bay, spent two hours learning how to do a proper walk-around of a readied spacecraft from the maintenance master-chief, who had enough tattoos to count as a Class A entertainment, and then went up to Space Ops to sit at Weps and watch very little happen. A bored tech showed her a simulation program for firing the main railguns, and she played with it for a while, but she was aware that in actual space combat, most of the decisions would be made by the AI, much faster and more reliably than a human could make them.

'Ms Nbaro,' the tech asked.

Elduras? Enduras? What's his name?

Space Ops was dark enough that she couldn't read the tape above his pocket.

'Yes, spacer?' she asked.

'Miz, is it true we launched super-fast to try and recover the time lost by the ... death ... of the *New York*?'

Nbaro laughed ruefully. 'I don't know, spacer. No one told me.'

'Yes, miz.' He stood over her. 'Here's the sim for running Space Ops as Lioness.'

'There's a sim for that?' she asked, and lost hours to the game.

In the ready room, the skipper ran a constant feed of City news, interspersed with mandatory training – sexual harassment holos, which Nbaro found dull and seldom to the actual point, and 'integrity' holos, which made her think of Thea's assertions about the patrician class.

Nbaro wasn't bored. There were duties and instructions at all hours, and then, when that routine might have begun to pall, they were falling into orbit around Barcino. Marca noticed that Thea went to work almost round the clock, and both her martial arts and her boarding party training vanished because everyone had too much work to do.

Barcino was a magnificent planet, about ten per cent larger than either Old Terra or New London. It had been settled in the same impulse as New London – the Desperate Diaspora of the mid-twenty-second century, as the oceans of Old Terra died and the climate began to resemble that of the Age of Chaos. Barcino had been settled from Spanish- and Portuguese-speaking territories – mostly Catalonia, Mexico, and the Azores. Barcino had almost twice the human population of New London, as well as the most productive agriculture in the DHC. Most of the planet's continents straddled the equator, and most of the open land had been converted to large-scale industrial farming. Marca had read claims that Barcino could sustainably support all twenty-six other worlds with her grain and meat products, if only she could ship the food fast enough.

Barcino wasn't just farmland, though. She had thirty super-cities, and an orbital called San Marti whose core had come from the same yards as City. After five days of almost non-stop cargo runs carrying, for the most part, rare citrus products and doubly rare spices like mastic and cinnamon that were special-ities on Barcino, Marca took a day of liberty and spent it with the New London officer, Richard Hanna. He was red-haired and entertaining, and they met on the liberty barge, a forty-human passenger boat that the *Athens* ran so that she could stay clear of docking at the station except when conducting cargo transfer.

'I guess I thought I'd just walk down the brow,' she admitted.

She and Hanna were strapped into crash-couches on the ferry. He turned his head to look at her.

'Master's being very cautious. We're not docking until we know what killed the *New York*, unless we're moving cargo, and even then we have Marines on the dockside. Barcino's not happy – the bars and brothels are losing business.'

Nbaro wasn't good at light conversation and she turned away, unable to find something else to discuss.

'How's moving cargo?' he asked.

She rolled back. There was no reason to be in a crash-couch; they were moving smoothly between the *Athens* and the station, but the DHC had rules and regulations about everything that had ever killed people.

'Just as brutal as the load at New London,' she said.

He nodded. 'It's funny. I'm ship's crew – Astrogation.

We basically took a week off in New London – I went and saw my folks.'

Nbaro nodded. 'But while we're lying in our couches waiting for insertion—'

'We're sweating our arses off watching the AI cook up an insertion point while we try to guess where we come out,' he said. 'Not to mention quarrelling with Engineering, which is an essential part of astrogation.' He smiled.

She smiled back.

See, this isn't hard.

In fact, it wasn't hard all day. They never committed to spending the day together, but their visit to the market led to a lunch in an orbital taverna, and then Hanna suggested they go planetside; the shuttles were free and frequent, and an hour later they were looking at the Cathedral of the Holy Cross.

'Almighty!' she said. 'This was built more than a thousand years ago. On Old Terra!'

A Free Believer nun took them on a tour and explained that, like many great cultural icons, the cathedral had been taken to pieces and sent into space as the Dark Time loomed and the oceans died.

'Incredible,' Hanna said. 'They built this and the *Athens*. What do we build now?'

The Free Believer nun was middle-aged and very know-ledgeable, and perhaps just a trifle amused at their youthful earnestness, but she made up for her matronising air by recommending a seafood restaurant.

'Seafood?' Hanna asked.

'Didn't you read the Bio briefing?' Nbaro asked. 'This sea was cleared and repopulated with Terran species. No one would do that now – the idea's terrifying. But they did it and got away with it, so we can eat shrimp.' She breathed in deeply over her plate. 'Real shrimp. I'm not even sure I like them, but …'

Hanna laughed. 'Never had a shrimp before,' he said. 'That's a lie. Never had a shrimp that grew up in open water before.'

'Saffron!' Nbaro said.

'Pepper,' Hanna said. 'We're in the very land of spices.'

They sat in the restaurant, watching the ocean and listening to the spoken Spanish around them and the crash of waves.

Much later, Hanna held out a glass of red wine.

'Could I interest you in sex?' he asked.

Nbaro bridled, fought it down, and shook her head.

'No thanks.'

'Drat,' Hanna said. 'Oh well.'

But he wasn't insulted, and they drank more wine and wandered through the quiet Old City for another hour before taking a shuttle back to the Orbital, San Marti. At the ship's airlock he took her hand and kissed it, very old-school, and she laughed.

And in the morning, ship-time, when Nbaro was burning off the wine with exercise in high *g*, she wondered.

Why didn't I? Totally like him.

I'm an idiot.

And that day when she went to lunch, he was sitting with Smoke and Fraser and Thea.

When Nbaro sat down, he said, 'I was just telling them how much fun you were.'

Thea rolled her eyes.

'That's me,' Nbaro said, self-consciously. 'Fun.'

The next few days were dreary, as they burned for their insertion point, and full of work – more so as the Master insisted on cutting the artificial gravity and exercising the ship under burn.

Nbaro was aware, perhaps from some long-lost tape at the Orphanage's virtual academy, that the artificial gravity of a greatship could only operate between zero *g* and about three gravities; over 3*g* something went wrong and the gravity would fluctuate in a very dangerous manner. For that reason, even aboard a greatship, the crews had to be prepared for hard burns of 4 g and more. Damage control parties had sleds like armoured wheelchairs to allow some limited function, and there were specially designated robots at fire stations that looked like low-slung air-cars in miniature.

Boarding parties, and their partners, anti-boarding parties, were also required to move through the ship, and fight, in relatively high g.

The Master was no sadist; he interrupted the burn frequently to give the crew a rest. And so Nbaro found herself learning about combat in corridors in 4 g, and then combat in a drop-shaft in zero g.

She learned that the egg-shaped nodes at almost every bulkhead were cluster drones – small, vicious anti-personnel drones with a wide range of sensors and the ability to stick to a target and then penetrate its armour. Each egg held hundreds of drones, and the drones themselves came in dozens of varieties. She learned that when she was the OP Force, her boarding party's Electro Magnetic Pulse gunner had to target the eggs and knock their contents out before they launched...

Which she learned when an exercise version with non-lethal remotes cracked open and four hundred remotes came at her team of six. Nbaro was the last member of her team standing, her sword cutting down the remotes until she missed two and was declared dead.

'Those things are insane,' she said to Locran, who by luck – or someone else's planning – was in her team.

He shrugged. 'Ship-to-ship fighting is insane,' he said.

'Have you been in a real fight?' she asked.

'When I was a new spacer on the *Arkansas*,' he said. 'During the Insurgency. One of the Torag ships came for us and put twenty boarding shuttles into our hull. I was shit-scared.'

His face was mottled, and sweat sprang to his forehead at the memory, she noticed.

'And?' she asked.

'They killed us all,' Locran said, his demeanour restored.

Nbaro blinked. 'You're an arsehat, Petty Officer Locran.'

He smiled. 'Nice of you to notice, miz.'

After two days of it, every muscle in Nbaro's body ached, and she wasn't even wearing armour, which everyone else in her team had. They were carrying fifteen kilos that she wasn't. She determined to work out more often.

Her tab gave an odd *BLLEEEeeeep*. It wasn't a tone she'd heard before.

Nbaro thumbed the screen.

'Midshipper Nbaro to the Command Bridge,' it said, as if this was an everyday event.

'Shit,' she muttered.

Clean uniform, Miz, Sabina said, helpfully.

She raced to her stateroom, unzipped her sweat-soaked ship's jumpsuit and pulled on her best flightsuit, with good embroidery and all her patches. She used water to make her hair as neat as she could and raced for the command bridge on the O-6 level, right at the top of the ship. She knew from the SOP that there was an O-7 level, but it was just an escape pod for the bridge.

Nbaro had never been to the command bridge before. The elevator looked like all the other elevators, and during the travel time from O-2 to O-6 she lost years of her life imagining which of her admittedly venial sins had brought her to the attention of the highest ranking officer on the ship.

Or... she thought suddenly at about O-5. *Or they just worked it out and the ship is outing me...*

When the doors opened, they opened on a closed iris valve lock, which then opened in a brilliant display of light on mirror-polished durabronze.

The bridge was... staggering.

The Master sat on a raised dais, a good three feet above the deck, in a contoured crash-couch that was built to allow him to see all the screens even at high *g*. Above him and at eye-line were another series of screens, and the final ones in the lower tiers were also visible thanks to careful placement. Officers and technicians sat in disciplined silence, heads down over their screens.

Everything was polished durabronze and dark blue velvet over black nanofibre and carbon laminates. The screens were lit in dark reds and glowing blues that gave the bridge a beautiful, textured light like the cathedral on Barcino. The light level was quite low, despite a lightboard to one side, and an enormous front-facing screen...

No, by the Almighty, that's a window! That's space!

She could see the mammoth sword-blade of the ship stretching forward to a remote point, and the star field above it.

Every screen was held to its station by the same antique metalwork that decorated the best portions of the ship, and all of it was lovingly polished.

Nbaro realised that she was standing with her mouth open. And the Master was looking at her.

'Um...' she began.

He was *old*. She knew that; Masters were always old. But Maestro Vettor Pisani looked as if he'd had two, or even three, rejuv treatments. His hair was very short and almost perfectly white. His skin was very dark, a uniform mahogany like the panel of wood in her stateroom. He had an enormous nose like a beak, which on his face looked both elegant and predatory.

'Ms Nbaro,' the Master said. His voice was soft, polite, and reserved.

She braced. 'Midshipper Nbaro reporting as ordered.'

The Master scanned his screens and then looked back to her. He had an old-fashioned earpiece in his right ear and a complex board, like an enormous wristwatch, on his left cuff.

He smiled. 'Welcome to the bridge.'

'Thank you, sir.'

'I wanted to meet you, Ms Nbaro.'

No way this is going to be good.

That's not an earpiece. That's a neural link.

He tapped a code into his wrist device and extended it to her.

'Is this you?' he asked. 'It's always worthwhile to be certain, don't you think?'

Nbaro's knees began to shake. She reached for the wrist device and it was all she could do to stand straight.

Fuck.

But it wasn't the chapel at the Orphanage that greeted her, or a spreadsheet of her demerits.

She watched a woman cutting at remotes as they attempted to take her down. In about four seconds, they got her.

'Yes, sir,' she said. 'That's me.'

'How many remotes did she kill, Hassan?' he called.

'Seven, sir,' a voice came from the lower tier of techs. Other people on the bridge chuckled, belying the impression she'd received of immense, restrictive discipline.

'Remotes are expensive,' the Master went on, quietly. 'In a practice like that, most people shoot them down with their exercise pistols. Am I right, midder?'

Nbaro didn't have an exercise pistol.

'Yes, sir,' she said, because there really wasn't another answer.

'And when some athletic midder starts hitting them with swords, they get damaged. Hassan, what's a new exercise remote cost?'

'About 170 ducats, sir. 'Cept we can't get no more until we dock back at City.'

The Master looked at her. 'Well? What do you have to say for yourself?'

She stood even straighter.

'I won't let it happen again, sir.'

Typically unfair. No one had told her not to use her sword.

The Master was laughing. After a moment, the whole bridge was laughing.

'Blessed gods,' the Master said. 'You think I'm going to come down on you?'

Nbaro couldn't imagine what the correct answer was, and her brain just sort of shut down.

'Nbaro, most of the crew has seen this vid by now. Shitsky, midder, you're going to have a cult following like Ladash.' He glanced at her. 'No exercise pistol? Where's your combat armour?'

'In repair. Sir.'

He nodded. 'Good. Well, I just wanted to see someone who was so fast she could carve up remotes. You like my bridge?'

'It's beautiful,' she said.

More laughter.

But the Master nodded, a different smile on his face.

'Yes. Beautiful. Yes, that's just what it is.' He scanned his screens again. 'Stay for a while. Hells, we have a window. It's the best reason to visit the bridge.'

Nbaro stood perfectly still for a bit, but no one seemed to object to her presence so she moved along one of the bulkheads and looked at several of the stations, all of which were duplicated elsewhere: Weapons, Cargo, Astrogation, Astrophysics, Space Ops. Space Ops was occupied by a spacer-tech she knew from the Space Ops command centre – Petty Officer Banderas.

Banderas raised her head and gave an encouraging look.

Then she moved over slightly, an obvious invitation. Nbaro went and sat with her.

'This is a repeater station?'

'Yes, miz. See?'

Her screen was split four ways, and she had a camera on the launch tubes, a 2D plot centred on the ship, a repeater for the Tower's board that showed upcoming launches, and a blank.

'During Space Operations that would double the Lioness's screens, so I know what they are looking at.'

Banderas sounded very confident. Smooth. Nbaro noted that.

Above them, the Master leaned out.

'Banderas, you know our sword girl?'

'She's qualing for Space Ops, sir,' Banderas said without taking her eyes off her screen.

'Good.'

The Master was still quiet, but his voice carried well.

A tall man was bent over, speaking to him – odd, in that the man wasn't in uniform. There were a handful of contractors aboard in corporate flightsuits – mostly avionics professionals Nbaro saw in the passageways. But this man was in fine clothes, the sort patricians wore in City: sombre breeches and a skintight vest over a white shirt; a long-coat in an almost invisible brocade.

Nbaro stayed a little longer, enjoying that miraculous forward window. But when she heard the Master order the bridge crew into vac suits for a drill, she went to the elevator.

The tall, skinny man was also waiting for the car to come up. Up close, his long coat was even more obviously expensive; made for him, it fell away almost to the floor.

He glanced at her nervously and then turned his head away.

The iris valve opened and Nbaro stepped through, and then the elevator doors opened behind it. She had a moment to think, *The bridge has its own airlock. Of course it does. And its own medbay.*

And it must rotate. Of course! When the ship flips its ends to brake, the bridge rotates on the elevator shaft.

She could see the lines on the deck.

163

The tall man was also looking at them. Then he stepped in behind her. The doors closed as she pressed O-2.

'I saw you…' he began. He sounded nervous.

Nbaro glanced at him.

'I saw you… fighting the remotes.' It was a struggle for him to get it out.

She nodded. She couldn't think of anything to say.

'It was very instructive,' he said.

The doors opened on to O-4 and closed again.

'Instructive?' she asked.

'It taught me that a human being could defeat a drone,' he said.

'But not eight drones.'

'Exactly. I learnt a great deal. Also, it was aesthetically pleasing.'

He was an *Augment*. Nbaro could see that now. They were not always good at shades of meaning, but then, it was rumoured that they didn't lie. His nanolink showed behind his left ear and one of his eyes was a replacement, allowing a direct feed into his visual centres.

She tried smiling. 'Thanks, I think.'

'This was meant as a sincere compliment,' he said, and then, 'I am not always certain that my comments are well received.'

The doors opened on O-2.

Some impulse drove her.

'I'm Marca Nbaro,' she said.

Almighty, I've lost my mind.

He smiled, if a single millimetre upturn in the corners of his mouth counted as a smile.

'Horatio Dorcas,' he said with a slight bow.

The doors closed between them.

Nbaro stood there for a moment, staring at the elevator's

closed outer doors. Then she put the name on her tab. Ran a search.

'Search Subject Not Found.'

He'd been on the *bridge*.

He couldn't be a stowaway.

Nbaro mentioned him to Thea over dinner, and she wasn't very interested.

'Ship's still full of contractors. Most of 'em won't get off until we reach Sahel.'

'A contractor in a thousand-ducat long-coat?' she said.

Thea waved a hand.

Hanna was eager to change the subject.

'Do you know that we have a pair of escorts?' he asked. 'Big ones. Military cruisers. Running silent.'

'See?' Thea said. 'There's so much we don't know.'

'Escorts!' Hanna said. 'No greatship has ever had escorts.'

Thea gave him a withering glance. 'You know that?'

Hanna was thoroughly abashed.

'No,' he admitted.

'So as far as we know, it's happened before, but no one talks about it.' She pointed at him. 'I'm just a dumb midshipper, and even I assume we have long-jump capable warships.'

Hanna sat back. 'Now I feel dumb,' he said.

He looked at Nbaro, and she found herself smiling at him. A man who admitted he was wrong?

I really am an idiot.

The third and fourth days out, Nbaro alternated Boarding Party practices, zero-*g* combat, a Damage Control refresher, and repeated watch-standing exercises, as well as an EVA with a senior chief petty officer from Engineering; *familiarisation,* they called it.

Nbaro had now passed enough of the checkpoints on her

qualification to be included on the watch-list, and she suspected her skipper had his thumb on the scales, putting her on once every rotation. She stopped reading her SOPs and her flight manuals and just dragged herself from one duty to the next.

Zero-*g* combat was intense, a little dangerous, and very exciting even in practice, though her zero-*g* skills left a great deal to be desired. Some of the Spacers and a few officers could move like fish in water; Nbaro was not one of them, and her leaps were always too hard, her landings always a little uncontrolled. She often died immediately upon landing, as she took half a second to stabilise.

She died a lot.

Nbaro liked the Combat Theory classes, though; she could envision them in terms of sword fighting, and she was proud as the legendary Lucifer when her refurbished space armour came back from Spacer Chu, the transparent blue xenoglas panels polished so that they glowed with their odd, very slight inner light. Her stretch-Kevlar was mostly new and a fine matt black. Chu had put a sticker on her breastplate with her name and her pilot's wings.

Nbaro went and stole pies immediately.

It was slightly anticlimactic when no one in her combat group noticed that she finally had armour.

After a hurried meal of something that seemed more like pressed fungal paste than seemed quite fair when they'd just been in port on the richest agricultural planet in the Human Sphere, she *ran* to Space Ops and managed to stay awake through an entire watch in which there was precisely one Space Ops event: a single Flight 8 shuttle testing an engine repair. Lieutenant Commander Dworkin, the Tower, let her launch it and then call the recovery. That kept her awake.

The next day Nbaro was on watch at the beginning of her day, and she was sent to work with Tower again, where an elderly

Lieutenant Commander introduced her to the Tower protocols in Space Traffic control with a pedantry that put her teeth on edge. She constantly wanted to say, 'I am a pilot, arsehat,' but she didn't, and as the long watch wore on and she learned more, Nbaro understood that the older woman probably felt that everyone needed a thorough briefing. Commander McGurty was one of those for whom the job was the whole of her life.

Then she was sent out on the hull in her EVA suit to learn a little about hull maintenance and deep-space welding. She stood on the hull in the shadow of the bridge superstructure and admired the universe and the endless veil of stars until her petty officer became concerned and raised her on comms.

'You all right, miz?' he asked.

'Really good, Petty Officer Deseronto.'

Nbaro split the rest of the day between her flight's maintenance shop, where she was learning the ropes, and the pistol range, where apparently the Master himself had ordered that she be instructed. A Marine gunnery sergeant, Drun, patiently taught her to load and fire a pistol, over and over, for four hours, until her head hurt and her hands hurt, but she could change clips while he fired off his own weapon next to her ear.

He smiled in the end and mentioned that he was not in her chain of command, and Nbaro didn't even stiffen. She was quite proud of herself.

'No thanks, Gunny,' she said. 'Excellent lesson, though.'

He gave her a wave, unoffended, and disappeared back down the corridor to the marine spaces on Third Deck.

Another day, and more high-*g* drills. Nbaro was on watch, with her own acceleration couch in Weps, and she now knew enough not to be intimidated by the screens. She leafed through every screen available to her until she found the Tactical Action Officer's plot and located the two cruisers.

So that was true.

And both of them were brand new, fifth generation battle-cruisers. Both of them had passive detection systems more advanced than the *Athens* and all the newer technology. Both of them had ellipses painted over them; when Nbaro rotated the view through three dimensions, they were like eggs.

'Probability ellipse,' she said to herself.

They weren't close; they were each a light second out, give or take a few thousand kilometres.

Two brand-new battlecruisers, escorting a greatship in friendly systems.

Someone was being very cautious.

'Will you … hum … have dinner with me again?' Hanna asked her.

'You're having dinner with me right now,' she replied, and Thea almost spat up her coffee.

'You used to be such a morose little thing,' Thea said.

'You just didn't understand my sense of humour,' Nbaro shot back.

Ko, the Flight 5 pilot, pointed at an empty place.

'Anyone sitting here?'

Hanna was shaking his head. 'You're taking your life in your hands, sitting there.'

Ko shrugged. 'Fighter pilots are renowned for their daring.' He sat. 'It's boring out between the stars.'

Thea made a face. 'Is that a pick-up line?'

Ko laughed. 'Now I'm screwed either way. But no. I just mean there's no flying.'

Marca smiled at Hanna. 'You mean the insertion to Haqq Algericas?' she asked.

Hanna grinned. 'Yeah.'

She didn't even have to force the smile. 'I'll think about it,' she drawled.

Ko looked at her. 'How's Space Ops?'

She nodded. 'You guys are flying tomorrow,' she said.

He shook his head. 'Nah, we're just on Insertion Alert. We sit in our cockpits until the insertion is done and there's no bad guys.'

'Oh,' she said.

He brightened. 'Hey, maybe there will be bad guys.'

'I don't think that would be good,' Thea said.

'Valid point,' Hanna said.

As it turned out, Marca was on watch for insertion. That made it a whole new experience. Every other insertion she'd flown, she'd been in her cabin, in her own crash-couch, and she'd had leisure to take her drugs and wake up.

But the jump to Haqq Algericas was in the middle of her watch, and so Nbaro was in the Weps couch, strapped in, and the needles moved through the stents in her suit and delivered the insertion cocktail. Some people liked it; some hated it. For her, it was like drinking too many cups of coffee: a sudden feeling of fatigue and jittery nerves; a strange feeling in her muscles and bones, as if she'd lifted weights.

Mpono was the Duty Officer, and Nbaro listened to them chatting with the Master on the command bridge while she looked for their escorts and then dialled her screens to the launch sequence, where she could see Alpha Echo 5–0–2, with 'Ko' stencilled under the cockpit of a matt-black warbird. A Gunslinger, the latest in DHC military technology.

'Fifteen minutes until Insertion,' Smoke said into the command circuit. 'Everyone take their drugs?'

A chorus of 'Yes, tir.'

The first of their two escorts hit its own insertion point and jumped. It didn't disappear immediately; first, its light and heat signature took almost two seconds to reach them, and second, jump was a quantum event and while it was instantaneous to the participant, it was not to the observer at either end.

The second escort began to fade.

Nbaro lay in her couch, contemplating *insertion*. She really should have reviewed the tapes a second time; the retired warrant officer who'd appeared at the Orphanage had just banged his podium and told them what to memorise for their exams. He hadn't explained anything. Useful enough – she'd passed. But now that she was in space…

Nbaro knew that some 'gates' were better for insertion than others, and that those gates could move, and that some points only 'inserted' to other points – but, because they were unreliable, they were not counted as gates. Every jump needed to be calculated in terms of the visible universe, the quantum universe, and the computer's best guess as to the relative positions of 'here' and 'there' in terms of *both* abstract simultaneity and relativity.

He said there's no proof we end up in the same universe we started in.

Computers couldn't guarantee *exactly* where you came out, which was why Astrogation aimed above or below the ecliptic and well out from the habitable zones. And insertion could add or dump velocity, which science was getting much better at predicting, for reasons she couldn't remember.

And everything in the Universe *moved*. Planets moved, stars moved, asteroids moved. Prediction in realtime of the movement of celestial bodies was one of the most difficult aspects of Astrogation.

And all the maths for insertion depends on the concept of a multiverse of infinite universes, each one flowing from the others at some unimaginable rate. Maybe in this one, I don't appear in an amateur pornography vid with a useless boy in a military chapel.

Ha.

Nbaro lay back and rotated the Weps screen until it was virtually over her head, so that she didn't have to move to see it.

'I could take a nap,' she said on Smoke's circuit.

'When I was a midder, all I ever wanted was sleep,' Smoke said. 'My spouse says you're one hell of a fencer.'

Nbaro had no response to that.

'Sixty seconds to jump,' Smoke said. 'Hats on, everyone.'

All command space crews went through jumps in vac suits and with their helmets closed. Nbaro closed her visor.

She tasted the air. Her new helmet was *much* better than the old one, but she could swear that a past owner had vomited into it. Perhaps many times.

'Jump in ten.' The Master's voice.

Nbaro was watching the Tactical Action Officer's plot.

'Nine, eight, seven...' the Master said.

Nbaro was tense – nervous. Was that just the drugs? This was the longest jump they'd made so far—

They jumped.

Nbaro got her eyes open.

There was a heavy weight on her chest and the tactical action plot was...

They'd reached Haqq Algericas. It said so on the screen. Only that screen was flashing red, and that made no sense unless it was damaged. They were moving quite fast, which perhaps Astrogation had predicted, but no one had told her; a long braking burn was going to be a pain.

'Stand by for high-*g* manoeuvres,' a voice said. 'This is a high *g* warning. Ten. Nine...'

The screens were flashing red because they were at Battle Stations.

No one was talking on any of her channels. Most people were still out.

Battle Stations!

Her couch turned on its gimbals, and the pressure on her chest increased. It was almost painful.

In moments she was having trouble breathing.

Shit . . .

Now launch the Insertion Alert 5.

Nbaro couldn't turn her head, and she knew nothing about launching when they were at high *g*.

She scanned her screens. They were at 4.4 *g*. Something gave in her neck when she turned her head too far – perhaps four centimetres.

Nbaro blinked through her helmet commands and engaged the Flight Deck comms channel.

'Alert 5, this is Lioness, over,' she said as calmly as she could manage.

'Lioness, this is Alert 5.'

Ko sounded incredibly calm. Nbaro was flooded with admiration.

'What are your launch parameters for *g* force?'

'Six point four, Lioness.'

Mpono's voice cut in. 'Alert 5, this is Lioness. We'll be cutting acceleration, launching you, and then rotating the ship for a hard decel. Over.'

'Copy. Turning and burning as soon as I launch,' repeated Ko.

Smoke spoke in her ear. 'Nbaro, good instinct to launch under *g*, but wrong. We can stop accelerating any time by asking the Master. *Then* we launch.'

Nbaro realised they were on a private channel and she felt . . .

'I'm an idiot,' she said aloud.

'Nope,' Mpono said. 'Just new. And you thought about it – your idea could have worked – and then acted. That's good.'

Data was flooding the ship as they went in system. They'd passed through Insertion at a very high speed, almost 0.2 c. Now they had to dump all that velocity, but at the moment it meant that their sensor arrays were pulling in data from the Haqq Algericas system, the quantum computers desperately trying to decode the blue shift as they went deeper and deeper into the system's datasphere.

Alarms sounded, and the Master's voice warned: 'Artificial gravity in one minute, for five minutes' duration. I say again, we will go to artificial gravity in one minute, for a duration of five minutes.'

A very slow minute passed.

The great weight lifted off her chest.

'Five minutes to pee,' Smoke called. 'Get it done, folks.'

'Allah is great,' muttered a tech.

'Oh, God.'

'Jesus.'

'Fuck me,' muttered someone with even less religious inclination.

Those simultaneous curses, from techs looking at their screens, were enough to stop most of the spacers who'd risen to stretch wounded muscles or visit the head.

Marca was very disciplined with her screen use; it was currently set to watch the Flight Deck, with a split screen to watch system traffic, most of its information four days old or more.

But many other techs, especially those with no real duties during insertion, were looking at newsfeeds – four days old – streaming out of Haqq Algericas. People had their tabs up to their faces; some, with implants, were reading straight off their retinas.

'But...' someone said. 'This can't be happening.'

'Get moving, friends,' Mpono said. 'We're turning and burning in four minutes thirty seconds, and your screens will still be there.'

Even then, some people didn't move.

Nbaro had a sense of foreboding, and it was confirmed when she turned her head and saw the reverse of the letters for *Hong Kong* reflected in the gold of the next station's visor.

She leant over.

Hong Kong reported destroyed, it said across Petty Officer Fisk's screen.

'Nbaro!' snapped Mpono. 'Get Alert 5 off the rails.'

'Yes, tir.'

'Get it done. Go ahead, Combat.'

Nbaro clicked over to another channel. The Tactical Action Officer was on the Combat Bridge, with the real weapons screens and techs.

Smoke was gone, but Nbaro knew the drill; she notified the bridge, found to her embarrassment that Mpono had already done that, and then she told the deck that Alert 5 was good to launch in thirty seconds.

She called Ko – if it was Ko.

'Alert 5, this is Lioness, over.'

'Lioness, this is Alert 5, over.'

Sounded like Ko; he was cheerful. Cheerful, while at Battle Stations immediately after a jump.

'Alert 5, I have your weight at …' She stared at her six-way split screen. 'I have you at 19192 kilos.'

'Roger, Lioness. Guess I should stop eating so much pie.' Pause. 'Over.'

'You are go for launch.'

'Roger, go for launch.'

Nbaro watched on the plat camera as he saluted, and his big Gunslinger attack craft hurtled off the rails and into the deep black of space.

She toggled Mpono. 'What about Alert 15?'

Mpono held up a physical hand. Then pointed and made the motion of firing a gun.

Nbaro toggled back. 'Upgrade the Insertion Alert 15 to Alert 5,' she said in every ready room.

Then she toggled to the alert pilot. 'Alert 15, this is Lioness, over.'

'Roger, Lioness, this is Alpha Echo 5–o–9.'

Ah, the Alert 15 is just a normal launch? Nbaro thought. *What don't I know here?*

'Alpha Echo 5–o–9, I'm upgrading your Alert 15 to Alert 5. How soon can you launch?'

'Any time, baby,' the pilot replied.

'Say again, Alpha Echo 5–o–9?' Nbaro said, just to be a pain in the arse.

'Uh, roger, Lioness, I'm good to go.'

It had to be Cortez. Nbaro rolled her eyes. Even in an emergency.

She informed the bridge, signalled the Flight Deck and moved the alert into the 'ready to launch' window on her screen with her light pencil.

Mpono came back up. 'We're rotating the ship to start a braking burn in about seventy seconds. Get him away.'

'Yes, tir,' she said.

'Flight Deck, this is Lioness, over.'

'Roger, Lioness.'

'Get the Alert 5 off the deck, chief.'

'Roger, Lioness.'

Back to the pilot. 'Alpha Echo 5–o–9, this is Lioness, over.

'Lioness, this is 5–o–9, over.'

'Call your weight, 5–o–9.'

'Roger, Lioness, I'm 19720 kilos, over.'

'5–o–9, I have your weight at…' Nbaro stared at her six-way split screen again. *How does Mpono do this all day?* 'I have you at 19720 kilos.'

'Roger, Lioness. Copy.'

'You are go for launch.'

'Roger, go for launch.'

On her wrist plate, the time until the ship rotated was counting down.

Mpono said, 'Do I need to ask the Master to hold the rotation?'

5–0–9 launched. Nbaro watched it go.

'It's away, tir.'

About fifteen seconds later, the ship began to rotate. The artificial gravity remained on, so that the rotation had a faintly impossible feel to it, as the stars swung around and they fell sunwards, stern first. But the railgun tubes worked in either direction, and in fifteen minutes the AI and Mpono had re-orientated all the magnets. Nbaro found a plat camera and, sure enough, the bridge had rotated and was once again facing in the direction of travel.

'Prepare for high-*g* burn,' the Master said.

Are we at war? What the hell's going on?

'Commander Mpono, are we launching anyone from my squadron?' Nbaro asked on the private channel.

'Good question. Wait one.'

Mpono was busy, so Nbaro toggled her squadron ready room.

'Truekner,' her skipper answered.

'Sir, this is Nbaro in Space Ops. How fast can you have two—'

'Two already crewed and ready to go. Guille and Storkel.'

'Thanks, sir.'

'No problem, Nbaro.'

Nbaro looked up. Out loud, she said, 'Truekner has two ready to launch.'

'Truekner's a fucking genius,' Mpono said. 'I'll ask the Master to hold the burn.'

Four minutes later, the two Flight 6 craft were launched into the Black.

Her couch rotated through 180 degrees, as did her screens.

And a huge weight descended on her chest.

It was a long, long watch. The deceleration was fatiguing and Nbaro was tempted to fall asleep, while the data on screen was so old as to be meaningless because they were four light hours out from the primary planet.

Like the rest of her watch, she spent the time using her various data feeds to read up on the news. A messenger boat had passed them by at least a day, so some of the news coming in was much more recent than other data in the same packet.

The *Hong Kong* was overdue, and a cloud of associated radioactive dust had been located in Ultra, one of the long-jump systems that the greatships navigated on their homeward route. Nbaro went back and forth between two reports, looking for anything that would indicate how the *Hong Kong* had died and what had killed her, or even how that information had become available.

Because the news came to them via New London, the files included grim reports of labour unrest and market failures throughout the DHC worlds as the loss of the greatships was totalled up by the financial markets, and the halt to xenoglas production intensified. There was other news: an insider trading scandal that threatened the political positions of three of the DHC board's seventeen members, and Senate demands on New London that the DHC investigate rumours of new alien contacts in the Anti-spinward marches. One of the opposition senators went so far as to claim that the DHC had lost control of the frontier. A DHC spokesman replied later the same day that, as the DHC was not and would not be a government, it controlled nothing.

But for the most part, the incoming news dealt with an entire culture's panic at losing two of their iconic vessels and their vast cargoes and the crews, taken from every level of human society – including the most privileged. Conspiracy theories reigned supreme, tying the losses to everything from internal sabotage to the dread forces of undiscovered aliens.

Nbaro finally went off watch with a vague feeling of unreality, a sort of loss of self that she hadn't experienced before. The Master stopped the ship's braking burn for ten minutes while the crew moved around and posts and watches were relieved. Nbaro fell asleep wondering where her laundry was, and only woke when Thea came in.

'Still at full alert?' she mumbled.

'Yah,' Thea drawled. 'We need a new alert level. The locals launched all their military boats as soon as they saw us come in system.'

Marca watched the local warships launch from their docks, scattering into the local equivalent of the asteroid belt. The data was hours old; the far-on spheres that the computer's holotank put on the ships were as big as planets, and indicated how far the ships might have moved since the last known location.

However, the potential hostility of the local navy was not the immediate problem. Their own velocity was. They were going so fast that they had to use the system to brake. Instead of 'coasting' down to the big orbital station in the L5 point of Haqq Algericas, they had to plot a course all the way in-system, slingshot the system's star and then out to a gas giant. It was the only way to slow down sufficiently at reasonable deceleration.

A journey of days would take weeks.

This was the sort of thing that made long-jump spaceflight erratic and affected shipping prices and cargo values; Nbaro had certainly heard of it happening. But that was nothing to the reported loss of the *Hong Kong*, and for almost three weeks, the crew of the *Athens* would be watching their screens and tabs and gossiping about what was killing humanity's greatest ships.

The death or loss of the *Hong Kong* was omnipresent and deeply depressing to everyone aboard the *Athens*, but Nbaro had a more pressing problem: none of her laundry was coming back.

She'd tailored all of her hand-me-down flightsuits herself and Chu had grudgingly embroidered them all; she should have had eight in total.

She had two. The other six, and three of her four shipboard jumpsuits, had vanished into the maw of the ship's laundry. Nbaro had posted queries on her tab and tried to go in person to the laundry office on the O-2 level and was met with stony indifference from the very junior spacers who handled such things.

'Sorry, miz,' they said. 'You need to go to Main Laundry.'

On the third visit, a harassed junior petty officer said, 'Chief Dornau might be able to help.'

Nbaro literally didn't have time to do any more, and she took to washing her few clothes in a sink and hanging them by one of her stateroom's air vents to dry, which took up time and earned glares of reproof from Drake.

But she was working too hard to care much, or give it too much thought.

The Master ordered Astrogation and Engineering and Cargo to perform complete equipment reviews, a gruelling job that ate into every spacer's entire watch and then some. The rumour mill said that the Master believed that the other ships had died because of an equipment failure. Or sabotage.

Hanna thought that sabotage was more likely, and he laid out his theory over pressed fungal sliders in the informal mess that most officers called the Dirtyshirt. The Dirtyshirt mess was on the O-1 level and resembled a magnificent dining room from the eyeline up – though, beneath the magnificent framed screens and acanthus leaves, brass, gold, and green-veined black marble, there were matt-black nanofibre tables and chairs and a set of machines and recyclers that produced food almost instantly, as long as quality was not needed. Everything came in bulbs; the food was mostly stews and curries, the drinks were odd, flat-tasting juices, weak teas and the omnipresent coffee to which Nbaro was finally growing used. It was a wardroom that officers could use in any uniform or no uniform, which was why it was called the Dirtyshirt.

Nbaro actually preferred the slightly more formal aft wardroom on the O-3 level, but her little group of junior officers had decided otherwise. Marca didn't often admit loneliness to herself, but it was nice to be part of a group, and Thea and Hanna and Ko were all much more important to her than better tea and silver mess service.

Ko had dark smudges under his eyes, as the greatship's escort fighters were flying round the shift clock and he was out for two long missions a day. Nbaro wasn't doing much better; the rotation now had her as co-pilot for two events a day, plus eight hours in Space Ops, plus her boarding training, damage control, and two courses the skipper had put her down for: a class in material maintenance and another on torpedo tactics, both on holo.

Hanna was working his entire rotation on reviewing every aspect of the programming of Morosini.

Thea was the only one getting any sleep, and she wasn't getting much; the Master had ordained a complete review of all the cargo manifests, and a physical inspection of every cargo space.

Ko, who was a senior lieutenant, shrugged.

'Could be worse,' he said. 'I'm the assistant maintenance officer for my flight and I'm a division officer with forty spacers. Lots of reports and, worse, promotion boards coming up ...'

Hanna nodded. 'I'm about ready to space myself,' he said. 'I can't see when I'm getting my promotion board stats into the computer.'

It was a miracle that had brought them all together – one moment in their fractal schedules when all of them could eat.

'I heard a rumour we aren't even taking liberty while we're

here,' Hanna said. 'Master's talking about doing the cargo exchange and leaving.'

'We're living in interesting times,' Thea said.

Cortez came and sat across from Thea. He looked at Nbaro.

'Was that you being Lioness?' he asked.

He was talking about something two hundred hours in the past. More.

'Yes,' she said. 'During insertion?'

He nodded. 'Sorry about the bad comms procedure.' He shrugged. 'I'm not my best after insertion, unlike the ever noble Lieutenant Ko.'

Nbaro shrugged. She'd decided that Cortez was all right, and she was in a forgiving mood.

'Me neither,' she agreed. 'I'm new and I made mistakes.'

He smiled, then – a real smile.

'That's how it goes,' he admitted.

Thea had not stopped talking for Cortez, and now she was developing her idea about interesting times.

'Look,' she said insistently. 'Half the problem here is that Haqq Algericas isn't DHC. It's independent – it's really a satellite of the SUA.'

Hanna made a face.

Nbaro bludgeoned her brain for the acronym.

'SUA?' she asked as Thea began her next point.

'*Sehemu mpya ya Ufansi wa Afrika,*' she said in a smooth accent. 'The New Africa Prosperity Sphere.'

'They're not a government,' Hanna said.

'The DHC isn't a government either,' Thea said. 'The Human Sphere is a set of voluntary trade associations.'

'Figure a Cargo officer would lecture us on trade,' Cortez said.

Thea rolled her eyes. 'Anyway,' she said, dismissing Hanna and Cortez, 'we're in SUA space with two gen-5 battlecruisers and a greatship and everyone's very, very nervous. The *Hong Kong* is missing and the *New York* is dead, unless that vid we saw is a fabrication.'

'Fabrication?' Ko asked.

Drake got a lazy little smile. Nbaro knew what that smile meant and was cautious around it.

Drake shrugged. 'I don't honestly think it is,' she said. 'But I'm trying to consider everything. Critically.'

'Like a patrician,' Hanna said.

Thea smiled. 'Exactly.'

Ko got up and stretched. He was tall, almost as tall as Commander Mpono. He was as handsome as an ancient god and he never seemed to play to it.

'Well, I have to walk,' he said. 'You just scared the shit out of me, Drake.'

'Good,' Thea said. 'I'm scaring myself.'

That seemed to take the sting out of the whole conversation; the tension dissolved.

'Could the SUA be responsible?' Hanna asked.

Thea shook her head. 'No way. They aren't all DHC, but they're bound to us by a hundred trade routes. And anyway, the *New York* went down the other side of Trade Point, and, unless my amateur maths is wrong, so did the *Hong Kong*. That's a year away, or even more.'

Hanna blinked. 'Right,' he said.

'SUA is only reacting to what they see, which is a very heavily armed force jumping in high c.' Thea shrugged. 'Our tech's a generation ahead of theirs – maybe two. In military stuff, if not in comms. So they have to mobilise their space forces immediately or we could, theoretically, just gun them down.'

'I get it,' Ko said. 'So I'm out there flying Space Patrol and they're reading me as a potential aggressor.'

'Roger that,' Thea said. 'If they see you at all.'

*

Another week: heavy braking burns every watch, and a level of fatigue that surpassed anything Nbaro had ever known.

She had Thea to talk to when she wasn't too tired; she saw Ko occasionally. She spent an entire event strapped in to 6–0–7 with the skipper, repeating Thea's musings.

Truekner listened with interest.

'Agreed to the SUA part,' he said. 'Although I'd say Ms Drake is a generation behind in her appreciation of SUA tech. I doubt they have anything to match a DHC battlecruiser, but their smallboys are as good as ours or better, and their information systems –' he glanced at her – 'are probably better. I don't want to fight the SUA, and I'm sure as shit they are not the ones killing our greatships.'

'Roger that, sir.'

'You can call me Skipper.' He had his visor up, and he smiled. 'I find your friend's suggestion that the death of the *New York* vid was a fabrication to be …' He paused a long time. 'Horrifying. Mostly because I never considered it.'

They were thousands of kilometres ahead of the *Athens*. The ship had slowed with a quick braking burn, paused, shot them off, and then accelerated just a little – a complex series of operations that allowed two torpedo-laden XC-3Cs to be in the dark, several thousand kilometres ahead of the greatship; never having lit their engines or even turned on their auxiliaries, they were virtually undetectable. It was cold, miserable duty, but it had the potential to save the ship or give an enemy a terrible surprise. They were moving only with the vector and velocity the railgun had imparted, and the greatship had only accelerated behind them to match their velocity exactly.

It was one of dozens of tactics they were practising every day.

'Want to hear some good news, Marca?'

'Maybe more than anything, Skipper,' she said.

'I have it on good authority that we will have planetside

liberty on Haqq,' he said. 'So I suspect that the Master and the SUA rep have come to an understanding.'

The nature of that understanding unfolded in her next Space Ops watch, when Nbaro saw that both of the battlecruisers had changed course and were making for a different orbit – refuelling at the gas giant, she guessed, looking at her holo projection.

About twelve hours later, the Master turned off the Battle Stations status and the ship dropped exhaustedly into routine operations, except for the flights. Because twenty hours after that, they were plotted to enter orbit over Haqq, and the cargo runs would begin.

Nbaro had slept a full eight hours, saw the flight schedule like an approaching storm, and decided that she had to find her uniforms.

The laundry was all the way below – Sixth Deck. Nbaro took a drop-shaft with a confidence she wouldn't have had three weeks before, and didn't bother with a handhold until she came to Fifth Deck.

The thing you have to keep telling yourself in zero g is that no gravity means that you don't accelerate by falling further, she thought.

The long drop *felt* dangerous, but the only velocity Nbaro had at the end was the velocity she'd imparted at the beginning of her fall, and she caught herself in a neat landing and then climbed down the last deck because she'd wanted a margin of error. She wasn't really *good* at zero g yet.

The Sixth Deck. It had high overheads and dusty murals and even higher knee-knockers, as if the designers had expected to have to separate one cargo hold from another …

Of course they did.

Nbaro stopped. She could see it: bulk cargoes like the grain they'd picked up on Barcino could be held in very cold temperatures – and maybe even in vacuum. Cheaper? She didn't know.

So much I don't know.

Nbaro passed a fabrication shop she didn't remember from her first visit, and realised that if the small hatch had been closed, she'd have assumed it was storage. Instead, peering in through the open hatch, she saw forty or more spacers working at various stations: lots of nanofabricators, but also one of the new 3D titanium printers which she recognized from a news vid sequence, as well as a silent and very old-fashioned lathe that turned metal at high rpm; Nbaro wondered if there was a blacksmith, somewhere.

'Help you, miz?' asked a senior petty officer. He was in a ship's jumper with so much dirt and oil on it that Nbaro couldn't read his rank, but he was probably a chief or a warrant.

'Never been here before, Chief.' Nbaro experimented with the title. 'Is that really a 3D titanium printer?'

'Yes, miz. Good eye.' He didn't quite smile, but he didn't seem annoyed.

'I'm headed to Laundry,' she said, somewhat inanely.

'Need an escort, miz?'

'No, Chief, I'm fine,' she said.

'Not really officer country,' he said. Kindly enough, she thought.

'I see nothing,' she commented.

In fact, Nbaro saw a few things that might give an officer pause. She smelt a little smoke, in fact. Hash? Marijuana? Or just some grease or oil she didn't recognise?

She also saw a young male spacer with a big bruise on his face. His half-open suit said 'Aquila' on the name tape. Workshop accident?

Hazing?

Not officer country.

Nbaro was balanced between the sense of justice and injustice that had brought her into conflict with the Orphanage, and the vague but real trust she had begun to place in the Service and the *Athens*.

She thought for a moment and came up with a non-intrusive plan.

'Have a good shift, Chief,' she said.

He nodded, and Nbaro slipped out, headed sternwards, alert to other wonders which might lurk behind the hatches that lined the passageway. Her tab buzzed in her pocket, and then buzzed again and again. The last time it had done that, she'd been syncing with City during docking.

Nbaro stopped outside the laundry and thumbed her tab. There were a dozen alerts, but none lined in red. So she ignored them. Instead, she keyed Hanna.

He answered. Hanna.

Know anyone in Engineering? she asked.

About half the officers, Hanna wrote agreeably.

Can you find out who's in charge of Fabrications on Sixth Deck?

He took his time answering, and then texted, On it.

Nbaro went into the main laundry shop. There wasn't even a counter to receive complaints, just dozens of very junior spacers, almost all new recruits, carrying bags of laundry – thousands of them. Of course. There would be about two thousand sets of laundry a day, she calculated in her head.

As she stood there, more than fifty ratings passed her, every one of them giving her a glance. She'd rarely felt more out of place in her entire life.

But... Nbaro grabbed a woman out of the line waiting to hand in their bags.

'Where do I find the work centre supervisor, spacer?' she asked.

The rating tried *not* to make eye contact.

'No idea, miz,' she mumbled.

So she tried again.

And again.

Nbaro was starting to become annoyed when a big woman in a ship's jumpsuit emerged from the steam of the laundry area.

'Miz?' she asked.

She wore chief petty officer stripes and stars and the tape on her chest said Dornau beneath the oil or sweat.

Marca smiled, mostly because smiling was her new way of doing business.

'All my laundry's gone missing—'

'Take it up with your laundry desk on your deck of residence,' the chief said.

'Done that, Chief,' she said.

The chief looked her up and down.

'Well, miz, not sure what I can do for you.' Her dismissal was startling.

'You can find my flightsuits,' Nbaro snapped.

The chief spread her hands, as if to explain.

'Ma'am,' she said formally, 'we've been under acceleration and braking burn for going on five weeks. Laundry isn't easy during high-g burn, miz. Stuff goes missing.'

Nbaro saw the other woman's bad eye contact and she reacted.

'Sorry, Chief. I don't believe you.'

They stood there, eye to eye.

'Maybe I didn't hear you right, miz,' the chief said.

Nbaro sighed. 'It's all tagged and tracked electronically, Chief. So ... I'd like my flightsuits back. If I get them back, I'll assume there's been a misunderstanding.' She smiled her best smile.

'This ain't officer country, miz. Maybe you shouldn't be here.' The chief's tone conveyed a definite threat.

Nbaro had seen all this before. The frightened recruits shuffling around them were like the new kids at the Orphanage, the senior petty officer the long-established bully...

'Maybe I shouldn't,' Nbaro nodded. 'And maybe,' she said softly, 'maybe I'm not someone to fuck with.'

The chief's stare was level. 'Way I hear it, you're the Orphan midder and no one will go to bat for you.' A long pause. 'Miz.'

Nbaro smiled, because everything was apparently *just* like the Orphanage, and that made it easy for her, but she tried one more time.

'Chief, do I take it you aren't going to lift a finger to find my missing clothes? That right?'

The chief said nothing.

'Chief, I know there's a black market in flight gear. And I'm missing my flightsuits. Are you seriously wanting me to bring this up with my skipper? Or can you just find or replace them, and we all walk away?'

Dornau didn't look flustered.

'Go fuck yourself, midder,' she said.

Nbaro was frustrated by the stupidity of the exchange. Dornau kept escalating.

As if we're enemies.

Nbaro leant closer, because the Orphanage Way was to escalate back and show no weakness.

'My skipper can call me midder. You can call me Ms Nbaro.'

The chief looked both ways. 'Or what, exactly?' Nbaro shrugged, conscious of being alone down here. 'Maybe I should break your neck and have all my nice recruits swear it was an accident. Something tells me no one would testify against me.'

The other woman moved and Nbaro got a little closer and her hands came up.

'Go for it, if you think you can take me,' she said.

'And lose my pension?' the chief snapped back. 'Fuck you. Miz.'

Nbaro crowded her again.

'Find my flightsuits, Chief.'

189

'You got no idea what you're getting into,' Dornau said. 'Just go back to your upper decks and fuck yourself.'

Nbaro swung back and Dornau flinched.

Nbaro shook her head, with a false smile that showed all her teeth.

'I can see how you got laundry duty, Chief. Do another stupid thing – like not return my laundered possessions – and you'll be the one *doing* the laundry. *Do you hear me?*'

The recruits were literally cowering.

Nbaro walked away, turning her back deliberately on the chief and counting on her reflexes to save her if she was attacked. She walked out into the passageway and headed sternwards, and when she was out of sight of the laundry, she stopped and shook.

I could have killed her.

I'm an idiot.

I'm not in the Orphanage. Not any more.

Nbaro looked back and saw two laundry recruits were watching her. She made her slightly unsteady way out of sight down the endless corridor.

She stopped at a cross-corridor, ducked down it five steps, and stopped and shook a little more.

What was that? Nbaro asked herself. *What made her behave that way? What could she really want with my flightsuits?*

The buzzer sounded and Nbaro pushed in to Smith's office. She was still shaking slightly, and she was surprised – shocked was more like it – to find Smith sitting with Dorcas.

Smith's eyes narrowed, and then he recognised her.

'Ms Nbaro,' he said. He looked at a computer screen.

Dorcas stood up. 'A pleasure, miz,' he said.

'You two know each other?' Smith said.

'We met in the bridge elevator,' Nbaro said.

There was an edge to Smith that hadn't been there in their last conversation; he didn't seem hesitant this time.

He swore. 'You made one trip to the bridge and you met Nbaro?' he shot at Dorcas.

'Yes. That is an accurate statement,' the Augment said.

Smith blinked. 'How can I help you, miz?'

Nbaro took a deep breath. 'I have a question, off the record.'

'Oh, good. I answer off-the-record questions all the time,' Smith said.

'If a chief petty officer threatens me and tells me I've no idea what I'm getting into, how seriously should I take her?' Nbaro asked.

Smith's eyes narrowed. 'Context?'

Nbaro made a face. 'A case of missing laundry. I suspect, based on her tension and body language, that she sold my flightsuits on the in-ship black market. Which I know exists, as another petty officer offered to sell me a helmet.'

Dorcas barked a humourless laugh. 'Well, we teach them to be merchants. Why shouldn't they buy and sell?'

Smith glanced at Dorcas. 'I'll ignore that.' He shook his head. 'Laundry. Dornau?'

'I was speaking hypothetically,' Nbaro said stiffly.

'All right then. Damn. Are you sure she threatened you?'

'Sir, I've been threatened many times, and by experts. I'm quite sure. And the recruits working in the laundry are learning some pretty fucked-up lessons in leadership.'

Smith nodded. 'I'll look into it.'

Dorcas glanced at her. 'Why *your* flightsuits?' he asked, and Smith looked over sharply. 'I mean, is anyone else missing flightsuits? They're embroidered, correct? I'm quite sure the one I saw you in had the name and emblems permanently adhered. The garment was tailored to fit you, and you have a unique body.'

'Unique?' Nbaro asked.

Smith smiled. 'It's just the way he speaks.'

Nbaro thought that the whole way that Smith spoke to Dorcas was odd, as if they were peers, or even... She gathered up her courage.

'Who are you, anyway?' she asked. 'You're almost the only person not in uniform on the ship, but you clearly have rank aboard...' She smiled in case he thought she meant offence.

He smiled back. It was an odd smile, as if it was a learned behaviour, not a natural primate reaction. It wasn't hesitant. It just wasn't quite... right.

Do I look like that when I smile? she wondered.

Smith was studying her, but spoke to Dorcas.

'I have curious but reliable reasons to trust Ms Nbaro. Though we really don't need anyone else...'

Dorcas was evaluating her; Nbaro suspected he had an implant, or even a neural lace, and was literally making a calculation.

'I'm a kind of mathematician,' he said. 'I'm also... perhaps the term xenobiologist would be accurate. Do you study history, Ms Nbaro?'

'Study might be a little strong,' Nbaro said. 'Though there are narratives and stories in history that I am drawn to—'

'The ones that most closely match your own experience? Yes, this is a common bias,' he agreed.

He seemed to be focused on something or someone that was not her.

'History?' she prompted.

His focus snapped back. 'I see myself as a cryptographer.'

Her incomprehension must have shown in her face.

'A long time ago, on Old Terra, power brokers discovered that they needed to communicate in codes. To preserve the secrecy and integrity of their communications.'

Nbaro nodded. She liked a history lesson, if it was succinct and to the point. 'I'd never thought of it. There must have been a first code. Nifty. Age of Chaos stuff?'

'Exactly. Some of the greatest minds of the late Middle Ages and early Renaissance ... Those terms themselves are open to argument ...' He waved a hand vaguely. 'Regardless, they invented codes. Increasingly complex codes.'

'Of course,' she said, to prompt him to continue.

'First there appeared people who wrote codes, and then those prepared to use their intellects to break the codes of others. As the codes proliferated, used by diplomats, soldiers, and bankers, code breaking became a profession. You may know that the term secretary implies a person who keeps things secret?'

Nbaro was keeping her eyes fixed on his nose, so that she didn't roll them. At the same time, she found the intensity of his manner – and his story – oddly charming.

'So you're a code-breaker,' she said.

He shrugged. 'Well, I work with mathematics and xeno-biology ...' he began, and then stopped, seeing Smith was flushed.

Nbaro looked from one to another.

'You're working to translate the language of the Starfish,' she said in amazement.

Smith sighed. 'That didn't take long,' he said. 'Ms Nbaro, I need you to sign something.'

He raised his tab, typed with one thumb, and pointed it at hers.

Meanwhile, Dorcas smiled. This was his real smile, she could tell.

'Exactly,' he said. 'But please, let me explain.'

'I'd like to stop you,' Smith said. 'But instead I'm going to make Ms Nbaro sign a non-disclosure agreement.'

'Stop me?' Dorcas asked.

'You aren't supposed to tell anyone!' Smith said. 'I thought you'd tell her your cover story. Why did I ever think you would remember to do that?'

'Nbaro isn't just anyone. She's quite intelligent.' Dorcas glanced at Smith. 'I ascertained that from the vid in which she killed the remotes.'

Nbaro couldn't stop the laugh. It wasn't even bitter. Dorcas was a remarkable person; he spoke the truth as he saw it without much filter, making him the worst spy imaginable. And she had thought he was some sort of DHC spy. Now she wondered what he really was.

Her tab beeped. Nbaro brought up the new document and was surprised to find that it was many screens long, and very detailed.

'You need to read it in full,' Smith said.

Dorcas went on, 'When we first encountered the Xenos known as the Starfish, our AIs felt that they had the ability to understand the signals, but all they got from the symbols they downloaded was gibberish...'

'Pattern analysis without meaning,' Smith muttered. 'For hundreds of years.'

Nbaro knew very little about the Starfish.

'Some people, very intelligent people, proposed that they didn't have language as we know it – they were telepathic, or vastly more intelligent than us.' Dorcas smiled.

'But you've cracked the code,' Nbaro said.

'There's a delicious irony,' Dorcas said, 'that one of the very few things the Starfish share with humans, given they're ammonia-breathing sea creatures who evolved under an ice sheet, is having bicameral brains. Or in their case, multi-cameral. Humans can think two things at once. Maybe the starfish can think five things, maybe ten... but I suspect two. Like us.'

Dorcas had a third kind of smile now. It was as if he was sharing a secret... and he was, but not the obvious secret of his work. Rather, he was imparting information that delighted him. While Nbaro was demonstrating her bicameral brain by listening to

Dorcas and analysing his body language while simultaneously reacting, at least inwardly, to the shock of his implication.

He can communicate with the Starfish.

Almighty.

Nbaro made herself smile back.

'And these bicameral brains...?'

'They're otherwise utterly different. For whatever reason, when one side of the Starfish brain creates a signal, the other half encrypts it and passes some kind of one-time key to the recipient – perhaps by touch? I really don't know... yet. But they share a message, which only the recipient has the means to decode. No other Starfish can understand what was said.'

'This is a theory,' Smith interrupted. 'Ms Nbaro, please read the agreement.'

'Surely any Starfish who receives the key can decode the message?' Nbaro asked, if only to show that she was keeping up.

Dorcas made a wry face. 'Exactly. I'm missing something there, and I lack the data to know what. Over the last two hundred years, the DHC has filmed the Starfish on their own side of the—'

'Please stop there, Dorcas, before you give away a vital secret of the Seventeen,' Smith said, and stood up. 'I'm sorry that I let this conversation continue. You must read and sign this, Ms Nbaro.'

'What – the cameras?' Dorcas waved his hand. 'They're unimportant.'

'I order you to stop,' Smith said firmly.

Dorcas took a breath and then his shoulders fell.

'Fine. If you insist.'

'I do,' Smith said.

Nbaro began to read the non-disclosure agreement. It was... draconian. It detailed ramifications including her expulsion, not just from the Service, but from the DHC, if she divulged any of…

…a very bland list of non-information.

'Welcome to my world,' Smith said, reading over her shoulder. 'I can't even disclose what you're not allowed to disclose.'

She blinked.

Then she read through the entire document again, slowly, while Smith and Dorcas had a spat that made them sound like an old married couple – clearly going over very old ground about secrecy and disclosure.

'You can have me killed?' she squeaked.

Smith shrugged. 'I wouldn't worry about that one.'

'You mean, you can't have me killed?'

'No, I mean that as an officer of Special Services, I could always have you killed if it was for the good of the polity.'

Nbaro digested that.

'Right,' she said.

And after a moment, put her thumb firmly on the screen of her tab until it beeped.

'As you're now read in to a compartmented programme, Ms Nbaro, I must first inform you that you are under no circumstances to allow yourself to be captured, and second, that you're going to share some social duties with me.' He grinned. 'Perhaps I'm overly fatalistic, but you're that rare thing – a person I have reason to trust. Because of your initial fracas, and… some other reasons. And Dorcas needs more people about him.'

Nbaro glanced at the man. 'I'm willing,' she said.

'Dorcas is willing, too,' the man said, and smiled.

Smith sighed. 'He's referring to an old—'

'Charles Dickens.' Nbaro was grinning now. The non-disclosure agreement had thrown her, but old books got her feet under her again. 'The Orphanage restricted our reading to classics whose rights were in the public domain, and thus free.'

'But no artistic work after 2253 ...' Dorcas said, and paused. 'Ah. I see.'

'I'm an old-fashioned girl.' Nbaro didn't even have to force her smile.

'They did real scientific research back then,' Dorcas said. 'Before it all fell in on them.'

'We do scientific research,' Smith said, as if it was his job to defend everything the DHC did, culture-wide.

Dorcas waved a hand dismissively, the most arrogant and annoying gesture that Nbaro had ever seen. Only a patrician born could manage to dismiss the entire scientific effort of 400 years with one finger flick.

'Do you have any idea how bad it was at the end of the Age of Chaos?' he asked.

'Old Terra's oceans died,' Nbaro said. 'Mostly. A billion people died, or more.'

'The effort that put us into space and got us off Old Terra left no room for real research,' Dorcas said. 'No one wants to admit it, but we're still coasting on their work. We've had *two hundred years* and we haven't cracked the Starfish, the only alien race we've encountered. The basis of our entire trade. Practically the underpinnings of our economy. Think about that.'

Nbaro did. It wasn't a pleasant thought.

She left the security station for the long walk forward to the drop-shafts. No one hindered her, although the junior spacers outside the laundry looked haunted. She knew that look. She'd worn it herself, for years. She hated it, and it took an effort of will not to stop and do something about it.

Returning to the familiarity of the O-2 level steadied her, and Nbaro realised that it was already home. Maybe the first home she'd ever had.

She got something to eat and noticed a lot of people bustling about, but she just wanted her bulb of curried goat and some green tea.

Back in her stateroom, Nbaro was washing one of her remaining flightsuits and contemplating how the laundry episode might play out as Thea came in, looked at her, and sat heavily on her acceleration couch.

'No luck?'

Nbaro considered various evasions and settled for 'Not yet'.

'I was *so* proud of getting you my brother's suits,' Drake muttered. Then with her usual mercurial change, she smiled. 'You religious?'

Marca shrugged. 'No straight answer.'

'Do tell,' Thea said.

'Why?' Nbaro asked. 'So you can tease me?'

'No, Orphan girl. 'Cause it's Christmas Eve. At least, ship-time.'

Marca smiled. 'I'd forgotten!'

'I'm going down to the Old Catholic chapel. I need a break.'

'Counting cargo?'

'No, I'm on the Market now.'

'Market?' Marca asked.

'We start marketing our cargo as soon as we come in system,' Thea said. 'Right?'

'I guess I've never thought about it,' Marca said. 'One of the hundreds of things always going on...'

'Too right, sister. Anyway, we send a list of what we have to sell and the bidding begins, and that's the only simple part of it. We have commodities on board, like xenoglas products, that will affect the values in this system to a greater or lesser degree depending on what quantity we have to trade. And... And the deaths of the *New York* and the *Hong Kong* have changed everything,' she said heavily.

Nbaro realised she wasn't dealing with the death of the

198

greatships at all well. Her mind just slid off the idea that they were gone.

Thea saw her blank reaction, and was angered by it.

'I'm probably going to piss you off, but do you really not care? Is it because your family's already dead? Almighty God, Nbaro – we've lost two of the ships that drive our ... our whole civilisation.'

Marca turned away and looked at the wall of stars that the screen was playing, in a silence which went on far too long. Long enough for Marca to think she needed a new stateroom-mate, and then time to think that really, actually, she liked Drake.

My parents are dead.

That was true.

The greatships are dead.

Also true.

Her mind sort of skipped over both sets of facts.

Behind her, Drake said, 'I'm sorry. Totally sorry.'

Nbaro nodded to the screen. She couldn't get her voice to work, and her throat felt heavy, as if she was getting a flu virus.

She blinked. 'I want to go to chapel.' Her voice sounded very odd.

'Good,' Drake said quietly. 'I also hope you plan to get me something for Christmas, because I got you something.'

The Old Catholic chapel was all the way forward on the First Deck, and it was as beautiful as the bridge, though in a different way. It held some remarkable pieces of art: a Virgin Mary statue from the eighteenth century, somewhere in Central America on Old Terra; a life-size Age of Chaos crucifix that was shocking because it was so realistic. The altar candles were the real thing and burned beeswax – or, just possibly, the 3D printers could print beeswax candles. That was the sort of information Nbaro liked to know.

'Isn't that a statue of the Buddha?' she asked.

Thea nodded. 'Regs say all chapels must be comfortable for use by any spacer of any sect,' she said. 'Each one has their own flavour, but it's a long way to the mosque in the stern. Buddhist temple is in officer country amidships ...'

Marca was consistently impressed by the way the DHC service was administered. But she had noticed that almost any institution created after the Age of Chaos had a great many insurances of fairness and equality built in.

The priest said the mass – not exactly the words that Nbaro knew, but when the priest consecrated the communion, she did it with all the familiar gestures – and Nbaro had a rare feeling of comfortable nostalgia. She noticed that there were a few people present whom she knew: a great many junior spacers, as well as her skipper, Commander Truekner, and several people she knew from Space Operations.

Afterwards there were little iced cakes and tiny glasses of champagne, and Nbaro drifted around, making herself smile.

Truekner was standing with the priest, who was now wearing a black ship's jumpsuit.

'Ms Nbaro. I hadn't realised you were Old Catholic.'

'Not sure what I am,' Marca said. 'I like the service.'

The priest gave her a nod that was almost a bow.

'That's fair enough,' she said. 'It's a pleasure having you here, miz.'

Nbaro managed a smile and something clicked in her mind – a decision made, or perhaps it was made back during the curious boredom, nostalgia and pleasure of the ritual.

'I enjoyed it,' she said, and meant it.

Drake was prepared to leave, and Marca learned, during a round of farewells, that Truekner knew Thea and all her brothers. Then they left together.

Nbaro really hadn't heard much of the service; she wasn't

really Old Catholic, although, of the various surviving religions, it was the one with which she was most familiar, and the ritual was comforting.

Enough to tell the truth, anyway.

'I love that chapel, even with the creepy, tortured Jesus,' Thea said. 'That thing bugs me. Like the sculptor watched a bunch of people get tortured to death to get the facial expression correct.'

Marca nodded. 'Age of Chaos. Could be true.'

'Yikes,' Thea said. 'Anyway—'

'Anyway,' Marca put in. 'I want to tell you something.'

They were back in their home passageway. They passed through an iris-hatch and over the knee-knockers.

'Something scary and serious?' Thea asked.

'Pretty much.'

'Does it start with the words, "I'm not in your chain of command"?' Thea asked, her eyes a little too bright.

'No,' Marca said and managed a laugh.

Thea laughed too. 'We're both tagged hetero or Morosini wouldn't have put us in the same stateroom.'

She popped their hatch and they went in. Thea sat on her rack, and Marca crammed herself into a chair.

'Close the hatch,' she said.

Thea did.

Marca crossed her legs and then stared at her hands.

'I'm sure you're tired of hearing this,' she said. 'But the Orphanage was ... terrible.'

'I get that,' Thea said.

Marca nodded. 'People did things to me. I did things to other people.' She looked up. 'I learned not to think about it much. I never think about my parents. I never think about the director of the Orphanage. I never think about the friend who was ...' She had to make herself say the words. 'Who was sold off as a sex worker.'

She met Thea's eyes. 'I'm sort of a monster,' she said. 'I mean, I function pretty well. I have emotions and I have empathy – I'm not a total write-off.'

Thea looked at her, and she seemed about to cry.

'All those memories are there – I can access them.' Marca said. 'I know it's my fault Sarah was sold. I led the little, pointless rebellion, and she paid for it.' She was really having trouble breathing now. 'I can tell you the story, and while I tell it, I feel ... terrible.' Thea was crying now. 'But in an hour it'll be gone. With my parents, and the dead people on the greatships, and the ships themselves. I guess it's a survival mechanism ...?'

Thea put her arms around her. Marca put her arms around Thea, and felt the slight detachment that she always felt when other people displayed emotion.

I've done my crying.

After a minute, Thea broke the hug, wiped her eyes, and shook her head.

'Oh, Marca, that's ... That's ...' Words escaped her. 'Let's not stay in here. Come with me. Let's get some food.'

After washing their faces, they walked down the passageway, and Marca said, 'I still don't understand about the market.'

'Ah,' Thea said. 'That's where I put my foot in it, as a child of privilege.'

Marca said *yes*, but only inside her head.

'I'll try to explain. You watching the vids?'

Marca shook her head.

'You know there's workers' riots on New London, eh?'

Marca felt her eyes widen and she shook her head again.

'A lot of stock values dropped like lead on a high-gravity planet,' Drake said. 'People are losing their jobs and vehicles and homes. Everything. Businesses are closing.'

In fact, Sabina had tried to brief her on this very thing a day before, and she'd shut the AI down.

'Almighty.'

'Exactly. It's the total loss of confidence – two greatships gone, two full cargoes of xenoglas for the factories and the replicators and the designers lost. So here, with our suddenly scarce cargo, our board wants us to charge an astronomical amount for xenoglas. Your suit of armour is worth twenty times what it was when I gave it to you.'

'Do you want it back?' Marca asked with a pang.

'Of course not!' Thea rolled her eyes twice. 'I'm telling you that every lump of the stuff is now worth a little more than gold by mass.'

'Oh.'

By this time, they were in the Dirtyshirt mess and Marca was drawing them both tea while Thea got food. It was traditionally Euro-American here, and festive – ersatz turkey and real mashed potatoes. Thick salty gravy.

Marca wolfed hers down.

'This is delicious,' she managed around a mouthful.

Thea pointed her fork. 'If anyone ever doubts your tales of horror from the Orphanage, they should watch you eat. Almighty, you're like a prey animal at a watering hole.' She smiled to show it was a joke. 'That's just the merchandise,' she said. 'We also sell shares in businesses and futures and cargo possibilities. And that gets complicated.'

Marca swung her head to one side. 'So ... the people who invested in the *Hong Kong* have lost it all?'

Thea locked eyes with her. 'I never thought of that. Oh, Almighty, the losses must have been staggering.'

Thea was shocked, but it prompted Marca to look at her tab. 'How do we know all this?' she asked.

'A messenger boat. Their messages hit us about four hours ago.'

Marca was already checking the alerts. Seven of them were the sub-AI that was tracking financial matters for Sabina.

All of them flagged purchases made by various Thornberg surrogates.

Nbaro collected all seven alerts and sent them to Smith. She added a quick note: Opportunity or planning?

Thea had her own tab out.

'SUA wants to force us to sell them some xenoglas at the old price,' she said.

'So?' Marca asked. 'I mean, there's just as much today as there was yesterday...'

Thea raised an eyebrow. 'See, it's not just about the amount yesterday or today. It's the amount tomorrow. The market is asking the question *will there ever be any more?* and that's the real danger.'

Marca and Thea looked at each other.

'Ouch,' Marca said.

There happens to be a polymath nine decks under my feet who thinks he can talk to the aliens, who we've never talked to before.

And now someone or something is killing our ships.

6

The cargo runs to Haqq Algericas were the unchangeable constant of Nbaro's next six working shifts. She stood just one watch under instruction in Space Operations, learning by mirroring the Tower, because a virus brought aboard by someone returning from a planet-side party had made a lot of pilots sick, and she was on the flight schedule all day, every day.

Haqq Algericas was a vast desert in the popular imagination, and as Nbaro landed all over the planet, delivering and collecting cargoes, she saw a great deal of sand and even flew through some of it, but the planet had marvellous green-grey oceans that looked a sparkling emerald from space, and modern industrial irrigation and careful maintenance for 400 years had turned vast swathes of the desert green. Landing near Dar was like increasing the resolution on a digital picture; from orbit, the whole area was a lurid green, but as she descended, that uniform green resolved into perfect circles of slightly different greens – hundreds of them, thousands, like pixels of life. A number of planets from the first expansion held alien life, from sulphur-based vent dwellers, to large mammal analogues in complex biomes out to Spinward on Lombardia. But Haqq Algericas had no life whatsoever on land, despite having oceans rich in alien microbe and algae analogues. Just Old Terran plants, human beings and the occasional pet.

And a set of alien ruins. Nbaro wanted to see them; everyone did.

She flew eight sorties, mostly with the skipper, but also with Guille and Didier. Didier was older; the Service was his second career, and he appeared unable to take the whole thing seriously. He was soft-spoken, humorous, and irreverent.

He was also an excellent pilot. In two sorties with him, Nbaro learned a lot about the smooth conduct of a flight; he had his own checklists and she was impressed with his processes.

Guille was polite, efficient, and by the book, and made Nbaro practise her emergency responses as if she was still a cadet. She resented Guille a little, but came to the conclusion that the lieutenant was ill at ease with her because she was so junior.

And maybe because I'm a woman, she thought.

There were plenty of women and androgyne/femmes in the Service, but they were still outnumbered by men and androgyne/hommes. And sometimes women were no better with women than men.

After a very brief rest, Nbaro was back with the skipper, Truekner, who smiled as she came into the EVA suit shop.

'Why's your flightsuit damp?' he asked.

She told him. At length. She saw no reason not to.

He looked to one side, scratching his jaw.

'That sucks,' he said. 'Listen, Guille just got this blasted crud. I need you to fly tomorrow, solo.'

She blinked.

'You'll be flying this whole mission today with me in the side seat. You're the pilot. OK?'

'Roger that, Skipper,' she said.

He nodded. 'Great. Because I'll be doing paperwork.'

Nbaro had nerves about it, and varying degrees of performance anxiety through all the preparations and the checklists and the engine start. Only when the big XC-3C hurtled down the tubes and spat out into the Black, the yoke alive and the ship responsive under her hands, did her anxiety fall away.

They were taking a mixed cargo of finished lenses and consumer electronics to one of the islands in the gigantic delta that was formed by the world's biggest river, which the first settlers had called the Nilus. Nbaro had laid in a course back on the ship, and now she triggered it, allowing the craft's computer to pick her route through typical upper-atmosphere high winds and turbulence.

Truekner had his tab on a kneeboard already and was bent over it, alternating between speaking and typing.

Nbaro kept her hands on the yoke through re-entry and then, once she had the bite of atmosphere on the flight surfaces, she relaxed and flew them down.

The skipper glanced at her.

'You listening?' he asked.

Nbaro started. She was above 20,000 m and there were no other craft in sight, so she turned and looked at him.

'No, sir,' she said. 'Should I be?'

He smiled. 'Good. Don't crash.'

Nbaro went back to flying, or rather, to watching the computer fly. When the weather proved worse than predicted at middle altitude she took control, more for the fun of it than out of distrust of the computer, and she made a smooth landing on a runway longer than some highway systems; it seemed to roll on forever towards the distant green sea. The Nilus was just off her right wing tip.

'It's going to take longer to taxi to the spaceport than to fly here from space,' Nbaro muttered.

'Saves a tonne of fuel, though,' the skipper said, not looking up.

Nbaro taxied along, watching the river from time to time. It, too, was bright green, and there was something in it that was alive; the surface would suddenly boil with movement, and then there'd be a swirl. A predator? A huge tail?

She turned under the Tower's direction and rolled to a hangar, or a warehouse.

For the first time in her many flights to Haqq, a customs officer was waiting. He downloaded her manifest and read it over carefully, and then he insisted on scanning every crate and recycle tub in her hold. He was perfectly polite, and so was his assistant, a tall, elegant woman wearing a headscarf of remarkable brilliance – so bright that Nbaro wondered if it had a nano-enhancement.

But they were efficient, and within fifteen minutes the man had expressed his satisfaction and flashed his official approval to her tab, and then the dockworkers began to unload with floating anti-grav dollies.

Everyone seemed a little on edge, but everyone had been on edge since the destruction of the *Hong Kong*, so Nbaro just sat in the pilot's lounge, drank a cup of excellent coffee – one of Haqq's best known exports – and then walked back to her plane, which Truekner had never left.

Nbaro looked over the oncoming cargo manifests, and met a very nervous local merchant, who wore a beautiful long linen robe, covered in embroidery. She was tall, a deep, dark skin colour accented by her pale clothing and gold accessories. She was shipping a cargo of coffee on speculation.

'Ma'am,' she said.

Nbaro made herself smile. 'How can I help you?'

'This coffee is very important to me,' the woman said. 'I am afraid...'

We are all afraid.

'This is a year's crop from my daughter's farm,' the woman said. 'I want to sell it for the best price.'

Nbaro nodded. 'Of course.'

'People tell me,' the woman said, 'if you get a crew to sell for you, it is better.'

Nbaro's smile fell.

'I don't know anything about selling coffee,' she said.

The woman leaned close. She smelled marvellous – spikenard and something equally rich and rare.

'I need sixteen ducats a kilo,' she said, as if she was whispering directions to a distant place. 'Twenty, if it can be done.'

Don't get involved.

Nbaro started to walk away and the woman took her arm and held her close.

'You take anything over nineteen,' she said. 'Please.'

Nbaro took out her tab and ran her thumb down the screen. She looked at the ship's systems, found the market, and looked at coffee.

She was in signal, so she called Thea.

'Small Cargo,' Thea said.

'It's Marca,' she said.

'What's up?'

'A trader's offering me a big consignment of coffee. She wants me to sell it and keep anything over nineteen a kilo.'

Somewhere high above her, Thea coughed. The pause lengthened.

'Is the coffee any good?' Thea asked.

'Smells heavenly,' she said.

'Samples can lie,' Thea said. 'How many kilos?'

Marca looked at the manifest. 'About 2700 kilos.'

'Gack. OK, do it. I'll go halves and help you sell it.' Pause. 'You understand that we're liable for it if we fail to sell it.'

Marca flinched. 'I couldn't—'

209

'Being a merchant means accepting risk. Profit without risk is one of the things our foremothers decided to be rid of after the Age of Chaos. We can do this.'

'I don't have—'

'Neither do I. That's why it's a risk.'

Silence.

'Roger. I'm in,' Marca said. 'You'll have to hold my hand.'

And there she was, trusting Thea. Again.

Maybe I'm an idiot. Maybe I'm a recovering sociopath.

Marca nodded. She tabbed the woman and they both thumb-printed the contracts.

'Bless you,' the woman said, and they shared a beautifully perfumed hug. Marca wasn't ordinarily given to hugs and found herself... moved.

And then the plane was loaded and Marca was back in the air, banking to avoid a thunder cell rising off the ocean. She headed for orbit.

She went straight to the Cargo office after checking in her ship, and Thea opened one of the coffee containers and tested it, by taking scoops out and making coffee.

'I'm on the edge of my responsibilities,' she admitted. 'But I'm allowed to open sealed containers and test samples,' she said, in justification.

'Most people can live without booze,' Marca said. 'But no one can go an hour without a rationalisation.'

Thea made a motion with both hands.

'I sure as hell can't,' she said. 'That's excellent coffee. When we sell it, let's keep fifty kilos for ourselves.'

'Fifty kilos?' Marca said, but even as she said the words, she realised that she was one month into a four-year cruise and coffee went fast.

'And maybe another fifty to sell to others on board,' Thea said, scenting an opportunity.

Marca floated back to EVA Riggers, got her gear off, and smiled at Chu.

'What's happening?'

'I passed my petty officer exam,' Chu said with a smile. 'And I owe you. How's your armour?'

'It's my favourite thing in the universe,' Nbaro said.

She tossed the spacer a smile that was mostly real and headed back to her stateroom to try and sleep.

Thea woke Nbaro up when she came in. They went to eat and found Hanna sitting alone, staring into space.

'Troubles?' Thea asked.

Hanna looked blank. 'Do we need more troubles?' he asked. 'Hey, Marca. What'd you want with Engineering?'

'I was down on Sixth Deck,' she said. It seemed as if it had been a month before. A lifetime.

Hanna raised an eyebrow. 'Only been there once,' he admitted. 'Like another world.'

The Dirtyshirt was almost empty. The people with the virus were confined to their staterooms, and there was now a raging, if not particularly dangerous, epidemic.

'While I was down there, I saw a spacer who looked like he'd been beaten.'

Hanna nodded. 'Best not to ask.'

Nbaro must have stiffened, because Drake pinched her.

'Hey, mighty paladin, calm down.'

Hanna shrugged. 'I'm not saying don't keep an eye on it. But... lower deck discipline is different than ours.'

'Are they different, too?' Nbaro asked. 'Maybe they don't feel pain like we do?'

'Fuck off,' Hanna snapped. 'That's out of line. I'm not in favour of hazing my spacers. I'm just saying...'

Thea pinched her again. 'Your high horse is showing,' she said.

'I've been hazed,' Nbaro said.

'Me, too.' Hanna met her eye. 'You asked for my help and I'll give it, but it comes with my advice. Don't get involved until you're sure, and then make double sure.'

Marca played with her curry.

'Yes, sir,' she said.

Hanna shook his head. 'Not an order. Just a suggestion.'

Nbaro nodded. But she was silent for the balance of the meal.

The next day Nbaro flew back to the delta, solo. She should have been anxious about it, but she wasn't; she rather enjoyed it. The ship's computer supported her with an automated co-pilot, and she liked that, too; she listened to music in the cockpit and went into the atmosphere on manual, flying the plane all the way to the landing. She purchased a twenty kilo parcel of cinnamon at the dockside and put it in the co-pilot seat, loaded another cargo and flew it home. She made her landing, and her only mistake was almost taxiing into the Flight 5 hangar. There were some raucous comments in her ears as she backed her plane onto the taxiway and the electromagnets took her to her true home.

Nbaro filled out her maintenance log while a work crew of spacers unloaded her cargo hold, and bounced into the ready room, where Guille asked her if she planned to join Flight 5. The skipper asked her if she thought she owned the spacecraft or could he borrow it for a while, and made a few other ancient jibes designed for junior pilots, which Nbaro made herself accept. At the Orphanage these would have been mortal insults – challenges to her status. Nbaro knew that this was different, but it was still a struggle not to respond.

Ko raised a hand in the corridor as Nbaro passed Flight 5 and she slapped it, the way they did at the Orphanage when they'd put one over on a teacher or a monitor.

'Nice landing,' Ko said.

'Thanks!' she said.

'Does that go on the Flight 6 board or the 5 board?' he asked with a smirk, and Nbaro smacked his shoulder. He laughed.

Her tab went off and she fished it out of a flightsuit pocket. It was Thea.

'You'll want to come to our space,' she said.

'Almost there,' Nbaro said, and trotted to their stateroom.

Hanging inside their door was all Nbaro's missing laundry.

'Damn,' Nbaro said.

'Exactly,' Drake said. 'Now you won't stay up half the night doing laundry in our sink.'

Nbaro started to apologise. But she went through the flight-suits, one by one.

'They're really mine,' she said. 'But—'

'You thought they'd send you fakes?' Drake asked.

Marca shrugged. 'I don't know what to think,' she admitted. 'I thought someone might have retailored others ...' She counted again. 'One missing. One of my original flightsuits is gone.'

Thea, like most people, had to count for herself.

'That's weird,' she said.

Marca wrote a text to Smith, noting the missing suit, and then showered before pulling on one of her new, clean suits. She felt like a queen.

Nbaro flew a second and then a third event, as Guille was confined to ready room work with her sinus infection and the skipper was flying other events. By the third solo event, some of the magic had worn off, and when she came back up the gravity well she was tired and the high-g launch hurt her right to her spine. There was also a troublesome red light on her board which the computer said Nbaro should override, so she did after enormous hesitation and three checks, but it still nagged at her all the way to her landing, which was still good.

Nbaro was bone-weary, and her boarding party group had a

drill organised which she seriously considered skipping; half the world was sick and she knew she could get away with it.

But putting on her armour gave her energy; she loved it, loved how it made her feel, and the way she looked in it.

Thea came in – she was working an extra half-shift. She collected her earbuds, paused in the hatchway, looked at her, and laughed.

'Yeah, that's your best look,' she said. 'Kinda hard to get off, though, if you want any fun on a date.'

'I'm leaving all that fun to you,' Marca said. 'I'm growing back my virginity.'

'Hanna's going to die of longing, then.'

Marca was too tired for teasing, and she walked with Thea back as far as Small Cargo, where Thea went back to work and Marca continued to the chain locker. She was slightly early for the drill, but there was some good sparring, which she discovered she needed, and a lesson in close fighting, including locks and throws.

Nbaro had a lot to learn. She spent half the class lying on the deck, and eventually she was sent to a chief petty officer named Chen for some remedial falling. He inflicted a long, hard lesson that caused her to sweat right through the Kevlar.

'Next time, let's do some of these throws in zero g, miz,' he said afterwards. 'You're fast as greased shit and you can handle it.'

Marca liked that phrase, and she liked Chief Chen, so she agreed.

They ended with the drill, a melee through three corridors with close pistol simulators. Nbaro was second in charge of a team, with Petty Officer Locran from her first day as her second; Captain Fraser was her team leader. Their mission was to EMP their target, and after a hard fight at a closing iris valve, she got her EMP-armed petty officer within range and he aced it in one shot, giving them a clean win with only three casualties, one of

214

whom was Midshipper Nbaro herself. It had been Fraser's plan, but all the spacers hand-slapped, because they'd been a good team with no heroes.

Then she fell into her rack as if she'd been hit with a hammer, and slept.

The wall screen flashed her back to wakefulness.

It wasn't a General Alert. It was, instead, a call from the Shipboard Security office. The winged lion symbol penetrated her sleep, and Nbaro was wide awake.

She pulled out her tab.

'Nbaro,' she said.

'Ms Nbaro, where are you now?'

Can't you tell? You must have this thing bugged. I thought that was the point.

'Stateroom. Sleeping.'

'May I speak to your stateroom-mate?' His voice sounded formal.

Nbaro woke Thea Drake, who was none too happy about it and said some unkind things until she saw the winged lion flashing on the screen.

Then she sat up hard enough to hit her head on the upper rack.

'Fuck,' she said. 'Hello. Drake here.'

'Ms Drake,' Smith said.

That was the last Nbaro heard, until Thea said, 'Of course she's here. And was here. I heard her come in from her boarding party drill. About 2200 hours. Yes, sir. Yes, sir.'

She looked up. Her eyes held a dozen questions.

Marca got back on. 'Sir?'

'Sorry, Ms Nbaro. Questions I had to ask, and I'll have more intrusive questions for you still.'

'Yes, sir.'

Nbaro had been in a solo flight for a day and a half; she couldn't imagine what she'd done. Her stomach churned.

'May I ask what this is about?' she said.

'Yes,' Smith said. 'Chief Dornau is dead.'

Nbaro stood over the corpse.

What was left of Chief Petty Officer Dornau lay in one of the breathable atmosphere cargo spaces on Sixth Deck. The space was loaded, deck to ceiling, with identical packing crates made of recycle; there were a staggering number of crates, in the three standard sizes: one metre cubes; four metre cubes, and the gigantic eight metre cubes that were the size of small houses and carried bulk cargo like rice or wheat or silicon beads. They were coloured and marked by their owners, and that made the space a remarkable piece of cubist art. The space was so vast that Nbaro had stepped into an elevator that ran along the bulkhead to the floor, and the size of the cargo area dwarfed her. It seemed inhuman, as if a titanic artist had experimented with coloured cubes.

Chief Dornau, on the other hand, might have been the work of the artist who did the crucifix in the Old Catholic chapel.

And something had eaten part of her. That was the worst.

Marca took one look and threw up. She did so into a bag, thoughtfully provided by Lieutenant Smith, and then she knelt on the cold porcelain deck plate for a bit, until she steadied.

'God,' she said.

'I beg leave to doubt it,' Smith responded. 'More likely, rats.'

'We have rats?'

Smith glanced at her. 'You should get out more often,' he said. 'This ship is its own ecosystem.'

Nbaro shuddered.

'Rats didn't kill her,' Smith went on. 'The single bullet at the base of her neck did that. Very professional.'

Marca had nothing to add.

Smith handed her the bag of her own vomit.

'Put this in a recycler,' he said, almost kindly.

Nbaro went out into the dark passageway, the main port-side artery, and found a recycler where it would be on any other deck, by the drop-shaft. She hurried back to Smith; she seldom felt fear like other people. But rats...

An entire ecosystem.

Formed over hundreds of years of bringing cargoes aboard from planets with alien biomes.

Smith hadn't moved.

'Do you think I did it?' she said.

Smith didn't turn his head. 'Nope,' he said.

Nbaro was overwhelmed with relief.

'I think it's probable that whoever did it wanted me to think of you, though,' he said.

He prodded a blood-soaked bundle that Nbaro had thought was part of the chief's clothing... or her entrails. It was all the same terrible colour.

So much blood...

Nbaro fought it down.

'That's your missing flightsuit,' Smith said.

'Oh. Almighty.' She blinked. Then: 'What the fuck?' she asked, her anger mounting.

Smith nodded slowly. 'Indeed. What the actual fuck?' He turned to her. 'You have access to a sidearm?'

'Yes, sir.'

'Take me to it.'

He locked the cargo hold hatch with an elaborate bronze lock in the form of a lion's head, and followed her.

Nbaro led him up the drop-shaft and, after making sure that Thea was dressed, she let him into their stateroom.

He took her pistol and, with apologies, Thea's as well.

'You had access to both,' he said. 'I'm not arresting you, but do not go ashore until I give you permission.'

'I'm walking in forty minutes,' Nbaro said. 'Cargo run.'

He thought it over for a moment.

'You may fly,' he said. 'Though I cannot rule you out, I don't actually think you're my target.'

'Yes, sir,' she said.

Target. Nice word.

Her next flight and recovery were some of Nbaro's worst hours in the Service. She couldn't forget the stripped flesh of the dead woman's face, the sheer amount of drying blood, the skittering noises among the endless crates. And she was afraid.

What if the murderer was clever enough to use my pistol? Or Thea's?

I would, if I were in that position.

Nbaro was lifting off again, this time with a full view of the magnificent ruins of a civilisation that had been dead for what xeno-archaeologists guessed to be more than a hundred thousand years. The ruins lay in circles: circular roads; circular foundations in a variation on extruded carbon fibre and sandstone that went down and down, layer after layer, and no other matching ruins anywhere on the planet.

Even in her anxiety and fear, Nbaro had the chance to think that the circles echoed, or were echoed by, the irrigation circles of their modern, human development.

Weird.

Then she was up the gravity well with her thoughts, and she almost forgot to deploy her magnetic couplers and felt like an idiot.

Nbaro didn't park in the wrong hangar, but the moment her craft came to a stop, her tab pinged.

Report to Special Services immediately.

She shuddered. And promptly spent an excessive amount of time filling out the maintenance forms on her tab, and filing them, and checking on her red light from the day before…

…before going straight from EVA, still dripping with sweat, to Sixth Deck.

Smith was sitting at his desk, working on a holographically projected interface, while Dorcas was doing something literally incomprehensible on the wall-mount interface.

Smith stood when she entered.

'Ms Nbaro.'

'Sir.'

'Ms Nbaro, I am officially removing you from the list of active files in the matter of the death of Chief Dornau,' he said, formally. 'You're allowed and encouraged to review the files I've kept, and while I would appreciate you allowing me to retain them for the duration of this investigation, I will destroy them or remand them to you if you require, in keeping with subject privacy regulations tag, tag.'

The word 'tag' was an activation and released an information glyph, which was appended to her affidavit on her tab.

Dorcas kept writing.

She blinked. 'You know I'm not guilty?' she asked.

'Know is too strong a word. However, your weapons were not used in the crime and certain circumstantial details don't work – not to mention that Captain Fraser, Chief Lu, and Ms Drake have established a timeline for you that makes your presence at the murder impossible.'

If I hadn't gone to Boarding Party, I'd have been alone in my stateroom for an hour.

Someone knew that about my schedule.

Someone who didn't know about Boarding Party.

'I'm willing for you to keep my data for the duration of your investigation,' Nbaro said, thumbing her tab and clicking a side button.

Smith nodded. 'Thanks.' He tried on a smile, didn't like it, and traded it for a more believable facial expression. 'You're released from my hold on your movements. I think you need some time off.'

'My flight is—'

'I happen to know Skipper Truekner is getting two pilots back on his list in six hours. By all means fly your next event. Then please consider going planet-side for a little rest and relaxation. I can tell you, in confidence, that we're only here for three more days. The Master is anxious to make up the time we lost for our system entry velocity and subsequent deceleration.'

Nbaro nodded. 'Thanks, sir,' she said. 'I want to see the alien ruins.'

'As do I,' Dorcas said.

She'd forgotten he was even there.

Smith nodded at her. 'Excellent,' he said, and her doom was sealed.

Nbaro's last event should have been either anticlimactic, or fun. But she was solo again, in the mysterious 6–0–7, the craft she'd handed in with a red light the day before. She was tired, and yet she was determined to check it carefully. Euphoria can be as exhausting as fear. Nbaro was very careful with her checklists; she was aware, now that she had been cleared, how much she had feared the system. She hadn't expected justice. And why should she?

Nbaro walked around her XC 3C. She was beginning to find the matt-black hull and its slightly odd, aerodynamic but asymmetrical shape beautiful – all a part of her feeling of being home, on the *Athens*.

She noted something above the co-pilot station, just aft of the canopy – something odd.

'Crew Chief?' Nbaro asked on the Maintenance channel.

'Roger, miz.'

'Chief, what's the little chef's hat thingy on my co-pilot station?'

'New antenna, miz. I can show you the work order...'

'Nah. I'm good. Does it do anything nifty?'

A laugh. 'Probably?' the chief said, and signed off.

Nbaro also noted a little ring of bright orange under the number 16 retractable electromagnetic coupler. She got in the craft, ran up the auxiliary power, and cycled the couplers: in and out, in and out.

'Chief?'

'Miz,' he said.

Nbaro turned and waved at the maintenance shop display above her. It wasn't really a window; it was a big screen that showed one side of the bulkhead to the other in real time.

'I've got a very slow hydraulics leak in the 16 coupler,' she said.

Pause.

'It's within tolerances,' the chief said. 'I have it noted.'

Nbaro shrugged in her EVA suit, completed her walk-around and buckled in, still thinking about fairness. Now, in the pleasure of having been found not guilty, she had to wonder if the system was actually fair.

She made the correct responses to the Tower, punched off the bow of the *Athens*, and let the computer calculate her re-entry.

Nbaro sat back, watching the curve of the planet become the horizon, and then the totality – tired enough, and happy enough, to find it all very beautiful, and to feel lucky.

'I'm sorry to interrupt you, Ms Nbaro,' said the computer.

Except it wasn't the computer's voice.

A light went on over the co-pilot's couch, and there, stretched full length, was a tall, skinny man with long, curly dark hair and a scarlet flightsuit. His nose was his most obvious feature, and if his appearance wasn't enough to cause her to flinch, he had a cat on his chest.

Nbaro could *almost* see through him, and gradually came to realise he was a holographic projection.

A very good, very lifelike projection.

'Who are you?'

She didn't quite say *who the fuck are you?* but her tone carried the message.

The man in red smiled. 'I'm a little disappointed, Ms Nbaro.'

'God almighty, you're Morosini,' she said.

'Francesco Morosini, my dear girl,' he said. 'I like to use both names when I'm "in person" so to speak.'

Nbaro had her hands clamped on the yoke that controlled the craft and she wasn't even flying it, which was probably good.

'Francesco Morosini, I prefer not to be referred to as "dear girl".' She kept her voice carefully neutral.

'Ahh,' he said, and stroked his cat. 'So noted. I am, or at least I model myself on, a man from another time.'

Nbaro blinked. Scanned her instruments.

'Perhaps you're wondering why I am here,' the AI said.

'Yes, sir.'

'That's a natural human reaction. I like to get to meet any new member of the crew. Also, your name has come through my systems so many times recently in so many different ways that I decided that it was time we had a chat.'

Christ! Now?

Marca looked at him, scanned her instruments, and looked again.

'Can you read my mind?' she asked.

Morosini stroked his cat. 'No, and yes,' he said. 'No, I cannot reach into your thoughts and follow them absolutely, like our mutual friend Dorcas breaking a code. That would be intrusive and clumsy and, if you'll pardon my saying so, very dull. All of you tend to think in depressingly scattershot ways that work for you but which are … ahem … trying, for us.'

'Ahh,' Marca said.

'On the other hand, even with a 0.6 second lag to communicate to the ship, I can read your every physiological sign in excruciating detail – hormonal levels, sweat gland reactions, electrochemical reactions, brain patterns, the amount of fungus under your left toenail, when your period will begin—'

Nbaro began to laugh.

'Now that is an interesting and unanticipated reaction,' Morosini said.

She was wearing a genuine smile; the laugh had been unplanned.

'Surveillance was everywhere at the Orphanage,' Nbaro said. 'And we fought a clandestine war for privacy. Here I am, escaped to the Service, and you have –' she loosened her straps and scanned her instruments – 'a level of surveillance the Orphanage would have killed for.'

'And this amuses you?'

'Only because in five short weeks, I've apparently become enamoured of my new prison. I'm amused at myself.' Marca stretched and then buckled back in. 'I need to take control back in about four minutes.'

Morosini nodded and stroked his cat. 'I should tell you that I find the amount of hydraulic fluid leaking in the electromagnetic retrieval system to be almost worthy of concern.' The AI paused as Nbaro scanned her data feed and brought up her hydraulics. 'But that is not my purpose here. You need to know that the latest messenger boat transmitted a great deal of data. Including a general transmission that was embedded in a routine logistics protocol.'

A screen replaced Morosini's head.

On it, Nbaro saw the nave of the chapel at the Orphanage.

A partly naked Nbaro leaned back against the altar, her face a mask of boredom that ill fitted with the rest of the frame.

She nodded. 'I've seen it a few times.'

Under the cool of her voice, the panic crept into her body.

Fuck, here we go.

'I blocked it,' Morosini said. 'I've also launched a little data-breach investigation. Actually, it's not that little – I've done the equivalent of launching a nuclear torpedo back down the link. You are Service, and I protect Service. Also, I've reviewed all of your records from birth, and the available data on the Orphanage.'

Here it comes. Except that he said I'm Service . . .

'You're an expert rebel,' Morosini said. 'You've a finely balanced sense of justice and you're a natural leader. You're very good at deception and making trouble.'

'Guilty as charged,' she said bravely.

'So far you have done none of these things on board the *Athens*,' the AI said. 'Though it's within the set of possibilities that you have, and I haven't detected them. Your avoidance of the Director of the Orphanage's efforts to destroy you was quite brilliant.'

'Thanks,' she said.

'I note and pass over some irregularity as to your service record . . .'

Her tension spiked, and she imagined how fast the AI was reading her reaction.

But the AI shook his leonine head. 'Ms Nbaro, now one of my personnel is dead, and though the evidence shows you were not involved, it is as plain as the holographic nose on my holographic face that someone is after you. I was very wary of allowing you aboard based on your record as a troublemaker. Now I perceive you as crew – and possibly as a very real asset. Do you wish to add anything?'

Nbaro had her hands on the yoke.

'You can sense my reactions,' Marca said. 'So I can't hide anything from you. All I have ever wanted is to be Service. Everything I did was to get *here*.'

The pause was longer than 0.6 seconds.

'Yes,' Morosini said. 'And that's why we will be friends. I am watching you, Nbaro, and that is, for the most part, for your own good.'

The craft's computer beeped, indicating the end of automatic piloting. The yoke stiffened under her hands, and the man in red was gone. The cat lasted a little longer.

Nbaro flew the atmospheric landing in a state of spiritual, if not physical, confusion, but training runs deep and she got her craft down and into the electromagnets without a bump. This field had rails to move her to her hangar, so that she had several minutes to run her post-flight checks and then to breathe deeply, splash a little water from her bottle on her face, and think.

Someone had tried to release the vid on her ship, and Morosini had blocked it.

Morosini knew that there were irregularities in her personnel record.

And at another level, *The hydraulic leak is getting worse, but still well within manageable levels.*

Nbaro watched the hangar come closer; behind the hangar, the night sky, a spread of alien constellations. Old Terran palm trees waved along the sides of the tracked taxiway.

She took a deep breath.

'Thank you, Messire Morosini,' she said.

'*Ah*,' said his voice. '*Messire? Very nice. You're quite welcome. Blackmail is ugly, and evil. Even an AI knows that. But elements of this attempt were unusual and further investigation is required.*'

Nbaro watched the instruments a little longer, until she thought the AI was gone, and unlocked her couch and harness.

She had a long list on her incoming manifest, including a number of parcels being collected for spacers. She ran down the list, then wandered through the brightly coloured recycle crates, trying not to think of the body, on a ceramic floor on Sixth Deck, huddled against an empty cargo crate. Eaten by rats.

It gave her a bad moment, but that was all. Nbaro turned her tab into a scanner and began scanning the float-pallets. Each anti-grav pallet had a set of codes that could be read by any scanning device; they were dead simple to program, and very difficult to hack.

Unfortunately, almost none of them matched her inbound manifest.

There followed two hours of the most torturous bureaucracy Nbaro had ever endured. She showed her manifest list over and over to a variety of officials, and eventually to the manager of the warehouse. She made repeated calls to Small Cargo, hoping for Thea, but she was repeatedly ignored until the petty officer who eventually took her link told her, in respectful terms, that a misload of the magnitude she was seeing wasn't possible.

The warehouse manager said the same, and commented on her junior rank. Nbaro began to be angry.

'Look,' she said.

She had a customs officer, a pair of local merchants, and the warehouse manager gathered around. Nbaro shone her tab on the scan code on the side of the float-pallet.

It threw up a list – about two tonnes of material. Most of her load.

Nbaro handed it to the warehouse manager.

'There's the manufactured cubic zirconium. See it? But nothing else on this manifest is mine. Saffron? Sounds wonderful. Not on my expected load. Salt? Do you see salt anywhere on my manifest? What about diodes? I don't even know what unprocessed silicon couplers are, but again, they're not on my manifest. Is this the load for a different sortie?'

The customs officer shrugged.

'I have all of these items on my list, and all of them are cleared for your ship,' she said. 'Why don't you just take them, eh?'

Nbaro was even considering it when the warehouse manager blinked.

'No. You're... You're right, Ms Nbaro. This is just plain wrong. And it's not entered this way in my system.' He was shaking his head. 'I want to unload this pallet and examine every item in it.'

The customs officer rolled her eyes.

'All of this material is cleared,' she repeated slowly and clearly. 'Why not sort it out on your ship, miz?'

Marca's tab made a purring vibration in her hand. She thumbed it.

'Nbaro.'

'Ms Nbaro, this is Tom Hughes in Cargo.'

'Yes, sir!'

Nbaro all but snapped to attention. She'd never met the well-liked, somewhat bluff captain who controlled the cargo section, but Thea spoke of him in awe.

'Run your situation by me, Nbaro. No rush.'

She turned and walked away from the four others, waving her hand vaguely.

'Sir, my form 1092 Alpha detailing anticipated cargo doesn't match their pallet. I'm standing here with the warehouse manager, who agrees this is wrong and just said he wants to open all the items on the pallet, and with the customs officer, who says every item is cleared and is pretty fucking eager for me to take the whole pallet. Pardon me.'

Pause.

'Nbaro, it is *possible* for 1092 Alphas not to match delivered cargo.'

227

'Yes, sir,' she said. 'Shall I accept it?'

'I don't suppose you have a scan of the pallet?'

'Here it is, sir.'

Nbaro fired it up the line with the press of a side button on her tab.

Long pause. Nbaro didn't like the way the customs officer was reacting, and the fatigue was pushing her down. Hard. She just wanted this to be over.

She wondered idly if Morosini was still listening.

'Nbaro, this is a bit of a situation. You're correct, most of those items are *not* on our manifest or among our expected deliveries. That's a simplification – but there are checksums and codes here that aren't right.'

Her back was suddenly cold. And the customs officer's repeated glances took on a more sinister meaning. Especially as she was now arguing vehemently against breaking the seals on the shipment and opening the parcels on the float-pallet.

And Nbaro didn't have a sidearm with her, or even a crowbar.

'Sir, I believe I may be in a hostile situation.'

'Roger, Nbaro. I'm calling the cavalry. Try not to escalate. You'll have backup in about seventeen minutes.'

Shit. Shit shit shit.

'That's a long time, sir.'

'I know, Nbaro. Do what you can.'

This could be nothing. But Hughes is as concerned as I am, because people don't hack into cargo manifests for nothing. It's smuggling, on a major scale, and if I wasn't so tired today I wouldn't even have run the numbers.

Nbaro turned and walked back to the group, closing her tab and making a face.

She was, in fact, not bad at deception. Or at rebellion. She had an expert opinion on that.

'No one on the *Athens* knows anything,' Nbaro said with a

carefully modulated whine. 'I'm on my third event of the day and I really don't want to fight this out all afternoon.'

The customs officer looked at her coldly – literally looking down her nose.

'But still you made all this fuss,' she said.

Nbaro allowed her face to register her jolt of annoyance.

'Nope,' she said. 'I noted the discrepancy. That's my *job*.' She looked around. 'Someone down here fucked up the load, so Ship's working on authorising me to bring the whole packet.'

The customs officer relaxed, but now the warehouse manager gave her a strange look, as if to say, *Hey, you got me into this*.

A minute passed.

'I'm going to run the preflights for my craft,' Nbaro said.

She walked around her XC-3C carefully, feeling paranoid, again spotting the replacement antenna which she was certain had been placed there to allow the AI to relay into her craft.

The Lord moves in mysterious ways.

It was from the old Bible, but it might as easily apply to AIs, the gods that humans had created.

There was a veritable puddle of bright orange goo under one of her electromagnetic couplers. As Nbaro saw it her tab beeped. There was a message from ground control, asking why she was taking so long and offering her various orbital windows.

The customs officer came over.

'I have other shuttles needing this dock,' she said. 'I need you to get your ship out of here.'

'Still waiting for clearance from the *Athens*.'

'I've given you clearance,' the woman said.

OK. I have a plan.

It will work, unless this pallet holds a bomb to kill me, in which case, I'm just surrendering.

'I'll take the load and get off your dock,' Nbaro said.

Was that relief in the haughty woman's face?

Nbaro watched the robots load her cargo hold with both pallets, and now, in the evening light, the bright colours of the recycle crates were lurid and threatening.

She climbed aboard, ran her numbers, filed a flight plan through her tab, saw her green lights, and did her preflight checks.

The rails took control of her craft and began to guide it on to the field.

In for a penny, in for a pound.

There were so many charming expressions from before the Age of Chaos.

Nbaro took a breath, then engaged comms.

'Tower, this is Alpha Foxtrot 6–0–7,' she said, and after a deep breath, 'Declaring an emergency on taxiway 3.'

'Roger, 6–0–7. What is the nature of your emergency?'

'Tower, I've got an electromagnetic coupler leaking hydraulics, over. I can feel it vibrate every time we move.'

'Roger, 6–0–7, we understand you have a hydraulics failure and a coupler problem. Are you in immediate danger?'

'That's negative, Tower. Only a problem for lift-off and recovery. I'm still safe on the ground. Can you shift me to an apron?'

'Roger wilco, 6–0–7. Looking for something nice. Got you. Turn at taxiway 0–9 left.'

'Roger, Tower. 0–9 left. Eyes on.'

Nbaro considered using her *White Rain* codeword, but this was a shipboard matter and she thought she'd handle it the ship way.

On her tab, Nbaro typed, I have claimed an in-craft emergency and will be parked on a spaceport apron.

Seconds later, text appeared.

We have your new location and will intercept in eight minutes. Hang tight.

'Morosini, what's going on?' she asked. *Worth a try.*

The delay was long enough that she thought she wouldn't get a reply.

'*We think there's a very real possibility you have a bomb on board,*' Morosini said. '*I'm running a fraction under sixteen per cent likely. I want you to stay in your acceleration couch ready to be punched out. Do you understand?*'

Nbaro was suddenly very, very afraid.

'Yes.' Then she said, 'Are you dropping Marines?'

'*Yes,*' Morosini said.

'Can you tell the field they're a repair crew?'

'*Perhaps,*' Morosini said. '*You're duplicitous.*'

'I could take off and dump the package in space.'

'*Then we won't know.*' Morosini was silent, and then said, '*I'm going off the air, lest they discern the level of our data feed and ask questions. Whoever they may be.*'

'Roger,' Nbaro said, but she could feel that the AI was gone.

Over the comms, Nbaro could hear the tower engaging with a drop-ship from the *Athens*. The drop-ship pilot said she was responding to an emergency call.

After a pause, she embroidered on that, adding something about a damaged spacecraft in a dangerous position in the open.

Tower didn't even argue. Nbaro sat on an empty apron, waiting for the flash of white that would mean that she was dead, and listening to the Tower find the descending drop-ship's story perfectly reasonable.

Not what she'd expected.

Nbaro was back to breathing normally. She was pretty sure that she'd played this as well as she could have with the cards she'd been given, and if there was a bomb in her hold, destined for the *Athens*, and the bastards blew it here, she'd have died for a good cause.

For the Service.

So weird, she thought. *I've found meaning.*

The drop-ship came down in smoke and thunder, and it hit harder than Nbaro had expected. Old-fashioned landing struts took the immense pressure, and the craft bounced even as people were coming out of it. She saw them clearly, because they had headlamps on – full breathing helmets, and armour. The drop-ship raised an incredible amount of sand and dust; it was only after a few seconds that Nbaro realised they still had their engines running and they were raising dust on purpose.

She opened her cargo bay and one of the Marines gave her a thumbs up.

Someone plugged straight into one of the external jacks.

'Ms Nbaro?'

'Speaking.'

'Gunny Drun, miz. We're going to take your cargo. Ship asks, how bad is the hydraulics leak?'

'I can fly her, Gunny.'

'Roger that, miz. Package is extracted.'

'Could be a bomb, Gunny.'

'I hear that, miz, but I have my orders. I'm leaving you a Marine who will pretend to be a mechanic. Can you get him home?'

'Roger that, Gunny.'

'Close your payload bay, miz. We're gone.'

Nbaro toggled the payload bay and the doors closed. She watched them close through the hydraulics subroutine, and noted that the leak was getting ever more real than she wanted it to be.

There was a man on her retractable lift-wing, and he opened the exterior hydraulics feed hatch. Nbaro gave him a thumbs up and when he'd climbed down, she opened the external hatch and heard him come in.

'Tower,' she said.

The drop-ship had already risen on a column of fire. Flight 1 was the drop-ship squadron, and Nbaro owed several people beers.

'What's your status, 6-o-7?'

'Tower, my dropped-in crew chief says I'm good to go – at least limp back to the *Athens*.'

'Roger, 6-o-7. Putting you back into the launch cycle. That was very impressive – never seen a drop-ship for a mechanical failure.'

'Service protects.'

Nbaro winked at the Marine, who was belting into what was usually her seat.

'I guess so. All right.' The last word drawled. 'You're good to go, and I'm turning on the electromagnetic rails. Tell me if there's a problem.'

A soft click as they began to move.

'What's your name?' Nbaro asked the Marine.

'Wilson,' the young man said. 'Akunje. Wilson Akunje.' He was grinning. 'Gunny says that might count as a combat drop.'

Nbaro smiled. They were sharing the joys of the very junior; someone might admit them to adulthood, if they were very lucky.

'Thanks, Wilson,' she said. 'I think you guys saved my ass.'

'Gunny says you saved everyone's ass ... or maybe you're too wet behind the ears to know what you're doing.' Akunje's grin was huge and infectious.

'Yep,' Marca said. 'At least one of those things is definitely true.'

Nbaro let the automated rails take them out on to the field, and then took off with the electromagnetic assist. There was a slight vibration to number 16, and she got an error message when she retracted the couplers.

'Now that's not good,' she said aloud. 'Wilson, do you have any spaceflight quals?'

233

He looked at her. 'No, miz.'

Nbaro nodded, mostly to herself, and ordered a camera to move to look at the coupler.

That took fifteen long seconds, after which the coupler appeared to be flush with the outer hull.

Nbaro set the computer to level flight at 10,000 m.

'It doesn't show as retracted and locked,' she said. 'Computer, run the diagnostic checklist.'

'Roger. Diagnostic says that there is a hydraulic leak in number 16. It is ninety-four per cent likely that leaking fluid has corroded the sensor that detects retraction and lock.'

Nbaro thought for a moment. There was no hurry; she had a full bag of fuel and time. But if the coupler was not fully retracted, her craft might ignite during its passage through the upper atmosphere. There were secondary problems, but she could deal with those later.

Akunje glanced at her. 'More trouble, miz?'

'Let's find out,' she said.

Nbaro summoned up her second mobile camera and ran it manually until it stood next to the first. Then she ran it back and forth over the tiny hatch that held the magnetic coupler.

From what she could see, the hatch was closed and locked; the weight of the magnetically attached mobile camera didn't even rattle the housing.

Nbaro called Lioness and explained, in detail. Then she sent the footage of the camera passing over the hatch.

'I'm satisfied the hatch is safe,' she said.

Lioness was silent, although Nbaro could hear the Space Operations officer breathing. She thought it was Mpono.

'Roger, Alpha Foxtrot 6–o–7. You are go for orbit.'

Nbaro took the yoke and flew the craft up into the upper atmosphere, and she didn't feel any trouble, so she fired up her manoeuvring thrusters, took the ship out of atmosphere and let the computer match orbits with the *Athens*. The ship was surrounded by traffic, though she noted that the Marine drop-ship from Flight 1 didn't show on her display. That was interesting.

'Lioness, this is 6–0–7, over.'

'Roger, 6–0–7.'

'Matching orbits and looking for home.'

'Roger. Stand by.'

Nbaro loosened her harness and stretched.

'Shit, what a day, Wilson.'

'No shit, miz.'

Nbaro was *happy*.

I am so weird.

Also, Akunje was utterly confident in her, and that, somehow, was boosting her confidence in herself.

'Alpha Foxtrot 6–0–7, passing your pattern.'

'Roger, Lioness,' Nbaro said, and let the computer fit them into the pattern of ships queuing to land on the *Athens*.

She called the break, passed across the *Athens* amidships in the customary way, with a magnificent view of the whole of the mighty greatship, its sword-blade length incredible at this angle and this close in. Below her, in terms of relative angle and motion, passed the vast, almost perfectly regular shape: a long sword with a stubby cross guard – the command section and superstructure; a hilt made of the four great main engines and their attendant reactors; and a pommel of the engine's flared drive cones. Light shone along her sides; there was the bridge, so close under her that between puffs of her manoeuvring thrusters Nbaro could almost imagine she could see the Master. The size of the greatship was … incredible …

Beyond, like the slave's reminder to the conqueror that he was but ash and dust, lay space. Its vastness dwarfed the greatship. Its perfect black made her hull seem garish; the stars outshone her array of portholes and lights.

Nbaro turned 6–0–7 and ran the pattern, braking slightly to slow relative to the greatship. She was piloting the craft directly, with the computer's overlay track visible on her head-up display but not engaged.

Nbaro turned at the base of the pattern, well within the computer's tolerance, and entered the probability cone around the stern where a landing was possible. The cone only existed in maths – but it was also on her head-up display, and she let it guide her in.

'Got you, Alpha Foxtrot 6–0–7. In the cone.'

'Roger, Cone.'

'Call the ball.'

'Roger, ball. Landing weight 17636, over.'

'Roger, Alpha Foxtrot 6–0–7.'

Nbaro toggled her electromagnetic couplers.

'Dirty up,' she said to herself, automatically.

'Alpha Foxtrot 6–0–7, you're tube 3.'

'Roger, tube 3,' Nbaro said, and indeed, the entrance to tube 3 was flashing a lurid green.

Only something went wrong. It was subtle – a silent, grinding, unexpected vibration.

She toggled her cameras.

Sixteen was about one third deployed, and so was … nine.

'Lioness, I've got a bad deployment of my electromagnetic couplers,' Nbaro said. 'LSO, I want to do this slow. Do you need me to go around?'

The Landing Officer was probably talking rapidly with Lioness. The stern was getting closer, and Nbaro decided to decelerate. It was easy to do; she had plenty of reaction mass, and she dumped some, killing her velocity relative to the great-ship's stern after checking the flight pattern to make sure she didn't have another craft right behind her. She didn't.

'Right, 6–0–7. Slow and steady.'

'Roger, ball.'

Nbaro fired another braking burn, knocking her relative velocity way, way down.

'Lock your harness,' she said kindly to her Marine.

'Yes, miz. Sorry, miz.'

Two more braking burns and her relative velocity was down around 0.25 metres per second. Nbaro *crept* into the gaping tunnel of the railgun tube.

Heavy vibrations started immediately, flinging the craft around by half-metre jerks as the couplers that were missing failed to line up with the powerful magnets in the tunnel.

And then something changed, and she was coasting smoothly again.

They turned off the electromagnets . . .

Shit.

'Need you to fly it all the way down!' Tower shouted.

But Nbaro already had control. She acted without thought and her computer helped her. They just barely tagged the top of the railgun tube, with a scraping sound, and then she had it.

Only after she was back in the centre of the tube, with her computer showing her the possible collision damage, did Nbaro discover that she was saying *shitshitshitshitshitshit* like a mantra as she flew, until she could kill the rest of her relative motion and let her wounded ship hang in the railgun tube. A small fleet of recovery vehicles seemed to leap from the walls.

'Was that a crash?' Akunje asked. 'Are you OK, miz?'

Nbaro was watching as half a dozen robot-mechs began to manoeuvre her craft.

'I'm OK,' she said. 'How are you doing?'

'I'm fine, miz.'

He didn't even sound scared.

*

Fifteen minutes later, Nbaro had her helmet under her arm and she was in Maintenance, where Chief Baluster was shaking his head over and over.

'My responsibility, miz,' he said.

The man was grey-faced – upset, worried, and angry at himself.

Nbaro didn't know what to say, because he had, in fact, assured her that the craft was safe.

'No one was hurt,' she said. 'And I don't think I hurt her much…'

Skipper Truekner came in from the elevator.

'You OK, Midder?' he asked.

'Yes, sir,' she said.

'You scared the crap out of me, Nbaro.'

He gave her a quick hug and she almost started to cry. She hadn't realised how much she was holding down until that moment.

But Nbaro had learnt not to cry in a hard school, and she blinked it back and said, 'I'm a big girl, for a midder, sir.'

He smiled. 'What'd she do to 6–0–7, Chief?'

Baluster shook his head. 'Sir, it's my fault.'

'What's the damage?'

'All the pilot-side antennas, and a new carbon panel over the rear crew compartment,' Baluster said.

Truekner nodded. 'We'll talk later,' he said. 'Ms Nbaro's wanted on the bridge.'

Nbaro followed Truekner to the elevator. She felt as if she was coated in clouds, or something.

The bridge? Why am I going to the bridge? Am I in trouble?

When she'd been very young, and still adapting to the Orphanage, Nbaro used to imagine very hard that she was somewhere else, and just stay there. She'd become very good at it – so good that ice-cold water thrown at her by various authority figures wouldn't snap her out of it, and at one point she'd been labelled mentally disabled.

Ah, the good old days.

Skipper Truekner was speaking. Nbaro found that with a little effort she could replay what he'd just said.

Something about the hydraulic leak.

'It didn't seem so bad when I did my walk-around,' she said.

Truekner made a face. 'Chief told you it was good to go,' he said. 'It's on the cameras.'

She looked away.

'Loyalty to a shipmate is a good thing,' Truekner said. 'But not if there's shoddy work involved.'

Nbaro thought about that as the elevator doors opened and she walked through the ready room and down the passage to EVA. She stripped out of her EVA suit and polished the visor on her helmet, functioning somewhat on automatic. Her tab chimed in one of her flightsuit pockets and she ignored it. Probably Sabina telling her what to wear.

She had the odd feeling that the spacers in EVA were watching her. She finished her visor, feeling a little self-conscious, and Carlson came and took all her gear.

'I'll hang that for you, miz,' he said softly.

Nbaro nodded. 'Thanks,' she said.

Truekner was waiting just outside, in the passageway; he was thumbprinting forms on his tab while he waited.

'Leave chits and shore-going requests,' he said. 'Let's go.'

They went to the outboard elevators and went up to the bridge level on the O-6. Nbaro had time to wonder about the escape pod on O-7. It had a lift button.

I need an escape pod.

The elevator doors opened and she followed her skipper out into the magnificent baroque space of the bridge. The huge nuquartz window showed Haqq Algericas filling two thirds of the window, her yellow desert continents interspersed with her green oceans, a magnificent jewelled pattern of fractal jade and gold.

Nbaro turned with Truekner and saluted the Master.

The Master was speaking rapidly, sub-vocalising with one hand touching his ear implant. He nodded at Truekner and smiled at her, and she relaxed. She stood by her skipper, but her eyes wandered the bridge. Every station was fully occupied, and Nbaro noted that Weps was not only occupied but active.

The elevator cycled, and three Marines appeared: a Gunnery Sergeant and two grunts, one of whom was Wilson Akunje.

Nbaro smiled at him. 'You've recovered from my landing,' she said.

Her eyes flicked to the NCO.

'Gunny Drun,' she said.

'Miz,' he said. She thought that he meant it pleasantly.

'Was that you in the rebreather? Did you come and get me in a drop-ship?'

'Did indeed, miz.'

Before he could say any more, the elevator cycled again, and another pilot emerged: Lieutenant McDonald. She was small and had bright red hair.

'Hey, Skipper Truekner,' she said.

He smiled at her. 'Doros, this is my new star midder, Marca Nbaro.'

The other pilot looked her over.

'Oh,' she said. 'Your craft broke, ch?'

'A small hydraulics failure,' Nbaro said.

She didn't like to be petty, but she had McDonald's number.

'So ...' the Master said. He'd run his acceleration couch around to face them and now he rose out of it. He was very tall and his nose was not unlike Morosini's.

All of them – her skipper, the three Marines, and the other pilot – stiffened to attention, so Marca did as well.

'That was some very effective work out there today,' he said. 'On behalf of the ship and the AI, I'd like to thank the six of you for some brave, dedicated actions and some very sharp thinking, especially from Ms Nbaro. Morosini says you acted in the best traditions of the Service. I'd like to add my thanks.'

They all stood, beaming.

'Gunny, tell us what you found,' the Master said.

'A nuke,' the Marine said. 'It's in the lab.'

The Master smiled, his lips thin and his expression bitter.

'I didn't want to let that thing on my ship, but the Special Services and the Science section were adamant,' he said. 'Someone tried to blow up this ship, ladies and gentlemen. Somebody meant us harm and didn't care what the collateral was.'

Nbaro was still thinking: *It was a nuke.*

'I want everyone on the ship to know what you did,' the Master said. 'It's been suggested to me that this might be a time for secrecy, but it seems better to me that every spacer knows what we're up against and that we're all on our guard.'

He reached up to his acceleration couch and took out a matt-black box.

'Midshipper Nbaro,' he said.

She stepped forward, and he pinned a small, jet-black medal on her chest, and she felt about a foot taller.

'All of you will receive citations,' he said. 'And Morosini and I have decided to rate that a combat drop. The risk was significant, and a successful outcome should not be viewed as reason not to reward your work.'

Akunje almost glowed with pleasure. McDonald blushed. Gunny Drun allowed himself a minute smile.

The Master shook hands with each one of them, starting with McDonald, and dismissed them to ride the lift down to the O-3 level together. McDonald got off first, and headed forward to the Flight 1 ready room. She didn't look back. The Marines went down to the lower decks.

Truekner smiled at her. 'Not bad, Nbaro. A Space Ops medal, a month into cruise?'

She smiled nervously.

'That was some seriously heads-up shit you did there, Midder. You made the flight proud, and as a reward you can have the two days off the flight schedule that you were going to get anyway.' He smiled. 'Get some sleep. For a pilot who just got a medal, you look like shit.'

'Yes, sir,' Nbaro said, her grin genuine, and headed aft.

Nbaro passed Ko outside Flight 5. He didn't say anything; he just slapped her back as she passed.

Her back was slapped a dozen times as she passed aft towards her stateroom, and when she was safely inside, she unpinned her medal and looked at it.

She didn't say anything. She just looked at it.

Her tab chimed again.

She had a message from Richard Hanna. She thumbed it up, and read it.

Want to go ashore together? I could buy a hero dinner.

Nbaro couldn't stop her grin. It was real. The medal was real. And already everyone knew.

And Morosini acted to protect her. I'm IN. Not OUT.

The Orphanage had never awarded anything to anyone, that she knew of.

She had a little trouble breathing, so she sat on Thea's rack and thumbed an answer to Hanna.

Absolutely.

Then Nbaro stripped and climbed into her own rack and fell asleep looking at her medal.

7

They went ashore in a landing barge with eighty other spacers, some well-dressed and others in disposable recycle clothes meant to be worn once and tossed – men and women intending to get drunk, get in a fight, or both. The woman next to Hanna wore recycle shorts and a stretch top that seemed to have been made for athletics. It showed off her back and arms, which were covered in tattoos, some of them holographic. She sat very stiffly and obviously resented being seated next to an officer.

The re-entry was bumpier than Marca felt it needed to be, but she'd never flown anything as big as the landing barge. Its lift surfaces were vast compared to her own craft, and she was in a generous mood.

'So, what are we going to do?' she asked.

'Am I allowed to tell you how beautiful you are?' Hanna asked.

Nbaro considered that a moment.

'I think I'd rather you didn't,' she said.

He looked out the window. When he'd regained his composure, he said, 'Well, I thought we'd go to the mosque first.'

'Mosque?'

'The Blue Mosque of Istanbul. It's impossibly ancient, all the way from Old Terra. Thea said...' He stopped.

'What did Thea say?' she asked.

'She said you liked old things.'

Marca nodded. 'I've never heard of the Blue Mosque,' she admitted. 'But I do like old things.'

'Then I thought we'd see the alien ruins.'

'Perfect,' she said.

'And then a romantic dinner.'

She smiled. 'It may just be dinner. But I'll keep an open mind.'

Hanna brightened. 'That was almost—'

'Careful now,' she said, and they both smiled.

The Blue Mosque was magnificent. When Nbaro had crossed the immense courtyard under the gaze of the incredible minarets, she took off her shoes and walked the carpeted interior, looking up at the glazed tiles.

'They say that the higher you go, the worse the tiles are,' Hanna said.

'Because the sultan knew we couldn't see them?'

'Because the sultan refused to allow for inflation, and the tile-makers felt underpaid the longer the project continued.'

'Someone did a great deal of reading,' Nbaro said.

'Someone did,' Hanna agreed.

'Why is it the Blue Mosque,' she asked when they were back outside.

'I'm not sure. The FAQs says it was illuminated with blue lights on Old Terra – I'm sure I'm missing something.' He shrugged.

Nbaro turned to take it all in. 'It's like the ship,' she said.

He looked a question.

'All the details. It's built to be staggering – magnificent.' She glanced at him and smiled. 'Never mind me. I'm just prone to talk.'

'I don't mind if you talk.'

And you feel that you get to give me permission to?

244

Shut up, brain. He's nice.

They walked across an immense square filled with fountains, and the gentle kiss of the mist off the fountains was refreshing. They had coffee at one side of the square and then boarded the maglev shuttle and flew underground through a hard vacuum tunnel, travelling the 700 km to the alien ruins in the delta.

The maglev tourist station had an incredible display where the escalators ran up to the surface from the deeply buried tunnels. The entire wall of the escalator, rising two hundred metres, exposed layers in the alien ruins, with dates superimposed in Traditional Chinese, Anglatin, Korean and Arabic.

'What happened to them?' Nbaro asked.

Hanna shook his head. 'No one knows. They were here for more than ten thousand years, but they didn't come from here, and then they were gone. So far, no one's found any other ruins of their civilisation here. I think I read that there's more somewhere else.'

'Ought to be easy to tell,' she said. 'Everything they built is a circle.'

When they emerged on the surface, Nbaro wished she'd worn a short athletic top like the woman on the landing barge. It was very hot, and she'd been in space for long enough to have forgotten what planetary environments were like.

The problem was that she owned so few items of clothing beyond her uniforms.

Nbaro bought a little umbrella, a silly thing with a local pop star's holographic image on it, but it kept the sun off. She wandered through the interlinked circles of the ruins, looking at the crumbling mats of carbon fibre so like and yet unlike their own; at the fused stone, and the complete lack of metal fittings.

There was a path to follow. Every few metres, a sign in nine languages warned them not to pick up souvenirs or take anything from the site. Nbaro looked at the scrap that she could see: minute scraps of what looked like old-fashioned petroleum-based plastics, or something like them; ceramics in brilliant colours . . .

'No metal at all?'

Hanna smiled. 'There are dozens of theories,' he said.

By then they had climbed a dozen steps to a nanofibre mesh platform with hard recycle walls and a low parapet to let tourists see out over the highest of the ruins – fused stone in the shape of what must have been a dome. Behind them, an artificial gravity elevator carried disabled tourists smoothly to the platform.

Nbaro could see the desert beyond, too, and a white haze of heat shimmer at the horizon. Closer in, there were no fewer than six different archaeological digs, each one with more than a dozen students.

'It's huge,' Hanna said suddenly.

It was huge. Nbaro understood the platform now; without it, seen only from ground level, no one could have imagined the scale of the ruin.

There was a busy plaque with a not particularly well-realised artist's impression of what the multiplicity of domes might have looked like when new. It ran a simulation, a bird's-eye view of the ruins as if they were a huge city. It had a glitch and a lot of bitmapping, but it was still interesting.

'Except that it was never new,' she muttered to herself. 'This place was ten thousand years old when it reached this level.'

Hanna shrugged. He was hot, and losing interest, whereas Nbaro was getting more interested by the moment.

'What happened with your sailor who was being hazed?' he asked.

Nbaro was still looking at the plaque, reading the comments in Anglic. 'I'm ashamed to say that I haven't checked back.'

'It's a busy life, being a hero,' Hanna said.

'Hero?'

'Didn't you get a medal from the Master yesterday?' he asked. 'I'm glad I asked you to dinner before I heard about the medal. I'd probably have...' He shrugged. 'Whatever.'

Nbaro knew he wanted to talk, but she didn't feel particularly heroic, and the alien ruins were probably the most fascinating thing she'd ever seen.

'We don't even know what they looked like?' she asked.

Hanna shrugged. 'Scientists,' he said, as if in disgust.

Nbaro wanted to walk around the path again, and he was willing enough, which was interesting, too. She was trying to judge his behaviour and how much she could lead him. He was higher in rank and older, and male. Gender differences weren't supposed to matter, but they always did, in her experience. On the other hand, he wanted her; his every movement indicated that.

She didn't want him.

It was too bad, as he was a far finer man than any of her ado-lescent crushes – indeed, he was almost remarkable. Attentive, polite, thoughtful...

But not for me. Tell him now? Later? Over dinner?
Dinner.

The second time around Nbaro found more to look at; she stopped and looked at a little pile of rubbish left by a group of xeno-archaeologists sifting material. There were dozens of tiny beads visible – all ceramic. Some had minute decorations on them.

Nbaro longed to grab one and keep it, but she didn't.

Hanna displayed a little impatience and she moved on.

Then Nbaro stopped at a wall of woven carbon fibre. The first time, she'd assumed it was a retaining wall erected by the archaeologists; this time, she realised that it was an alien artifact two metres long.

'Almighty!' Nbaro breathed. 'It looks just like ours!'

Hanna was gazing out over the ruin.

'Which makes it pretty dull.'

'Dull?' she asked. 'Ninety thousand years ago, a bunch of aliens made a carbon-fibre wall that looks like ours? That's dull?'

He smiled. 'Yes?' he said, wistfully.

He really was a fairly good person, for a man. Nbaro laughed, and he laughed with her, and it settled her mind. He really just wanted the sex, and he was agreeable about it. Better than many.

Not good enough any more.

Later, they went into the Haqq Kerdoba souk, which was close to the maglev and which his tab said had the best food. They wandered the souk for an hour, exploring the vendors, who ranged from two dangerous-looking adolescents selling illegal ghat to goldsmiths with a fortune in magnificent wares and bolts of silk and synthisilk from a dozen planets. The souk radiated mercantile prowess; twice Nbaro stopped just to listen to people haggle.

There were artists and street-singers and two women with a holographic display of the animals of Old Terra that was remarkable and very beautiful. An old man sold salt that he mined himself in the desert. A calligrapher demonstrated classic Arabic calligraphy. He wrote her a line from the Holy Koran in a beautiful, tiny script and handed it to her with a flourish, and then suggested that his brother-in-law, the goldsmith in the next street, could sell her a perfect pendant in which to keep it.

To Hanna's amusement, Nbaro walked straight over, looked at the little golden amulets, and chose one. It was not cheap, but she had five weeks' pay, so she bought an amulet shaped like a half-moon, and a gold chain, and hung it round her neck.

She was very happy.

Or maybe I don't tell him, she thought. *Maybe I just don't tell him that he doesn't stir me, and we have many good times like this one.*

The goldsmith recommended a restaurant to Hanna, and seemed a trifle put out when Nbaro paid for her own amulet, rather than his paying. Or perhaps she imagined that.

She shopped her way through the women's souk, having left Hanna at the entrance; he said he'd look at carpets, and there was an abundance of carpets to see. Every stall was like a little shop, the walls made of carpets, most with dressing rooms and mirrors, and all with a smell of perfume and spice that enthralled her. There were a few men inside, but only a few; it was mostly women shopping for clothes, and women selling them. It was very old-fashioned and bi-gendered, but in a romantic way, not a gender bias way – or perhaps its very antiquity caused her to forgive it.

Local women smiled at Nbaro; she smiled back.

She found a silk jumpsuit. It was clearly modelled on the lines of a ship's suit, like the best of high fashion in City, but with decorative mesh and pockets. The embroidery had been done by hand. It was a dark gold, which complemented the brown of her skin and hair, and it had dark blue accents.

Nbaro loved it. She tried it on and it fitted. The woman who kept the stall paid her a thousand compliments, and told her that men would follow her home, which didn't sound appealing at all, but was probably meant kindly.

'How much?' she asked.

Asmahan, the shop owner, smiled.

'For you? I should give it to you to adorn the world.'

Her smile was false and predatory, and Marca rather liked her for it. Or at least, felt comforted by her. Here was a familiar part of her childhood: haggling.

She smiled. 'I couldn't allow your family to starve,' she said.

Asmahan smiled so that her well made-up dimples showed.

'Perhaps one hundred DHC ducats, then.'

I can afford that warred with *That must be the tourist price.*

Nbaro kept any hint of annoyance out of her voice.

'Oh,' she said sadly. 'I'm so sorry.'

She stripped out of the beautiful thing, only now realising that the bust was lined in the same blue silk and beautifully finished, even though no one would ever see it.

Nbaro handled it carefully, aware of a feeling of the weight of the silk in her hand.

The woman made a face.

'What do you think it is worth?' She clearly thought that Marca came from a culture that didn't haggle. 'All of the finishing was done by human hand. The lining is real silk. The exterior is synthisilk and will never wear out.'

Nbaro looked at the collar. It was true. She could see the faint irregularity of the stitches.

It didn't *look like* high fashion at home. It was the real thing. In her hand.

'I could possibly go as high as twenty DHC ducats,' she said. 'In cash.'

Even under her cosmetics, Asmahan flushed.

'That is an insult to the labour to make it,' she said. 'I could possibly cover the expense at ninety ducats.'

Marca shook her head, mostly to hide her smile of enjoyment.

'I could never afford so much. And my friend is waiting.'

Nbaro pulled on her shorts and noticed that her legs were sunburnt. It didn't show much, but the prickly pain above her knees was the giveaway.

She'd only ever heard about sunburn before…

'He'll wait for you,' Asmahan said, effortlessly guessing the gender of her friend. 'Where are you from?'

'City, in the New London system,' she said.

Asmahan tilted her head. 'Are you misleading an old woman, spacer? City people don't haggle like Bedou!'

Marca allowed her smile to show. 'I could perhaps go as high as thirty.'

'Now we see it!' The local woman laughed. 'I am Asmahan. Do you like sweet tea?'

'I'm Marca, and I might!'

The woman snapped her fingers and a young girl came and heard a whispered command while Marca finished getting dressed.

'That bra does not fit you properly,' the older woman said. 'Also, it is cheap.'

'I lead a very active life,' Marca said.

She'd never given much thought to underclothes; that was more Thea's department.

'Try this,' Asmahan said. 'And this, and this. Try them all. No two women are the same, under God.'

All three fitted better than anything the Service had provided her. She did one of her sword kata.

Unbelievable. It was like discovering an alien technology.

Nbaro wondered if Hanna was angry to be delayed, but this was too good an opportunity to be missed, and she tried each one for the proprietress. She now had half a dozen local women as observers, and the shopkeeper from another stall bringing her underwear.

They were unanimous in choosing for her.

Tea came.

One of the women offered, through Asmahan, to have her servant tell Marca's man that she was trying on clothes, and she laughed and accepted, almost tempted to emotion. What had she done, that these women would be so friendly to her?

Adding three bras and the matching panties to her pile restarted the haggle. Tea came; Nbaro drank hers with gusto, and they went back and forth with the spectators adding comments, some quite ribald, others supportive.

In the end, for eighty DHC ducats, she owned everything.

'For another thirty,' the older woman said, 'I will have a second made in contrasting colours by tomorrow, delivered to your ship.'

'You are the very queen of merchants,' Marca said. 'I bow before you. As I am but a poor spacer, I cannot fight you any more. I accept.'

Asmahan grinned, kissed her on both cheeks, and then caught her shoulder.

'You must wear it now,' she said. 'I promise that he will forgive you any delay, if only you wear it.'

'You'll want nicer shoes,' said another woman from further along the souk.

In the end Nbaro had dark brown boots, not utterly unlike ship's boots, but slimmer and with a small heel, and a purity of line that made her feet look delicate when in fact they were not. She haggled automatically. The woman told her that she made the shoes herself, and showed her a woman's slipper she was making in the back, which also allowed Marca to see the three children working leather. That struck her hard.

But the children all smiled and chattered at her, and while Nbaro tried the boots on, the oldest girl asked her a hundred questions about space.

In the end, the shoemaker conceded very little, and one of the local women, the spectators, told her that she was careful in setting her prices.

Marca paid, again in cash. Then, dressed more beautifully than she'd ever been in her life, she walked out the gate of the women's souk and found Hanna seated in a coffee shop with fifty other men. He was reading his tab.

He looked up. 'Took you long ... God Almighty, you look like some goddess come to Earth.'

She smiled. *That* was a new experience.

*

The restaurant proved to be both very good and full of tourists, many of whom were her fellow spacers.

'Do they just send all the tourists here?' Richard asked. 'We could go somewhere else.'

Nbaro shrugged. 'It's beautiful,' she said.

It was, too; there were rows of tables outside, in the clear warm desert air, under strings of coloured lanterns, and there were enough local people to suggest that it wasn't bad or entirely fake.

A robot seated them, spoke some empty platitudes and offered the menus in the form of sigils that they could access from their tabs. Both of them had a local beer, dry and delicious in the heated air.

Sabina said *'The Biryani is very well thought of. The curry's have many compliments on juried systems...'*

'Shush,' Nbaro said, her coded word.

Richard looked at her with something like worship, and she found it hard to meet his eyes. Instead, she concentrated on deciphering the menu and using her tab to translate. Richard had a second beer.

'This thing with cashews and dates sounds like heaven,' she was saying, when Lieutenant Smith appeared at her table.

'May we join you?' he asked. He was with Dorcas.

She rose. 'Of course, sir.'

Hanna had excellent manners. His annoyance only showed for a heartbeat and then he was on his feet.

'Sir?' he asked.

Nbaro felt responsible for the introductions.

'Lieutenant Hanna, of Astrogation. Lieutenant Smith, of Security.' Smith shot her a glance of gratitude. 'And Messire Dorcas, a contractor I've done some work with,' she added.

Richard was still shaking hands with Dorcas as Smith smiled at her.

'The hero of the hour,' he said.

Hanna raised an eyebrow. 'If you're from Security,' he said, 'How the fuck did someone almost get a bomb aboard in the first place?'

Hanna had drunk a couple of beers, and it showed.

Heads turned at his tone. The restaurant was full, and most of the people on the patio were sailors.

'Above my pay grade, I'm afraid,' Smith said, and the moment passed.

'Did you go to the ruins?' Dorcas demanded, ignoring the questions in the air around him.

She was wondering why no one had spoken to her about the bomb, and she suddenly wondered if this was the shipboard etiquette; she'd lived through something, and they left her alone with it. *Curious.*

'I did,' Nbaro said.

'I found them incredibly stimulating,' he said. 'Look at this.'

Dorcas reached into a pocket. He was modishly dressed in a tight black waistcoat with mock-armour Kevlar and carbon-fibre reinforcements over a tight white shirt and breeches with boots; his long-coat was a single layer of well-cut silk and proclaimed his status to anyone watching. It was a dark khaki, and had embroidered acanthus leaves like those on the ships in matching silk floss, so that the embroidery was invisible from a metre away.

The very height of City fashion. He must be old money. Nbaro narrowed her eyes, wondering who he really was.

Smith, like Hanna, wore an open-collared shirt and nondescript shorts, and looked like a tourist on vacation.

Dorcas produced a long twist of carbon fibre that must have come from the edge of something, as one side of it was burnt or compressed into a tight, closed edge and had decoration.

'You stole an artifact?' Marca asked.

'There's thousands of twists of this material,' Dorcas said.

254

'They won't miss one. Anyway, I want to study it – I doubt they have anyone like me on their teams.'

Hanna was gazing off into space.

'I'm Devid,' Smith said to Hanna.

'Richard,' Hanna responded, as everyone sat. 'Wine, or beer?'

'It's the decoration that excited me,' Dorcas said.

'His first name is Horatio, and he cannot be stopped,' Smith said.

'Or rather, the *not*-decoration. I believe I can prove that it is not a decoration.' Dorcas looked at her, as if noticing her for the first time. 'This suit becomes you, Nbaro. You look splendid.'

Nbaro felt herself blush, and wondered at it. But then she ignored him and looked at what he had seen.

There were circles – really, white dots. But when Nbaro looked carefully, she could see that the dots fell in a recurring pattern, and were sometimes doubled, like a number 8 coloured in, except even those sometimes had pieces missing...

She grinned. 'It's writing,' she said.

Dorcas chuckled. 'You're really quite intelligent.'

'We can't be the first people to have worked out that this is a code,' she said.

Dorcas shrugged. 'It's hard for me to guess what other people do or don't know. I'm often disappointed.'

Smith tried not to choke on his tea.

'But you enjoyed the archaeology site?' she suggested.

'Goodness, yes. It was amazing. Remarkable. I need another day to study it and I intend to ask Morosini to let me stay here.'

Hanna turned. 'You... You *know* Morosini? You speak to him?'

Dorcas nodded. 'Oh, yes.'

Smith cleared his throat. 'I'd prefer wine, although I seem to remember the Prophet not being too keen on the juice of the grape.

I wonder how the Islamic authorities here feel? Is it an issue? It's on the menu. Are they against it?'

Dorcas spread his hands. 'Not always or everywhere. Persia was always famous for its wines.' He winced, and Nbaro got the strong impression Smith had kicked him, under the table. 'Ow. Damn it, Smith, am I doing it again?'

'Very much so,' Smith said.

'But you asked...' Dorcas said.

'I didn't, actually. Regardless, my tab says that we may drink wine to our heart's content. Out in the countryside there are people who might feel differently, but here, it's not an issue.'

'What were you doing?' Marca asked.

Horatio Dorcas smiled. 'Apparently I frequently give long, prosy answers to questions that other people feel didn't need an answer, or possibly weren't actual questions, a concept that makes no sense to me.'

Marca nodded. 'What else did you see in the ruins?'

Dorcas talked about the width of the doorways as an indication of the size of the aliens.

'Where did they go?' Hanna asked, trying to join the conversation.

'It would be useful if someone could give us a map of the coastlines from fifty to one hundred thousand years ago,' Dorcas said.

Wine came, and eventually dinner. Dorcas dominated the conversation and patronised everyone, but Nbaro forgave him, mostly because what he had to say was so interesting. Hanna and Smith seemed to like each other, and from time to time Dorcas realised what he was doing, apologised, and a more normal conversation would propagate for a few moments, until some new idea struck him.

As they finished their food, a half-dozen science techs from the ship, with Yu among them, stopped by to congratulate Nbaro and all of them seemed to know Dorcas, and in no time they'd ordered pitchers of wine and fruit juice and were sitting in a circle. And later still, she was dancing with Richard while Yu ordered another round of pitchers.

'I somehow imagined having you all to myself,' he said.

'I have exactly zero experience of being popular,' she admitted. *Not strictly true. Of being popular while not being in command, perhaps.*

'Dorcas is an arse.'

'No!' she said. 'No, he's just peculiar. I like him.'

'Of course you do. He's interested in archaeology.' Hanna was letting his annoyance show and she felt the needle swing back away from him. Also, he was less interested in her, the person, and more interested in what was under her silk suit.

Sigh. Of course, I bought the silk suit . . .

Other people started dancing; she saw Spacer Chu dancing with one of the techs from Space Ops, and Yu asked her to dance.

She agreed.

He was a much better dancer than Hanna; really, too good for her. But she enjoyed the dance, which was fast and complex; she was learning it as she went and she made a dozen mistakes and Yu just laughed and pushed her back to her place in the pattern, which was fun. She danced the next with him after making him promise to do the same dance again, and she learned it fast enough that she barely stumbled, and some people even stopped to watch them.

Yu bowed and wiped sweat off his brow. 'Thanks,' he said.

'Thank you. You're an excellent teacher.'

He grinned. 'I ought to be. I run a dance class while we're in the Deep Black. You should come. You move beautifully and you learn fast.'

Nbaro agreed that she *should* come.

She sat down and drank some more wine and fruit juice, which was delicious. Smith went and danced with someone she didn't know, a tall, handsome science tech. They looked almost too good together.

'Rudyard Singh Agam,' Dorcas said. 'One of the senior lab techs from Science. He's also quite intelligent.'

'Devid's lover?'

'Hmm. It's more complicated than that and I don't always follow along. It's tedious.'

Nbaro smiled. 'Fair,' she said. 'I'm guessing that Science people are outside the ranks and chain of command system?'

Dorcas looked at her as if she wasn't actually all that intelligent after all.

'Science is its own department, across the DHC,' he said. 'They're not even part of the Service.'

Marca thought it was odd that he sounded as if *he was.*

She looked around. The wine was getting to her, and she wasn't paying enough attention.

'Did Richard leave?' she asked.

Dorcas made a face. 'Yes. I'd say he was uncomfortable with you dancing with Steven Yu.' He shrugged. 'Some things I understand,' he added.

Nbaro felt her throat go heavy.

Later, she was crushed between Dorcas and Smith in a packed maglev car headed for the spaceport, and then, feeling a little queasy, she was strapped into an acceleration couch on a landing barge, survived a bumpy trip to orbit and staggered across the brow, managed a completely unnecessary salute, as she wasn't in uniform, and made her way to her stateroom.

Thea was lying on her rack, reading from her tab.

'Someone had fun,' she said. 'Someone looks fantastic. What the hell are you wearing?'

'Someone did, indeed, have fun,' Marca agreed, stripping

out of her new silk suit and hanging it carefully, despite her drunkenness. 'Where were you?'

'Working.' Thea rolled over. 'Cargo's great, right up until everyone else is enjoying shore leave and you're following the local markets trying to sell one more parcel of whatever. Listen, what'd you say to Rick Hanna?'

Marca told her the story.

Thea made a sound. 'I thought better of him. Oh, well.'

'I danced with Yu and then with Gunny Drun. Can I be arrested for that?'

Thea laughed. 'Only for bad taste. Drun's a shark. He's just in it for the sex.'

Marca nodded, drank water, and then drank more water.

'I still don't want any of them.'

Thea lay back with her tab. 'Sadly, I'm coming around to your point of view. Or maybe work just drowns out my hormones.' There was a pause. 'Damn, those are nice boots.'

'Or maybe we've only been in space for a month,' Marca said, climbing into her rack for some sleep, glorious sleep.

The next day, the greatship advised that shore leave would be authorised for twelve more hours, ship-time. Before Marca could even sign out, Smith called her.

He looked as if his night had been even longer than hers.

'I need a favour, Ms Nbaro,' he said.

Given that he had helped prevent the vid of her most humiliating moment from going to the ship, Nbaro felt beneficent, despite the slightest lingering headache.

'Dorcas apparently ignored a standing order and left the ship on the morning barge. If you could, would you join Dorcas at the alien ruins and—'

'Keep an eye on him?'

'Exactly,' Smith said, and rung off.

While you lie in bed with your lover, she thought, but it wasn't bitter.

Marca signed out and went ashore by herself. She worried a little on the way down; about Richard, about finding Dorcas, a needle in the proverbial sandstorm; and she listened to the sailors around her talking about the possibility that a bomb had almost gotten them. Certainly the shore-going security was the most complex she'd seen in her very limited time, and their were *marines* in *armour* at the shore patrol station. But once she was past the security station she was back in the wonderful heat, and this time she mag-leved straight to the ruins and spent five hours walking them. She was aware that Dorcas was there; he was almost always in sight – tall, civilian, fashionable, and mostly doing things he oughtn't, like crossing the barriers into the archaeological zones to speak to the students. She carefully avoided him; twice she saw him being escorted away by local security officers. She had a pleasant day, and she got to know the ruins well, but she never quite let him out of her sight, and he never noticed her.

But in the middle of the afternoon something changed, because he looked up from a wire-mesh sorting frame and waved at her as if they were old friends. He approached her and asked her to share a meal, and they went to the tourist restaurant located where everyone could see out over the ruins. The food was of the lacklustre variety known as interstellar, by which restaurateurs generally meant a bland mix of acceptable cultural compromises that was the same everywhere among the sixty-six fully settled worlds: hamburgers, curries, chow meins and sushi, as well as a bewildering variety of vegan tofus with various cultural flavourings.

The view was stupendous, though, and as the sun set over the desert and the ruins, hyenas – real ones – howled in the distance.

After Nbaro had looked hyenas up on her tab, she shook her head.

'Why on earth would anyone import hyenas?' she asked.

Dorcas was drinking a cocktail. 'I suspect this is one of those questions that I'm not supposed to answer.'

'Not at all. Please, be my guest,' she said.

'Hyenas fill a complex scavenger spot in an ecological niche system,' Dorcas said. 'I imagine they were chosen for their sheer adaptability. And look, they've adapted.'

'Yesterday, why did you want to see a chart of the coastline from fifty thousand years ago?' she asked.

He shrugged. 'Perhaps there are more ruins under the sea?' he asked. 'Maybe the oceans rose, or the river is covering another set of ruins – or five? Rivers change course.'

Nbaro nodded. She hadn't known that, because her useless Orphanage education hadn't covered anything like plate tectonics or how rivers lived and died. She read an article about it on her tab while he looked out over the ruins. Sabina steered her quietly as she read.

It was, in every way, much more relaxing than sitting with Richard Hanna.

Their food came, and they ate in companionable silence, which, after a while, seemed remarkable to Marca. But she let it go on, and watched the local star set over the ruins in a ball of fire.

Immediately, it began to get cold.

'I think I'll head back,' she said.

He appeared to wake up.

'What, no dancing tonight?'

Just when Dorcas appears to be inhuman, you discover that he's watching everything.

Nbaro laughed. 'No. I made a spectacle of myself.'

He shrugged. 'Yes and no.' It was fascinating how seldom he

made concessions for his listeners; he seemed to speak only the truth as he saw it. 'But people liked watching you dance.' He paused. 'I did.'

Nbaro didn't know what to make of that, so she paid her bill and rose.

He tilted his head to one side, like a particularly intelligent pet.

'May I come? Or would you rather be alone?'

She thought about it; decided he meant what he said.

'I'd rather be alone just now,' she said.

He nodded – almost a bow. 'I'll take the next train, then. There's another in twenty-three minutes.'

Nbaro left him contemplating the ruins. He called to the waiter, and when she looked back, he was smoking from a water pipe.

It was full dark by the time Nbaro entered the mag-lev station for the spaceport through a beautiful arcade lined with fountains. She paused to look up at the stars before she walked in, tabbed her ID through the system at the robust security kiosk, and went to an elegant neo-Arabic waiting room while the landing boat was prepped for the return to space. In one corner there was a marble plaque with a holographic direction arrow indicating the direction of Mecca, on Old Terra; in a small alcove across the waiting room, a holograph played the news.

Nbaro watched the spacers come in, some hurrying, some drunk or drugged, a few with local people who embraced them, sometimes erotically, sometimes just in sadness. It hadn't occurred to her that some of their crew might be from Haqq, but it was obvious that more than a few of the men and women catching the landing boat were locals, or had local ties.

She glanced back at the holonews, thinking of the shoemaker's daughter and her interest in space.

'In other news,' the slightly accented female voice of authority said, 'another murder in the Maghreb Arcology brings the total there to seven in the last month.'

It was juried news; the comments of the jury, who were listed on her tab as four other journalists, two legal professionals and two Islamic clerics, were played down the right side of the screen in Arabic and Anglatin; there was a tab code to get any of them full screen.

'Fatimah bint Laden Sayyid was gunned down at the door to her apartment. The killers then entered her apartment and killed both of her children and her husband, Mohammed bin Awad. White phosphorus was used to burn the apartment out completely.'

A picture of a middle-aged, stern-looking woman in a uniform appeared. Nbaro recognised her with a shock that went right to her heart. She was suddenly standing, arms outstretched, ready to fight or run.

'Ms Sayyid was a veteran officer of the Planetary Customs Authority. Her killing was claimed by the Wahhabi Underground, a fringe anti-government fundamentalist group. Her husband was a senior police officer with Office 2, the planetary counter-narcotics directorate, but he was not mentioned in the group's announcement.'

Marca tabbed through the comments from the jurors; one of the journalists noted that Ms Sayyid was under investigation by the DHC and the Planetary Office of Security, as well as the SUA's diplomatic police, and had been on forced leave.

Sabina copied the article, the photos, and the comment to Lieutenant Smith.

Then she noted one of the imams had written a long comment. It took a moment and a thumb drag to translate it from classical Arabic to Anglic. It said: 'All forms of killing are repugnant to Allah and to Islam except in a few unique circumstances. Terrorism is nothing but a form of vigilante criminality, and all murder is a sin. The Wahhabi Underground itself was destroyed by Planetary Security in the well-known Ramadan Raid of 2887. This terrible killing has been conducted by a copycat group who have stolen their name.'

Nbaro looked up the Ramadan Raid, and found that local security forces had cornered violent rebels in a fairly remote farming area south-east of the capital. Thirty-seven men and nine women were killed in the raid. Four wounded men were taken prisoner, interrogated, and later shot by firing squad.

She sent it all to Smith.

Are you with Dorcas? Smith asked.

Not any more, she answered.

Please find him immediately, Smith sent.

Nbaro tabbed Dorcas, who responded almost immediately that he was inbound on the maglev.

I'll have him in sight in three minutes, she sent.

Nothing came back. Her heartbeat increased.

Nbaro got up and walked over to the Shore Patrol station outside the waiting room. There was an officer she didn't know, but then, there were thousands of spacers she hadn't met. She had a Marine in armour and a spacer in a ship's suit wearing a sidearm, a boarding pistol. It looked dangerous.

Nbaro walked back out under the sky towards the maglev station across the fountain square.

Get him aboard by any means necessary.

She typed back, *On it.*

Passengers, all of them Service, came pouring out of the maglev the moment it arrived; the last train before the landing boat leapt into the sky. Drunk or sober, happy or glum, tall, short, every colour and gender and choice and mood, they poured out and headed for the shuttle's waiting room.

And there he was – taller than most, in a long-coat against the chill night air.

The moment he saw her, he waved.

'Did I tell you that I gave the University of Terra's dig that piece of carbon fibre that I found?'

'Stole,' she said, putting her arm through his.

Nbaro tugged him along, watching the galleries by the maglev station, and she saw something move. Pattern recognition told her that there was a ...

... , man ...

... with ...

... a ...

... rifle ...

There was a flash.

It was a slug-thrower firing, and Dorcas was frozen in place.

The next slug passed so close by her face that Nbaro heard the buzz, felt the trace of movement in the air.

She threw herself on him, and took both of them down, yelling *Brace!* as if they were on the ship.

He grunted.

To her complete surprise, he rolled out from under her.

There were three rapid flashes, like a strobe. The shooter was at least fifty metres away – perhaps more like a hundred.

Now Nbaro heard the shots. The spacers panicked, running for the Spaceport building. They screamed, like one monstrous, many-headed beast, a hydra of fear.

Dorcas rolled out to her left and turned, still prone. He had a small, very flat pistol in his hand, but the shooter was covered by the gallery and far enough away that, unless he had a thermal scope, his shots would be wasted.

'Come on,' she said.

Nbaro grabbed Dorcas's free hand and pulled.

He followed her, and the pistol vanished.

'You're allowed to carry a gun?' she asked. 'On someone else's planet?'

He didn't answer.

'They were shooting at you,' Nbaro said. 'I'm not imagining that, correct?' She knew she sounded a little shrill.

The armoured Marine was trying to force his way through the crowd, but with so many people moving around them Nbaro could no longer see how an assassin could get Dorcas, so she ignored the Marine.

Two local police officers in good xenoglas body armour appeared from a side hallway and shoved out into the fountain court. They'd probably watched the whole thing on cameras.

A dozen more shore patrol emerged from a room behind the SP deck, and the officer used an augment on her helmet.

'STOP RUNNING! HALT WHERE YOU ARE!'

Training told. Even drunk, terrified spacers came to a halt.

The Marine reached the doors to the vast fountain yard and hit some sort of lever. The doors closed.

Dorcas smiled at her. 'You're a person of many talents, Ms Nbaro,' he said.

'Smith was very worried about you,' she said.

'He ought to be,' Dorcas said, a little too smug. 'He left me to my own devices. He's not supposed to do that.'

'I had you in sight all day,' she said. 'At his request.'

He glanced at her. 'You did?'

'I did.'

8

The outbound trip towards their next insertion was relatively short. Haqq Algericas was part of the SUA, at least in part because the other two habitable planets of the SUA were only one system away, both in the same system – the only instance in the Human Sphere of two habitable planets in the Goldilocks zone of a single star.

The trip from Haqq to the SUA's home system of Sahel was plotted at just two weeks, and they were going to be frantic weeks. Sahel was one of the richest centres in Human Space and the ingoing and out-flowing cargo was immense; it was like a second Load. Nbaro looked at her schedule: two weeks of standing her watches, going to classes on Tactics and various Boarding Party clashes, as well as some Damage Control and a class on basic ship's systems – all required stuff that Nbaro had been too busy to take before. In between classes, she was tasked with helping with maintenance on the various spacecraft in her flight and had some hope of getting eight hours of sleep a night.

The virus that had come aboard at Haqq was running its course; most of the ship had at least mild encounters with it. Nbaro was ordered to visit medbay, where a space surgeon from Science gave her a battery of blood tests and scans that took less than two minutes, and mused out loud about the source of the virus. After that, she was injected with a nanobot and then a narrow spectrum anti-viral that she worked into her muscles with push-ups. That night, she discovered that Thea had done the same.

Truekner said that Sahel would be intense. He held an all-pilots meeting in the ready room as soon as they were under way, and he and Skipper Tremaine from Flight 8 went over the cargo plan for moving everything on and off Sahel. Tremaine was as tall as Truekner, as thin as Smoke, and one of the few combat veterans on the ship; she'd piloted a torpedo craft in the Beta War and had a sort of mythic aura about her.

'Even with the sky hook this is going to be hard as hell, friends,' Tremaine said. 'And after the bastards tried to nuke us, we're going to do this with *lots* of security.'

Nbaro downloaded the flight schedule, noting that she was flying up to four missions a day, every day, for six straight days. Mostly she was on as co-pilot, but she saw she was also listed as pilot almost every day, usually with the skipper as co-pilot. She had a nine-hour mission with Smoke where she was pilot.

Odd. Very long flight.

Truekner leant over. 'Nbaro, I need you to get qualified as a mission commander. You're the only pilot not qualed.'

She sighed. 'Yes, sir.'

He smiled slightly, but otherwise ignored the sigh.

'How's tactics?' he asked.

Nbaro was, at least on paper, the Assistant Tactics Officer.

'Good?' she said, as she wasn't sure what to say.

Nbaro made time before her next Boarding Party class to visit the Special Security office on Sixth Deck. Smith buzzed her in.

'I owe you several layers of thanks,' he said. 'And I've been too busy and too embarrassed to make them.'

She smiled. 'Was it good for you?' she asked in a suggestive voice.

He rolled his eyes. 'Yes?' he said.

They both laughed.

'I admit that I chose a *carpe diem* moment over my duty and I'm a fool for it,' he said.

He seemed much more like the man she'd met the first day. Nbaro wondered what might mark the changes; people were complicated, and they often had hidden lives – happy, sad, angry, in love, depressed, sulky…

'I was happy to help out,' she said.

'The shooter was engaged and killed by local security forces,' Smith said. 'I need to show you something ugly.'

He held out a tab. It was an odd tab, made of metal, with armoured corners.

'This is covered by your non-disclosure agreement,' he said.

On the screen, it was night in the fountain court.

After a long hesitation, the camera refocused and Nbaro was looking at a man in a long robe, with a rifle. It was an old-fashioned slug-thrower, with a sling, and he was in a hurry. He leaned against one of the pillars supporting the arches, shouldered the rifle, and fired one shot. Then he cursed; that much was obvious. He changed a setting with his thumb and fired a burst, the muzzle flash strobing against the darkness.

He shook his head, visibly anxious, and he dropped the rifle, picked it up, tried to sling it, and looked up.

Then he pulled a tab from his pocket and spoke into it.

Another figure entered the frame further along the pillared arcade.

The assassin turned.

The new figure raised a pistol and fired. Twice, and then twice more.

Another person entered the frame from the fountain court side, and ran to the now-prone assassin. She knelt, and said something. The assassin's mouth opened…

She put her gun to his head and shot him.

Marca almost dropped the metal tab.

'Exactly,' Smith said. 'And there's more – the virus currently making its way through our pilots and Cargo personnel is almost certainly engineered.'

'What?'

Smith spread his hands. 'Science is pretty sure we're looking at a fairly sophisticated plague attack. A two-part virus. First part makes you sick. Second part kills you.'

'Almighty.' Nbaro paused. 'Is that why I just got shots in medbay?'

'Yes,' he said. 'And we've got sniffers at the airlocks to detect it, if they try to get the second part of the virus aboard. And to see who does it, and how.'

She met his eye. 'Ugh.'

'We're at the centre of a co-ordinated set of attacks, and we have to wonder if this is how the *New York* or the *Hong Kong* were taken down. Morosini reported a very serious hacking attempt that compromised one of our landing boats. He isolated it, but it's going to have to be destroyed. Morosini thinks the nuke was a distraction.'

'How was a landing boat compromised?'

There's a million ducats going up in smoke.

'The attack was hidden in the automated landing sequence interaction with the Spaceport.'

She looked at him.

Why are you telling me all this? she wondered, and answered: *Why not? He needs someone, and I'm safe.*

'Why does Dorcas have a gun?' she asked.

He went to a cabinet and unlocked it with a very old-fashioned key.

'Same reason I'm giving you one, and the authorisation to carry it. Marca, someone is trying to stop us from reaching Trade

Point. I have to assume that's because of Dorcas. He's the most obvious vector, and the attack on Haqq was aimed at him.'

'Or me,' she said.

'Fair,' Smith said. 'But no matter how clever and elegant you are, Nbaro, you're a midshipper.'

She nodded. 'Thornberg would like me dead.'

'Consider the cost to Thornberg of getting a message here far enough ahead of the ship to set up an assassination. Occam's razor says it's Dorcas, although I'll keep my mind open.' He nodded. 'This is an Egg.' He passed it across.

It was small and light, and bore only the most casual resemblance to a pistol, in the grip.

'This is railgun technology. Hold the trigger down and it will throw a continuous stream of flechettes until the supply is exhausted. Range is quite decent – at up to fifty metres it's a killing machine. Not much use against armour, though. Or at long ranges. Good in hard vacuum, no real recoil and won't puncture the fabric of a hull.'

Nbaro took it, a light blinked, and her tab pulsed twice on the desk.

'All yours,' Smith said. 'Wear it all the time.'

'And you're just trusting me with this lethal force?' she asked, a little more sharply than she meant.

He shrugged. 'First, Morosini suggested it. Second, I'm getting fairly desperate. Which may have been part of my romantic entanglement. Two of our greatships are dead, and we're under almost constant low-level attack. In effect, the DHC is at war – we just don't know with whom, or why.'

Nbaro sat back; suddenly the pistol had lost its charm as a toy.

'So arming you is one of my many acts of desperation. I'm supposed to have had a partner, but Dorcas is temporarily confined to his berth. The people who planned my part of this mission never imagined ... this.'

She met his eyes. 'I'm just a midder,' she said. 'But I'll help as much as I can.'

'Someone killed Dornau, right here on the ship,' he said. 'I'm going to catch that person before we reach Sahel.'

'Do you think the SUA is responsible?'

He sighed. 'Honestly? Haqq Algericas had its fingerprints all over those operations – a customs officer, an assassin killed under one of our cameras by local security, a traffic control computer infected with a piece of malignant code intended to hack Morosini.' He shrugged, setting his lips. 'Maybe I'm just stubborn, but it's too neat. And Haqq needs us. Haqq runs on trade – they need our biologicals and they crave our luxury goods.'

'And you're telling me all this because ...?'

He smiled. 'I suspect I'm high on the list to be killed. Once they shot Dornau, it was a race between me and them.' He nodded. 'If they kill me, you and Dorcas are going to take over.' He held up a hand. 'Morosini chose you. Don't even ask.'

'I'd prefer to keep flying,' she said.

Smith smiled bitterly. 'I'll see if I can stay alive, then.'

Tactics class was as complicated and exciting as talking to Smith. The tactics of space combat were not fully established; Nbaro knew that much from the Orphanage. At the end of the Age of Chaos, humanity had been unwilling to contemplate new conflict, and that hesitation had prevented or minimised interstellar combats for 300 years. The Powhattan War between 普天下 Pǔ Tiān Xià (known through most of DHC space as PTX or 'the Empire') and the SUA had gone through two phases, but it had never been fully hot, and both sides had declined a fleet engagement. The Beta War had seen one of the original settlement worlds, Beta, attempt to charge tariffs on passage through their system, which was part of the easiest access to Old Terra. DHC vessels had fought two actions before arbitrators had negotiated an agreement. In addition, there had been dozens of fights between the smaller planets over very little, usually a single ship on each side: the famous clash between the UNS *Exeter* and the Starfish cruiser out at the very edge of explored space, and a dozen anti-piracy actions against various foes that were dreadfully one-sided once the pirates were run down.

Most DHC ships were merchants with large cargo holds. As such, and because they were developed to service low-technology worlds with minimal spaceport facilities, the greatships had dozens of small craft, from military fighters and electronic warfare gunboats, through the various cargo shuttles that could also carry heavy torpedoes, right up through the small spaceships, like the pinnaces. DHC doctrine was to fight battles well out into space, far from the mother ship, with small craft.

The greatships themselves could pack a hefty punch, and the same railguns that launched the spacecraft could throw enormous payloads. Of course, the ships used this capability to place selected robust loads into orbits, or even to send them to the ground, but in combat, a railgun load of reactive sand or cluster bomblets with proximity fuses could devastate an entire enemy fleet. A greatship could lay an extensive and utterly deadly minefield in a matter of hours, and could manufacture everything she needed to do so on board.

Greatships were poised to dominate the fleet actions that had never happened, and in response torpedoes grew ever smaller and space-stealth technologies improved, as did competing heat and anti-heat detection technologies. Pirates tended to favour small, stealthy craft with internal heat sinks and complex background-matching external systems, and lured their unwary targets close to a planet or an asteroid belt that could hide their signature until they attacked. Their favourite weapons were railgun-deployed torpedoes that would only ignite their engines in the final sequence and be invisible until then.

The detection of such silent killers had fallen increasingly to the various spacecraft that the greatships carried, and to purpose-built pirate killers like the two battlecruisers that continued to escort the *Athens*.

There was an enormous amount of data, and like the alien ruins, Marca found it so fascinating that Thea would come in and find her watching the ship's camera footage of the *Exeter* confrontation again and again.

'We won that encounter!' Thea said. 'And we won two hundred years ago!'

'Starfish ships are filled with liquid ammonia,' Marca said. 'Starfish grow up in pressure many times our Terran gravity. They can take a much higher acceleration than we can. They should have smoked the *Esperance*. Instead, Captain Hae Yon bluffed them, got a torpedo in them, and then rescued them.'

It was a famous story: the human ship first won the ship-to-ship fight and then towed the damaged alien ship to its nearby station.

'They fired first,' Thea said.

Marca watched it happen, using screen data from the tactical display of the ship's captain, that had become public information during her court martial.

Later, when Marca came in from her workout, Thea was just going on duty. They were two days out from Insertion and Thea had dark smudges under her eyes.

'I can't decide which to ask about first,' she said when Marca slipped in. 'About the new underwear, or the gun.'

Marca sighed. 'Please don't ask about the gun,' she said. 'The underwear is marvellous. I had no idea that bras could fit.'

Thea laughed. 'And you have to talk to Richard Hanna,' she said.

'He walked off and left me!' Marca said defensively.

'Concur,' Thea said, as if it was a tactics situation. 'Despite which—'

274

'Fine,' Marca said.

Nbaro changed and went to lead a boarding party in a corridor that was already compromised by a damage control situation. The scenarios were growing more complicated – more ominous, as if the mission planners were responding to the threats to the ship.

After class, she approached Captain Fraser.

'A word, sir?' she asked.

He nodded.

'I was thinking in Tactics class, sir. If we had to fight the Starfish—'

'God forbid. But yes.' He didn't smile.

'Their ships are flooded with liquid ammonia.' Marca waved her arms as if she was swimming.

'They are,' he said. 'I don't think we could operate in their environment, even in full EVA suits.'

'But if they could come alongside us to board,' she said, 'could they flood part of our ship with ammonia?'

Fraser turned and looked at her. 'You have a terrible mind, Nbaro.'

'It'd make a horrible reaction scenario.'

'God help us.' Fraser nodded. 'We've enough to worry about with feral human adversaries.'

'Yes, sir,' she said.

'But thanks for the nightmare.'

'Any time, sir.'

The next day, after a long watch and a stilted meal with Thea and Richard and Yu, Nbaro went to the Marine Shack on Third Deck, found Gunny Drun and got him to find her time on the Marine firing range. He expressed no surprise whatsoever that she had the Egg, and he knew exactly how it worked, including its power requirements. He asked her no questions, and took her through stripping and rebuilding it.

275

'You're not going to ask where I got this?' she asked.

He pointed at the handgrip.

'The grip reads biometric data,' he said with his Old Terran drawl. 'The biometric data is checked against Morosini. So you're authorised. That's enough.'

Nbaro fired off magazine after magazine. The barrel rise was bad; as the electromagnets grew stronger during a long burst, the whole weapon wanted to twist in her hand, and anything metal tended to be attracted to it. It was also bad for tabs.

Drun showed her various ways of wearing her holster. He loved to shoot, and was happy to let her share his passion.

When Nbaro was done, he pointed at her weapon.

'Just remember that if you're exposed to any EMP,' he said, 'then it's nothing but a piece of ceramic and dead superconductor.'

Nbaro went to Space Ops and served a Tower watch with only one event. Her tab reminded her that she had a mandatory EVA event, her bi-weekly trip outside to remain inside safety qualifications. The *Athens* was very strict about outside procedures, because spacers had died on the last cruise.

Every day Nbaro felt she was further behind: too many qualifications, too many lessons, too much to learn, and never enough time.

Thea felt the same. She'd stopped dressing carefully, stopped doing her hair, stopped experimenting with even a trace of cosmetics. She didn't always shower when she got up, and sometimes she'd just zip up her ship's suit and head out to work. Dinners with friends vanished; all of them simply grabbed bulbs of something edible and returned to work, to study, to sleep.

Mpono grinned at her once, in the ready room.

'You think this is bad,' she said. 'Wait until we're in the Deep Black and you have nothing to do for weeks at a time. That's worse.'

Nbaro didn't think it was so bad. She loved the Boarding

Party classes – loved the fighting, loved the game of it. She loved Tactics, and even Ship's Systems was interesting enough; it was fascinating to learn how things worked, even if the Service was a little light on *why* they worked. They spent four classes working on the artificial gravity systems, and none of them explained the twenty-sixth century breakthrough in high-energy physics that made both insertion-style spaceflight and gravity-defying technologies possible.

But Nbaro learnt how to operate most artificial gravity equipment and how to change the solid-state black boxes that allowed it to run. She learned a lot more than she wanted to about nanobots, in everything from fabrication to medicine, and then she learned what happened when nanotechnology failed, and how to clean it up.

Nbaro lay awake imagining holding various parts of the ship against assault, and then, imagined taking those same parts against her own defensive plan. She ran checklists in her head, imagining various spaceflight emergencies and Space Operations procedural scenarios until she fell asleep, exhausted but satisfied that she was ready to face whatever test might be thrown at her.

She and Thea were both in their racks for the insertion, and they slept through it. Four insertions into her career, and sleep was more important than experiencing the acme of human spaceflight technology.

Nbaro went on watch with Commander Mpono, who nodded at her in a distracted way while downloading news from a juried service.

'The last time, no?' Smoke said. 'After Sahel, we start long-jumping. We'll *be* the news after this. No messenger boats arriving in our time bubble.'

'Time bubble?' Nbaro asked.

Mpono shrugged. 'It's a service term, really. When we left New London, we carried a bubble of New London time with us, as if

277

we carried some of their air. Right? And at Barcino, we got the bubble updated – fresh news from home. We were still in New London's bubble. Then at Haqq, someone got a messenger boat there ahead of us, but it was still from our time, or a few weeks later. But after this, four straight long-jumps and no worlds in any system. We're going hundreds of light years and when we push in system at Draconis Prime, we're entering their time bubble, because New London's will no longer have any meaning to us.'

Marca swallowed that. 'OK,' she said slowly. 'Time dilation …'

Mpono shook their head. 'Even back before spaceflight, people on opposite sides of the ocean didn't always imagine themselves as being on the same day or at the same time until communications enabled them to talk together.'

Marca had doubts. 'They had dates and times – newspapers had dates. I've seen photos.'

Mpono sighed. 'My point, *Midder*, is that simultaneity is not reality. When we're done with our round trip, almost four years will have passed for New London, their time. It will be about three years for us, our time. See? And more importantly, when you come back, things will have changed in ways you cannot predict. People change, places change …'

'Sounds wonderful,' Nbaro said, and started reading her tab.

The news was still bad. But at least they didn't arrive in system to reports of the death of another greatship and the consequent emergencies. In the officers' mess, speculation about the *Dubai* – which ought to be out past Far Point – was rife, as well as a certain fatalism about their own prospects.

The economic news from New London was still bad. The news here was only three days newer than what they'd left behind in Haqq, but the vids of near riot conditions in the government centre of New London were hard for many of the crew to watch. Tumbling shares in various trade markets through ten star systems contributed to the feeling of panic, while AIs and human 'experts' speculated about possible developments, including the abandonment of the long trade routes and the elimination of the miraculous xenoglas as a commodity.

'They're writing us off,' Marca said, watching one debate unfold. 'Smoke, it's as if they've already declared us dead.'

Smoke lifted their head from their comms.

'I saw that,' they said. 'Don't let it get to you.'

Easier said than done, Nbaro thought.

Up close, Sahel was magnificent: a sapphire shot through with milky white clouds and brown-green continents, the whole so Earth-like that Nbaro had to look carefully to not see the familiar outlines of Old Terra's continents on her surface.

Sahel had more open water than Old Terra, and a little less land mass, most of it concentrated like a belt along the equator, with strings of islands into the northern and southern zones like the spiral arms of the galaxy. Her biome was healthy, with alien plants and animals that had mostly been given Swahili or Bemba or Hausa or Yoruba names. Several big mammal analogues roamed the central plains, mostly eating what appeared to be plants.

In fact, many, many things about the life on Sahel were very definitely alien, and yet, at first glance, humanity had made the locale fit with their origins in Africa. The first colonists had made every effort to avoid the mistakes made on Old Terra. As farmland was laid out and cities were established, so were reserves and routes for the local life; xenobiologists flocked to Sahel and studied it before intensive colonisation took place.

Although Sahel offered remarkable evidence of parallel evolution, nothing was really the same. Terran life forms could take no sustenance from eating either the plants or animals on Sahel, and early disasters involving the rapid colonisation of some parts of Sahel by Terran fungus indicated that the two biomes would mostly do each other harm. Because of which, or perhaps despite it, humanity flourished without destroying what had come before.

Sahel and her sister world in the same system, Madagascar, were two of the richest and most technologically advanced planets in the Human Sphere, on a par with New London, Vera Cruz, or Palace in Pŭ Tiān Xià. With Haqq Algericas, they formed the SUA – a socialist-democratic government – and all three worlds' economies remained members of the DHC. The legalese of understanding true membership in the DHC bored Nbaro in ways that understanding tactics or how to repair the auxiliary power unit on her XC-3C never bored her.

But the planet was beautiful.

Sahel had a number of features that distinguished her, besides her Earth-like colouring. For one thing, her system was rich in asteroids – and thus metals. There were dozens of orbitals and two big hubs in long, lazy orbits, originally placed to service the mining industry and now huge, healthy habitats in their own right. Nairobi was reputed to be the most populated city in space after City, and Mombasa, while much smaller, had an elite space tourism industry unlike anything in any other system.

Sahel had a massive orbital, Kilimanjaro, that hosted the sky hook, a cable freight and a passage elevator that ran from the equator on the surface up to Kilimanjaro, where there were docking facilities developed exclusively for the greatships. The DHC had its own bonded warehouses on the station.

The traffic in-system was staggering compared to Haqq, where the tactical action screens had only displayed perhaps fifty contacts. Here at Sahel, they were flooded with contacts as soon as they arrived, and now, close in to Kili and matching orbits, they were in a cloud of thousands of ships from tiny private shuttles to massive ore freighters coming in from the belt. A PTX merchant was one spot ahead of them in the docking pattern, their ship more than half the size of the greatship. The Tactical Action Officer said the ship was less than ten years old.

Mpono brought the ship up on full magnification.

'See the insertion vanes?' they said. 'See how they've extended the stern to separate the vanes further from the drive?' They pointed again.

'She's a long-jumper,' Nbaro said.

'She's got a lot of teeth,' muttered the TAO on comms.

Smoke ignored the TAO and went back to vanes.

'Exactly. That's the new design. In a hundred years, the great-ships will be outclassed and these whippersnappers will jump further for less mass.'

They both grinned to see the beauty of the PTX 'merchant', but like all of them, Nbaro loved her huge ship and didn't like the trend in shipbuilding.

There wasn't much for Space Operations to do except watch the docking.

'We're going to launch Cargo Ops while docked to the station?' Nbaro asked.

Smoke nodded. 'Yes, and it allows a nasty level of outside control. Only Station knows where all these rock-hoppers and private shuttles are, and only Station has control, so we're basic-ally just an airport and they're the traffic authority. In effect, we hand off the moment a craft launches.'

'So we're just Tower?'

'Exactly. You're getting a handle on this.' Smoke smiled.

'And we launch at low velocity.' Marca sighed. 'And we just trust them? After someone tried to put a bomb aboard at Haqq?'

'Very low, so we don't interfere with anyone else's launches and to allow time for a human-to-human handoff on launch.' Smoke leaned back. 'We have a few tricks up our sleeve. But yes; we have to trust them. We can't conduct the whole load from space. We have to dock. It's a cargo thing.'

In the next four hours, as the cargo schedule commenced, Marca first observed it and then directed it, interacting with Kili Control and passing over launched spacecraft. It was smooth with the experience of many repetitions, and she ended her watch by going down to the Fourth Deck freight dock and watching the largest eight metre cargo pallets as they were moved on artificial gravity out onto the vast Station Deck and then into the Beanstalk, the freight elevator to planet side.

The Master was there, watching his cargo being moved in person. Nbaro noticed that he was wearing a sidearm. There were Marines on the dock, and she was interested to see that she had a Boarding Party schedule overlaid on her flight schedule for the next six days.

Nbaro waited to see the sky hook descend. She had no real reason to watch it, and she knew she wouldn't see much, but the presence of more than a hundred crew members on the freezing cold dockside indicated that she wasn't alone in wanting to watch one of the galaxy's only sky hooks.

Richard Hanna walked up to her. In a fairly stiff way, he said, 'I want to say I'm sorry.'

Nbaro couldn't decide if a smile was called for.

'I'm sorry, too,' she said.

'I didn't know what to do. You weren't enjoying my company.'

He was so ... earnest about it. He meant what he was saying. But he was also just jealous, and he'd had no reason to be jealous. And it was all too far out of her experience, and in a way that she couldn't quite access, like a hatch that wouldn't open, Nbaro didn't care enough to force it.

'I'm sorry, Richard.' She turned to face him. 'It doesn't work,' she said.

'I got that,' he said. 'If you prefer Yu—'

'I don't prefer anyone!' she said with too much emphasis. 'I'm just not ...'

I'm not a prey animal. I'm not ready to be hunted. Fuck off.

'I enjoy spending time with you, but I don't have romantic inclinations.'

Possibly ever.

He looked Nbaro in the eye for a long time – time enough for her to get colder and wonder if the elevator was going to leave and she'd miss it.

'Damn,' he said. 'Well, Marca, I enjoy spending time with you, and I do have romantic inclinations.' He managed a smile, and rose in her estimation. 'But I'll do my best to keep them in check.'

Nbaro made herself smile. It wasn't that hard.

'Thanks.'

He nodded. 'We should walk over there or we're going to miss it.'

The elevator moved, like the whole floor of the station dock dropping away from them, and vanished.

'It's not really gone,' Dorcas said behind them.

Hanna laughed aloud. 'Must he?' he asked her quietly.

'Yes,' she said.

Dorcas went on, 'It goes down to a huge airlock, and then it can fall through gravity in a vacuum – less friction, less drag.'

Hanna was interested, despite himself.

'And of course, it's providing most of the power to raise the one on the other side,' Dorcas added.

'Why do I have to fly round the clock if we have this technological marvel?' Marca asked.

'It's easier and cheaper to move smaller cargo by shuttle,' he said. 'Anyway, insurers hate the sky hook and no one will move xenoglas on it. Mostly, that's what you'll be delivering – finished xenoglas parts for aerospace.'

'It must be nice to know everything,' Hanna said.

Dorcas gave him a look. 'My only wisdom lies in knowing how little I know.'

'That's me, told,' Hanna said when the tall man walked away.

Two midshippers and a junior lieutenant walked up and began an animated discussion of possible plotting error in astrogation that was so intensely technical that Marca decided to edge away. She waved at Hanna, inwardly delighted at their resolution, or what she hoped was a resolution.

Dorcas was watching the great cables of the elevator; they were jet-black and probably made from something insanely technical, and Nbaro was daring herself to ask him about them.

'Morosini's cloned himself,' Dorcas said.

She blinked.

'We're sitting alongside a foreign station and, after the biological attack and the hacking attempt at Haqq, Morosini's decided to assume that we'll get hit here. He's cloned himself and his clone is dealing with the station from behind an air-gapped firewall.'

'Why are you telling me this?' she asked.

'Because both Morosini and Smith view us as their backstop. In emergency, break glass and pull handle and out we pop. That sort of thing. Morosini wants us to know he's got a counter-intelligence program running too – a sub-AI.'

'I still don't get it. Why us? Why me?'

Nbaro looked around guiltily; any Orphanage graduate knew about directional mics.

'I'm brilliant and you're lucky.'

'That makes sense,' Marca said, 'If we enlisted Thea, then we'd have someone with a social IQ on the team, too.'

Dorcas blinked. 'Was that sarcasm?'

'Might have been,' she said. 'I'm walking in thirty minutes.'

'I was hoping you'd want to go see one of the game parks.'

'Find me in five days and I'm your woman,' she said.

'Hmm,' Dorcas said. 'I might be done with alien elephants by then.'

'My loss, I'm sure.'

They both smiled.

Nbaro got back into the body of the ship with something like relief. It was warm and safe, and the engraved acanthus leaves and painted birds and angels were reassuring after the cold, stark dockside.

Nbaro's first mission was a simple drop down into atmosphere, where she was assigned to land at one of the industrial space-ports that ringed the megacity of New Soweto. From space, as the megacity was in darkness, it looked like a haze of light bigger than anything on New London, and the air traffic was as thick in the atmosphere as the space traffic at Kili Station.

Nbaro was co-pilot with the skipper, so all she had to do was keep the communications flow going. Lubumbashi Control picked them up from Kili Control, and they landed on an ultra-modern magnetic rail system that mimicked the ship's launch and landing tubes but with a much more comfortable deceleration.

'I hate letting a computer fly my craft,' Skipper Truekner said.

Landing into the rail system was all automated. Despite his words, he leant back and let go of the yoke after the green light on the computer said that Lubumbashi Control had the landing.

'So,' he said. 'How's Tactics?'

'Really fun,' she said.

'That's an excellent answer. What's fun about it?'

'It's a game,' she said. 'I like games.'

He nodded, scanned his instruments by old training, and tried not to watch the landing lights that the craft was approaching at breakneck speed.

'It's not a game when people die,' he said. 'I know, I know. I'm paid to say that sort of thing to junior officers, OK? What have you learned that interests you?'

'A lot about using the railguns to launch us,' Nbaro said.

285

'I've been thinking about ways to put a reflective or obscuring cloud just in front of us, so that we can make a burn or two without being seen.'

He looked interested.

'If one tube launched sand while the other tube launched one of ours,' she said. 'Or just one second behind, to leave behind a pre-laid screen.'

'I'm liking all that.'

'I've been looking for ways to run cold, to hide manoeuvres, to hide even the launch of the torpedo. It's all fun.'

'Somehow I knew you were the right person for the job,' he said. 'And ... we're down.'

They'd missed the landing. Nbaro laughed.

'It's funny,' she said. 'It's funny how little we actually know about how to fight a war in space.'

Truekner was raising his couch.

'It's a fine thing,' he said. 'We're really just a glorified merchant marine. War in space is a terrible idea. People will die, ships will die ...'

'You think it's coming, don't you, sir?'

'Why do you ask that, Nbaro?'

She looked over at him. 'I see you worry. Sir.'

He nodded. 'The *New York* and the *Hong Kong*,' he said. 'Every day I expect to hear it's the *Dubai*, too.' He shrugged. 'Yeah, kid. Someone's coming for us. I want to be ready. You know why I always have two birds on the line every time we go to Battle Stations? I'm practising for the time it's real. You know why we always load with torpedoes? Because we're practising for the time it's real. Even down to loading the damn torpedoes.'

'Yes, sir.'

He shrugged, unbuckling his harness. 'I'm just a crazy old man.'

'Yes, sir.'

The cargo load here was automated – no visible customs, just a mobile gantry that included robot arms. The pallets in 6–o–5's belly were removed and new pallets put in, and a hundred thousand ducats' worth of xenoglas-based widgets were delivered, signed for, and a cargo of high-end electronics headed for orbit. Nbaro checked it all against projected manifest.

Sabina did most of the work, and beeped her approval.

'They don't even need us,' Truekner said. 'We could just send the birds empty.'

Her next flight was with Didier. He was entertaining, and perfectly happy to give over his control to Lubumbashi, and they did two drops together, gathering cargoes. Nbaro did nothing but talk on her radio and put her thumbprint on a cargo tab.

It might have been boring, but the views from space were incredible, and Sahel was fascinating. Even the warehouses had a faint alien smell – something hard to place, like a stale sulphur smell with a hint of allspice.

A shockingly busy Space Ops watch with Ko as her Lioness, coaching her on being Tower because he had nothing else to do. Nbaro looked forward to serving with him because he was easy to talk to, but the constant stream of events, and even visiting dignitaries coming aboard in their own shuttles, kept both of them too busy to chatter or even snark – an art form that Marca was learning, from Thea, was a useful way of communicating with peers.

Ko let her run the watch for almost half an hour while he discussed diplomatic procedures with Morosini and the Master, and only took Lioness back to bring the President of Sahel's private space shuttle aboard with due ceremony, which included a Marine guard, in polished armour and led by Major Darkstar, greeting the president as he left his shuttle in Hangar 1. They watched it on one of the plat cameras, and Nbaro finally managed to slip some of her snark in as the president of the SUA made a distant and easy target. She made Ko laugh, and then the watch was over and she could sleep.

The next day was like a 3D printer's duplicate – the same flight to the same field and the same communications. Nbaro had Cortez as her watch officer in Space Ops, and even without a diplomatic visitor they were insanely busy. Cortez was, by his own admission, relatively new; he wanted to be hands-on, and mostly Nbaro fetched coffee and food.

'When do you take your test?' he asked at the end of watch. 'Ko says you're smooth – and he's the best.'

She glowed. 'No idea,' she said.

'You aren't sweet on Ko?' Cortez asked.

'Not sweet on anybody, bro.'

He smiled. 'Good, because he's got a mate and he's a one-mate kind of guy. Trust me, I know.'

'I'll bet you say that to all the girls,' she said.

He nodded. 'Only the ones who look like they're falling for Ko.'

The next day brought her a long mission with Commander Mpono. They were in Mpono's craft, 6-o-2, with their name painted under the cockpit. They lingered over their walk-around as if they were in no hurry to make their flight time.

Finally they strapped in and Nbaro lit up the auxiliaries to get the computer to link to the ship.

'You know we're going to my home?' Mpono said.

'No, tir,' Nbaro didn't know what to say.

'It's always weird, going home,' Mpono said. 'Anyway, let's do it.'

It proved to be both amazing and dull – her first really long space flight since the *New York* died. They had a cargo: xenoglas parts for hi-tech mining operations bound for Ndola Station, an orbital placed to support mining operations on two big, rich nickel-iron asteroids in the belt. Ndola had been a mine, once, and had been hollowed out in the course of her history. First she had gone from mine to refinery, and then a spaceport grew, and a dockside, and eventually, an entire habitat.

It was a long flight and required some exact rationing of fuel. Ordinarily, the *Athens* could have shot the craft in exactly the right direction and all they would have had to do was decelerate into their landing, but the traffic control rules around Kili Station forced them to go the whole way on thrusters. They did time their launch with the station's rotation to get a little velocity, which reduced the nine-hour trip to a mere seven hours.

It was dull, in a way; but the view was splendid, and Nbaro enjoyed Mpono's company.

'I think this is what I imagined when I was at the Orphanage,' she said.

Mpono was reading from their tab.

'Hours of boredom on a cargo-hauler?' they said. 'Damn, that's a weak-ass imagination.'

'Space!' Marca replied. 'Alien worlds! The Deep Black out there ... The PTX ship, the sky hook ... and yes, even this.'

'There's something refreshing about having someone aboard who still thinks this is fun,' Mpono said.

'Don't you?'

Mpono sighed. 'Ask me on the way back.'

Nbaro noted that they referred to the ship as home, not Ndola Station.

They matched velocities neatly, and Mpono exchanged pleasantries with the station control in Bemba, to the delight of the station's tower, who chuckled as he slipped back to Anglatin for the docking permissions. They got a station-side hangar, and their cargo was valuable enough that the receiver paid to have the hangar brought up to atmosphere for the unload, which was done, not by robots, but by people.

On their appearance, Mpono was mobbed as if they were a vid star. As soon as they took off their helmet, people came from all directions; some were family, because Nbaro was introduced, and some were Mpono's friends. There was food, and a surprising amount of rum, which Nbaro kept refusing because she had to fly, but the smell was tantalising. Now she understood why she was listed as pilot with Smoke as co-pilot. It was Smoke's homecoming party.

The xenoglas parts were taken away and a small consignment of ore loaded.

'It's gold,' Marca said.

'Not surprised. They get some gold out of these rocks.' Mpono smiled. 'Anyway, gold is pretty much the same as any other cargo.'

'Not when you have 400 kilos of it,' Marca said.

She went to look at it, just to say she'd seen 400 kilos of gold, and one of the locals knelt with her, looking up into the gleaming cargo bay. He was dark, like his African forebears, and tall, like Mpono, but his hair was golden. Not blond – gold.

'That's our gold,' he said with a huge smile. 'We sweated and we gulped air and, by God, we got it done. An' more where that come from, eh?' He looked at her. 'Where you from?'

'City,' she said.

'Ahh, that's nice. Nice place. Been twice. Learned to weld with the xenoglas, *eh bien?*'

He seemed pleased, and his smile was infectious.

Meanwhile Smoke was exchanging a long hug with someone as tall as they were.

'That's their mum,' her new friend said. 'I'm James.'

'Hello, James, I'm Marca.'

'Let me get you some rum and a curry.'

'No rum for me, thanks. I'm flying.'

'Big girl like you can fly with some rum in her, I bet,' he said.

'You're a gold miner?' she asked.

'What gave me away?' he asked, pretending to be offended. 'Was it my accent?'

He was funny, and very smooth.

'Is that gold dust in your hair?' she asked.

'Nanoplated to the hair itself,' he said. 'Some biochemical shit that keeps the hairs from growing longer for a while. Costs a mint.' He grinned. 'You like?'

'It's ... remarkable,' she said.

'Not sure that's good,' he said, wincing.

James introduced her to a hundred people in fifteen minutes – a blur of faces, all ages. The little pressurised hangar had become a party, with music utterly unlike the music of the streets of City, and spices, roasting meat, human sweat.

People were dancing; Nbaro danced with James, and then with a younger man whose hair was just as gold, then an older man who was called away. The food was fabulous; Nbaro ate skewer after shawarma and relished it all. It was fresh food – the meat had the toughness that almost guaranteed that it was real, the vegetables had a vitality that even the best hydroponics lacked.

James nodded at her second shawarma, which was over-packed with something that might actually be arugula.

'That shit's so real that my mum was washing *dirt* off it last night,' he said. 'We paid big baksheesh for this food. Jan Mpono's the fucking hero, right? Homecoming, they.'

'They are the best officer I serve under,' Marca said.

She tried to explain Space Ops to James, who was well into his third rum punch and whose hands tended to reach for her. And yet, she found his vague amorousness ... more fun? Less intrusive? ... than Hanna's approaches. He was somehow harmless and attractive at the same time. She patted his hands away with something akin to regret.

'I have to fly,' she said.

'You really need to come back here when you don't have to fly,' he said.

291

Nbaro met his bold eye. 'Might do,' she said with a smile that she . . . meant.

She met Mpono's mother immediately after – a mature woman with Mpono's good looks and elongated height.

'You take care of my baby,' she said to Marca, as if a midder could do anything to protect a full commander. Her hug was effusive and all-enveloping. 'Do you like the food? James says you eat like a machine.'

'I love it, ma'am,' she said.

Ruby, Mpono's mother, beamed.

'Have some rice,' she said. 'Did you try the rum?'

'Nbaro can't have rum any more than I can,' Smoke said with some exasperation.

'I can drill a micron-wide hole between two protons and never change their spin,' James said. 'And that's after five or six cups o' rum.'

'Perhaps you can,' Smoke said. 'But I can't, and anyway, the Service is quite explicit.'

'Explicit,' Ruby said. 'Such a word, baby.'

Mpono rolled their eyes like an angry teenager.

'But they *love* you,' Marca found herself saying to her pilot.

'I find it wearing,' Mpono said. 'I see them once every four or five years, and I'd like to spend a day with Mum and not be the centre of a block party. And my half-brother all but pulled your clothes off on the spot. That annoyed me.'

'I liked him,' Marca said. 'And he took no for an answer.'

There was a long silence, punctuated by a checklist as they neared their turnover midpoint from acceleration to deceleration. The station had launched them with plenty of delta v so they had more fuel to spend decelerating, making the whole trip back faster.

'I don't know why I'm telling you all this,' Mpono admitted.

For her part, Marca found it odd to have her idol displaying anger, annoyance, and even hurt. She admired the 'gyne – their demeanour, their confidence, their aura of command, their years of experience. This Mpono, with more fragility and complications, was of a different order.

'I think people find it easy to talk to me,' Marca said.

'You have a way of giving your whole concentration to another person. I see you do it in Space Ops. It's as if you're an antenna, and you're set only to receive.'

Marca smiled, not sure how to take that.

'Anyway, my mum loved you. You ate and danced and apparently flirted with James without giving anything away – you may achieve legendary status.'

'Are all your family gold miners?' Marca asked.

'No, the gold's recent,' Mpono said. 'And so's the money. My mum and da were part of a line marriage of miners. Even a generation ago, miners died like . . . well, like workers in the Age of Chaos, eh?'

Marca noted with some secret amusement that the bantering tone and the slight patois of Ndola Station had crept into Mpono's diction. She'd never heard it before.

'What's a line marriage?' she asked.

'Line marriages are when there's more than two or three people. And it's not the same as polygamy either – that shit's usually all about men. This is a kind of pragmatic response to life in low *g* and high danger – five women, seven men, all the kids in common. It meant that there were always adults to raise the kids, eh? Unlikely they'd all die in one go. Harsh life, mining nickel and iron for fairly low pay-offs. But when the orbital expansions started at Sahel, we suddenly had the best iron and we had a smelter. My mum and her sisters knew it was coming, went to City, took courses, and became a smelting co-operative that could manufacture industrial alloys.'

'Ah,' Marca said.

'Exactly. So miners started moving their cargoes to Ndola and our station expanded and suddenly we had a little money. Mum raised me to go to Service. She's a natural patrician – always has her eye on the long prize. Then Dad found gold.'

Marca could see the irony.

'Now we're rich enough that Mum may actually choose to *be* a patrician.' Mpono shrugged.

'A million ducats,' Marca breathed.

'Fifty million, if you want to ennoble your whole line,' Mpono said.

'Almighty,' Marca said.

'Ten thousand kilos of refined industrial gold,' Mpono said.

'Hard to imagine that much…'

'Mum's probably got it in storage,' Mpono said. 'Do you know how many people are patricians in the DHC?'

'A few thousand…'

'A little more than a million,' Mpono said. 'We're at something like one hundred and forty billion in the DHC. 普天下 Pǔ Tiān Xià has twice that.'

Unlike most DSC spacers, Mpono always pronounced the Empire's Mandarin name exactly, so that Nbaro could all but see the characters. People in the SUA lived closer to the Empire and knew it better.

Smoke leant back. 'And to think – back in the Age of Chaos they thought the human race was about to die out?'

'I've read Valsequez,' Marca said.

'Good. Most people don't. Anyway, you're patrician yourself, aren't you?'

Nbaro had a moment of near panic. She'd never mentioned it on board ship.

294

'I'm a penniless patrician who went to a prison school,' she said, a little more bitterly than she'd intended.

Mpono nodded. 'I hear you, but honey – your ancestors were masters of greatships, maybe even admirals. There was an Nbaro Doje, wasn't there? Director of the Board?'

'Yes, tir.'

'Smoke – for God's sake, honey. Don't call me tir.'

'Smoke,' Marca said. It just sounded unnatural to her.

'My point, here, Marca, is that however much you downplay it, you're a patrician and any kids you shell out will be patricians, which means that, far from being penniless, you're fifty million ducats ahead of my mum. You pay different taxes and you have a preferential promotion rate in the Service and you can serve in the Senate and the Great Council.' They shrugged. 'The DHC has still got one foot in the Age of Chaos.'

Marca hadn't thought of it that way before.

'What do you mean?'

'Our society is all about fairness and levelling,' Smoke said. 'But the DHC still runs on social classes. We have guaranteed minimum income, funded retraining, and uniform health care which our ancestors couldn't have dreamt of, and yet we still have patricians who can make economic decisions that affect planets they've never visited.'

'And your mum's planning to buy in,' Marca said.

Mpono grinned. 'I know. It's a hypocritical argument for me to make, because as soon as she buys in, I'll probably make captain and benefit from the system.'

They were watching the instruments as the ship performed its mid-flight flip to decelerate.

Nbaro rubbed the bridge of her nose with two fingers; was that eyestrain from watching the instruments too closely, or something else?

'There's an item in the juried newsfeed, an editorial piece

claiming that the bar to patrician status is too low and too many people are getting in.'

Mpono smiled wolfishly. 'Anyone inside the fold always wants to shut the gate.'

As soon as they were within tab range, Marca's tab gave a clear ring; she answered it to find Thea looking at her.

'Just in time. I have a buyer for our coffee. I need your agreement.'

Marca nodded. 'How much?'

'Forty-three a kilo.'

'Almighty! Thea, that's insane …'

'Just tell me how pretty, skinny, tall, and smart I am,' Thea said. 'Tell me early and often.'

'Of course I accept.'

'We'll lose about five a kilo on that in delivery charges,' Thea said. 'I can arrange for you to deliver it tomorrow. You're the pilot of record on a small cargo headed for the resort orbital.'

'Fun!' Marca said. She meant it.

They were on their landing procedures, but Marca interrupted her checklist to say, 'I'm starting my rise to fortune with my first cargo sale.'

'Good for you,' Smoke said. 'Tell me when you're ready to buy some gold and I'll make sure you get a good price.'

'I'm more interested in where you got your flight jacket,' Marca admitted.

Smoke nodded. 'Right there on Kili Station. I can take you there.'

'After tomorrow, I'll have the money to buy one.'

'I'm not sure this is how the ancients thought socialism was going to work,' Smoke said, and began their final approach.

9

Mombasa Orbital was a luxury resort even from the outside, where vast, expensive canopies of xenoglas and other exotic materials decorated the exterior skin of the orbital like illuminated soap bubbles. Everything about the massive wheel of the station was polished, decorated, elegant and at the cutting edge of technology. Alpha Foxtrot 6–o–4 landed in an automated tube of jet-black nanofibre whose magnets nested the shuttle so softly that even Marca, who was pilot, was not exactly sure when they came to a stop.

Truekner was her co-pilot and had spent the flight doing his tab work, mostly on personnel files. Spacer evaluations were due shortly after they left the system, with officer fitness reports due two weeks later, and the skipper was deep in the process. He didn't even look up during landing and docking.

Even the shuttle terminal was elegant, in wood grain that looked real and matt black with inlaid bronze accents that were reminiscent of the greatships. The wood was everywhere; only when Nbaro met with her merchant contact did the androgyne explain to her that these were Desdemona-wood, a tree analogue with wood-like properties that was native to Madagascar. It was something like rosewood – which was common enough on

297

the greatship – except that it had an opalescent shimmer in low light that was both alien and thrilling.

Koinet Legishon was the name of her contact, and they had beautiful manners and were dressed in long, elegant robes with beads of gold woven in their hair that made Marca feel tawdry in her flightsuit, and garish with all her patches. But Koinet was mostly interested in tasting her coffee, which they did in a small coffee tavern on the main concourse of the orbital's promenade, a ring added inside the docking ring so that the elite patrons could sit in comfort away from the hoi polloi of the docks.

Marca sat in a deep, comfortable armchair that adjusted automatically to her height and weight and shape. Skipper Truekner, who'd accepted greetings with his usual courtesy, sat down, apologised for having so much work, and went back to his tab.

Koinet went behind a counter. There was one human employee and a number of robots and sub-AIs to wait on customers, but the androgyne had their own key of some sort. They brushed aside the automatic help to fetch a coffee grinder and a number of other devices, and they proceeded to measure off a kilo of coffee and grind it three different ways.

First, they produced an espresso from an ancient and very beautiful brass and brushed aluminium steamer. Truekner drank his without looking up; Koinet drank theirs in a single gulp, and Marca took hers in three long sips.

It was delicious, she thought, but she wasn't the buyer.

Then Koinet took some ground to a powder, placed it in water and brought it slowly to something short of a boil. It produced a dense, rich foam, and they handed her a spoonful, took some, and made an appreciative noise.

'This is from Haqq?' they asked.

'No,' Nbaro said. 'A private grower on Barcino.'

Thea had given her a script.

Koinet nodded.

The last grounds, the most coarsely ground, went into a press. Koinet asked Marca questions about the greatship and told her a little about the Mombasa orbital while they waited.

'I don't think anyone planned it to be a resort,' they said. 'But when the sulphur played out, and the industry demands changed, they had to try something or it would become a ghost. And one thing it had that was built in by the designers was a place to swim. Not a lot of those in space, eh?'

The core of the orbital was a huge column of water that included an entire Old Terra-based marine biology structure, with everything from starfish to dolphins and the largest live coral reef outside the Sol system. Marca watched the dolphins hunting as she tried her third coffee.

Koinet was leaning on a railing next to her.

'You know that before the Age of Chaos, they speculated that dolphins would make great space pilots?' they said.

'I didn't know that,' Marca admitted.

'Have you read any pre-spaceflight literature?'

'Probably too much,' she admitted. 'I loved *Middlemarch*. George Eliot.' Nbaro glanced at the Mombasan.

'Loved it,' they said. 'It's odd – they are suffused with misogyny and racism and yet they are so poignant and so descriptive, as if the authors had nothing but time to pour out their hearts.'

'I confess that when I read *Little Women*, I wondered if we've advanced as far as we claim,' she said.

'And no one has yet written a book called *Little Androgynes*,' Koinet said. 'We are sometimes the aliens among you.' They waved a hand. 'I don't mean to make you uncomfortable. You are easy to talk to.'

Marca smiled, because that's what Smoke had said. She was beginning to think it might be true.

'Your coffee is indeed excellent,' Koinet said. 'It's not as strong an espresso as we'd hoped, but the mid-range is excellent.

I'm going to lower my offer to forty a kilo, with an additional rider that if you'll sell us the supplier's details, we'll either offer you a small royalty or a flat finder's fee.'

Nothing in her briefing from Thea covered lowering the offer. And Nbaro *liked* Koinet.

Damn.

The charge on an in-system call to Thea would be ... high. Not prohibitively so, but enough money to make her hesitate.

Do the numbers, Nbaro thought.

The value of 2300 kilos at forty ducats a kilo was 92,000 ducats, less five ducats a kilo shipping, and less twenty ducats a kilo to the farmer. Her share of the profit at this price would be roughly 5000 ducats for about ten hours of work.

A little more than two months' pay.

'I'd like forty-two,' she said.

Koinet looked surprised.

'Ah, I'm not here to bargain,' they said. 'I have tested ...'

Nbaro nodded. 'I'm afraid we both made some assumptions, then. Will you be covering the shipping charges to move the coffee here and back to the ship?'

Truekner looked up from his tab. His look was amused, and also ... respectful.

Koinet produced a strikingly modern tab from their robes; it appeared to be a single slab of crystal.

They smiled ruefully. 'Apparently,' they said, 'I will take your cargo. At forty-one.'

Nbaro put a hand on their sleeve. 'I accept your forty-one. And let me say – that extra ducat per kilo will go to the farmer, not to me or my partner.'

Koinet frowned. 'You are merely consignees?'

'We're the ones taking the risk.'

Koinet nodded again. 'And the name of the supplier?'

'I have to ask my partner,' Nbaro said. 'I give you my word

that if she agrees, you shall have the name, for a royalty to be negotiated.'

'That is satisfactory.' They snapped their fingers, and a small drone appeared from outside, on the concourse, and flew in to land on their table. 'I have brought you a small gift,' they said.

Nbaro looked at Truekner, who nodded.

The drone opened to reveal a book; it wasn't really paper, but a sealed recycle finished like paper, and it was very elegant.

'I hope you like Jane Austen,' they said.

'I do!' she said.

Afterwards, after they'd exchanged thumbprints on three different contracts and Koinet had sub-designated for the other shippers on her cargo list and accepted all her parcels, the cargo load began.

Koinet and Marca strolled the concourse together. It was breathtaking; the designers had correctly aligned opulence and openness. It was the only wheel orbital Marca had seen where almost the entire sweep of the station was open inside, so that she could see all the way to the curved horizon from the promenade. The walls were lined with balconies and elaborate walkways and internal elevators, apartments and shops and tavernas, and every one of them had a view of that central column of water and the magnificent animals living there. Elevators ran through the water volume, and several maglev train lines.

'We keep asking Old Terra for a whale,' Koinet said. 'They claim our environment is too small, and yet most of their survival areas are no larger. Give us a pod, and we'll have a whole population in twenty years.'

'And then what?' she asked.

They shrugged. 'There's a dead inland sea on Mara, with a whole consortium looking to lower the salinity, introduce plankton and make it Terran sea habitat about 400 kilometres by 300. We could be the seed.'

Nbaro smiled. 'You dream big.'

Koinet nodded. 'Look around you,' they said. 'A hundred years ago, this was a failing mining orbital in a backwater system.'

She nodded. 'Human Space is changing.'

'And you are a patrician, Ms Nbaro. I looked into you. In time, perhaps you will be in politics. We want friends.'

Marca's world was getting more complicated by the day. And Koinet didn't seem like the kind of person to whom she could plead her poverty, especially after driving such a good deal on the coffee. In fact, she wondered if the entire purchase had been a set-up for Koinet to meet her.

'Do you know Jan Mpono?' Nbaro asked.

'We know her mother,' Koinet answered. 'She vouched for you. May I send you our thoughts on the whales?'

'Absolutely,' Marca said. 'Just understand, I'm not anyone. Yet.'

Koinet turned to her and put their hands together formally, and bowed.

'We are adept at making wagers and investments,' they said. 'I represent a group, of course. We own a good portion of this orbital and we have other interests. You appear ... an overlooked asset – perhaps a unique opportunity.'

Nbaro drew back.

They shook their head. 'We mean no offence and we're loyal DHC partners.'

'Who are *we*?' Nbaro asked.

They smiled. 'Call us the Mombasa Conglomerate. Ask Mpono.'

Nbaro bowed. 'I will. And I'll read your proposal about the whales.'

*

Back in the spacecraft, Nbaro got them off the orbital and into space, and then sat back into her acceleration couch with a sigh.

'What did you think of Tir Koinet?'

'High-end merchant type,' Truekner said. 'Gunning to make their fifty million and buy in. What were they buttering you up for?'

'My eventual vote in council,' she said.

They coasted along for a bit.

'I wouldn't be surprised if you made the Great Council,' Truekner said.

'I have no family and no money.'

'Hunh.' Truekner glanced at his tab. 'But you are *the* Nbaro, are you not? The head of your line?'

'Yes.'

'It's an old line. And you must have cousins ...?'

'Not many. Most of them went down with my parents.'

'But some. So you could probably assemble patronage. I'm a commoner, and I'm probably at my maximum rank in service. But I know how this is done, and so do lots of other folks. Your friend Ms Drake, for one. When you get back from cruise, you'll want to start picking up the reins of your line and looking—'

Nbaro was suddenly fighting back tears.

'Looking to make Thornberg play my sex-vid to the Great Council?' she asked.

Truekner was silent for a while, as the great emptiness of space passed across their screens, vast and inscrutable, and throwing brief human concerns into sharp contrast with its magnificent indifference.

'I take your point,' he said. 'On the other hand, you already have a medal, and Service is its own family. I'm not the spin doctor that you need, but I'm guessing that four years hence, someone smart could laugh that vid off, with her medals and

303

her veteran status, as the high jinks of an adolescent who grew into a salty officer. Edgy risk-taker, ram'em, damn'em.'

Nbaro was wiping the tears away ineffectually; in the zero g of the float before deceleration, they collected around the eyes. It was all very inefficient and a nasty comment on the fitness of the genome for space.

'How many old-family line-heads are there, anyway?' Truekner asked. 'Fewer than a thousand?'

Nbaro had never given it much thought, because to think about her status was to start a cascade of thoughts about loss and dead parents and the Orphanage. Now, in the relative emotional comfort of a spacecraft with Skipper Truekner, she looked into that abyss.

'About seven hundred,' she agreed.

'So if you chose to take your place, you'd be someone very quickly indeed. Which is why the conglomerate wants your friendship. Maybe it's why Thornberg has been so set against you.'

Nbaro nodded. She was coming to understand Thorberg and the Orphanage better all the time. Thornberg wanted *to own her.* He'd tried to break her, and then to capture her, and when that failed, he was willing to settle for blackmail. He'd never really cared about her accusations about his malfeasance. That was a red herring.

He wanted her name.

Why, though? Just money?

Nbaro finally had to use the special cloth for wiping her visor. It was hyper-absorbent, and it dealt with the tear-ball.

'I think I'll hire you as my campaign manager,' she said. 'Sir.'

Truekner nodded, as if that was a genuine offer.

'Let's make sure we survive the trip, then,' he said.

*

Nbaro didn't have time to meet Thea, or even talk between events; she was out of one craft and into another with Guille as pilot.

Today's Guille was more relaxed and far less into her usual teacher/student role, and they made two deliveries, one planet-side, then up out of the gravity well to a small orbital that handled freight forwarding for Madagascar, and back to the ship. Nbaro had never had such a good time with Guille.

She landed to find Thea waiting for her in the ready room, and the two went to EVA together.

'So?' Thea asked. 'I saw the contracts. You got forty-one. That's great. What happened?'

Marca told her the whole story, and Thea was interested.

'My mum warned me about this,' she said. 'About how some of the out-planets see us as future allies. Which I guess we might be. I'm certainly pro-whale, but then, let's be honest, isn't everyone? Though a plot to save whales could just be a nice cover story, right?'

'Exactly. Anyway, beans and bullets first. They want the name of the farmer.'

Nbaro explained, and Thea nodded.

'All good. An arrangement where everybody wins.'

Marca sent Thea the sub-contract, and Thea ran it through a routine that checked contracts for unique occurrences. Of course, Sabina had already checked it too.

'One per cent royalty is pretty standard,' she said. 'Let me do this part, OK?'

'All yours,' Nbaro said. 'Do I have the money in my account?'

'We need to register a partnership,' Thea said.

In fifteen minutes, with Spacer Chu as a witness, they had registered, paid a fee, and divided their first profit. Each of them left a thousand ducats in the newly created joint account.

'Let's face it,' Thea said. 'With me in Cargo and you flying,

305

we ought to be able to do this over and over again. We should find ourselves a nice little opportunity here in Sahel.'

'Gold?' Marca asked.

'We don't have the money to buy enough gold for it to work,' Thea said. 'But some entertainment electronics for the far stars?'

'I'm in. Here – I'll only take a thousand and leave the rest in our partnership.'

'I'll leave the same amount in, and look around for something good.'

'If I can, I'll go and pick it up,' Marca said, and they shook hands.

Day four at Sahel started with her first ever flight with Storkel, who was one of the few spacers who had been born on Old Terra. People said it was all right to ask Storkel about Old Terra, and he told stories throughout two long delivery events – stories as alien as the Starfish: about fishing in the ocean from an open boat, and storms at sea, and the geyser outside his parents' house – a house his family had owned for more than a thousand years, on an island called Iceland.

Storkel was one of the most striking people Nbaro had ever met – pale and blond, but with distinctly slanted eyes. And he was an excellent storyteller. When it was her turn to speak, she mentioned the SUA plans for whales, and he was instantly enthusiastic.

'Old Terra's oceans almost died,' he said. 'In fact, I think it's realistic to say that they *did* die. Most of them. The Far North struggled through, and some of the Pacific, and eventually they'll reseed the rest, I guess.' He raised his hands from the yoke to waggle them. 'Whales are massive, and wondrous,' he added. 'They're like space.'

'Like space?' Nbaro asked.

'When you look at space – really look at it – you know how small you really are, right?'

She nodded. 'Too true.'

'That's whales. One passed under my dad's boat once. It was probably forty feet down, and I suddenly knew how small I really was.'

The rest of the mission passed quickly enough: a load of quantum computer components for the far stars. They picked them up directly from an orbiting factory. Then Storkel landed them, and they ate bulbs of curry in maintenance while their craft was turned around. Every craft in the flight was in space or waiting to launch, and maintenance was running like a well-oiled machine. Nbaro stayed small and watched while she sucked down food and much-needed coffee. Terrible coffee, compared to what she'd had the day before.

Thea tabbed her.

'I have our electronics,' she said. 'Virtual play decks and some other interesting hardware, all self-powering off the owner's movements.'

'That ought to be popular at Far Point,' Marca said.

'And robust. We got a good deal, because I learned a terrible truth about the manufacturers. They want the robust models shipped out so they can sell a less sturdy version in system, and people will have to replace them more often.'

'Whereas out in the far systems…'

'Exactly. Four years until they get a replacement. Bad for the market share.' Thea laughed. 'Age of Chaos shit. Crass manipulative capitalism. Anyway, I'm buying us in for about fifty-five hundred, OK?'

'OK,' Marca said.

It was all pretend, anyway – they were gambling with money she'd never really earned, or held in her hand.

The electronics were waiting for her at Mtwara Orbital, and Nbaro collected them with a thumbprint, in a very unglamorous red recycle container, and then Storkel flew them around the planet to Zanzibar Orbital, where they collected a fortune in ground and cast lenses for high-end optics. Their human contact joked several times about making a careful landing, and Storkel did, coming back to the *Athens* at less than a metre a second so that the magnets slowed them like the gentle rocking of a baby's cradle. Then they turned around *again* for a drop down into the atmosphere to take a consignment of xenoglas to a customer who didn't trust the sky hook.

They were going to take off empty.

Storkel was as interested in cargo as Nbaro, and together they prowled the warehouse, asking the computer and the human merchant about various parcels.

Finally they found a standard recycle container with two dozen EVA suits with built-in nanoprocessor medkits and radiation hardening. They were intended for science teams in hazardous environments, and their armoured cloth outer layer incorporated the company's patented xenoglas fibre.

The merchant looked at his tab.

'Busted deal. Meant for the science team on the *Hong Kong* but they didn't take delivery. No reason given.' He looked again. 'Looks like it got bumped back by the freight elevator. The sky hook.' He shrugged. 'Automation doesn't always work.'

Marca called Thea, and Thea spoke first to Small Cargo and then, to her own amazement, straight to Morosini.

'We'll take 'em,' she said. 'There's a finder's fee, that's all we get.'

'Split with Storkel,' Marca said.

They went for orbit loaded with expensive EVA suits and matching helmets; at twenty thousand ducats a suit, Nbaro couldn't have bought them anyway. But the *Athens* could.

She and Storkel split a thousand ducats, which was a nice bonus and made him smile.

'Smoke said you were fun to fly with,' Storkel said, 'but she didn't mention that you have the very luck of the Irish, eh?'

'What was lucky about the Irish?' Nbaro asked.

'No idea, since they got invaded all the time.'

Nbaro crashed after Tactics, Damage Control and Boarding Party; got six hours of sleep, and woke to a damage control drill that woke her in a panic and had her standing in the middle of her stateroom, unable to identify where she was for ten long seconds.

The drill was intense but mercifully brief, and she was clean and in one of her shore-going silk suits in time to meet Smoke at the Fourth Deck airlock.

Mpono smiled at her. 'Is this a date?' they asked. 'I don't incline to your sort, but you look very nice.'

Nbaro smiled; perhaps blushed a little.

'I'm a little short on clothes,' she admitted. 'I bought this on Haqq.'

'It's a little too formal for me,' Smoke said. 'But hand-sewn silk is not a bad message to send to dockside shopkeepers. Let's go.'

Smoke took her along the ring of spacers' shops that lined the dockside ring of Kili Station. Many were corporate brands known throughout the Human Space, and some were purely there for space tourists, but Smoke took her to a shop that sold EVA boots that fitted, as well as custom-sized uniform boots for ship wear that were manufactured by a fabricator, while you waited, to your exact measurements. Nbaro bought a pair, and two more flightsuits, which came tailored and fitted to her small waist and broad hips. Finally, well down the curve of the dock, she bought a flight jacket and watched with immense pleasure as a machine produced her Flight 6 patch, her wings, and a name patch, all to go on the expensive, fireproof carbon-fibre shell. In a side room, the sub-AI scanned her, both undressed and in her flightsuit, and produced a flight jacket that fitted her *exactly*. While they waited, they wandered the shop looking at its museum-like exhibits, which included a 600-year-old US Navy flight jacket.

'They made them from *animals*?' Nbaro asked.

'Sheep's hair collars,' Smoke said. 'Cowhide shell. Remember, before you judge – cowhide was more fireproof than most of their fabrics.'

'The cows might not have agreed,' Nbaro said.

'You ate meat at my party on Ndola.'

'I can think one thing and do another, like everyone else,' Nbaro said, and Smoke laughed.

The price shocked her, but everything on Kili Station cost too much, and anyway, she could afford it. Smoke laughed when she hesitated.

'You'll have nowhere to spend it for about a year,' they said.

'Right.' Marca thumbprinted the form.

An hour later, they strolled back along the concourse. Nbaro wanted to wear the jacket, but it was in a bag that was itself a thing of beauty – a custom helmet bag that the shop had given her.

Nbaro was due for watch with Mpono in second shift, and they were going to do something first with Captain Fraser, so she went to one of the dockside bars, bought a glass of wine, and watched people for a while before calling Dorcas.

'Looks like I have a day off tomorrow,' she said to his message computer.

Then Nbaro paid a small fee to have her table provide local news, and she took it in, curated by Sabina. Much of it made no sense, and there was a sea of political information about upcoming local elections and redistribution of seats according to changing orbital populations that she knew nothing about. She read several nested articles about new ship designs with interest, and spent an hour reading up on the Mombassa Conglomerate, which proved to own everything from real estate on Old Terra to a controlling interest in the Mombasa Orbital and a new dockyard facility that was being billed as a second Kili Station.

She looked up when Dorcas sat down.

'Uh, hello,' she said. 'I never realised that there was *so much money* before.'

He was reading the table. 'It's because they trade with the DHC and with 普天下 Pǔ Tiān Xià,' he said, as if Nbaro had asked a question. 'They're expanding at an incredible rate – I think they must be on for twelve per cent growth.'

She leaned back. 'How did you find me?'

He shrugged. 'I asked Smith where you were.'

'Didn't it occur to you that I might enjoy being alone?' she asked.

He looked at her for a moment, head slightly to one side.

'Damn,' he said. 'No. Never occurred to me.'

'Well, that's honest.'

He got up. 'Apologies, Marca. Yes, I'm available tomorrow.'

'Hey, you're here. Tell me about 普天下 Pǔ Tian Xià?'

Nbaro tried to pronounce it carefully, the way Smoke and Dorcas both did.

He sat back down and ordered a rum punch.

'普天下 Pǔ Tiān Xià controls as large a region as the DHC. Both of them have relatively unproductive fringe colony worlds, but that's the nature of the expansion game, isn't it?'

'Is it?'

Talking to Dorcas was like rabbit-holing on the information web.

He looked at her, eyes narrowing.

'Are you teasing me?' he asked.

She shook her head and hid a smile behind her wine.

'Nope.'

'Think of the colonies as an investment that eventually pays off when they can be included in the trade system and have something to trade,' he said. 'Of course, they'll always pay for luxuries from the inner systems, but they have to have something the inner systems want too, right? Only, that development takes time, so for several generations, colonies are just resource pits. They depend on the resources of the mainframe.'

'I see that,' Nbaro said. 'And 普天下 Pǔ Tiān Xià?'

'Well, they have as many systems as we do,' he said. 'But they don't have xenoglas. They keep trying to invent xenoglas substitutes, but then, so do we … Anyway, Powhattan and Sahel are the crossroads between Palace and City.'

Nbaro drank down her wine.

'I have to go on watch,' she said, with real regret.

'There's another 普天下 Pǔ Tiān Xià ship out there,' he said. 'It's coming into dock, and Smith thinks it's going to dock right next to us.'

'So we'll be docked between two of their ships?'

'That's what we see. Morosini knows. I left you a note in your onboard log, but face to face is much nicer.' He nodded. 'And more secret, despite routine eavesdropping.'

Nbaro sighed. 'Ouch,' she said, looking at the docking bay configurations. 'Where are our battlecruisers?'

Dorcas looked around. 'This is not the place to discuss them. But they're … lurking.'

'Not good,' she said.

'Morosini is worried. And the bio-sniffer has detected the second part of the virus about forty times now. Someone must be fairly frustrated that we're not currently dying of a plague.'

Nbaro looked down at the Mombasa Conglomerate data.

'These people approached me,' she said.

'Really?' Dorcas asked. 'Fascinating.'

'They think I'm a good bet for Great Council,' she said.

'Or Doje,' he said. 'I'm with them. Please keep your eyes open on watch, Marca. Those EVA suits you bought?'

'Yeah?'

'They're a clue. A forgotten relic of whatever happened to the *Hong Kong*. Or that's what Morosini thinks.' He got up as Nbaro rose. 'I may have insufficient data to make a prediction, but I'll wager that there will be an attack on the *Athens* in the next twelve hours.'

'Not good for our *safari* tomorrow,' she said.

He smiled. 'Let's get through today.'

Nbaro walked briskly along the curving surface of the dock, noting that there were armed SUA soldiers at most of the cargo and passenger hatches, and came to the *Athens* brow. She slipped past a crowd of tourists gawking at the greatship, tabbed her ID, and walked aboard. Glancing back, Nbaro saw Lieutenant Svaro, the man who had been on watch the day she signed aboard, standing in a first class uniform, and she waved.

He smiled. 'Have a good time?' he asked.

She nodded and flourished her flight jacket.

He made a gesture, half wave, half salute.

'I have to go and herd cats,' he said. 'My third tour group today. Never seen so many tourists.'

Nbaro headed towards the drop-shafts and her stateroom, thinking, *If we're facing a fight, why are we allowing tourists aboard?*

And something bothered her about the tourists.

Nbaro wore her new flight jacket into Space Ops, aware that ancient soldiers had dressed up to fight. It hid her shoulder holster beautifully, and the outer shell was close to armour.

Also, she loved it.

I am suddenly a material girl, she thought.

When she entered, the watch officer was Lieutenant Commander Dawa, and Commander Lee from Flight 5 was Tower. Lee waved; Dawa briefed Nbaro as if as she was the oncoming watch officer, and she had to explain that she was only under instruction.

He nodded. 'I know, Midder,' he said, as if her rank gave away her inexperience, which, while it was annoying, was also true. 'But more people in the loop can't be bad.'

'I'm told there's a second PTX ship docking next to us,' Nbaro said.

'Shit,' he said. 'Says who?'

'Morosini.'

He read a screen.

'You're a well-informed junior. Thanks.' He read his screen again. 'Shit.'

'I'm going to sit at Weps,' she said. 'If you don't mind.'

'Good thought,' he said, already talking to the Tactical Action Officer in the Combat Centre.

Nbaro went to the empty Weps station. They were a shore watch, but with the modification that they had spacecraft to launch and recover. The other command centres would barely be manned; Bridge and Combat would have skeleton crews and Engineering would be almost empty.

Her Weps station was mostly a repeater; no one fired weapons from Space Operations. But Nbaro signed out a VR helmet anyway, so she could 'see' the system in real time – or the real time that Morosini lived in. The VR helmet projected the status around the station across her reality, and the VR image was semi-transparent so she could still interact with her station and those around her. She'd used it a dozen times; she was by no means expert, but she knew what buttons to press.

Nbaro pushed her tab functions to a head-up display in the VR. Dorcas pinged her almost immediately.

She was surprised to see him appear in three artificial dimensions of virtual reality.

'Neural lace,' he said. 'I'm always in VR and in reality. And Morosini's reality.'

'I'm on watch,' she said.

'This isn't a social call,' Dorcas said. 'People just died in a terrorist attack on Kili Station. Smith thinks they went for the Control Module. Be advised.'

Nbaro raised her VR visor and glanced at the Lioness station. Mpono had just walked in, a bulb of coffee in one hand and a headset in the other. Dawa was leaning forward, watching something.

'Lioness, there's a situation on the station,' she said.

And, like a gunshot, something came together in her mind. *All the tourists in the queue had been of military age.*

'I'm seeing a report from security,' Dawa said. 'Nothing to do with us.' He paused. 'Whereas that PTX ship is docking *right now*.'

Nbaro flipped her visor down, and saw the second Pǔ Tiān Xià ship gliding into the angled dock position next to the *Athens*. The *Athens* was more than twice as long, but the two PTX ships were still enormous, dwarfing any other ships in the station dock.

Suddenly, there was a man in red with a cat standing next to her station, and he was the most sharply defined presence she'd ever seen in VR.

'Morosini,' she said.

'*I'm under attack*,' he said.

Nbaro knew he must be saying this to every watch officer on duty and to the bridge at the same time – it wasn't just her – but her adrenaline surged.

Behind her, Mpono was just settling into the lioness chair.

'We're under attack,' Marca said loudly.

Mpono looked at her, and suddenly all their screens flashed red.

Battle Stations. This is not a drill.

Stand by for acceleration.

Ship Integrity in sixty seconds.

Battle Stations. This is not a drill.

Nbaro was on the comms with station, and station was not responding.

There was *someone* on the bridge. The Master's voice said, 'Kili Station, this is *Athens* Command. Emergency breakaway in ten, nine, all lines dropped, seven, we have cargo bay sealed, five, four, brow sealed, two, one.'

'You fucking can't! Stop!' shouted the station. The voice sounded angry and, somehow, not like the station. 'You'll blow the whole deck!'

'Emergency breakaway. Emergency breakaway.'

The greatship shuddered.

Almighty. We're breaking away from a station with a million people aboard, with no warning.

Her board lit up with comm requests.

Her board lit green in four places. Weapons were hot. Somewhere in Combat, they had warmed the main railguns and all the point defence turrets.

Nbaro was having a little trouble taking in the rate of change, the volume of data. She'd only arrived for her watch six minutes ago. Now she was ...

'We're taking fire, repeat, taking fire.'

That was the TAO in the Combat Information Centre. She sounded calm and rational.

Marca could feel the *Athens* taking hits. On her VR, she saw red lines – small-calibre railguns, she guessed, firing from the flanks of the recently arrived PTX freighter...

Only it wasn't a freighter. It was a Q-ship – a disguised warship. Nbaro could see the disguised turrets emerging from the ship's shell, firing, and vanishing, the smoothness of their operation almost organic.

Mpono's voice – private comms.

'I'm behind... What the fuck?' they asked.

'Launch all the alerts,' Nbaro said. 'We're under attack, tir.'

Mpono sat back as if they'd been shot; it was only ten seconds since they'd sat down. Then they raised a hand.

'Listen up!' they roared. 'Full launch!'

Every hand in Space Ops went up. It was a drill they practised. 'Now!'

The hands came down. Every head went down to its screen. Orders rolled out as Lioness launched the Alert 5 as soon as the bow had cleared the station. It wasn't Ko; it was Talhoffer, a woman Nbaro had only met once.

Ko's voice in her headset. 'I'm armed and hot. Launch me.'

'This is Alpha Foxtrot 6–0–1, armed and hot, ready to launch.'

Mpono was talking to Ko, so Nbaro took a moment to talk to her skipper.

'Roger, 6–0–1, you are two to launch.'

The Tactical Action Officer said, 'Weapons Free on my command. Target the—'

Morosini's voice said, *'No fire,'* his calm inhumanity cutting across every channel.

The TAO said, 'Roger, *Athens* Command. I hear you. We are taking fire and—'

'I forbid you to fire,' Morosini said.

In VR, the man in red with the cat was still standing there.

'It's too complicated to explain,' he said.

What if he's compromised? she thought.

'*Athens* Command, this is TAO requesting human command override.'

Is that even a thing? Human command override?

Morosini said, '*They must not fire. That's what the enemy wants – a space fight here in the heart of SUA space. They tried to hack me and only got my clone, who I have just eliminated. They have full control of the weapons systems on the Jian Ye, but only for another eighteen or nineteen seconds. We are not under attack from the 普天下 Pŭ Tiān Xià. This is not a war. I repeat, this is not a war.*'

'Don't fire!' Nbaro shouted over the Weps frequency.

'I'm taking command from Auxilliary Control,' said another voice. 'This is Captain Aadavan, taking command. Prepare to open fire on all PTX units...'

She was thinking more clearly than she'd ever thought in her life. She could see how the attacks might be coming together...

Nbaro thought of the tourists in the queue. A crowd of military age.

And Smith suggesting that he was next.

And Aadavan taking command from Morosini...

How big is this? she thought, then: *Better hanged for a lion than a lamb.*

Nbaro toggled her comms with the Marine detachment.

'Gunny Drun,' said her friend. 'What's up, miz...?'

'Gunny, I need a fire team to deploy. I think we have enemy boarders loose on the ship—'

'On my way,' he said, instead of asking for an explanation.

In VR Nbaro said, 'Morosini, I think we have armed adversaries already on board.'

Morosini looked at her in VR.

'*Of course*' He nodded. '*My clone was more compromised than I thought. Of course.*'

He vanished.

The TAO said '*Athens* Command! Come in! Damn it, Lioness,

318

I've lost contact with the bridge. Is Auxilliary Control in command? Come in!'

Dorcas reappeared in VR. 'You're about to be attacked. Do you have your weapon?'

'What?' Nbaro asked, having trouble processing it all.

Ko was launching, the next spacecraft moving onto the rails; Nbaro could see movement in a Sixth Deck corridor as she conjured up the cameras there. The TAO was sounding strident, her voice higher.

'Do I have weapons free or not, damn it!' she spat.

Then something hit Space Ops. Nbaro didn't see it; she only saw the flash of blue light and white-hot metal sprayed and Commander Lee was hit, her suit leaking blood. The Tower console had a perfect round hole that matched one above her to the right, and then another in the deck. Air began to shriek out.

'Outside Space Ops,' Dorcas said, and gave her a window showing the passageway. It was full of tourists...

'Shit,' Nbaro said. She said it several times, but she was moving, and her brain was working.

Those were definitely not tourists. And they were armed...

They were affixing something to the big armoured door that led into Space Ops.

Nbaro saw it all, as if her head was a tactical display. And she knew the solutions – all of them, as if they were written inside her VR helmet. It was remarkable, to think so clearly.

'Everyone down!' Nbaro roared over the shriek of air emptying through the hole.

She was already off her couch and she ran to the hatch. Smoke was flat on their acceleration couch, bleeding in several places; blood was literally running off their holed acceleration couch. And she couldn't stop to help them. Lee was badly wounded; perhaps dieing.

Not my job right now.

The pistol was in her hand.

'Dorcas!' Nbaro barked. 'Give me the drones at Port Side Aft frame 366.'

'You have them.'

'Close the iris valves either side of our passageway.'

'Ahead of you.'

Nbaro looked at the corridor outside with her VR visor, and the swarm of angry men, all of them now pointing at the closed airlock doors at either end of the section of passageway. She saw no bystanders, and they were seconds from firing the charge on her hatch. She had a clear view; it was a shaped charge with a magnet. She'd handled the DHC version in drills, to do just this – blow an armoured hatch.

'Launch!' she said.

The drones burst out of their housings – the size of children's balls. A man yelled silently in VR, except that Nbaro could hear his shout even through the armoured door.

'Fire!' she said.

The drones detonated, and she heard the muffled screams.

Behind her, a spacer had reached Commander Mpono with a medkit in his hand. Another was kneeling by Lee.

'Auxiliary Control just went off the air,' Chief Kelly reported from the bridge repeater. 'I think you blew all the wiring on O-3 level, ma'am.' Kelly, at least, sounded calm. Behind him, another Spacer was putting an emergency patch on the hole in the overhead, but the air loss had already stopped. Damage control was underway on the hull.

Nbaro took a breath, steadying herself. The drones had destroyed most of the cameras in the passageway, but she could see enough.

She cycled the door, and it swung inwards.

There were three men still standing, all looking at her. They'd been protected from the drones by the slight inset of the door, and Nbaro was ready for them.

She shot the first one from about ten centimetres away, because he was pressed against the door, and he all but stumbled in, and then the second, and the third, her pistol firing a continuous stream of flechettes like a liquid knife.

Nbaro stepped to her right, fanning the corridor with her flechettes, and slammed the armoured door closed again. The first man had fallen into Space Ops and the door hit his head and outflung arm. She kicked him, hard, rolled him back, and the hatch slammed closed.

Moving the dying man took long enough that Nbaro had to face the results of her drone attack. The corridor was a charnel house, a sticky abattoir she'd remember for the rest of her days, but she already had lock boxes to hold the other traumas, and this could join them: the Orphanage; Sarah being torn away; Salim in a pool of his own blood…

Focus.

Nbaro looked at the VR instead of the reality behind it. Morosini, or the Bridge, had rolled the ship and dropped them out of the line of fire of the docked PTX ship unless it, too, broke its connection to the station.

Two Gunslingers had launched. They were now between the station and the greatship, which was below the plane of the station's docking bays.

Morosini said, '*I may lose artificial gravity soon. The Combat Information Centre is under attack.*'

Nbaro was trying to access the bridge.

'You still believe we should not fire?'

Nbaro saw the PTX Q-ship launch two torpedoes on her VR visor and she designated the torpedoes hostile for the Gunslingers.

'Weapons free,' she said. 'Torpedoes only. Repeat, torpedoes only.'

'Roger, Lioness,' Talhoffer said.

The torpedoes should have had three-second burns, but they'd been fired softly, the same way the spacecraft had been launched from the *Athens*, and they had to burn just to get velocity; they also had to fly a sharp curve from their launch that cost them time.

They began to accelerate, and the *Athens* was only three kilometres from the station.

She was betting their lives and her career, such it was, on Morosini. Aadavan in Aux Con... probably didn't have the whole story. Gods, or Morosini was already hacked.

God.

'Don't—' Morosini said.

'Human override!' Nbaro shouted.

A muffled *bang*.

'Dorcas?'

He appeared in VR with a pistol in each hand.

'A little busy here,' he said.

'I need to see CIC and the passageway outside,' she said. 'I no longer have any visual feeds...'

He waved a pistol as if it was a magic wand, and Nbaro had the passageway: eight men. No women – whoever these bastards were, they were all men.

The armoured door into CIC was open – blown open. There was smoke in the air and the camera picture was poor and the angle was not what she would have liked, but someone in CIC was holding out.

'Dorcas, close the iris valves at...'

Almighty God, what frame number?

'Got it. CIC, both ends.'

322

Nbaro watched on her screen, as the drones tore into them. Apparently no one had warned them about the drones.

The Gunslingers downed the two torpedoes and she shut off their weapons free.

'Bridge,' Nbaro said.

Morosini reappeared and said, *'At the moment, I'm the bridge.'* He looked bad – bitmapped and tattered.

'What's the status of the PTX ship?' she asked.

Nbaro toggled up her ship-wide comms. She was a midshipper, one of the lowest officers on the ship. But desperate times demanded desperate measures.

Morosini was silent.

'Boarding parties, this is your Alpha Papa event, repeat, Alpha Papa. Captain Fraser to Space Ops.'

Morosini appeared. *'I overestimated the capabilities of PTX military intelligence. The hackers still control her weapons systems, but not of the second ship, which is under lockdown and whose captain is screaming at the Yung Li. If the conflict continues, they may join the engagement in our defence.'* His voice sounded heavy, robotic; not at all like his usually cultured, Italianate demeanor.

Nbaro looked back over Space Ops and identified Chief Petty Officer Kelly.

'Chief, can you take Lioness?'

Chief Kelly had blood on his face and all down one side, and had clearly taken some spalling from the railgun hit.

'Yes, miz.'

'Good. You have Space Ops.'

'Yes, miz.'

Nbaro looked down at Mpono, but they were unconscious.

'Show me the bridge?' she said through her VR connection.

Morosini said, *'I have no connection to the bridge.'*

'Give me Gunny Drun, comms.'

'Miz?'

323

'Gunny. Situation?'

'Four dead bogeys and a lot of hurt spacers,' he said. 'Sixth Deck is pretty bad. We're securing it as we go. Not yet to Special Services.'

'Roger.'

Morosini was with Nbaro in the VR as she put her hand on the hatch access panel.

'Where are you going?' Morosini asked.

'I'm going to take any boarding party volunteers who come this way and clear the passageway to CIC,' she said.

'*I must advise against that*,' Morosini said.

'Why?'

'*At the moment, you are the sole line-of-command officer that I can reach. You are the commander of the Athens.*'

TAO was down; Master and Bridge were off the air, the link to Aux Con was destroyed; Lioness was unconscious.

'Shit,' Nbaro said.

But she tabbed the door anyway.

It slid open and the dead men seemed to push into Space Ops. Nbaro waved at Kristianopoulis, the comms petty officer.

'Close the hatch behind me,' she said.

Nbaro grabbed the corpse of the small man she'd shot point-blank and rolled him off the second so that he was clear of the hatch.

She stepped over the first pile of corpses, her pistol covering the corridor, and then moved aft towards the CIC.

She took cover and tabbed the iris open.

Blue coveralls – two in armour. A boarding party team. Nbaro lowered her pistol, and the surprised-looking petty officer looked as if she'd seen a ghost.

'Who's in charge?' Nbaro barked, hoping that she didn't sound desperate, but they were all junior spacers, bar the single petty officer. She put the armoured people in front and sketched the

324

situation briefly. She was heartened by their reaction – anger, determination.

'We have to take down anyone we come across,' Nbaro said. 'They don't have armour and they don't know much about the ship.'

'We'll just fuckin' teach 'em,' growled the petty officer.

She gathered them in two sticks – short files that could stay together and support each other, even in smoke or low visibility – and then had them tab the next iris valve.

Someone fired at them. Heavy slug-thrower, automatic fire, some of it going into the overhead, and a lot of ricochets. Her people went into cover; only the petty officer in armour leant out and got hit. She wasn't wounded, but she was knocked flat.

Nbaro could see the shooter, twenty frames away.

She went forward, jumped the knee-knocker, and as her adversary leant out...

She fanned flechettes across his position, fell forward, rolled into cover, and struggled to her feet.

No return fire.

Trap? Or dead?

Only one way to be sure.

'Follow me!' Nbaro roared. Terror and courage became the same thing, and she charged.

She burst from cover. She hurdled the next knee-knocker and the dying man behind it. He had a small-calibre pistol in his waistband and Nbaro took it.

Shoot him in the head?

No.

Nbaro had reached the closed iris valve that separated her from the passageway in front of CIC. Her boarding party was catching up, and there were two more in armour, both petty officers.

One was Locran. She'd seldom been so happy to see a familiar face.

'Miz,' he said, as if this sort of thing happened every day.

'Petty Officer Locran,' she said. 'We need to retake CIC. Dorcas?'

'Here,' he said in VR.

'I need to see CIC.'

'I really must teach you to do this for yourself,' he said. 'There.'

Nbaro was watching through two cameras, one either side of the TAO console; it was disorientating. So was the blood and the death... the TAO was dead; the attackers had shot everyone in the CIC. The insurgents themselves didn't look good – half a dozen men planting what had to be charges, and one trying to...

'Dorcas, isolate CIC from Morosini,' Nbaro said.

'Did it four minutes ago,' he said smugly.

'Locran, we're attacking straight through into CIC. When we open this iris valve, I'll lead us—'

'Best let me lead, miz,' Locran said. 'You're an officer, and I have armour... miz.'

Nbaro took a breath. She *wanted* to lead the way. Ordering Locran to lead the way felt... terrible. She shook her head, but only at herself.

'Right. You'll lead us straight in. No hesitation, understood? Shoot 'em. Locran, go low through the CIC hatch. You – Painter? You go high. Anyone have a grenade?'

No one did.

'Dorcas?'

'Yes?'

'Can you fly two drones into CIC and detonate them?'

Two long seconds.

'You think we have no friendlies alive?'

'They shot them all.' Nbaro said it coldly.

Dorcas waved a hand and fire seemed to flow from it.

'Detonation...'

'Go!' Nbaro yelled, and tabbed the iris valve.

'Now,' Dorcas said.

Locran and Painter went through the opening passageway hatch. Nbaro followed, already aware that she hadn't set an order for the rest of the stick.

I'm an idiot.

Morosini said, '*I really don't recommend*—'

She took the VR helmet off and dropped it.

Locran arrived at the bent hatch of CIC, the blackening and distortion clearly showing in a single glance what the door bombs could do – and would have done to Space Operations. Painter was slow, having tripped over a body, and was visibly alarmed by the corpses. Locran threw himself across the hatch's lintel, prone, and fired in with a shotgun.

Painter fought through her disorientation and her rising gorge, fired a boarding pistol at waist height into CIC, went over Locran and into the room.

She was hit. Nbaro saw her stagger and get hit a second time.

Painter was dropping as Nbaro went over the knee-knocker behind her. She had the flat pistol set for three-round bursts, and she identified one shooter and dropped him before Painter ceased to offer her cover. Nbaro went left, behind the torpedo station. They'd shot the torpedo watch officer, a warrant officer with thirty years' experience, and he lay glassy-eyed in his acceleration couch, his face and neck a bloody mess.

Nbaro guessed their attackers didn't know CIC the way she did – didn't know that the various computerised stations had a gap underneath them. She dropped all the way to the floor and shot a pair of bare tourist legs, and then another. When the first fell, she shot him as he writhed on the deck. Then she rolled over and stripped off her precious flight jacket, which had a burn

327

mark up the back. She was bleeding in several places – from ricochets or spalding from one of the railgun hits, she didn't know. Everything was focused, laser-tight, on the moment at hand.

Nbaro wriggled under the torpedo console. She just fitted, and adrenaline and will and some torn clothing got her into the next aisle. She rolled right and almost shot Locran.

'Clear,' he said. He was bleeding.

'Painter?'

'Didn't crack her armour. Took two in the chest, though.' Locran said the last with a sort of wry experienced look. 'Lot of cracked ribs.'

Nbaro got to her feet, aware that she'd torn her flightsuit all the way down the back, and she moved to the first enemy and kicked his gun away. Then the second.

'Miz, I'm still the one wearing armour,' Locran said.

Nbaro cleared the third.

'Good point,' she said.

Her hands had just started to shake, and abruptly she could barely stand.

They went from body to body. Two were alive, one with his jaw shot away. The other had a grenade, and Locran shot him before he activated it.

He looked down at the dead man.

'Shit,' he said.

His one word, and his look at the dead man, encompassed a world of disgust – and empathy. The dead man was perhaps sixteen years old; he'd lain, badly wounded, with his grenade, waiting to take someone with him, and he'd botched it and died.

'Shit,' agreed Nbaro, who was shaking like a leaf now.

Locran nodded to her; she'd seldom communicated so much with so few words. The dead invaders were all terribly young, all except the computer or comms expert, dead at the comms station, ripped to pieces by Painter's boarding pistol. He was heavily tattooed and, judging from the glint of metal inside his ruined skull, had possessed a neural lace.

Nbaro was thinking twenty things at once, but what she said was, 'Who are they?'

'Hold on a second, miz,' Locran said.

He reached into his coverall, produced a roll of emergency tape, and taped the back of her flightsuit closed. He smiled. His hands were also shaking, but he didn't drop the tape, or the small knife he'd apparently pulled out of the air.

'CIC secure,' Nbaro said into her tab before she realised that she hadn't called anyone, and the VR visor was out in the passageway with the other dead.

She didn't even know how to tab Morosini.

Nbaro went back into the passageway, seeing her boarding party had secured both ends as far as the mess and Space Ops. She tried to ignore the human wreckage made by the drones and she got the VR helmet back on, noticing that one of her hands was covered in blood, sticky with it, and her flightsuit...

'CIC secure,' she said again.

Morosini nodded. '*Your orders?*'

Nbaro took a deep breath. She still had the local tactical display available on VR; they were fifteen kilometres from the station and pulling away.

'I think we should hover at a reasonable distance to have sufficient time to react to a railgun or missile attack.'

'*Concur,*' Morosini said. '*One hundred kilometres?*'

'Take us out to one hundred kilometres,' she said. 'And below – off axis.'

'*Very well,*' Morosini said.

'Are you injured?' she asked.

'*Yes, I am. Several ways.*'

329

'I think we need to retake the bridge,' she said. 'What's the PTX ship's status?'

'The Command Deck has been retaken. Kili Station is demanding that they allow a station security team aboard. The PTX authorities are refusing.'

'And we've not fired?' she asked.

'Your Gunslingers fired anti-missiles to kill the torpedoes,' Morosini said.

Nbaro sighed. 'There must be an officer senior to me.'

'And as soon as one reports in, I'll put her in charge,' Morosini promised.

Nbaro stood up straighter. She was a few frames from her stateroom.

'The XO is in Aux Con. Can you reach him?'

'No,' Morosini said.

'Then we have to retake the bridge. You don't even have cameras?'

'No,' Morosini said.

'Dorcas?'

'I'm here,' he said.

It was odd. He was standing there in VR, and so was Morosini with his cat, who looked … bad.

The *cat* looked better. Less fuzzy, crisper, as if the cat had better resolution in VR.

Nbaro scooped up her armour and her sword, and dragged herself out of her stateroom and back down the corridor.

'Dorcas, did Drun get to you?'

'Like the proverbial cavalry,' Dorcas said. 'Smith is hit.'

'Care to speculate on what's happening on the bridge?'

'Morosini can't see there because he cut himself off from it. Danger of contamination.'

Dorcas sounded exactly as he always did, and that steadied her.

'OK.'

Marca was gathering boarding parties as she went.

She saw Captain Fraser outside Space Ops. He looked pale, like any normal person standing amid the cooling destruction of a dozen human lives.

'Thank God, sir,' she said. 'You're in command.'

'Command?' Fraser said. 'Of the boarding parties.'

'Of the ship.'

He shook his head. 'No. I'm an astrophysicist, not a line officer.'

'Shit,' she said.

He gave her a look. 'Who's commanding the *Athens*?'

'I am,' she said miserably.

Fraser nodded. 'Very well, miz.'

Nbaro looked at him and straightened up.

'We need to retake the bridge,' she said.

Fraser was fully armoured.

'I've practised it a dozen times,' he said.

'I'm with you. Just give me time to get into my armour.'

'With due respect, miz,' Fraser said, 'no. You manage the ship from Space Ops. We'll take the bridge.'

Nbaro looked back at Locran, who had someone's emergency dressing on his right bicep and was standing with a shotgun over his left shoulder. He nodded.

'Yes, miz,' he said, in the way that spacers could imply pending disapproval with an affirmative. Then he pulled her flight jacket out of his breastplate and handed it to her. 'You dropped this, miz.'

She smiled. 'Thanks, Locran.'

She turned back to Fraser. 'Sir, they seem to have very little shipboard experience. They have no armour, but they have advanced computer penetration devices and shocking number of small explosives. I think their are about sixty, all told.

331

They came in as tourists, and there may have been assault boats on the hull; I can't know.'

Fraser nodded. 'Got it.' He put a hand on her shoulder. 'You're bleeding.'

'I'm fine,' she said. 'Mostly.'

Nbaro got into her armour anyway, and took the Lioness couch in Space Ops, which was still sticky with Mpono's blood. A dozen medical techs were triaging and clearing the wounded.

'I need one person for CIC,' Nbaro said, recovering a little after a spacer handed her a bulb of hot coffee. 'We've a wounded enemy there. Jaw shot away. I need him alive. Take someone with a gun.'

A tech saluted and collected a Marine...

Marines?

Major Darkstar came in, took the weapons console, and began working the screens.

'I guess this is the bridge, right now,' Nbaro said aloud.

Darkstar looked at her. 'I have weapons, miz,' they said. 'All green and hot. Your orders?'

'We're not shooting back, no matter what the provocation, unless Morosini and I order it,' Nbaro said.

Nicely put, Morosini said in her ear.

Marca settled back and did something familiar.

'Alpha Echo 5-o-2, what is your status, over?'

'Lioness, good to hear the sound of your voice. We're between you and the station, manoeuvring to keep that position, over.'

'Roger, 5-o-2. We had a bit of difficulty here – seems to be resolved. Please cover our movements if the bogeys try another torpedo, over?'

'Roger that, Lioness.'

Nbaro looked at the space around the station and saw two other ships had broken free and were running; one was already moving under heavy *g*, directly away towards... somewhere.

Running could indicate guilt or fear. Nbaro didn't know. She toggled main comms and Kristianopoulis nodded and pointed at her.

'Kili Station, this is *Athens*, over,' Nbaro said.

Long pause.

'*Athens*, this is Kili Station.' No apologies, no further information.

'Kili Station, we have been attacked in cyberspace, attacked by boarding parties, and have taken fire and torpedoes from the PTX ship. Do you copy, Kili Station?'

'*Athens*, we have cameras on almost every angle of the disturbance—'

Nbaro cut Kili Station off. 'We have a dozen or more dead, Kili Station, and you have half our crew still in your corridors.'

Pause. 'Kili Station does not hold *Athens* responsible in any way for today's actions. Likewise, Kili Station was not the instigator of the attack. Our investigation is ongoing.'

Dorcas appeared in VR. 'Captain Fraser is asking Morosini to vent all the air from the Bridge,' he said.

'Concur,' Nbaro said. 'Dorcas, can you do that without Morosini having to ... I don't know. Contaminate himself?'

Dorcas raised both hands like a man casting a spell in a vid. 'Got it.'

Nbaro raised Fraser. 'Are you going in from outside?'

He didn't grin, but he was wearing his armour over a vac suit on a side screen thoughtfully provided by Morosini.

'Yes, miz. And we have a little surprise – there's a hatch onto the Bridge from medical. And another from the escape pod on O-7.'

'Good hunting' Nbaro said, for lack of something better.

Ten minutes later, and somewhat anticlimactically, Fraser was on the Bridge.

'Master's alive, but in no condition to command,' he said. 'So's everyone else but the signals yeoman. They're going to need oxygen for a while.' He sighed, but he looked... happy. 'And we'll need to repair the window.'

Their Marines had slapped an emergency airlock over the big window, cut a hole in it, and gone in.

'Practised this a hundred times,' Major Darkstar said. In their clipped, professional tone, they went on, 'And this is why we practise. So nothing goes wrong.'

Marine fire teams began a clear and secure operation on every deck.

Medical teams fanned out behind them.

Damage control went to work.

Nbaro spent another hour doing nothing but managing damage control; Morosini had a bias towards his own self-protection and the restoration of circuits, and she overrode him once to get the holes leaking air patched first. A bomb-detection unit began to sweep the ship, starting in CIC. Dorcas came to Space Operations briefly, and then went back out, headed for the Bridge with some kind of elaborate computer equipment. Science teams tested for biological and chemical weapons left behind – poisons, traces...

Nbaro gave almost no orders after the initial assignment of damage control teams. She talked to the four deployed spacecraft, then sent out her own squadron's alerts, and finally launched one of the two pinnaces, noting that the other was not there. By the time the pinnace was crewed and launched, the holes in the hull had been patched and a lieutenant commander had been found at his battle station as a damage control officer. He came into Space Ops looking tired.

Nbaro sprang to her feet.

'Sir,' she said. 'You have command.'

'Allah be praised,' he said. 'You were *commanding the ship*?'

334

Nbaro managed a smile. 'Yes, sir.'

He nodded.

'All yours,' she said.

'I see,' he said, and she saw the weight of it settle on him.

About ten minutes later marines restored comms to Aux Con and a very angry Captain Aadavan took command. From the harsh gravel of his voice, Nbaro assumed he'd been shouting at a dead comm unit for hours.

10

'I think the technical term for it is a clusterfuck,' Dorcas said.

He was sitting at the end of Smith's autodoc in Medical.
Nbaro was sitting next to Smith, who was mostly a disembodied
head emerging from what looked like a large clamshell.

He made a noise.

Dorcas leaned towards him and then nodded.

'Yes, they made more mistakes than we made, but the whole
attack was ridiculously elaborate.'

'And they almost got us anyway,' Smith whispered. 'And God,
we were unprepared. Even after the nuke. I was looking too low.
Big and elaborate, that's ...'

'Three things saved us,' Dorcas said. 'They never considered
that their precious hacking team was taking down Morosini's
clone, even though firewall cloning is a tried and true defence.
And their attack on and from the station went off almost two
minutes early and gave us warning. Nbaro and I saw right
through it—'

'I didn't!' Nbaro said.

'You did too!' Dorcas said. 'You spotted the tourists ...'

'Luck,' she said.

Dorcas shrugged. 'And the two Gunslingers destroyed the

336

incoming torpedoes. Which, let me add, wouldn't have crippled a greatship, but they'd have hurt us.'

'And the explosions would have damaged the station,' Nbaro said.

Dorcas nodded. 'Yes. That's true.'

'And you took a prisoner,' Smith whispered.

Dorcas pointed. 'She did.'

'Again, it was luck,' she said. 'They all had poison capsules. The poor man had his lower jaw shot away so he couldn't suicide. All the rest did, including everyone who took the Bridge.'

Dorcas smiled a nasty little smile. It wasn't an expression that Marca liked. 'I don't think that they suicided,' he said. 'I think they were pushed.'

'Pushed?' she asked.

'A signal that triggered the suicide capsules.'

Marca shuddered.

'Anyway, why didn't they kill everyone on the Bridge, when they'd killed everyone in CIC?' Dorcas asked, arms spread wide.

Nbaro knew that one.

'Morosini says they were supposed to ransom the Master. And they were trying to take Morosini out right up until the end.'

'Or scuttle the ship,' Dorcas said. 'Because all of this was intended to end in the destruction of the *Athens*.' He was looking out into the medbay. 'Or they expected to be rescued, and to take the Bridge crew as hostages. Yes, that must be it – one of those fast freighters which undocked was with them…'

Nbaro cursed. 'I could have sent a torpedo into one.'

Very weakly, Smith said, 'No.'

Nbaro looked at him, but Yu came and put a hand on her shoulder.

'He can't take any more today,' Yu said. 'And I have too many casualties to allow you to make more work for me.'

*

The *Athens* hung twenty kilometres off the station; that was the closest the Master and Morosini would approach. Their own landing barges went back and forth with the spacers who'd been on liberty ashore on Sahel or the orbitals, and Nbaro flew a dozen emergency drops to the surface, picking up spacers stranded by the crisis or cargoes that had expected more time to prepare. It was mostly electronic and nano wizardry intended for Starfish trade, much of it built specifically for the Starfish, based on guesses and diagrams.

The landing barges and the cargo shuttles also carried raw materials. The *Athens* had been hit, hard. She needed repairs, and new equipment. The entire Combat Information Centre was a write-off; Space Ops wasn't much better and the Bridge needed work, so the Master took advantage of the hi-tech industries of Sahel to purchase new equipment, with Morosini's ghostly hand on his shoulder throughout. Every spacer coming aboard, and every item of equipment or material purchased, was inspected by both people and machines. The greatship's external control interfaces, like docking and landing protocols, were twinned off into a new sub-AI who was given some autonomy, christened Contarini, and allowed only to function on the other side of an air-gap from Morosini, so that there was no obvious conduit into the ship for a hacker.

An aura of crisis penetrated everything from meals to dreams, and Nbaro was especially hard hit. It wasn't the people she'd killed ...

Or maybe it was. What she remembered best was shooting a man under the Weps console, and then, when he fell screaming to the deck, shooting him again. Without a thought, at the time. It made no difference that she knew full well he'd have suicided anyway. Morosini and Dorcas said all of the suicide pills were remotely controlled – not that the attack teams had known that. There were never going to have been any survivors.

Nbaro spent too much time lying on her rack, *not sleeping*. Her best sleep aid was the book she'd been given on the Mombasa Orbital, and she read *Pride and Prejudice* slowly and carefully, afraid of what she'd have to think about when the last lovely page was turned. She was trying not to read faster when Thea spoke up from below her.

'If I'd known what a hero you'd turn out to be, I'd have been nicer to you,' she said.

She was at the stateroom's desk, working on cargo, with dark circles under her eyes.

A surprising number of Cargo officers had been killed or badly wounded in the incursion. Thea had been ashore, buying souvenirs on the station concourse. She'd been one of the first to return, and she'd been working ever since.

Nbaro shook her head. 'I wasn't a hero. I did most of it wrong.'

'Honey, you're the *only* person who thinks so,' Thea said. 'And that flight jacket is beautiful. I'm jealous.'

'I owned it for one hour and got a burn across the back.'

'Shit, girl, a burn? From when you fought off the bad guys and held the *Athens* and saved the day? That burn?' Thea turned.

Nbaro was having a bad moment. The dead in the corridor. The boy with his jaw shot away. Over three ship days, they'd only grown worse, and Thea saw it.

She came and wrapped her arms around Marca.

'You OK?'

'Nope,' Marca said.

'Fair.'

Marca thought that it was pleasant to be hugged, and also that the hug went on too long, but she was awkward about such things and knew it. As if Thea sensed her thoughts, she let go.

'You getting some counselling?'

Marca took a deep breath and pinched the bridge of her nose between two fingers.

'Yes,' she said.

She made one more atmospheric landing, this one as the pilot with Guille as co-pilot. Guille kept looking at her as if longing to ask questions, and Nbaro found it trying, but flying the spacecraft still had its attractions, and she lost herself in technical minutiae.

After the flight she lay on her rack and thought too much. In the end, she went to her medkit and took a sleeping dram. The sounds of the ship were omnipresent: the hum of the drives; the voices in the passageway; the repair parties cleaning away the scars her combat decisions had left. Somewhere far forward, a grinder was working ...

Nbaro awoke to a different ship. The sense of emergency had lightened; the ship was outbound, and she'd slept through the Master's announcements about a burial service in space. Thea filled her in, and she wore her dress uniform for the first time – a short dark jacket and matching, very old-fashioned, trousers. The entire ship's company turned out in the largest hold on Seventh Deck, one of the great cargo holds, and the sheer size of the space added its own sense of awe. There were cargo containers against the far bulkheads, but the centre of the space was empty enough that the whole crew, minus a hundred or so on necessary work, could form up by divisions.

The Master spoke about duty, and about what the DHC stood for in space, and about the shared danger and triumph of being a crew.

When he was done, he read off the names of the slain. Nbaro was moved to sudden tears when she heard that Lieutenant Anthony Svaro had been killed.

One by one, the coffins were shot off into space.

When all fifty-three of the dead were gone, the Master went back to the small podium.

340

'It has been suggested,' he began, and there was a gentle rustle, like a breeze over flags. 'It has been suggested,' he began again, 'that we turn back to New London.'

He looked out over his crew, and Nbaro felt as if he was looking at her.

'We will not return to New London,' he said. 'Not when tens, even hundreds of thousands of people, are depending on us. We have to assume that we will be attacked again. We will have to be clever as well as brave. We will have to take careful precautions and watch over each other, and keep one hand and one eye for the ship at all times, because we need each other to survive this, and we need her to get us home.'

He looked them over.

'But she will get us home. And we'll go home, not with our tails between our legs, but with our holds full of xenoglas, having performed the mission we were assigned. Now, three cheers for the *Athens*.'

The cheers were deafening even in the great hold.

The run out to Insertion was long, because they were about to make a long-jump.

'It's the second longest insertion of the trip,' Hanna said. 'It's not as long as the jump into Lighthouse, but it's long.'

The shipboard routine was returning and, despite death and injury, they were slipping back into a normality aboard. The damage control parties had given way to actual repair parties, and Engineering and Facility Maintenance were fully employed, but Small Cargo was all but shut down. Flight was virtually on vacation, except for Nbaro's usual round of Damage Control and Boarding Party and Tactics classes, and the upcoming evaluations and fitness reports.

Marca smiled at Hanna. Her notoriety as the midder who'd commanded the ship was still running hot, but Hanna, whatever

341

his failings, treated her the same way he'd treated her since the beginning. He might be in love with her, but he was easier to talk to now.

Thea was eating her second slice of chocolate pie.

Yu looked as if his patients had beaten him with sticks. His pale skin was sallow, his eyes puffy, and he moved as if he was hurt.

Ko and Cortez now usually sat with them; sometimes Talhoffer and Mpono joined them, and Captain Fraser too. Mpono had their neck in a mobile brace and some remarkable scars, but they were already back on light duty.

But today it was just them, and Hanna was explaining space travel.

'You know how long-jump astrogation works, right?' he asked, and Yu laughed.

'Nope,' he said. 'Dammit, Jim, I'm a doctor, not a...'

Ko waggled a hand. 'I passed it at the academy,' he admitted.

Nbaro shrugged. 'I watched a vid about it. Please, Richard, tell us how space travel works.'

'You're cruel,' Thea said.

'Learned from you,' Marca shot back, and Thea smiled. It was true; Marca had learned this kind of teasing from Thea.

'If only Mr Dorcas were here to help me explain,' Hanna said.

'Mr Dorcas is my friend and I'll defend him,' Nbaro said.

'Right,' Hanna said. 'Anyway... remember the Big Bang?'

'I wasn't there,' Cortez said. 'I was born afterwards.'

'There's always someone. Right, so in the first milliseconds after the Big Bang, there was no time... and before you say it, I know, I know, so how could there be milliseconds, right? Anyway, for some amount of time, the universe functioned under very different laws, or perhaps no laws that we'd understand. And then things calmed down and the laws of physics precipitated out of chaos and dark matter.'

'You're making this shit up,' Thea said.

'Yeah, well, I had to see if you were awake.' Hanna grinned at her.

Richard is flirting with Thea.

Nbaro hadn't seen that coming and for a moment she felt a sense of… loss. But then a sense of release, too.

'Anyway… in that time, before the rule of law, exotic matter was created. Scientists call these particles "relics".'

Thea leaned forward. 'I remember this page in the text on my tab. My crazy room-mate asked the instructor if they were like saints' relics and he got a demerit.'

Hanna looked… entranced.

He's just realised she's flirting with him.

'So… despite the rule of physics, these relics still exist, spread far and wide throughout the universe – indeed, the multiverse. And every relic is connected, by its exoticness—'

'Is that a technical state? Exoticness?' Cortez asked.

Ko punched him in the arm. 'When Drake does it, she's cute. When you do it, you're an arsehat,' he said.

Cortez rubbed his arm.

Hanna went on, 'Every relic is connected to Artifact Space. That's the spacetime of the first milliseconds. It's not like our spacetime. So when we make an insertion, which isn't even exactly what we're doing, we're using our vanes to find enough relics to build the course we want in the direction we want, and it has to be very precise. When we've collected enough relic matter, we can use it to open a window into, and pass through, Artifact Space. Right?'

Nbaro nodded. 'Actually, Richard, you're better than the vid I watched. You make sense.'

Thea was interested, despite herself. She leaned forward.

'Then…' she said, 'why are we never exactly sure where we'll come out, or how fast we're going?'

'Quantum entanglement,' Hanna said. 'We're the observer and the participant at the same time – we affect everything. The further we want to go, the more relics we have to collect, the more unreliable the interaction and the faster, in real space, we have to go. Then, the more tightly we control the velocity of our arrival, the less control we have over the position of our arrival, and vice versa. There's an element that I'd call luck, and another of experience. Veteran astrogators who've made a run a dozen times always outperform newbies.'

'So... how long is this jump?' Thea asked.

Hanna smiled. 'How long is a piece of string?' He raised his hands as if to fend her off. 'We're aiming for about 104 light years. This is where we jump off into the Deep Black, friends. Until this, we've been in home space.' He waved a hand. 'And the other thing is the actual astrogation part. Everything moves. Not just the Relic particles and the vents into Artifact Space, although they definitely move. But planets and moons and stars themselves. And when you are defying time...'

'Defying time?' Nbaro asked.

'You know how physics works, right?' Richard asked, and Nbaro thought that he wasn't so different from Dorcas, now that he was on his intellectual home ground.

Ko either ignored the exchange or caught Nbaro's poisonous glance and decided to defuse a little. He glanced at Nbaro. 'Home space? Shit, if this was home space, give me the Deep Black. Maybe no one will try to kill us there.'

Nbaro raised an eyebrow at him. 'Or maybe they're waiting for us, the way they waited for the *Hong Kong* and the *New York*.'

'You're cheerful,' Ko said.

She frowned. 'Someone's ahead of us – they were ahead of us at Sahel. They were ahead of the other ships. In relativistic time,' she glanced at Hanna, who had the good grace to look away, 'that means that this … conspiracy against us … is more than five years old.'

Hanna looked at her. 'I hadn't thought of that,' he said.

Repair work became her day-to-day norm; often, it was work for which Nbaro had no training, so she'd help by moving a grav-sled up and down a passageway, loaded with nanofibre repair fabric and followed up by enthusiastic volunteers who could make repairs to the decorative bronze work and the murals and accents. Most of these repairs were on her own passageway, as the detonation of the anti-personnel drones had stripped two sections of passageway, cutting most of the power conduits and even the airflow.

Sleeping became even more difficult, as welding and nanoreader repairs and their attendant scents and sounds filled the passageway at all hours.

And then suddenly, at the ship's direction, Nbaro became the officer in charge of the various data-processing tech and fabricators rebuilding the Space Operations Centre in the first shift. Space Operations was totally closed off, and all Space Ops functions were being run from the Bridge. They were still taking on cargo from some of the Sahel System's outer orbitals, and they had a major pulse of flight activity coming up when they would take on fuel at the gas giant, Obatala. But they had two weeks of travel to reach the giant, and Nbaro was in over her head from the beginning, reading manuals all night in an attempt to understand the new stations being installed, all matt black plastic and sleek contours. She was pleased, as the new weapons station was taken from its foamed recycle crate, that despite having less than a week to produce it, Sahel's factories had given their new tech a brushed bronze decorative edging marked with etched acanthus leaves. Despite their ultra-modern appearance, the new consoles had some cultural references to the *Athens*.

Likewise, Nbaro and the junior lieutenant assigned to the duty in the second shift pored over photographs and room models, trying to restore something of the look of the former Space Operations. Thea, who was an expert amateur data miner, found them a 200-year-old vid of Space Operations underway from an ancient documentary. Morosini, who seemed almost chatty with Nbaro now, worked with the old vid to create a 3D simulation on which they could base their redesign. It was work far outside Nbaro's competence, and she and Lieutenant Qaqqaq complained to each other constantly and drew on anyone on the ship who had any experience in installation.

'I'm really a robotics engineer,' Qaqqaq said. 'Not an interior designer.'

'At least you're some kind of engineer,' Nbaro said. 'I'm a pilot.'

Dorcas was the most helpful, but Thea was a close second, arriving in the working space unannounced to show them paint chips kept in Maintenance for a hundred years – or to share a schematic she'd found in a database, showing the complete fresco plan for the O-3 level. Morosini, who was still struggling to recover his own system's architecture, admitted his surprise at some of the physical artifacts that Thea recovered.

The work moved from outer shell, where the titanium and extruded diamond was repaired, restored or replaced, to the fibre-optic cables, electricals, and microtubes laid in sheets below the plastic sub-flooring. Nbaro was used to stepping over coils of cable, and was amazed to think that the new Space Ops might have smooth floors.

Electricians' mates, borrowed from the ship and all the flights, checked each cable run and nanotube against the housings and consoles, lighting, and every other working mechanism that would require power. Nbaro was almost saddened to lose the snakelike coils of cable that had lain on the old floor – evidence of hundreds of years of upgrades and alterations swept away in a single disaster.

When the power runs, air and heating ducts, and nanotubes were laid, work moved more swiftly. The floor was laid, composed of the original hexagonally embossed black carbon fibre, lovingly reproduced by onboard fabricators to exact specifications laid down by Morosini, and installed by their work crews with adhesives from their stores. With the flooring down, the new stations were installed, as well as the mounts for acceleration couches, themselves all new and requiring their own attachments, from automated medkits to ship's air for emergencies.

Despite the complexity, Morosini's involvement and Dorcas's extensive automated checklists made it all flow quickly once the floor was down. Hundreds of crew people participated, and Qaqqaq told her that many were volunteers working in their off-hours, eager to take part in the restoration.

Qaqqaq was a little in awe of Nbaro to start with, and Nbaro was finding her status as a cult hero to be detrimental to anything like a normal life. Spacers brought her cookies and bulbs of coffee; her laundry was suddenly done in a couple of hours and re-hung in her stateroom as if she was the Master. Even Major Darkstar treated her with elaborate courtesy that she found difficult to accept. It had its uses; her people worked on the restoration project with inhuman energy, but Qaqqaq's diffidence, considering that the short, muscular, and very effective woman was senior to her, was more complicated. But as the first week of work moved into the second, Qaqqaq became more human and occasionally even overrode Nbaro and gave an order.

Nine days after the first work party had begun stripping out all the damaged material, the Space Ops work was complete. Everything gleamed; the new consoles, which had a uniformity of manufacture and design that had been utterly lacking in the former space, glowed with dull red and vivid blue indicator lights. A new, large, automated vidscreen and holotank table filled the centre of a ring of stations, and the Space Ops watch officer would now sit in the middle of the holo projections, able to rotate through a projection of tactical space in 360 degrees. Overhead, xenoglas conduits provided a rich golden light while also carrying data, and on the bulkheads, the original motifs had been meticulously repainted, the outlines of the original images reproduced by Morosini's replicators in wallpaper sheets, based on the designs Thea had found.

The space was beautiful, and more importantly, fully functional. The Master came down to inaugurate Space Operations, and more than a hundred crew-people crammed into the small space.

He stood by the command couch and smiled like a boy, despite his age.

'They're fools if they think we can't do this,' he said. 'Do those set against us think that when we repair, we don't make ourselves better? Stronger?' He turned all the way around. 'I'd like to thank everyone who's worked here. Morosini has told me how this became an all-hands activity, and shipmates, that shows how fine a crew you are. This is our ship – our home. They hurt us, but by the gods, we've recovered well.'

He nodded to Lieutenant Qaqqaq. 'I'd like to express my especial thanks to Lieutenant Qaqqaq of Engineering and Midshipper Nbaro for making this happen so quickly and efficiently,' he said. 'And since their last watch was interrupted by the attack, I'd like to ask Commander Mpono to take the Con.'

Mpono grinned. All of their bandages were gone; they'd spent two days in an autodoc and had served five days of light duty. They looked thin but recovered.

They lay down. 'Wow,' they said. 'This is comfortable!'

Everyone laughed.

Mpono rotated their command couch like a small child playing with an office chair, and the Master reset the watch, appointing all of the spacers who'd been on watch during the attack to pick up the watch schedule.

He waved to Nbaro.

'If you'd be kind enough to take Tower, Ms Nbaro?'

Nbaro sat in the number two position, and there was applause. She flushed at it.

But she knew they meant it.

The heavy workload continued through the refuelling operations at Obatala; Nbaro flew three events a day, scooping hydrogen for the ship's great fuel tanks or flying packaged food cargoes from the orbital's vast hydroponics arrays, which were themselves platforms with artificial sunlight. The ship was buying packaged spacer food, and she had some dark ideas about why.

In four days of refuelling, Nbaro was pilot once; otherwise, she was co-pilot, handling communications and the details of refuelling while her pilot, usually the skipper, flew.

'You know you're going to get a medal,' Skipper Truekner said.

'I'd think a lot of people will be getting medals,' Nbaro said.

Truekner looked over at her. 'I was right about you,' he said. 'You have the makings of an excellent officer.'

She glowed.

'The Master's going to hold your award for a little. Trust me, that's entirely to your benefit.'

Nbaro scanned her instruments and then turned her head. Their visors were open and she could see his face.

'I don't really need another award,' she said.

'Morosini thinks you saved the ship,' Truekner said. 'Honestly, people dream of doing what you did.'

I dreamt of it too. Somehow, I did it. And I'm still an idiot about so much . . .

'Is this my fitness report?' Nbaro asked, in the teasing tone she'd learned from Thea. Teasing could cover all kinds of nerves.

Truekner laughed. 'I never thought of doing fitness reports during operations, but damn, it makes sense, eh? Side by side, staring into space?' His tone changed. 'If this were your fitness report, Ms Nbaro, I'd say that you had the makings of an excellent officer and had my highest recommendation for early promotion. But I would offer you two pieces of advice.'

Gulp.

'First, don't let it go to your head. I suspect the Master put you on the restoration of Space Operations to keep you humble, and he's damn good at what he does. The border between competence and arrogance is a knife-edge – be wary.'

'Yes, sir.'

'And second, almost the opposite advice, but hells, Nbaro, we're dichotomous creatures. You have a darkness in you – it's the damned Orphanage, no doubt about it. But you've done… amazing, brave, brilliant things. I can't order you to lighten up on yourself, but I'd strongly recommend that you start giving Ms Nbaro some credit for her successes. And perhaps get some sleep.'

Nbaro's lips curled.

'You think we can't hear you every time you say *I'm an idiot*?' he asked.

'Ouch,' she said.

'We're *all* idiots. Viewed by that remorseless logic, we're all incompetents, struggling to fake competence. Lighten up. You're working too hard, and I don't mean the flight schedule.'

Nbaro thought, *Which of the things you've assigned me shall I stop doing?*, but managed not to say it. She knew he meant well.

'Also…' he said, and the humour was back in his voice.

'Yes, sir?'

'You may have saved the ship, but you still need a lot of flight time, especially in atmosphere, so how about taking the craft so that I can do some tabwork?'

And then they were outward bound for Insertion. Nbaro received her formal test date for the qualification to function as Tower and she took it, three days from Insertion, before a board of four officers, all of whom she knew. Despite the overwhelming tension of preparing for the examination, she managed to answer all of their questions, and they passed her without consultation. Her friends, now including Naisha Qaqqaq, threw her a small party in the formal mess, complete with cake, and she took slices of it to Chu and the rest of the spacers in EVA.

Nbaro stopped dreaming about the dead. Part of her was a little appalled to learn that the horror of instant, violent death had cost her about two weeks' sleep and now seemed less omnipresent than some of her older, unresolved horrors.

One day before Insertion, and Nbaro was invited to dine with the Master. She wore her dress uniform, and arrived on the O-5 level where the Master's stateroom and mess were located, to be ushered by an android mess servant into a magnificent, neo-baroque space decorated with dark wood panelling all the way from Old Terra. An oil painting of a woman in ancient court dress hung on one wall and another of a river in a well-wooded wilderness in a planetary environment probably on Old Terra. There was a long table between and a large fireplace, almost as big as her rack, with a fire burning in the grate. Nbaro assumed it was a holo-image, but it felt warm, and it threw a beautiful light.

While she stood nervously by a seat which had her name on a small card, trying to decide whether she should sit or stand, the elevator door opened and Dorcas emerged with the android.

'Ms Nbaro!' he said. 'You never visit.'

She smiled to see him.

'Mister Dorcas,' she said. 'The drop-shafts work equally well in either direction.'

Dorcas bowed. He was wearing a black singlet, almost skin-tight but with a number of real pockets, and over it a long formal coat that hung from his shoulders like a cloak. No matter what Dorcas wore, he managed to make it look like some fashion from bygone ages, which was impressive given his neural lace and obvious infosphere manipulation skills.

He was also so tall that he made her feel small, and Nbaro wasn't really small.

'How is Lieutenant Smith?' she asked.

'Not good. We should have left him on Sahel, only both Morosini and Smith himself assumed that someone would find him there and kill him, or worse.'

'Worse?'

'Kidnapping, interrogation, humiliation.'

Nbaro swallowed.

Dorcas nodded. 'Whereas I'm fitted with a device allowing Morosini to kill me remotely.'

She blinked. 'But if Morosini is compromised…'

'Indeed,' he said, with a smile. 'You might have been said to have saved my life, by storming CIC.'

'I doubt—'

'Honestly, as a savant I'm usually the least socialised animal in any room, but you're the worst person at accepting a compliment or accolade that I know.'

'Perhaps I'm just modest,' she snapped.

'I doubt it,' Dorcas said. 'Anyway, Smith is recovering well enough, but his spine was injured. There's no real solution besides a regrowth that's going to take months. And then a massive rework of his musculature, as he'll have significant atrophy. Indeed, he already does. Yu is working on it.'

'I'll visit,' she said.

'Please,' Dorcas said. 'Lieutenant Smith values you highly. As I've said before ...'

The door – a real door, a beautiful wood-panelled door, and not a hatch – behind the head of the table opened, and the Master came in, wearing a flightsuit. He pulled back the heavy chair and sat.

'Please,' he said. 'Be seated.'

The Master surprised her by offering a brief Old Catholic prayer, and the androids served food: a pasta with spicy and excellent sausage; a salad with mushrooms cooked in breadcrumbs over arugala; and finally a pastry confection from before the Age of Chaos – something full of confectioner's cream that was so beautiful Marca didn't want to eat it ... until she took a bite. And then she devoured it.

'You're probably wondering why I've called you both here,' the Master said.

'Not at all,' Dorcas said. 'We're the closest to a Special Service team you have, and we're the only ones—'

The Master laughed aloud. 'Mister Dorcas, that was a deliberately ironical conversational device.'

'Ah,' Dorcas said. 'Of course it was. Sir.'

The Master sat back and pushed his plate away.

'How's Lieutenant Smith?' he asked.

Dorcas repeated what he'd said to Marca.

The Master steepled his hands. 'I've also invited Morosini to join us.'

A light flashed in the overhead, and the man in red sat at the other end of the table, his cat in his lap. The quality of the holographic projection was superb.

'I'm usually present, one way or another,' the AI said.

'I've invited both of you, first, to congratulate you on having

353

saved the ship,' the Master said. 'But more immediately, to discuss some possibilities. Morosini?'

The AI appeared to sit back in a relaxed, human manner. He patted his cat, which glared at him and took a swipe at his hand.

'We need to consider whether the facility of Lighthouse has been destroyed,' Morosini said.

'Lighthouse?' Nbaro asked. 'Sir?'

Dorcas glanced at her, as if disappointed. 'Lighthouse is a single station in the dark,' he said. 'Its only real purpose is to provide a jump point for this route.'

Nbaro took that in, or rather, added it to something Hanna had said about their course.

'I understand,' she said.

She looked at Dorcas and their eyes met. In a flash, Nbaro realised they had reached the same conclusion independently.

What does it say that I think like Dorcas?

Pisani, the Master, also sat back.

'You two don't look as shocked as I want you to look,' he said.

Dorcas made a face. 'They've had at least five years to get ahead of us.'

He looked at Nbaro, throwing her the conversational ball.

'On a positive side ...' she said, and faltered.

'Positive?' Pisani said. 'I'm all ears.'

They were all looking at her.

'From a tactical point of view,' Nbaro said, 'and I'm a dumb midder, so pardon me if this all sounds foolish ...'

Morosini raised an eyebrow.

Nbaro cleared her throat. 'The way in which the attacks were conducted suggests to me that these plans were laid down a while ago, and they didn't change their operational doctrine to deal with the possibility that, once other greatships were destroyed, we'd be on high alert.'

Morosini nodded.

354

'So while they're ahead, in terms of having made plans, they're also behind, because the layered nature of their attacks have left them with their worst possible outcome – we are alive, and alert.'

She'd started hesitantly, but Morosini's look gave her confidence.

'Exactly,' Morosini said. 'Go on, Nbaro.'

'Why?' she asked. 'Surely you've all worked it out?' She looked at the Master. 'I'm sorry, sir, but I'm not sure why I'm here.'

Pisani shrugged. 'Because I ordered it,' he said simply. Then he gave her a thin-lipped smile. 'Your modesty is noted. Please continue.'

Morosini spoke up. 'I missed the tourists, Ms Nbaro, and you and Dorcas didn't. I console myself that my facilities were very limited for a number of compelling reasons, but there remain holes in my deductive and inductive processes. If AIs were perfect, I'd remind you, we'd crew the ship and you could sit home.'

Pisani smiled. 'The time may come for that,' he said, 'But for now, we're here, and you are, Ms Nbaro, part of my operational planning team. Please relax and tell us your thoughts.'

Nbaro nodded her head very slightly.

'Yes. Ah … thanks. Er …' She took a breath. 'The scale and disregard for casualties of the Sahel … incidents … suggests an adversary with absolutely no moral compass.'

'Yes,' Dorcas agreed. 'May I?'

'Please.'

Nbaro relaxed back into her chair. If she had enormous hesitation about trying her thoughts on the Master and the ship's AI, Dorcas clearly had none.

He waved a hand and a holo of Kili Station appeared.

'Here's us in dock,' he said. 'Here are the two 普天下 Pǔ Tiān Xià ships. Here's the opening of the attack seen from the station.' He stopped the replay. 'If we hadn't broken dock, there's about a four point two per cent chance of our being destroyed at the dock. Higher if the boarding parties had five more minutes to do their work – much higher if their two-part virus attack had worked.'

He dismissed the holo with a wave of his hand in favour of an enhanced 2D view of the ship from above, with a set of rings drawn around the ship's reactors.

'If the ship and her reactors were destroyed,' he said, 'we would have taken the station with us. Because of the station's rotation, the initial explosion would have peeled the outer ring away like the rind of a fruit, leaving the central core to fall into an uncontrollable spin and descend into the atmosphere. Total destruction would have taken about three hours.' He looked up. 'That's a million dead. Without counting the crews of all the other ships, and anyone planet-side who's beneath the rain of debris.'

'Jesus,' Pisani said. 'Nbaro?'

'Sir, I didn't have this level of research ready. I was merely confident that our attackers didn't give a shit if they killed the station … Pardon me – if it meant they got us.' She felt herself flush.

Pisani laughed. 'I just like you better and better, Midder.' Then he folded the smile away. 'So …' He looked at Morosini. 'Any idea what's going on?'

Morosini pointed languidly at Dorcas.

'Initially,' he said, 'Smith and I assumed that all of this was aimed at Dorcas.'

Pisani clearly knew all about Dorcas. He nodded.

'Right.'

Nbaro wished she knew more.

'But the sheer scale of the attack at Sahel has undermined my confidence.'

'Wait,' Nbaro realised that she'd spoken aloud.

'Yes?' Morosini said.

356

In for a penny, in for a pound.

'Is there someone like Dorcas on every greatship?'

Dorcas steepled his hands and looked thoughtful.

Pisani smiled.

Morosini shrugged, and petted his cat.

'No,' he said. 'But—'

Dorcas had the effrontery to cut the AI off.

'Let's say that hypothetically, word of my research leaked about six years ago,' he said.

Nbaro worked it out in her head. 'So you're the target, but they don't know which ship you're on,' she said.

'Exactly,' Morosini said. 'What does that tell you, Ms Nbaro?'

She was so interested in the data that she forgot to be nervous.

'It means that we're being attacked by someone inside the DHC. Someone who stands to lose everything when Dorcas does whatever he's going to do.'

Dorcas looked amused. 'What am I going to do?'

Pisani raised a hand. 'I don't think—'

Dorcas ignored the most powerful man on the ship.

'Think about it, Marca,' he said.

'You're going to talk to the Starfish,' she said. 'Sir, I've already signed the non-disclosure agreement.'

Pisani looked at Dorcas. 'Mister Dorcas, I realise that you are an exceptional individual, and I respect your talents, but if you cut me off in my own spaces again...'

Dorcas nodded, with real contrition. 'I apologise, sir. But I want to see if Ms Nbaro and I have reached the same conclusions – surely that's the purpose of having her here.'

Pisani sat back again. 'Very well,' he said.

But that time had been useful, because now she got it.

'And if you can talk to them,' she said, 'you can ask them how xenoglas is made.'

Dorcas nodded. 'That's one of many possible questions.

357

We could ask to move Trade Point, we could change the conditions of trade. Who knows what will happen when our communication can move beyond numbers and pictures? Especially as our pictures seem to puzzle them, and theirs are mostly incomprehensible gibberish.'

'Almighty,' Nbaro said. Then, 'What if they've blown Trade Point?'

Pisani, whose skin was naturally a medium brown, could be seen to pale.

But Morosini shook his head. 'Never,' he said. 'We're playing against someone bidding for a monopolistic power from the old Age of Chaos days, but they still want to control the trade. They won't kill the goose.'

'But they might take out Lighthouse and Far Point?' Pisani asked.

Dorcas spoke up. 'Yes. We should expect them to be gone.'

Pisani showed the first sign of strain Nbaro had ever seen in the man. He threw himself back in his chair, and said, 'Fuck.'

Morosini nodded. 'Can we make it to Trade Point without either of those trading stops?'

Pisani had turned his head away.

'You tell me,' he said.

Morosini moved the cat on his lap, for all the world like a real person with a big, heavy cat on his thighs.

'We'll have to refuel the hard way,' he said. 'Food will be tight and ...' He shrugged. 'You'll see a gradual degradation in everything. Air, water, recycle, crew morale.'

'I've already crammed the corridors with food,' the Master said.

Indeed, Nbaro had seen the pallets stacked along every side passage, and knew that all the holds were full of pallets, as was one huge bulkhead of the Hangar Deck. She'd brought some of it aboard herself, and not understood what she was transporting.

'It can be done,' Morosini said. 'But I'd recommend that we start moving and braking hard, to reduce the time and save the larger supplies. One *g* acceleration is all very well…'

Pisani glanced around the table. 'I'll take her up to the anti-grav limits, but not beyond until our wounded start recovering.'

Morosini nodded, and Nbaro had the sense that this argument had already taken place.

Dorcas leaned forward. 'Sir, based on the murder of Chief Dornau, I have to believe that we also have adversary forces on board this ship. Lieutenant Smith was investigating them when he was attacked. And more may have come aboard with the attackers and gone to ground.'

Morosini looked at the nails of his right hand, and Nbaro wondered about the AI's self-programming. Who was 'Morosini'? And who added in the cat and his vanity?

'Lieutenant Smith believed that there was a relatively harmless black market aboard, and that a cell working for our adversary was embedded within it.' Morosini looked up.

The Master looked at Dorcas. 'Do you have the skill set to continue Smith's investigations?'

'I do,' Dorcas said.

'I think that's your first priority,' the Master said.

'I also need to prepare my programs and my hardware for the Starfish,' Dorcas said.

They locked eyes.

'If I may be so bold, sir, Ms Nbaro is already read in to the programme, and there won't be a great many flight operations in the Deep Black. Perhaps she could be seconded to me?'

Morosini nodded. 'Exactly.'

The Master was not best pleased, but his control over his face was excellent; he was two hundred years old, or older. So instead he fingered his chin.

'Ms Nbaro?' he asked.

She looked at Dorcas. 'I've absolutely no skills in this direction,' she began.

Dorcas shrugged. 'You're intelligent,' he said, as if that was the measure of a person. 'And you, at least, have demonstrated beyond a shadow of a doubt that you are not involved in this.'

The Master glanced at her. 'Ms Nbaro, spacers are as superstitious as our forebears who sailed the seas of Old Terra. And you, miz, are *lucky*. You've become something of a talisman for this ship – indeed, my *only* hesitation in committing you to this course of action is that your loss would be a devastating morale blow. But we need some luck. I don't deny that you work hard and have real skills, Nbaro, but even in the restoration of Space Operations, Qaqqaq says that things consistently worked out in your favour – delivery schedules, lost parts found, schematics uncovered and so on. Spacers believe in luck. Hells, miz, *I* believe in luck. And we could use it.'

Nbaro looked down. Her cheeks were burning.

'Very well.'

Morosini said, 'As you always like to do your research, Marca, I've sent your tab two introductory courses on investigation.'

The Master nodded and pushed back his heavy chair.

'Very well. We'll meet again after insertion. I'm going to add the Executive Officer and Major Darkstar to this group. We'll know a great deal after our next insertion, but this one...'

'Dark system,' Dorcas agreed. 'There's a drone navigational beacon and a drone lifeboat station.'

'One more thing,' Morosini said.

The Master had been about to rise; he settled back down.

'The Sahel messenger boat carrying our dispatches was destroyed about ninety seconds ago,' Morosini said. 'By one of the two ships that broke station and ran when we did.'

Dorcas made a whistling sound.

Pisani stood – so they all did.

'Shipmates,' he said, 'we are at war. It's not the old kind of war, with fleets and lines of battle – it's viruses and computer hacking and misinformation and terrorism, but it's war all the same. Proceed accordingly. Catch me that cell of saboteurs. By any means necessary. Which reminds me ... The prisoner?'

'We're regrowing his jaw and he's being treated humanely.' Dorcas shrugged. 'When he can speak, he'll be interrogated.'

'That's it, then, unless Morosini has more.'

Morosini was still seated. He petted his cat.

'Nothing for now,' he said. 'Worth noting, though, that Sahel is launching military spacecraft. They appear to be accusing the PTX of complicity.'

The Master shook his head. 'And?' he asked impatiently.

'I gravely doubt that PTX has anything to do with this,' the AI said. 'Less than a ten per cent chance. But Sahel's reaction will provoke a counter-reaction.'

They were all standing.

Dorcas said, 'Am I correct in saying that all of our information on that messenger boat was one-time encrypted, so it's truly lost? They can't just upload it on to the next shuttle?'

'Correct,' Morosini said.

The Master gave a very slight smile. 'I have an ace up my sleeve,' he said. 'We'll proceed to Insertion.'

'Aye, aye, sir.'

Nbaro was not slated to be on watch for insertion, so she followed Yu's medical advice and took a heavy sleeping dose, took her insertion drugs after a big meal of Venetian-style fish soup in the nicer wardroom, and lay down.

She was asleep almost instantly, and her dreams were convoluted: chases and pursuits through the corridors of the ship; a long fall down a drop-shaft that left her on the streets of City behind the Orphanage, where her secret route led her off the ancient fire escape into the corridors of the second district. Something was hunting her, and she was hunting something; it was a race of sorts, with terror behind her and anger ahead.

And then, somehow, Nbaro was in one of the City canals, the hard-vacuum shafts and byways that permeated every level, allowing small spacecraft to move freely through City. She was piloting one of them, through a long, long canal, and her skill wasn't up to the task and she was bumping the sides, cracking the thick xenoglas and endangering everyone with her poor manoeuvring. The sides, rushing past her, were not the xenoglas of a City tube, either; they were alive with a fractal cancer of deep black stalks and tentacles and growths that grew denser and more insistent the further down the canal she flew, reaching for her, reaching, reaching . . .

Nbaro awoke, drenched in sweat.

'Have I mentioned that you're the worst room-mate ever?' Thea asked from the lower rack. 'You were screaming.'

'Christ,' Marca swore.

She rubbed her eyes. Rolled over and looked out of her privacy tent at the cabin's screen.

They were in normal space. Nbaro tabbed through to the navigational screen: they were in Gliese 433, where a dim red dwarf star had a Neptune-sized outer planet in the Goldilocks zone and a close-in large planet that was inside what, in Old Terra's system, would have been the orbit of Mercury. It was big and hot. The system didn't have a usable gas giant for refuelling, and the big planet in the 'habitable' zone had proved to be far too massive, with far too much gravity to support a human population; even attempts to mine its admittedly rich metals had failed.

Nbaro thumbed down to the navigational beacons.

All of them were operable. Even half-asleep, she could think tactically. She wrote Dorcas a message asking if the beacons could be used to track them, and whether hostile interference with them could be detected.

Then she read her manuals for an hour. They were dull even by her own standards, and more committed to teaching her about the legalities of handling evidence than about the actual techniques of investigation.

The ship was moving very fast, and they would not be slowing down beyond the bare minimum needed to keep their next insertion from going into the red zone, from which ships did not return. Nbaro knew that much about astrogation: ships that inserted above about $0.35c$ could emerge with velocities that were unrecoverable; a velocity of $0.88c$ could take years to slow from, and would burn more fuel than a big ship could carry, dooming the crew to a relativistic ghost-ship existence. It had happened, several times. She toyed with her screen controls, doing the maths; it looked as if they would need thirty-eight days of braking at $3g$ to slow to an acceptable insertion speed.

Nbaro checked the plot and saw that the navigator's calculation was closer to seventy days.

'That's why I'm not in Astrogation,' she said softly, and went back to her investigation manual, which put her to sleep after an hour.

She woke to morning, ship-time, and managed to have breakfast before her Tactics class, which was about the minutiae of operating sand casters and other screening techniques. They were promised a tour of CIC to look at the consoles in operation as soon as the Combat Information Centre was repaired and fully operable again.

Nbaro left her class with most of the other line-of-command midshippers and her tab went off when she stopped to talk with Andrei Gorshokov; he was in Flight 5, and just starting his Space Operations qualification cycle.

'Give me a moment,' she said.

It was Qaqqaq.

'Am I right that you have an EVA patch and your qual is up to date?' she asked.

'Yes, ma'am,' Marca replied.

'Can I use you on an EVA work party? We're wickedly short-handed, and it's just a routine check on the patches over the combat damage.'

'Yes, ma'am.'

'I'll tab you your times and I'll brief you in person. I'll be outside, too.'

'Thanks, ma'am.'

Nbaro went back to Andrei.

'It's not all that hard—'

Andrei shrugged. 'No one's making it very easy, either,' he said. 'My skipper doesn't seem to care where I start. She said to ask you.'

Marca laughed. 'Skipper Truekner makes it pretty easy. Come with me.'

She took Gorshokov into Space Operations, where Tad Dworkin was the watch officer. She introduced the young man, and Dworkin tabbed him the routine qualification sheets and the checklist.

'Another one on the watch list,' Dworkin said. 'I can't wait. We're short-handed as it is.'

He smiled at Nbaro, and she remembered when she'd thought of him as distant and a little scary. Was that really only forty-five days ago?

'It's beautiful,' Gorshokov said when they were back in the passageway. He looked star-struck. 'That's the best space on the ship.'

His praise was sweet, and Marca grinned at him.

'I like it too. My second home.'

'How close are you to your full qual?' Gorshokov asked.

'I can't even take the test until I pass for lieutenant,' Nbaro said.

Gorshokov shrugged. 'Midshipper's salute,' he said, and they both laughed. He went on, 'My father was a warrant officer. He told me that if I worked *really*, *really hard* and did everything I was told, I'd make lieutenant in eighteen months.'

She nodded.

And then he said, 'Though you can probably do fuck all and ignore your superiors, and you'll still probably make lieutenant in eighteen months.' He spread his hands. 'You're the hero of the ship, and I like to sleep in.'

She shook her head. 'We'll make lieutenant the same day, and you'll still be senior to me, because you are Academy.'

He shrugged. 'Thanks for the help. Really. Thea said you were nice, and look, you are. I appreciate it.'

Nbaro nodded, already thinking about her EVA suit. She went into the riggers' shop to find Chu had it all laid out, though Carlson gave her a look and didn't answer her greeting. She had four minutes until she was due on the hull.

It was beautiful out on the hull. The red dwarf was so dark, and they were so far out in its system, that Nbaro couldn't pick it out until she asked her helmet to give her a pointer on the HUD; the blue-green Neptune-sized planet, which most people called Torrent, was more visible.

She had all the patch locations in her suit's computer, and her task was simple: to examine each of them visually and with a data-recorder that was locked into her suit's left arm like an extra hand.

Nbaro had her usual religious, mystical reaction to being outside the hull; she stood still, her magnetic boots locked to the hull, for seven long minutes by her suit's clock, just watching the heavens. It was utterly unlike watching deep space on a screen.

It went on forever, in perfect clarity.

It reminded her how small she was. And the ship – she could see the navigational lights forward and above her on the Bridge, and a few lights aft, where Qaqqaq led a work party towards the silent drives. Otherwise, the hull was in darkness. The distant red dwarf and the big blue-green planet were too far away to give the impression that they were in a star system.

It was very lonely, and the universe was vast.

Then Nbaro manoeuvred to her inspection areas. Each of them held its own challenges: one was located in an area of vent outlets lined in carbon fibre where her boots wouldn't grip, and she had to use a carefully attached line to move across the surface of the hull to the patch. She took pictures, a vid recording, and she looked at it from various angles in the light of her suit torch before using the line to exit the non-metal area. Then she clumped across the deck to the next indication on her head-up display. This one was inside a niche, which had been made to allow for the widest firing angles of a close-in weapon for point defence. The little domed cylinder sat in the niche like an ancient religious statue in a cathedral; the CIW hadn't been damaged, but a railgun round had come in at a high angle and gone into the hull behind it, so that she had to attach herself to the CIW and then work her way in.

'Engineering, this is EVA 3–4.'

'3–4, go ahead.'

'Maybe I'm being too careful, Engineering…'

'No such thing as too careful, 3–4.'

'Can we shut down –' Nbaro read the turret's ID off the canopy – 'Close-in weapon turret 5–9–4–8?'

'I copy 5–9–4–8.'

'Roger.' She waited.

'Should be seeing a red light on the maintenance screen low and inboard.'

'I see it. Red light.'

'Roger. You're good to go, 3–4.'

Nbaro pulled herself in behind the turret, surprisingly aware that despite the turret being off, any movement on its part would crush her into the back of the niche in seconds.

Really easy to die out here, she thought. The words of her first EVA instructor.

Nbaro found the patch, took pictures and vid, and shone her torch on it from various angles. It was not nearly as neat as the first patch, but then, she suspected it had been done during combat, by a spacer who had every reason to fear that the turret would turn and crush him. She made a note.

People were brave, that was a truth. Someone had come out here while Nbaro was leading a boarding party; someone had risked a messy death to get a patch on the hole. That seemed braver, somehow, than just shooting people.

She had a moment, thinking about shooting people. And dead people.

And brave people.

'3–4, this is Engineering, over? You green and green, 3–4?'

'Roger,' she acknowledged.

The evidence of her life at the Orphanage – that people were shitty animals who seized every opportunity to behave badly, with a handful of exceptions – was not borne out by the ship, where people behaved nobly, with a handful of exceptions.

Interesting.

Nbaro backed out, after a terror-inducing half-second where something in her suit got caught on the turret.

'Check in, 3–4.' That was Qaqqaq.

'Just finished my second inspection, ma'am.'

'You just said "Interesting" out loud on the command line,' Qaqqaq said.

'Sorry, ma'am.'

Nbaro hauled herself out of the niche, retrieved her safety line, and toggled her main communications.

'Engineering, this is 3–4, over,' she said.

'Roger, 3–4. What's up?'

'All clear of the turret,' she said.

'Roger, I read you as clear of turret 5–9–4–8.'

'Correct.'

'Should have a green light and be responsive now, over.'

The turret vibrated, rotated perhaps three centimetres right and left, up and down, and a telltale glowed green.

'She's good,' Nbaro reported, and began a longer trek, headed forward along the hull. She passed under the gleaming arch that held the Bridge and Master's quarters and Astrogation, and her third task required that she find a spot almost halfway up the superstructure. She reorientated herself and climbed it, walking up and then safety-lining to the safety ladder before she found the railgun round that had missed the Bridge by only a few metres. The patch was neat and quite expert; Nbaro filmed it and walked around the Bridge wing and peeked at the Bridge window, where a work party of four spacers had a massive airlock-tent over the whole front of the Bridge.

Then she walked back to the main hull and around it 180 degrees, and began checking the exit patches of the three entries. The depleted uranium rounds were moving so fast when fired from electromagnetic systems and had so much kinetic energy that they usually passed all the way through a ship, even a ship as large as the *Athens*.

Morosini had given them a lesson in tactics. The AI had dropped them away from the station stern first, the moment he broke with the dock; he'd shielded the engines and the reactors from the railguns within seconds. All of the hits had been well forward of the parts of the ship that could be most critically damaged.

Those were the aspects of piloting that a human couldn't manage in real time; the split-second decision from the moment thrusters were engaged had probably saved the ship and the station.

Nbaro found the exit patch for the round that had hit Space Operations – another neat patch, on the side that had been away from the engagement. The repair team had clearly felt safer. She could see it in the way that the edges of the patch were finished.

Her suit was heating slightly, and Nbaro ran over the controls, looked around for a heat source, worried a little, and called it in.

'3–4, we copy your suit building heat. Think you should come inside.'

'I only have one more patch . . .'

'3–4, recommend you come inside immediately. Your HUD should be displaying the closest airlock.'

Nbaro saw it, well off sternwards down the hull. But her last patch was just forward, and there was an airlock at the base of the Bridge superstructure.

She ignored Engineering Control and went forward, watching the thermometer. It climbed a little, then seemed steady.

The exit wound for the round that had penetrated below the Bridge was just above her. Nbaro moved steadily, one foot, the other foot, as she'd been taught in EVA.

'3–4, what's your status?'

'Just checking my last patch,' she said.

'3–4, didn't I order you inside?' Control asked.

'Sorry, sir, I heard a recommendation not an order, and I chose to finish my task.'

Nbaro was feeling the heat now, but she was ten metres from her last hole.

She took two more careful steps, and then she saw it – a big, ugly patch. Nbaro snapped a picture, then another, and when she ran her data recorder over it, it registered residual O_2.

A leak.

Nbaro sent the data to Engineering, and took her vid. It was definitely unpleasant in her suit. She had the airlock in sight, perhaps one hundred and fifty metres forward, and she began to move towards it.

'3–4, I'm ordering you in,' Qaqqaq said.

'Yes, ma'am. I'm on my way.'

Qaqqaq was on a private channel.

'When Engineering makes a recommendation, they mean it as an order,' she said.

Then they should say so.

'Apologies, ma'am. Did you see the slow leak on the patch?'

'Yes, Nbaro. I saw it. Good work. Now get your arse inside. Agloolik, girl! You're over fifty degrees!'

Nbaro was feeling distinctly queasy, and the sweat was pooling in various parts of her suit, making her feel as if she was swimming.

Fifty metres.

Shit.

Nbaro was having trouble moving now. Something was definitely wrong.

Qaqqaq again. 'Nbaro! Your EVA pack is malfunctioning. I recommend . . .' She sounded very professional. 'I recommend you jettison it and get in that airlock.'

Nbaro didn't think she knew how to *jettison* her source of air and temperature control.

'How, ma'am?' she asked.

Thirty metres. And she was still slowing down.

'Emergency procedure, Nbaro. Tab one, left side.'

Nbaro opened the HUD tab, and read the procedure. It was short.

Thirty metres. She took a step.

ISOLATE EVA PACK.

Done. Nbaro now had no air and no heating system and no way to dump heat, either.

The EVA PACK light went from amber to red.

Her helmet flashed, warning her that this course of action would limit her to the air in her suit.

Nbaro took another step, and another. It was still hot; she felt as if her back was on fire. Something smelled wrong.

WARNING – EJECTION HAS VELOCITY VECTOR.

Nbaro clicked the override with her tongue and chinned the EJECT EVA PACK button…

She was blown face down onto the deck and then she bounced.

Away from the hull.

The ejection of the pack had knocked her off her feet and cost her her link to the hull. Sheer luck saved her. An external antenna rose next to her; she brushed it, and her desperate fingers closed around it.

'Almighty,' Nbaro said weakly, as the antenna took her whole mass. But it held; she pulled herself down. She was lighter now, and no cooler; vacuum didn't allow her to cool.

Her boots locked to the hull.

Twenty-five metres.

Nbaro no longer had comms – that was all in her EVA pack, except a tiny helmet radio that was only line of sight.

Fifteen metres. The airlock was visible, and lit.

Nbaro was having trouble concentrating on the whole idea of the airlock, and she wondered how long she'd been without air, and she wondered why Andrei Gorshokov had been so friendly, and she wondered if the bad guys could use a navigation beacon to track their ship, and she wondered if someone had rigged her suit to kill her.

Nbaro was still fifteen metres from the airlock. She'd stopped moving.

I'm an idiot.

Don't die because you're an idiot.

Nbaro shuffled forward, which seemed the right thing to do. The heat was overwhelming, but lack of oxygen was taking over as the critical problem.

Ten metres.

Concentrate.

She remembered being beaten at the Orphanage – an exercise in endurance. You set your mind a certain way, and you made it through. Some didn't.

I did.

Don't die. They win if you die.

Fuck them.

Nbaro had reached bright lights. She turned her head, suddenly aware, in a burst of adrenaline, that she was *inside the airlock*, standing there like a fool.

She hit the tag-plate and closed the airlock doors behind her. Then she passed out.

Nbaro woke inside an autodoc with Dorcas and Thea and Qaqqaq around her.

'Algoolik, Nbaro, you were almost a fucking statistic and my career would have been ruined,' Qaqqaq said. 'Also, your friends might miss you.'

Thea smiled. 'I'd get more sleep,' she said. 'But then I'd miss all the excitement, and you *are* my business partner.'

Dorcas just read the screens. 'You have second degree burns over most of your back and a number of other small injuries,' he said.

Qaqqaq nodded. 'I won't put this in my report. But damn. When Engineering Control orders you inside, you go.' She leant over. 'The leak wasn't that important.'

Nbaro tried to ask what had happened, but the sedation was too heavy.

And then she was gone again.

*

And back. It was exactly like the last time, and for a moment all the intervening time was gone and Nbaro was new aboard the ship, and Thornberg had just tried to kidnap her.

Thea was there, and Yu, to add to her sense of disorientation, but then it all came back in a rush, an accelerating rush that unfolded like a rapid-fire vid.

'What happened?' she asked.

Once again, Nbaro was sitting naked on the fold-out bed on the autodoc, but now Yu's presence didn't trouble her much – just an uneasy feeling when he glanced at her. He was putting something on her back that felt like oily sunscreen.

'All this dead skin has already peeled once,' he said. 'It may peel again, and it will be itchy as hell. That's a scientific term.'

Thea smiled. 'I brought your best underwear,' she said.

'I think wearing a bra is going to be miserable,' Yu said.

Nbaro ignored him and nodded to Thea.

'What happened?'

Thea said, 'You should ask Dorcas. That boy's either very sweet on you, or he's a very strange obsessive. He's been in our stateroom about twenty times. He's been out on the hull looking at where you had your accident, too.'

Nbaro, despite her acute discomfort, had to smile at the idea of Dorcas being sweet on her.

Yu was wrong about the bra strap; it wasn't as annoying as the itch she couldn't quite reach. She got dressed.

'How long was I out?'

'I kept you out for three days,' Yu said. 'You were nearing exhaustion and you need to eat properly, and I decided that you needed the rest. Also, it allowed me to get the inflammation under control.'

Nbaro smiled. 'Thanks. I feel ... great!'

'That's sleep,' Thea said. 'You should try it. Hey, I joined a boarding party.'

Marca zipped up her flightsuit and shook hands with Yu.

'Really, thanks.'

He gave her a lopsided grin. 'Any time you feel the need to get a critical injury, I'm here for you,' he said. 'You should try my dance class.'

Thea laughed. 'We're in the Deep Black now,' she said. 'Dance sounds as sane as anything else.'

Marca followed Thea out into the corridor and caught up on the events of the past few days. Marca also looked at her tab, and began answering queries, most of them from Mpono and Skipper Truekner, both of whom she answered immediately.

She stopped at the drop-shaft.

'While I'm here, I should see Smith,' she said. 'You're doing Boarding Party? Do you like it?'

'Very much. It feeds my inner adrenaline junkie, I think.' Thea nodded. 'Also, I'm sleeping with Richard Hanna,' she said in an odd voice. Strained. Worried. Very unnatural.

Marca took several steps towards the medbay where Smith would be – the main medical space.

Nbaro had a great many thoughts in three steps.

She turned around to see Thea watching her with ... concern? Fear?

'That's great,' she said. 'You really like him?'

'It sort of snuck up on me,' Thea said. 'While I was coaching him on dating you.'

Marca smiled. 'I didn't click with him. To be honest, I'm not sure how clicky I am.' She shrugged and her back spoke out in itches. 'I'm damaged goods.'

Thea made a face. 'I feel ... bad? Or just strange? The whole thing is odd.'

'I hope it's not *that* odd,' Marca said.

Thea smiled. 'Hey, I taught you how to deliver those lines.'

Marca surprised herself by stepping forward and putting her arms around Thea.

'We're fine,' Thea said. 'Also, you're not damaged goods. You're brilliant.'

She put her arms around Marca, and Marca gave a squawk like an angry cat and almost threw Thea against the corridor's bulkhead.

'Oh, your back!'

'Oh, my back.' Marca managed a smile.

She went into the main medbay. There were still a dozen of the wounded from the attack in recovery, as well as the worst-hit crewer from the virus, an older petty officer who'd nearly died. She was fully clam-shelled, isolated by her autodoc.

Yu already stood over Smith, and he smiled at her.

Smith lay on the fold-out table, and he was very pale. He glanced at Nbaro.

'Come back when I'm decent, will you?' he asked.

'Of course,' Nbaro said, embarrassed and backing out.

Yu said something, and Smith laughed.

'I'll go visit Dorcas,' she said to Thea, once she was safely outside again.

'You OK to wander around? Shouldn't you be wearing your gun?' she whispered.

'I wouldn't trust me with a gun right now,' she said. 'Everything's a little muzzy.'

Nonetheless, Nbaro navigated the drop-shaft with ease and landed neatly on the Sixth Deck platform and began the trudge aft along the starboard side passageway, passing Laundry and the huge cargo bay in which Dornau's corpse had been found, and the fabrication shop, whose hatch was open. Nbaro looked inside and didn't see the spacer who'd had facial bruising.

She saw something rat-shaped moving along the corridor

ahead of her and smelled an odd, musky scent that she found very disturbing, and she almost turned back. But she made it to the brass Lion plaque and the hatch opened as soon as she put her palm on the palm plate.

Dorcas was inside, wearing a collarless shirt and breeches with boots. He had a succession of computing devices open on Smith's worktable, and the wall screen had been divided into a dozen different images.

'Ms Nbaro,' he said, rising. In doing so, he managed to knock one of his small devices onto the deck. 'I'm sorry,' he said, his long form diving for the hand-held computer.

Nbaro wanted to hug *him*. He was comforting, somehow, despite his odd speech patterns and aristocratic airs and his obvious arrogance.

'Thea says you're looking into what happened to me?' she asked.

He pointed her to a seat, as if she needed the invitation, and sat himself, then swivelled his seat to face the screens.

'Lieutenant Qaqqaq and the EVA riggers have reported that you damaged your EVA pack while moving around the close-in weapon's turret.' He pointed at a still image on one of his screens and tapped it. It was a vid, and it showed her, at a clumsy angle – the camera was obviously intended to watch the turret, not her. 'Right here, it's possible you hit the turret's edge with the flanges on your heat exchange. See?'

'I do see,' she said. 'So, an accident, and my own fault?'

'It's possible,' he said. 'Here you are in your EVA suit, emerging onto the hull – here you are from the opposite side. There's your EVA pack. All intact. At this point, your pack looks good, and I assume, as you're an intelligent person, that you inspect your gear before you go out.'

Nbaro blinked. 'I can't remember...'

He waved at another screen.

'You did,' he said.

There she was, chatting with Chu, and Carlson was walking away. She was examining every inch of the suit.

'I'm not such an idiot,' she said.

'So let's look at the next sequence,' Dorcas said.

'Can I ask an enormous favour?'

'You can ask,' Dorcas said.

'Will you scratch my lower back?' she asked.

He laughed. 'Skin peeling?'

He came around the table, reorientating one of the screens as he came. He sat behind her and scratched her back in the wrong place and she directed his hand.

'Watch what happens,' he said.

There she was, on a hull camera, plodding across the gently curving surface. From the angle, Nbaro thought the camera was mounted on the superstructure and was slightly above her.

There was a flash behind her. The camera seemed to malfunction, the screen went black, and then, as it returned, it had to refocus on the hull and then on her.

Nbaro plodded on, stopped, and turned slightly.

Dorcas pointed around her at the time hack on the screen.

'That's you, calling in your suit temperature,' he said.

'What was the flash?'

Dorcas nodded, and switched to another camera. There was a flash on that camera as well. And he stopped and played it back, and then again.

'There was no flash,' he said. 'No one remembers a flash.'

'What the hells?' she asked.

He pointed at the screens.

'The vids have all been tampered,' he said. 'Someone shot your EVA pack with a laser...' He paused. 'That's only a hypothesis, not a fact.'

'Tampered?'

'Yes.'

Dorcas was now scratching exactly where she needed a scratch, but all too soon the scratch was painful. Nbaro wriggled, and he stopped.

He rose from behind her.

'Did anyone retrieve my EVA pack?' she asked.

He showed her another camera view.

'You'd been in the airlock for about fifteen seconds at this point,' he said, and showed her the tiny point of reflected light that was her EVA pack wandering away from the ship.

There was a small flash and then ...

It was gone.

'Engineering says that shouldn't happen, no matter what you do to an EVA pack,' Dorcas said.

She nodded. 'Someone tried to kill me.'

'They tried to kill me, too,' Dorcas said. 'A poisoned needle in the catch of my tab's faceplate.' He showed her.

'Almighty!' she muttered. 'I'll never touch anything again.'

'Exactly. I think it's time we catch them. I need to get back to my real work.'

'The Starfish language,' she said.

'It's far more than that. May I show you?' he asked.

Nbaro sat back into the cushions of the acceleration couch. 'Please.'

He nodded. 'You know that when we're at Trade Point, we pass material back and forth through a sort of airlock. I suppose they call it an ammonia lock.' Dorcas smiled at his own joke.

She smiled, too.

'Do you know what we trade to them for their precious xenoglas?' he asked.

'High-end electronics?' she asked.

'Some, with varying degrees of success. It's very difficult for us to deal with creatures who don't communicate their desires,

378

and who also do not appear to wear clothes or any personal adornment. Hells, Nbaro, we don't even know if they have … personality? Individuality?'

She nodded in appreciation. 'So what do we send them, then?'

'It's a state secret. But mostly, just gold. Pure, refined gold.' Dorcas laced his fingers behind his head.

Nbaro suddenly realised that she had to have known this – or she should have guessed it. They'd loaded immense quantities of gold at Sahel. And, come to think of it, she'd often wondered why the price of gold remained so high …

'So Sahel—'

'It's the vital trade stop. Luxuries and hi-tech industrials taken to Sahel for gold. Gold to the aliens for xenoglas. Xenoglas to New London for hi-tech industrial use.'

Nbaro was rubbing her back against the fabric of the couch like a cat rolling on the floor.

'The gold …'

'I'm going to assume that the Starfish knew about gold before they met us – they must have had some. But it's extremely rare – as it would be on an ammonia-oceanic moon, say. On the other hand, we have tonnes of the stuff, and nine of ten systems can mine more.'

'What do they use it for?' she asked.

'Do you realise how little we know about them?' Dorcas said, his lecturer voice coming to the fore. He tagged a screen and an article appeared. 'There's a considerable body of scholarship, most of it supposition and foolish theorising, I'm sorry to say. But this paper is what started my own studies, and it's almost a hundred years old. It's about their biology.'

Nbaro nodded, reading the abstract.

He went on, 'We got several desiccated corpses from the first space battle. We didn't return them – a fairly natural reaction, given that our people had to assume that the Starfish might be a major threat. They've been exhaustively studied, probed, analysed – after all, the Starfish are the only other fully sentient beings we've encountered.'

Nbaro felt as if she was waiting for the verdict at a murder trial.

'And?'

Dorcas glanced at her. 'The xenobiologist in question, Prof Marilyn Horton, posited that the Starfish race was hundreds of millions of years old, and had re-evolved for a second and even a third environment.'

She considered that idea. 'Hundreds of millions of years?'

'As in – they evolved somewhere, and then moved somewhere else, and then possibly to a third place.'

'Then why isn't their tech unimaginably beyond ours?' she asked.

'Why indeed?' he asked. 'Why don't they have colonies on every ammonia world? Why didn't they blow the *Esperance* out of space? What is xenoglas?' He shook his head. 'Honestly, we were better at this kind of science before the Age of Chaos. Pure science. It's hard to get the DHC to fund anything esoteric, and even when you'd think that the xenoglas companies would do anything – pay anything – to know more about its production, my research has all been funded by intelligence funds.' He shook his head. 'Regardless. I'm being very scattershot. You have that effect on me, Nbaro.'

'I make you want to lecture me?' Nbaro asked, channelling Thea Drake.

He laughed. 'Yes. That too. At any rate … You asked, in a way, about my work. I'm out of my depth – I'm building a robot starfish.'

He took her into the workshop. Nbaro could tell that it was principally an armoury; one wall was festooned with dozens of weapons, most of them slug-throwers, matt black or darkly blued against the black carbon-fibre wall.

On the worktable was a complex mechanical exoskeleton. She could see the two starfish conjoined at the central hub immediately; other parts made less sense.

'It's much too small,' she said. 'Isn't it?'

'I don't want it to seem threatening,' he said. 'And I don't want to insult them, either. I have to hope they aren't iconoclasts.'

Nbaro barked a laugh.

'I'll put a skin over it. Horton says they can't distinguish colour the way we do, which makes sense. Their side of the partition at Trade Point is a dark soup, and we're not even sure if they have lights.'

'What do they see?' she asked.

'Heat,' he replied. 'Light may actually blind them. I'm asking the Master to issue night vision goggles for all hands and run our side of the station in main spectrum darkness.'

She nodded. 'No one's tried all this already?'

'Depressing, ain't it?' he said in his upper-class accent. 'The powers that be are happy with the way it all works – xenoglas for gold is a tremendous trade, for us. But I'll tell you the real secret, Nbaro – it's all coming apart anyway.'

Nbaro was playing with the double starfish articulation.

He leaned over her. 'I have extensive vids of their movements,' he said. 'I tried for authenticity.'

Nbaro nodded. He was very close to her, and she didn't feel the need to sink a knife into him.

Interesting.

'Why is it coming apart?' she asked.

'New ship designs – better computational powers, better access to Artifact Space. You saw the 普天下 Pǔ Tiān Xià ship designs? In ten years, or a hundred at the outside, every trader who wants to will be able to long-jump to Trade Point. The DHC xenoglas monopoly will come to an end. And out to Anti-spinward, in the marches beyond Alexandria, no one cares about xenoglas. They're expanding so fast that they may suddenly become the Human Space, and we'll be a backwater – Old Terra and New London and Palace and Sahel. Or rather, the arm of Human Space out there will just grow and grow, and it won't take the DHC with it. You know they say that out beyond New Texas they've encountered another alien race, or even a group of races? And the leading edge of human settlement to Anti-spinward is about five years' travel from City.'

She nodded. 'I read about it back at New London.'

'And the greatships themselves are *old*.'

He was looking at his mechanical starfish.

'What's it for?' she asked. 'Are you actually going to send it to their side of the station?'

He smiled. 'It's the only way I can test my language theory. You see, Professor Horton included an analysis of the excretion pods she believed that she saw at the terminus of each of their six arms on both sides of the sensory cylinder. She said, right then, a hundred years ago, that she thought the excretions were part of their communications suite.'

He indicated the mechanical pods on every limb of his robot starfish.

'I need help with all this – my robotics and mechanical feedback controls are not good. I need to be able to react almost instantly to whatever the real Starfish do. I need to be able to read the ammonia around them for trace chemicals, and then to produce my own.'

Nbaro put a hand on one of his.

'Qaqqaq is a robotics engineer.'

He looked at her, and his smile was enormous.

'Of course she is,' he breathed. He turned away, and stared

382

at the gun wall for a moment. 'She'll have to be read in. And Smith will have a proverbial cow.'

Marca shrugged. 'And...?'

He turned back. 'Excellent point. It's weeks before we have him back.'

'Why, though?' Nbaro asked, looking at the double starfish on the armoury table. 'Why would they have a double cipher just to communicate?'

He shook his head. 'I have no idea.'

She stared off into nothing and scratched her back slowly.

'Me, neither.' Nbaro nodded, mostly to the thoughts in her own head, circling back to the beginning of their conversation. 'So. We have an infiltrator...'

'Exactly. I have thoughts – but they all involve an immense amount of computer time.'

'Can I help?'

'I *need* you to help. Hold on.'

He went to the workbench where the robot starfish lay, picked up a small black box and thumbed an analogue switch.

'Now we're covered in white noise,' he said. 'Morosini is compromised.'

Nbaro snapped back so fast that she hit her shoulder on the edge of the gun wall.

'This tells me a dozen things, but first and foremost, that our infiltrator is not some amateurish thug. This is an operative with serious data-war skills who most likely came aboard with software already tuned to Morosini. Because AIs should be tamper-proof.'

'Fuck,' she said, because she couldn't think of a better way to express her feelings.

'I've been suspicious since Sahel, but the incident on the hull proves it. Smith should have been suspicious when there were

383

no cameras on the murder in hold 61X, but he didn't read the data that way.'

Nbaro blanked out the sense of horror that Morosini, who she liked better than many humans, had been altered or tampered with. She shut that down, and let her mind attack the problem.

'One thing that comes immediately to me,' she said, 'is that if Dornau met this infiltrator in 61X and was murdered, she'd probably met him there before.'

'I already had that thought. I found eleven other failures in the camera and no footage of either of them.'

'Shit.'

'Yes. Our opponent is very good, and very thorough, and has the power to tell Morosini not to watch them. It's a miracle you and I aren't dead. I have to posit that our operative has other, bigger problems.'

Nbaro leant forwards. 'My second thought,' she whispered, 'is that we can trap him.'

Her face was perhaps fifteen centimetres from his.

He blinked. 'Trap how?' he asked very softly.

Days became weeks.

Nbaro flew only what the Service required for her piloting skills to remain safe; almost no one flew for anything else. The repairs on the Bridge and CIC were completed, and both spaces, as well as Space Operations, were opened to the full crew for a day so that everyone could see how beautifully the repairs had been made.

Nbaro spent more and more of her available time in the unarmed combat classes offered by the Marines. Every combat class left her tired and yet somehow happier – and she found running on high-*g* treadmills dull. Thea joined her and proved to have excellent skills learned in dance, as well as a better zero *g* sense.

Boarding Party sessions had more of an edge to them, as a quarter of the students had participated in some part of the fighting on board and everything was far more real now. The same was true for Damage Control exercises, in which everyone participated with a new determination. Lieutenant Smith improved, and Lieutenant Qaqqaq was read in to Dorcas's ultra-secret programme and began work on the starfish. Marca had reason to know this; she spent her spare time, something she had for the first time, visiting Dorcas and holding tools for them while they worked, and burrowing through hundreds of vids looking for any sign that the operative they were hunting had made a mistake. She reviewed every vid that Dorcas had tagged for signs of tampering, and pointed out a pattern: early on, the adversary had made beautiful patches to cover his absence. In the 61X cargo hold, for example. But in later tampers, there were just seconds of black, as if they were in too much of hurry to do a good job.

The prisoner's jaw was mostly regrown, and Dorcas asked the Master to put a pair of Marines on the medbay.

It was all very routine work. Nbaro mostly enjoyed it.

Morosini had them conduct high-g braking burns from time to time; her back itched and another layer of skin came off, and Nbaro learnt to throw an opponent in one g or zero g with equal facility. One afternoon, after two hours with a sword in her hand, Thea said, 'And now I guess I'll have to buy my own sword. I blame you.'

They both laughed.

The Master had two more meetings with his planning team, and Nbaro met the XO Captain Rajiv Aadavan, a darkly handsome man who was as tall as Dorcas. He had a brilliant smile and piercing brown eyes, and she thought he might be the handsomest male she'd ever laid eyes on, but there was something... indefinable about him that reminded her of the Orphanage – some emotional distance. He was the Executive

Officer, the second in command of the *Athens*, and in the fullness of time, he'd be the Master of a greatship. He was also the tall man she'd met in the blue-tile on her first day aboard, which seemed to have been many years ago.

'Here's the midder who commanded the *Athens*,' he said when he met her. Somehow, it didn't sound like a compliment.

Nbaro also met Althea Dukas, the Chief Engineer, who was also a captain. She was small and on her third rejuvenation and she looked like anyone's favourite great-aunt. She had an air of competence and likeability that was a relief after Aadavan's distance. She spoke with a very slight Greek accent and had, like Thor Storkel, come from Old Terra. Marca knew that Qaqqaq worshipped her, and she was sharp and to the point in meetings.

At the end of the third meeting, the Master smiled down the table.

'I have a happy announcement,' he said, and slid a small box to Marca along the well-polished table. 'Given the breadth of your current duties and proven abilities, we've seen fit to give you an acting order to lieutenant. Effective this minute.'

'So noted,' Morosini said.

'It's not your actual promotion – you still have to pass the test. However,' he said, 'no one doubts you'll pass, and a ship's acting order will give you seniority from this date.'

Nbaro was stunned. *Stunned*.

'A very rare honour,' Aadavan said in a voice which might have suggested that he didn't approve.

'Give them here, *agapete mou*,' the chief engineer said.

With deft fingers, she pulled the gold buttons of a midshipper off Nbaro's flightsuit collar and pushed in the little gold lions of the DHC, marking her as a lieutenant.

Dorcas beamed as if he'd thought of the whole thing.

Marca didn't really believe it until Thea did a double take in their stateroom.

386

'Fuck me,' she said. 'You're a lieutenant?'

'No, I'm impersonating an officer,' Marca said. 'Almighty, Thea. They just pinned the rank on me.'

Thea kissed her on both cheeks and then, fairly painfully, slammed a hand into one of the little lions so that it bit into her neck.

'Ow!' Marca spat. 'What the fuck?'

Thea grinned. 'Get used to it,' she said. 'Academy tradition.'

And so it proved. By the time Marca took her long-awaited Space Operations examination, just after the insertion into Lighthouse, her neck looked as if she'd been in a fight with a dozen vampires. Even relatively staid and normal officers like Lieutenant Ahmad made time to slap her neck and then offer her congratulations.

And Midshipper Gorshokov called her 'ma'am', which was... very odd.

In the whirl of preparing for the exam and a sudden change in responsibilities even in her flight, Nbaro missed the transfer of the prisoner from the medbay. Once again she was asleep for the insertion. And even in the nervous tension of the last moments of her preparations, she was aware that Lighthouse Station was not responding.

As they'd predicted.

Nbaro hadn't wanted to be right.

She also knew that they'd picked up more velocity in their insertion than Astrogation had predicted, and they had another long deceleration ahead of them. This was why these cruises took years – long-jumping required months of deceleration afterwards.

Meanwhile, the ship tried to raise Lighthouse Station, a small orbital, mostly DHC personnel, but with a population of almost ten thousand. Lighthouse orbited a magnificent gas giant, the major refuelling point for the region, which glowed an almost perfect white.

Nbaro sat, or rather, stood, her examination in Space Operations itself, surrounded by all the spacers who usually sat at their consoles. As there were no flight events scheduled, they were able to run simulation after simulation: a refuelling mishap; an accident in the launch tubes; a battle damage scenario where her launch mechanisms went down one by one, and she had to keep moving events and shuttling her spacecraft; a major landing accident where a Flight 8 shuttle hit the stern of the *Athens* ... She began to get things wrong in the last one, and she saw it on the faces of her board.

Nbaro took a deep breath, thought it through, and changed her answer, recovering the bodies of the dead pilot and co-pilot, informing the Bridge ...

Eventually it was over. She'd sweated through her jumpsuit and her back burned like fire.

Dworkin was the Chief Examining Officer. He smiled at her. 'Give us a minute, Lieutenant,' he said.

Not good.

When Nbaro had taken the Tower exam, she'd passed immediately.

She went out into the passageway and blinked at the sudden memory ... The hatch, and shooting a man at a range of ten centimetres; the look in his eyes ...

Nbaro turned away and looked somewhere else. She looked at the mural across the passageway – at the nymphs. At the polished bronze.

I can take the exam again. Hardly the end of the world.

Nbaro thought of all the places she'd gone wrong: the launch cycle she'd battered her way through in the combat scenario, which could have gone faster and more efficiently if she'd paid attention to the repair reports ...

'Come back now, Lieutenant,' Petty Officer Banderas said, leaning out into the corridor.

The woman smiled shyly. Marca made herself smile back, although her lips felt like lead.

She took a deep breath and raised her head, ready to be brave in her defeat.

Inside, her board had gathered around the command chair. They were all laughing – not at her; someone had just made a joke.

Dworkin whirled the chair to face her.

'So …' he said. 'You know you passed, right?'

All the wind went out of her.

Mpono came to her aid.

'Of course she didn't know,' they said. 'No one ever does.'

Dworkin nodded. 'Well, we had to pass you. We're so short on watch officers we don't care how many spacecraft you crash …'

They were all smiling. Not for the first or last time, Nbaro had to remember how different their idea of humour was; they hadn't survived the Orphanage, and they thought this sort of banter was funny.

She made herself smile.

And an hour later, Nbaro was Lioness, alone in the command crash-couch.

Somewhat anticlimactically, there were no flight events what-soever in her first watch.

More watches passed. Nbaro trained with her sword every day, wrestled and threw her companions, fought exercise fires and began to use a tactical simulator to explore larger space actions. It was becoming increasingly clear to her that actual space actions alternated boredom with action too fast for people to direct; everything needed to be pre-planned. One of their first exercises was a head-on engagement at 0.18 c; the closing speed meant that anything not directed by a computer never got off a shot.

Lesson learned.

Nbaro was coming off watch when her tab went off, and she looked down.

Battle Stations.

Nbaro was fifteen steps from EVA, and she had her flight gear on before her tab stopped flashing. She never made it to the ready room, because Skipper Truekner met her in front of the elevator.

'You're with me,' he said.

They were away as the ship ordered all personnel to crash-couches and warned them to brace for evasive action in two minutes.

They bolted through Maintenance, out onto the surface of the hangar bay and performed a very rapid inspection of 6-0-5. When the AG went down, they were already strapped into their acceleration couches on board, and the magnetic rail system was moving them smoothly out into their launch position.

They launched cold, no engines, while the railgun tube next to them threw foil bomblets into space in front of them. A screen blossomed on her Electronic Counter Measures suite as the bomblets released their chaff across about 3000 km² of space.

Space having no atmosphere, the chaff moved forward at a constant velocity in front of the greatship as Nbaro deployed her attack craft behind the screen.

'Exercise,' breathed her skipper.

She found that she could breathe.

'How do you know?' she asked.

'No second chaff deployment,' he said. 'Plus I just heard Tower use the word "exercise" and then try to cover it up.'

Nbaro rolled her head so that her helmet stayed against the headrest in case of sudden acceleration.

'Almighty,' she muttered.

'Exactly,' he said.

'I guess I wasn't the first to think of deploying behind a wall of clutter.'

He smiled. 'No. But I liked how quickly you imagined it. Have you and Suleimani gotten together lately?'

'No, sir,' she allowed.

I'm a little busy.

'Well, in between moments of saving the universe,' the skipper said, 'see if you can work in a tactics briefing for the flight, eh?'

Five shifts later, Nbaro was asleep in her rack when the alarm sounded. This time, she was among the last pilots into her gear, and she found herself with Suleimani, way at the back of the queue to launch. Nbaro had never flown with her, but it all went as well as a desperate emergency launch could go, and she and Suleimani spent the whole flight working up a tactics briefing on close-in torpedo launch tactics. Nbaro learned that Suleimani's name was Zeynep, she was a devout New Muslim, and was inclined to other women. She was very easy to talk to, and Marca found herself telling Orphanage stories she hadn't shared with anyone else, even Thea.

'How come we've never flown together before?' Marca asked.

Suleimani shrugged. 'I'm preparing for my lieutenant commander exams,' she said. 'I've been down in Engineering, working on my qualifications there.'

'I hear that.'

Nbaro told the tale of her Space Operations board, and then Zeynep told hers, and they laughed outrageously over the stupid things they'd done under pressure.

It was a good flight, made better when Skipper Truekner sent them a tab about the quality of their briefing.

And there was still no response from Lighthouse.

The planned braking burns grew more frequent, as if the Master was in more of a hurry to slow them down, and in the operational planning team, they debated investigating Lighthouse. They'd have to move off their path – that is, away from the most efficient path to their next jump – and they'd have to slow down a great deal more to do it, in addition to potentially endangering the ship. Even to send in a landing barge full of investigators and then collect it again further down track, the maths was bad, as the Astrogator said somewhat lugubriously.

Through the whole debate, Nbaro couldn't take her eyes off Morosini.

He didn't have his cat.

Nbaro didn't know what that meant, but she couldn't imagine that it was a good thing.

'If we slow enough to dock,' the Astrogator said, 'we add at least seventeen days to our plot.'

The Master glanced at Morosini, who was ... fidgeting.

Shit.

'If we don't, we may be condemning ten thousand of our own to death,' the Master said. 'I have nothing in my orders to cover this.'

Nbaro waited to hear someone else say it, and then, very hesitantly, she raised a hand.

'Lieutenant?' the Master asked, his use of her lowly rank almost chilling.

'Sir, it seems to me—'

'A midshipper acting as an officer,' said the XO.

She sat up.

'Yes, sir. It seems to me that we can blast one of Flight 6's XC-3Cs out of the railguns and they can carry enough fuel to decelerate, and at least make a fly-by, with discretion to land.'

'Why one of yours, Marca?' the Master asked.

'We can refuel in space,' Nbaro said. 'So we could shoot off a second full of hydrogen…' She thought. 'I'd need to do a lot of plotting, but I think we can do it. We might need two fuel birds to get the third in and out of the station. But it's just a refuelling exercise, really. The big Flight 8 shuttles can also probably do it,' she added.

The Master looked at her for a long time – long enough that Nbaro assumed she'd said something really stupid.

'And that's why we have you here,' he said. 'Get me Tremaine and Truekner, in my office, one hour.'

Having had the idea, Nbaro was more than a little disappointed that she wasn't going. But Truekner, who was in charge of the refuelling operation, chose to go with his most experienced pilots across the board, and that left her at home.

As it proved, they launched Tremaine in a big Flight 8 shuttle, unarmed but with a fire team of Marines in armoured zero-*g* suits, with Dorcas in lieu of an investigator. No fewer than *four* Flight 6 tankers full of hydrogen would allow the unlucky crew of the Flight 8 shuttle to decelerate *hard* and then, if required, accelerate just as hard, while the *Athens* remained on course.

The manoeuvre was called a chainsaw; the tankers refuelled each other so that the fourth bird, Commander Truekner's, could be on station to refuel the big shuttle as she came off the station.

Nbaro did what she could to help, found she was in the way, went to Space Operations, where she was due to take Mpono's watch in an hour, and stood around until Guille asked her to go and entertain herself and not make trouble.

She was almost to her stateroom when her tab alarmed.

She looked down, expecting to see that they were going to Battle Stations.

Instead, Nbaro saw her trap had been sprung.

Her screen was flashing, and it was showing a frame reference on Third Deck.

She ran to the drop-shaft, hurdling knee-knockers and leaping into the drop-shaft like a madwoman. She was going too fast, but she braked a little by running her hands along the drop-shaft's walls, and caught herself at Third Deck without much pain. Nbaro was on the wrong side – port instead of starboard – and about two hundred frames too far aft.

She ran across the first cross-corridor, passing a set of science labs she'd never seen before. Rudyard Singh Agam stepped out of a hatch, yelped, and got out of her way. She raced to the junction with the starboard side corridor, and turned left towards the bow.

There was a spacer twenty frames in front of her, hurrying towards her. He looked up…

Nbaro reached for her pistol inside her flight jacket.

So did he.

She would never have been able to describe how she knew that this was their infiltrator, but part of it was his lack of military bearing; he was too fluid, too casual, and, despite whatever training he'd had, he reacted the moment he saw *her*.

Because she was on his target list.

The flat black pistol came into her hand like a friend, the fruit of a thousand repetitions, and she jumped a knee-knocker.

He was just as fast and he fired first. A small-calibre slug-thrower.

Nbaro continued moving forward, straight at him. She pressed the trigger – three-round burst – and hit him.

He flinched.

Nbaro took another stride forward, the gun recycled.

He shot her and hit.

She took the hit in her chest and staggered, then stepped forward with her right leg, aimed for his centre of mass, and put all three flechettes into him.

He went down.

Nbaro slumped against the next knee-knocker, leant in to very close range, and blew his lower jaw off.

Then, as her vision tunnelled, she called Dorcas.

That was foolish, as he was getting ready to launch. He didn't answer.

Nbaro tabbed the Marine Shack and got Darkstar.

'I'm hit,' she said, and gave her location.

'On the way,' the major said calmly.

Her infiltrator screamed, and screamed again, and Nbaro had to get the pistol away from him. As she'd suspected, he was attempting suicide.

'No way,' she said. 'No fucking way.'

Nbaro lay, panting, trying to get air, and thought it through. There was a lot of blood, and curiously, she felt ... very clear. Was that bad?

She and Dorcas had laid a trap for the next person to tamper with Morosini. It took some coding and some persuasion, but it relied on the fact that, whatever this bastard had just done, he'd need to cover his tracks. That's how he'd fallen into their data trap.

What had he just done?

Nbaro looked him over ruthlessly while he screamed.

The hydraulic fluid on his boots was obvious, and he was wearing flight deck boots – that is, boots that could be worn in hard vacuum.

She tabbed for the Bridge.

She got the signals yeoman.

'I need the Master, immediately.'

'On the way, ma'am,' the signals officer said.

'Master,' Pisani said.

'Sir, I've caught a saboteur and I believe he's tampered with one of the spacecraft,' Nbaro said.

'Right. Operational hold.'

'Yes, sir.'

Nbaro heard it on her Space Operations channel: all craft were to hold in place. Guille, the Lioness, sounded as if she'd been carved from ice – voice calm, ordering all craft to hold in place.

Nbaro called Lioness.

'Ma'am, I believe it's a bomb. Probably on a Flight 6 spacecraft.'

Nbaro thought about that, and then knew the truth.

It was on the Flight 8 shuttle.

Dorcas was the target. Of course he was.

'Belay that, Lioness. Target is the Flight 8 shuttle.'

'You sure, Nbaro?'

'No, ma'am, but I'm betting the farm on it.'

'Roger.'

Nbaro's vision was tunnelling again and she was losing control of her right arm, which held her tab. It tumbled out of her hand. She had the pistol in her left.

Was the infiltrator moving?

He was still screaming, but the passageway seemed far away.

Then someone was leaning over her, slapping a dressing on her side. Agam. Smith's friend. Nbaro tried to say 'thank you', and she tried to smile, because this wasn't the Orphanage. This was Service, and these people were her people, and she was perfectly willing to die for them, the family she'd never had. She wanted to tell Agam that she was happy, fucking *happy*, to die for the ship. For him and Smith and Dorcas and Drake and Chu...

Instead, Nbaro gurgled a little, and there was blood in her mouth, and she was gone.

II

'This is getting old,' Thea said.

Marca was once again sitting naked on the folding cot of an autodoc.

'At least all my burns have healed,' she managed.

'You almost fucking died,' Thea said. 'You had a bullet in your chest, right below your heart.'

That made something come into her throat; made it hard to swallow.

Thea sighed. 'Well, get dressed. Helping you back to our cabin is pretty much my entire duty schedule for the day.'

This time Nbaro was in a private bay, and this time she had two Marine guards on her hatch. They saluted her when she emerged, and she went and visited Smith immediately. He had his own Marine guards, and so did her saboteur.

Gunny Drun saluted her crisply. He was in full armour with his helmet on and Nbaro was in a flightsuit; she returned his salute with a nod.

'Gunny,' she said.

'You look like shit, ma'am,' he said with a twinkle in his eye.

'The other guy's right there,' she said, pointing at the infiltrator.

'I saw the film,' he said. 'You have big balls, ma'am. Any time you want, the whiskey's on me.'

'Deal, Gunny. I am definitely owed a drink by the universe.'

'Yes ma'am.'

His grin was infectious; his praise was sweet. Nbaro had a lingering thread of feeling, from when she was sure she was dying… that she loved them all.

'I took the liberty of recharging your pistol,' he said. 'Which, begging your pardon, you gundecked.'

Nbaro smiled and shook her head.

I'm still an idiot.

'How many charges did I have left?' she asked.

His smile didn't change. 'Three.'

She nodded.

Drun laughed. 'You are something. Ma'am.'

'Something,' she agreed, and went to Smith.

He looked much better.

'You got him.'

'If there's just one,' she said.

He nodded. 'Master thinks there's more than one,' he said, waving his chin at the Marines. 'He came for a visit.'

Nbaro nodded. 'I'm pretty sure we're winning,' she said softly.

'Winning?' he asked. 'I'll settle for not losing.'

Nbaro nodded. She sat with him awhile, but as she no longer trusted Morosini, she didn't talk about anything important, and he read her well and answered in kind.

She'd been out for three days. Three days during which the bomb on the Flight 8 shuttle had been found and the crew rescued. Another shuttle had been prepped, the maths redone, and the whole package relaunched, cutting the shuttle's time on station to a sliver.

They would be gone for eighteen days and a few hours, if all went well; longer if they chose to dock with the apparently dead orbital.

Her second day after confinement, Nbaro moved both prisoners. It was Dorcas's idea originally; he'd thought to shuffle them around the ship into prepared spaces whose cameras and sensing devices were separated from the ship by an air-gap. They had thirty-six such spaces, and a Marine fire team that moved around among them. It was a baited trap, Nbaro knew, and when she deliberately allowed Morosini a glimpse of where the prisoners were being moved, she felt as if she was betraying a friend.

She dreamt of his cat.

Where was his cat?

And the next day, in between shifts, Nbaro sat with the two prisoners. The infiltrator was awake, his face cradled in an elaborate regrowth mask. He was a man of middle build, with strong Han features. Major Darkstar sat by their autodoc and read through long word lists. It was the most benign interrogation she'd ever heard of, but as the autodoc was attached to every part of the prisoner's body and could function as a massive human reaction analysis tool, Darkstar used it as a lie detector.

Nbaro deliberately allowed their other prisoner to be present for it, and he was also closely monitored.

She watched the strain in his face. Watched the dawning awareness of what was happening in the infiltrator's face.

Nbaro reported in person to the Master, using the black box that Dorcas had built.

'Our infiltrator is a PTX officer,' she said.

'Ahh,' the Master said. '*Odio*. Are you sure?'

She nodded. 'About eighty per cent sure, with a limited possibility that he was extensively trained to mimic a PTX officer.'

The Master looked quite old – tired – and then his eyes came up to hers.

'And the other prisoner?'

'They haven't attempted to speak or transfer information in any way.'

He nodded.

'I've been through the infiltrator's cabin. He shared a bunk room with five other sailors and nothing he had is of any interest. I suspect that he had another space aboard – a hidey-hole – and he must have some kind of device to help him … sabotage Morosini. I can't imagine he could hold the codes in his head.'

'I could,' the Master said, indicating his neural connection.

'No hardware inside him,' she said.

'Keep looking,' the Master said in his soft voice. 'Morosini is in danger of disassociation because of our distrust. And we've removed so many functions from his control that he's … not himself at the moment.'

'And his cat?'

'Tom? I won't theorise about Tom.' The Master smiled slightly. 'I take Tom's absence as the only positive sign.'

And with that enigmatic comment, he dismissed her.

The routine work never stopped: Tactics class, where they were investigating three-dimensional manoeuvres and the different terrains of space; Boarding Party, which was now drilling them on the minutiae of going through hatches and doors; Space Ops, where her watches were the only time Nbaro could see outside the ship. The Flight 8 shuttle was deep in the gas giant's gravity well, sending a constant stream of data that went, for the most part, to Science and Intelligence. It was obvious to all that the station had been severely damaged; there was some debate as to whether it was worth their time to decelerate and board.

From Space Ops, Nbaro could also see the two battlecruisers who'd made the long-jumps with the *Athens* and were now running in the same system, but separated by hundreds of thousands of kilometres. They were both running silently, visible only by the minute difference in temperature between their heat-sinked hulls and refrigerated outer skins, and the vast void of space.

Mpono and one of the TAOs had come up with a passive scan to look for other bodies in the system that resembled the two DHC battlecruisers, on the assumption that the DHC was not alone in possessing the technology. They had discovered nothing, but they used optical and thermal arrays carefully, with massive processing power behind them. They used sensors located well apart in the whole length of the ship as phased arrays to make the instruments as sensitive as possible – even rotating the ship between burns so that the whole hull could be used to help focus.

It was such a useful idea, and one that used the vast length of the ship to best advantage, that any spare time Nbaro might have had was spent on EVAs to install new sensors on the outer hull.

Zero-g combat, a sword practice, some firearms practice with Gunny Drun. And in between all these activities, Nbaro tried to be an investigator. Most of her investigations were done from her stateroom, on screen, combing the data she had available – reviewing every altered vid on Morosini's database, trying to find another pattern.

Nbaro had a growing sense, with far too little supporting data, that if the infiltrator had a hidden hideout, it had been close to where Dornau's body had been found. In fact, she began to speculate about the cargo containers, because any four by four by four metre container or larger might be...

Anything. And there were hundreds, if not thousands, of large containers in every hold.

Nbaro set daily traps for a second infiltrator, especially if they were bent on freeing or killing their associate, while Major

401

Darkstar continued various associative interrogation techniques, and she reminded herself to be patient.

The shuttles fell sunwards, decelerating.

Nbaro was on watch in the ready room, a dull job at the best of times, when she remembered the EVA suits that had been bound for the *Hong Kong*. She spent a fruitless two hours searching them; she enlisted Petty Officer Locran, because he worked in Intelligence, to help her, and they disassembled every suit and searched it. She learned a great deal about the latest model EVA suits and she began to lust after one, but there were no smoking-gun clues embedded in the suits.

When Locran was gone, Nbaro took one that fitted her to the EVA riggers and asked Chu to check it out. She left a note for the Master, explaining why she'd taken one, and privately wondered if she was allowing greed for new gear to cloud her thinking. But she couldn't rid herself of the notion that the suits were the clue she needed.

Petty Officer Carlson was avoiding her, which she puzzled over. His behaviour was consistent across several visits, and led her to wonder if the infiltrator had ties to the on board black market, just as Smith had guessed a month before. Nbaro left Dorcas a note on the subject, thinking of him with some pity – eighteen boring days, mostly in a vac suit, unwashed, pulling high *g* all the way.

He proved her speculations correct by answering her almost immediately, if one allowed for a forty-minute time lag.

Ask Smith. But it might be worth pulling Carlson in and asking some questions.

Nbaro went and visited Smith after Tactics. He was exercising on a complex machine that appeared to use rubber bands to torture the unfit, and he smiled.

'I think you've just rescued me,' he said. 'I cannot believe how weak I've become.'

She nodded. 'You'll get it back,' she said.

He lay on the bench, head down.

'If I live long enough,' he agreed. 'Tell me *your* woes.'

Nbaro explained about the infiltrator, and her theory that Carlson might be linked to Dornau and the black market. And then she spoke of Carlson's behaviour.

'We have no evidence,' Smith said, 'and we're an investigatory organisation within the laws of the DHC. We need evidence.'

Nbaro chewed on that for her next two shifts, and then began to trawl her vid files for Carlson. He was so easy to find that she felt a fool for not thinking of it before; she could use recognition software to follow him almost anywhere in the ship.

She was sitting in warm, freshly cleaned sweats at the desk in her stateroom, when it occurred to her to see if her two investigations – Carlson's movements, and security camera irregularities – could be made to run together.

Nbaro asked the vid system to show her any visits that Carlson had made to the 6IX cargo hold.

I'm an idiot, she said to herself as she watched the vids.

But I'm catching on.

Nbaro reported to Smith in Medical, and showed him.

'Arrest him?' she asked.

Smith hummed a little. 'I need to get back to work before they give you my job,' he said. 'But no. Let's let him run with a monitor. Look, this is going to be a lot of work – I'll split it with you. We need to establish his routine, and then look into any variations from it. Ordinarily I'd ask Morosini. You know he's been maimed…'

'I know.' Nbaro *liked* Morosini. 'I don't think we can do that. Not yet.'

'I agree. If we can clean out these vipers then we can, indeed, restore Morosini.' He sighed. 'Don't go. They'll make me exercise again.'

Another watch, and the Flight 8 shuttle made the decision to make a full deceleration and dock; perhaps the decision had been made while Nbaro was asleep. That put Dorcas's return at least nine days away. The *Athens* was performing periodic high-burn decelerations herself, and she was constantly decelerating at between one and two *g*, depending on other factors; when she was at 2 *g* the artificial gravity felt queasy, somehow. And Morosini's malaise was felt throughout the ship; Thea felt it, and Hanna, and Locran.

Is this how the other ships began to die?

The landing party began to send live vid, with a forty-minute delay, of the station. They were grim, empty corridors, sealed spaces full of the dead. Nbaro saw the marine lieutenant's report; he was hollow-eyed and haunted.

'Explosive decompression,' he said, 'commensurate with a surprise attack. Radiation is high – a nuke close in, is my guess. Some people survived for a little while, but not very long – and they must have known they were already dead.'

Nbaro was sitting in the Master's briefing room, watching the Marine officer's report projected on the wall that had held the ancient woman's portrait until a screen deployed.

'The EMP destroyed most of the digital data,' the Marine said. 'I'm sending copies of some of the hard copy we're finding.'

Dorcas had sent a private report as well. He looked alert, and less haunted than the Marine, but he sounded subdued, and less patronising.

'All the evidence points to a trio of 普天下 Pǔ Tiān Xià cruisers,' he said. 'Though it makes no sense. Dozens of techs survived the attack, realised that their digital equipment was fried, and spent what were literally their last hours documenting the attack. Photos to follow.'

The photos were of handwritten documents. There was, of course, no vid – no replay of the attack.

No unimpeachable witness.

The Master whistled softly. He looked at Morosini.

The XO sat up.

'I guess we're at war with the Empire,' he said.

Morosini was hesitant; he seemed out of focus, and he still had no cat, and nothing about him seemed right.

'It makes no sense,' he echoed Dorcas.

'Seems pretty obvious,' the Chief Engineer said. 'They came after us at Sahel and they took out the station at Lighthouse. They're trying to kill the trade route.'

Nbaro missed Dorcas because he made her bolder.

'Sir, if I may…' she said, too softly.

But the Master looked at her. 'Go ahead, Lieutenant.'

Nbaro sat forward. 'A great deal of our actual, hard evidence on the attacks at Sahel points to…' She looked around. 'To a faction within the DHC being responsible.'

Morosini nodded.

'A faction looking to make sensational profits on the xenoglas trade – perhaps,' she said, speaking carefully, 'a faction looking to change the governance of the DHC.'

Nbaro looked around. Aadavan, the XO, looked positively inimical. Dukas, the Chief Engineer, looked puzzled.

Aadavan glanced at her, his handsome face bland. 'Occam's razor, Miz Nbaro. The PTX is shooting at us. We don't need an adolescent conspiracy theory.'

'We saw signs of a PTX faction fight on the docks at Sahel,' she said. 'I suspect they might have a rogue faction as well.'

The Master sat back and steepled his hands.

'I'm following,' he said.

'If this were as simple as war with PTX, I'd have expected unanimity among their ships at Sahel,' she said. 'Sir.'

The Master looked at her with his mild old eyes.

'Interesting,' he said. 'But you must admit, hardly conclusive.'

He looked around. 'In seven or eight days, we go to Insertion for Shannon's Star. Another long-jump.' He waved a hand and the holotank appeared over the table. 'After Shannon's Star we're inserting for Draconis, which has a route back into PTX space. After that, we *still* have five insertions to Trade Point.'

'We could still turn back,' Aadavan said. 'We cannot fight the whole PTX navy.'

'You heard Nbaro,' the Master said. 'She doesn't think we're facing the whole navy.'

Aadavan glanced at her and then back to the Master.

'Pardon me, sir, but Nbaro is a jumped-up midshipper with no experience as either an investigator or intelligence analyst. I can't put any faith in anything she says. And neither should you.'

The Master nodded. 'But she's lucky,' Pisani said. 'Anyway, I've already said I'm not turning back.'

Aadavan shrugged. 'I thought you were seeking advice.'

'You were mistaken,' the Master said. 'I was explaining the risk and the duration of the risk. If there is a trio of rogue PTX cruisers out here, that represents a real problem, but scarcely an insurmountable one.'

He looked at Nbaro.

'It would be useful to know how big this rogue faction might be,' he said. 'Our escorts can't sail beyond Far Point. We'll be alone for the last three insertions.'

Nbaro felt the hairs prickle on the back of her neck.

'Oh,' she said. And then, 'Sir, I'm doing my best.'

Nbaro was tempted to say, *Everything Aadavan says is true!* but she was coming to really dislike the XO and anyway, she had something more useful to add.

'Sir, Lieutenant Smith is returning to duty soon, and I have consulted him on every step of this. We have some ideas of where to go from here. That's all I should say at this time.'

Aadavan gave her an odd look.

The Master nodded crisply, and his quiet voice was kind.

'Tell Lieutenant Smith I miss him,' he said. 'Perhaps I'll go and visit him today.'

Trying to keep her tone light, she said, 'He'd enjoy that, sir, especially if you could interrupt his physical therapy.'

The Master laughed bitterly. 'Ouch. I know what that's like.'

Aadavan was still looking at her.

'Any idea why it's called Draconis?' Nbaro asked Drake.

She was leaning on Drake's counter in Small Cargo, drinking her coffee. Their coffee.

'You could look it up on your tab.' Drake produced her own and said, 'Draconis.'

'Would it help if I said, up until a few months ago, I'd never had a tab?'

'No,' Thea said. 'Anyway ... Oh. Huge solar flares, like a dragon's breath. Regular as clockwork. Apparently a very odd development for a small star. See? You can just look things up.'

Nbaro read Drake's tab. 'Couple of million people,' she said.

'Customers,' Thea said. 'Where you going?'

'I need to get down to Sixth Deck before we burn again.'

'Are you sure there's nothing else I can look up for you?' Thea asked sweetly.

'You said you had something to show me?' Nbaro asked.

Major Darkstar was sitting at one of the consoles. Nbaro slipped into the seat Nbaro thought of as Dorcas's while Darkstar, also now read in to the Special Service's programme, leaned over their screen. It was heavily encrypted, and thus slower and somehow more primitive than most digital data.

There were the two prisoners. They were in the dark, to allow them to sleep; of course, the vid had very sensitive infrared recording apparatus, and they were visible even inside their confining autodocs, like unborn babies in sonograms.

Nbaro saw them straining towards one another, reaching with their free hands, and when that failed, as they were too far apart, the vid recorded the very faint sound of knocking. A code...

'I have it all,' Darkstar said. 'Shall I separate them?'

'Until Dorcas returns and breaks their code, I'd say yes,' Nbaro answered.

The Marine nodded.

But in that moment, watching them strain silently towards each other, trying to communicate, Nbaro had realised something profound. And perhaps terrible.

And she had no one to tell.

Naisha Qaqqaq called Nbaro and she made the journey all the way to Sixth Deck Aft to see the Engineering officer.

'Two things,' Qaqqaq said. 'First...' She tossed a small machine, no bigger than an insect, on the worktable. 'That camera was set to watch the outer door here. Attached with organic gum. So I doubt it's been there long.'

Nbaro sat down at one of the systems, called up her log of vids and rotated through ship's cameras until she got to various passageway cameras in Sixth Deck Aft.

She saw a symbol on the third camera that she'd never seen before, and she pointed it out to Qaqqaq.

She sat down. 'It means someone else is on the system,' she said.

Nbaro brought up the third camera in the passageway to find that it was black – its vid slicked for ten hours.

She skipped forward two cameras immediately. She was dexterous in doing so, because she'd been through so many vid logs now that she knew most of the camera locations by heart.

She was greeted with a furtive figure in a contractor's jumpsuit moving along the corridor, passing directly under the camera.

The vid went dark.

'Shit,' Nbaro said, but her fingers were already flying on the holoboard.

'Get this on your tab,' she said to Qaqqaq.

The engineer pulled out her tab and shot a still image with a flash and then steadied.

Nbaro brought up the next camera, and there was the contractor coming down the passageway. Nbaro knew who he was already: Carlson.

He raised his head and the screen went black.

'Someone's working right now,' Nbaro said savagely. 'Killing the vid system.'

'I got that one,' Qaqqaq said.

'Last camera.'

Nbaro was trying to guess how long it would have taken Carlson to walk to the Special Service's hatchway. Forty seconds, she guessed, and typed it in.

The vid started, showing an empty passageway. Then went black.

'Shit.'

Qaqqaq showed her the playback. Nbaro ran it, and then, on a hunch, went to the playback she'd found the day before.

Erased. Her smoking gun had been deleted from the system … except for the copy she'd made to show Lieutenant Smith. Nbaro looked at it on her tab and breathed again.

'Good catch with the spy camera,' she told Qaqqaq. 'What's the second thing?'

Qaqqaq said, 'It's about the sensors, and trying to locate enemy ships running dark.'

'Sure,' Nbaro said.

Qaqqaq had led the work party that had attached new sensor packages at either end of the ship to widen the angle between detectors, however slightly.

'If using the length of the ship creates a noticeably better lens,' she said, 'then what if we fabricate drones to toss into space. We could create a line of the damned things 5000 kilometres across.'

'Even better if you could put them out by spacecraft. We could drop them behind us ...'

'Perfect.' Qaqqaq was taking notes. 'Then you could angle your detector cloud. Give them a tiny propulsion system and you can redirect them at least once.'

'Some of this must exist already,' Nbaro said. 'Our XC-3Cs carry an array of active sensors – radar and ladar – that we could dump into space and then use to fix a target without giving the ship's location away.'

She brought a schematic up on her tab and handed it over to Qaqqaq.

'I'll bet I could just modify a few of these,' she said.

Nbaro, who'd given far too much thought to how to find enemy cruisers running dark, nodded eagerly.

'I'll get you a remote sensor.'

Nbaro was Lioness for the shift that should have fallen half a day before the insertion, except that Mpono, working with the Master and Space Operations, launched another Flight 6 tanker that allowed all the spacecraft to match velocities faster and more accurately, and saved them almost half a day.

Suddenly, Nbaro would be Lioness for a watch with all the landing events and the insertion.

No one offered to hold her hand, so Nbaro assumed that she'd survive. She spent the hour before her watch started running a simulation of the launch cycle in a new system that the Master had promulgated. They were to enter the Shannon's Star system at Battle Stations and ready to fight.

She learnt the sequence by heart. And recorded her part so that she could send it out automatically upon insertion.

And then she was in the chair and it was all happening.

The landing spacecraft came aboard without mishap, and each one got a ship-wide cheer as they came aboard: first the tankers, one by one; Skipper Truekner had been out for sixteen days in a tiny cockpit on a small spacecraft, and everyone on the *Athens* knew how brutal that must have been.

Once Truekner had been aboard for ten minutes, Nbaro sent him a comms request. She asked Mpono to prepare an Insertion Alert for two spacecraft, and to inform her as soon as the newly landed Flight 6 spacecraft were cleared by Maintenance.

She did the same for the Flight 5 and Flight 3 Alerts.

She called Astrogation and got a countdown to Insertion with fifty-three minutes to go, which she sent to her main board so she'd have it on her display.

Flight 5 had two officers walking to their Alerts; Commander Talhoffer and another woman Nbaro didn't know at all. She put them first on her rapid launch programme, loaded to intercept incoming anti-ship missiles.

Sixteen minutes to Insertion. The landing barge from Flight 1 came into her area of control, got the numbers, called the ball and came aboard to a loud cheer.

As soon as the railgun was clear of the landing barge, Nbaro began to move her alerts on to the rails. She sent her launch schedule up to the Bridge and got a curt 'Good' from the Master.

Morosini didn't come and visit her.

Nbaro called Mpono, who was already in their spacecraft.

'Tir, do you have any of Qaqqaq's new sensor arrays aboard?'

'I have four. We're going to test them, regardless of what we find out there. Suleimani will do the same.'

'Good to hear, 6–0–2.'

Nbaro ran her own checklist.

Four minutes until Insertion.

'Take your drugs, everyone,' she said.

At two minutes, the Master came on.

'Listen up, shipmates,' he said. 'In two minutes we're inserting into a system that may have enemy ships waiting for us. Our escorts are ready and we're ready. Remember that we are the best ship and the best crew. Remember your duty. That is all.'

Nbaro had a moment to wonder how many crews had heard those words, or words like them. In space and, before that, on oceans.

She drank a little water, sat back in her acceleration couch...

Checked in with all five of her Alert pilots.

'Good to go.'

Here we go, then.

Insertion.

Shannon's Star. Nbaro wasn't even particularly muzzy; she felt more as if she'd drifted off a moment and was waking up in embarrassment, except she'd never been asleep.

She fired off her pre-recorded Alert launch sequence. She'd recorded the entire procedure so that it would run without her, and the pilots had pre-transmitted their take-off mass.

The ship shuddered slightly, as Alpha Echo 5–0–1 shot out of the bow, engines off, invisible to almost any detection. Four seconds later, Commander Talhoffer in 5–0–2 joined her.

The TAO was warming up the sensor array and Nbaro was looking over her screens, looking for enemy ships, looking...

She looked down at her own board and toggled her approval

for Mpono to launch. The railguns were cycling at the battle speed, not the safe, 'normal duty' speed.

Once again, they were moving fast, although not as fast as on the last insertion. Nbaro noted that they were approximately as far out as Jupiter would be in Old Terra's system – well out of the local sun's gravity well. Shannon's Star was another red dwarf, which was hardly surprising since they were the commonest stars in the whole spiral arm.

Almost no traffic, and the only incoming traffic was the blue-shifted data from the navigational beacons.

The TAO tagged something. Nbaro saw it happen in real time because her eyes were on the tactical screen; she looked up at the holo display to see something well across the system. A *long* way away. Seventy light minutes.

Nbaro knew from their astrogation plot that the new tag was roughly where they would expect to make their own insertion for Draconis.

She approved her fourth launch in forty seconds, as Suleimani went hurtling down the railgun track and vanished into the dark.

Nbaro looked at the ID tag on the TAO plot. She expanded it until she could see two blurry far-on spheres. The information was eighty-four minutes old, blurred by maths, blurred by distance and time and the computer's interpretation of their own deceleration. It reminded her of those evil problems on her maths boards at the Orphanage.

If a starship enters a system and begins a 6 g deceleration immediately, and a second starship at distance x ...

Nbaro toggled the TAO.

'If one of my birds does a burn,' she said, 'I can widen your lens and give you a better resolution.'

The TAO sounded gruff.

'If the thing works,' she said. 'Anyway, we've left enough Cherenkov radiation to guarantee that everyone in the system saw us arrive. Or rather, *will see us* when the light of that radiation reaches them.'

Nbaro toggled to Smoke. 'Alpha Foxtrot 6–o–2, this is Lioness, over.'

'Roger, Lioness, this is 6–o–2, go ahead.'

'Light 'em up, 6–o–2.'

'Roger, Lioness. Wait one.'

Somewhere off in space, Smoke pulled back the yoke and engaged their thrusters, and the spacecraft accelerated on a new vector, separating rapidly from the greatship. If Mpono followed the tactical drill, they were accelerating on an orthogonal vector – in effect, climbing 'up' above the system's elliptical plane.

About sixty seconds later, a younger voice full of excitement said, 'One away.'

That was almost certainly Eyre.

Nbaro toggled 6–o–5, Suliemani, and authorised the same manoeuvre, except that Suleimani's off-angle turn took her below the elliptical plane.

'Almighty,' the TAO said.

At the TAO repeater, Petty Officer Banderas gave an un-muffled whoop.

'Two away,' Eyre said, thousands of kilometres away. 'One is hot.'

'That's *fucking* amazing,' the TAO said.

Nbaro looked up to see Lieutenant Qaqqaq lying on the spare acceleration couch, beaming with happiness.

'One away,' said Suleimani's sensor operator.

'We're about to have a lens 500 kilometres across,' Nbaro said to no one in particular.

'Record this,' snapped the Master on the Command channel.

The other sensors came online, and suddenly the resolution on the two unidentified shapes eighty light minutes away improved dramatically.

The fifth sensor, and then the sixth, came online.

'PTX heavy cruisers,' the TAO said. 'Three of them. Running cold and dark. Amazing.'

Astrogation tagged them: *24 days ahead of us. About to insert for Draconis.*

Seventh sensor.

'There they go,' Banderas said, and the TAO in her earpiece said, 'They just inserted. Well, actually, they inserted eighty-one minutes ago.' And then, 'Look at that resolution.'

The Master came on.

'TAO, that means they might not have seen us jump in-system.'

'Roger that,' the TAO said after a moment. 'Morosini, confirm?'

Morosini appeared, a pale ghost of his formerly robust scarlet self.

'Confirm. They should have hit Insertion almost forty minutes before we arrived in system.'

'Ma'am?' Banderas asked. 'How is that possible? If we can see them, surely they can see us?'

Nbaro smiled with the memory of getting this wrong on a test.

'In their frame of reference, we're not here yet,' she said. 'In our frame of reference, they left the system before we arrived, but their light and radio waves and heat signatures are just reaching us now.'

Banderas came back, 'There's something wrong with the profile of those cruisers, ma'am. It's like they're too long.'

Nbaro went private with Banderas.

'Send it to Intel,' she said.

On the Command channel, the Master sounded grimly satisfied.

'Astrogation, give me the max-burn profile to get to a safe insertion for Draconis.'

Astrogation came back after a twenty-second delay.

'Assuming 6 g all the way with periodic zero g for breaks?'

'I think that's about all we can take, Astrogation.' He went on, 'I'm concerned that if these three took out Lighthouse, they might not scruple at Far Point.'

'Understood,' Astrogation said. 'I can get us into an insertion in sixteen days.'

'Try ten gees,' the Master said.

'Not much better, but a lot more spacers are injured or even dead ... Eleven days?'

'Morosini?' the Master asked.

'We can't get there in time to save Far Point,' Morosini said. 'But given their current course and speed, sixteen days would get us in system in time to record them if they're in range of the Draconis station. And with respect, Master, the planet at Draconis is probably too big and too populous for some cruisers to destroy.' The fragile AI seemed to be thinking. 'I can't imagine what they would accomplish by attacking a human population centre.'

The Master said, 'I have yet to see any limitations of size or empathy on this bunch. Sixteen days it is. Make it so.'

Nine days at 6 g was going to be like hell come to space. Nbaro finished her watch at 6 g and heard the warnings – twenty minutes at artificial gravity.

She went straight to Sixth Deck, and found Darkstar in the acceleration couch and no sign of Dorcas. Nbaro cursed and ran for the drop-shaft and her own rack. She got in and lashed down with only a few seconds to spare, before the other five Nbaros sat on her couch as full deceleration returned.

'Cut that a little close, didn't you?' Thea asked.

She grunted.

Half an hour later, and Dorcas contacted her on her tab.

I learned so much. Still sorting my data.

Nbaro wrote, *Read my Carlson file.*

He wrote, *I will. I have an entire ship's manifest for the* Hong Kong. *And all the navigational information for the three enemy ships. They failed to clear out the buffers on the . . .*

She stared at the tab, willing him to go on, straining her neck in 6 g.

Carlson killed Dornau? You are quite brilliant.

Nbaro typed back, *Only Smith knows. I'm trying to find the last infiltrator. And their allies. And their equipment locker.*

He typed, *I need to read all of this properly.*

Six hours of torture and bad sleep later and he typed, *I think I have our infiltrator's hideout.*

Nbaro turned her head far enough to look at the digital still he'd tabbed her. It was from a surveillance camera, and it was in Cargo on Seventh Deck – Hold 61X, where Dornau's corpse had been found.

She hit *play* and the scene went black.

She laughed, despite the 6 g.

'That's not going to work this time,' she said.

'Are you going to talk in your sleep all night?' Thea asked.

'Maybe,' Marca said.

She typed back, *You are also brilliant.*

I know, he responded.

I think I know why the Starfish communicate the way they do, she put in, laboriously, as they had some fluctuation in their deceleration.

You already had my full attention. But now I'm thinking of crawling up there to your stateroom, he typed, so rapidly that she laughed.

'Gack! Marca, do you have someone up there with you?' Thea gasped. 'No sex in high *g*.'

Nbaro started typing.

The Starfish were either prisoners or slaves. For a long, long time. Long enough to develop an entire biomechanical approach to secret communications.

Silence. The sound of some ship-part under stress, giving off a periodic clacking noise, and something further along the passageway that was loose and sliding along the flood under the deceleration, slamming into the bulkheads. A mop? A bucket?

And a vibration Nbaro had never heard before.

That's incredible. And obvious. Damn. How did you figure that out?

I watched our prisoners attempt to communicate, she typed.

And then, when he didn't answer right away, Nbaro drifted off into a desperately uncomfortable sleep.

She awoke to the bells from her tab.

In one hour the Master is giving us a one-hour break. Be ready. You and I and a Marine team are going into Hold 61X.

12

Nbaro took four minutes to shower and two more to get into a clean flightsuit, and then Thea helped her put on her armour.

'What the fuck is going on?' Thea asked.

'Some shit,' Marca said.

'I have armour and a sidearm,' Thea said. 'And I'm on the list for boarding party. And I'm a lot better in zero *g* than you.'

So Marca spent three more minutes helping Thea into her armour, and then the two of them went to the drop-shaft and dropped down to Sixth Deck.

Smith was there, with Dorcas and four Marines led by Drun. Drun nodded to Nbaro, and his eyes flicked to Drake.

'Ms Drake,' he said.

'Gunny,' she replied.

Smith raised an eyebrow.

Nbaro felt defensive.

'She's trained and available,' she said. 'Also, it's hard to hide anything from your room-mate.'

Smith nodded to Drun.

Drun grinned. 'It's fine, sir. Ms Drake, you're the rearguard, holding the hatch in case this all goes to shit. Now I don't have to leave a Marine at the hatch.' He pointed down the passageway. 'Lieutenant Smith took out all the cameras.'

Smith shrugged. 'Someone on this ship is rotten,' he said. 'Until I know who, I don't want them using Morosini against us.'

Drun looked at Nbaro. 'I'm inclined to let you be armed, ma'am, as I've seen you shoot. But my fire team has trained for this exact mission, and in my eyes you're not a shooter unless something goes seriously wrong. Do you copy?'

She nodded. 'Understood, Gunny.'

He handed her a battle gun: a short, boxy carbine with internal dampers and an optics system and a lot of other very useful auxiliary gear. One of the other Marines – Wilson Akunje, no less – adjusted the stock to fit against her armour.

Drun and Smith checked the time on their tabs.

Drun looked them over.

'So – here it is. Stick goes through the door and secures the entry area. Assuming no enemy contact, Mr Dorcas enters behind us with the sweeper and starts the tech sweep. When he locates the target, we isolate it with lines of fire. Akunje has the autogun, Juarez has the elephant gun. Assad and McDonald are with me. After that we're playing this by ear – if we have to crack it, I have a door charge. Nbaro is overwatch, Drake is rearguard. Lieutenant Smith is in overall command, I'm in tactical command. Everyone ready?'

Akunje shook his head. 'Lieutenant Smith is in overall command, but—?'

'I mean I give the orders. Lieutenant Smith can tell us to press, or withdraw, or change targets. In effect, he tells me what to achieve, and I tell you how to achieve it, Akunje.'

'Got it. Sir.'

'Anyone else?'

He looked around. Juarez looked keen; she was smiling. Akunje looked intense and focused.

Nbaro raised her hand.

'The bad guys know we're coming,' she said. 'Maybe not here and now, but soon.'

Drun nodded. 'Got that.'

'We need whatever's in that hiding place,' she said. 'What's our plan to take it intact?'

Drun was all business. 'Juarez can kill a tank through the side of one of those cargo containers.'

Juarez nodded. 'Just show me the heat spike, ma'am. I'll do the rest.'

Dorcas looked at Nbaro. 'In other words, we're not taking prisoners.'

Drun's face didn't change. 'You didn't specify that as a desired outcome. Sir.'

Smith shook his head. 'No, I did not. Let's go.'

'Ready?' Drun asked.

The Marines formed in a tight stick at the door, and suddenly their weapons looked lethal, aimed with intent. Drake knew her role, and was already covering the corridor behind them, pressed against the bulkhead between Smith and Dorcas.

'Three, two, one,' Drun called softly.

'Go!'

The hatch opened, and the four Marines went through so fast it surprised Nbaro.

'We're in,' Drun said.

Dorcas slipped in. He had what looked like a rifle, except that it had sensors and even, apparently, a microphone. His left hand worked on a holographic keypad as he crossed the threshold.

The lights in the hold had been disabled by Dorcas so that they advanced into darkness. Nbaro had IR goggles on her helmet, and she flipped them down to peer into the darkness. Smith pressed her into a kneeling position by the hatch.

The space was vast – at least 500 metres long and almost twenty metres high. Most of the space was stacked to the overhead with regulation crates in the standard DHC cargo sizes. The cargo brought aboard at New London and Sahel was, for the most part, stacked according to the system to which it would be delivered, and then by stability. The cargo-handling computer was one of the ship's most important, and Cargo had hundreds of spacers, from the administrative officers like Thea all the way to the men and women who drove the grav lifts and tagged the cargo or moved it depending on dozens of factors.

Cargo manifests were further complicated by the fact that every spacer, regardless of rank, was allowed a two-metre shipping container for private trade – an ancient privilege that was one of the major reasons that the DHC Service had such an easy time recruiting. Some spacers sold their cargo space to someone else; even at a standard rate, that was equivalent to several years' pay. Others became small, independent merchants: a two-metre cube and some careful investments could make a spacer's fortune.

But the private cargoes could play havoc with the computerised system, and Smith had uncovered some illegalities early in the cruise, in a separate investigation. Now his investigations were paying off, in that they were aware of dozens of uncounted containers in Hold 61X.

Nbaro thought about all of that while she watched the Marines cover Dorcas.

Drun ghosted forward from cover to cover. The containers were stacked in blocks, eight metres by eight metres, like giant puzzle blocks. Some were stacked up to sixteen metres, and all of the crates in the top section had heavy nanofibre arms connecting them to the rigid beams of the overhead. The standardised cargo containers locked together electromagnetically and mechanically, but they were also locked into the deck, bulkheads and overhead, and packing regulations required the contents to be stable to $15g$.

The gaps or walkways between the stacks were a uniform

two metres, wide enough for the heaviest grav sleds. The main corridor down the centre was four metres across.

Juarez used a derrick to climb to the top of the nearest stack, and then she moved along the tops, passing around the supporting girders and using a carbonfibre beam to cross the main corridor high above Drun. Akunje was right by Dorcas, the muzzle of his autogun tracking in concert with his IR goggles.

Dorcas had moved well down the main corridor and come to one of the many cross-junctions. His sensor swept back and forth, back and forth …

And stopped. He took another step, his figure glowing green in Nbaro's optics, Akunje so close to him that the two were almost a single image.

'I have a possible,' Dorcas said.

There was a burst of fire. It happened too fast for Nbaro to react, or even drop to the deck. She was standing by the first row of crates, only about two metres from where Dornau's body had been found, and her ears were ringing despite her helmet. The gunfire was brutally loud in the enclosed space. A cargo crate by her head splintered.

'Sound off!' Drun's voice.

'Roger,' Akunje said. 'I've got Mister Dorcas.'

'Roger,' Juarez said.

'Roger,' McDonald said.

'Roger,' Assad said.

'Roger,' Nbaro said.

Drun went forward very cautiously. Nbaro watched him move, and only after reading his orientation did she see the downed figure, and the bright heat signature – a partially opened door with a dead body holding it open.

Drun knelt.

'Got her, Juarez,' he said. 'Akunje scored too. Nice job, team.'

Nbaro was still trying to see.

Smith's voice: 'OK. Let's see what we've got. Gunny, secure a perimeter.'

'Always,' Drun said. 'Sir.'

Nbaro slipped forward, cradling her carbine. She met Dorcas, who was leaning against a cargo container.

'You OK?'

Nbaro couldn't read his face on IR. But his tone was flat.

'I thought I was dead,' he said. 'But it turned out someone else was dead.'

She put a hand on his shoulder, and then went to the door.

Smith said, 'I've cut access to the cameras in 61X. Lights.'

The lights came on and Nbaro flipped up her IR, after-images from the flare of light dancing across her retinas. She blinked and looked at the dead woman. She was small, heavily muscled, and wore very expensive body armour with xenoglas inserts. Smith bent over, photographed her open eyes, and ran them to ID her.

Drun spoke on the Command circuit.

'She had a tripwire and a detection system. Akunje bypassed the tripwire through good tactical awareness, but the motion detector alerted her and she tried for a shot.'

Juarez's heavy rifle had killed her right through her armour. Akunje had hit her twice between the armoured plates.

'Don't fuck with the Marines,' Nbaro said softly.

'Truer words, ma'am,' Drun answered.

Nbaro was inside a cargo container that was a full four metres by four metres. Smaller than the smallest of the controlled housing apartments in City. Larger than her own cabin nine decks above.

There was a small acceleration couch, some food storage, and a computer: a small unit with a holoscreen.

Dorcas was searching the dead woman's pockets and produced her tab.

For the next thirty minutes, with Smith advising, they opened every container, laid out every item they found, opened food containers and sent hundreds of items aft to the Special Services office and lab.

'Eight minutes to deceleration,' Drun said.

'I've got a work party trying to access 62X,' Drake reported. 'I hid my gun and said the passageway was closed until further notice. A mouthy rating tells me we should have declared this area locked out if we were working here. She was pissed.'

'Good job, miz,' Drun said. 'We'll be finished soon.'

Fifteen minutes later, Drake and Nbaro were out of their armour, and pinned in their racks by the deceleration.

'I heard the shooting,' Drake said. 'What's going on?'

Nbaro pondered different answers. And then said, 'We still have some enemies aboard.'

'I sorta figured that out,' Drake whispered.

At the next pause in the braking burn, Smith arrested Carlson. The prisoners were separated, and Dorcas vanished into his own information-warfare world. His only communication to Nbaro said, *I think I have the codes to Morosini.*

Nbaro found that she was praying.

Constant deceleration at 6 g was so exhausting that it was all any of them could do to eat, perform the bare minimum duties, and sleep. On the third day of deceleration, Nbaro was Lioness for a full watch under deceleration, and there wasn't enough to do; the grinding pressure of the burn combined with the boredom to make the watch last for what seemed like several eternities.

Nbaro played with the various instruments, watching the two friendly battlecruisers. The sensor arrays dropped almost half a million kilometres astern still functioned, and she was able to use them to watch the battlecruisers and her own ship, and she was astounded at the resolution. But, of course, the millions of kilometres made for a two-way time lag...

She wrote a congratulatory note to Qaqqaq.

Her back hurt. And she wanted to talk to someone.

Eventually, the minutes ticked down and Guille relieved her in the zero-*g* interval. She managed to wolf down a bulb of curry, Drake made them excellent coffee, and then they were back in their racks.

'This is boring,' she said.

'No shit,' Thea said.

For her next awake shift, Nbaro saw that she was on the flight schedule for the insertion alert into Draconis, and her adrenaline peaked without her leaving her rack. Like every spacer on the ship, she'd rigged her tab to lock into a space in the overhead so she could read or play games or respond to texts without turning her head in the nanofoam of the acceleration couch. She tabbed her receipt and acknowledgement immediately.

So, two endless days later, Nbaro was in the co-pilot couch on Alpha Foxtrot 6–o–6, with Skipper Truekner in the pilot couch next to her, and Indra next to Eyre in the back seats. They listened to the Master's brief message together as the countdown to Insertion ran on.

'We might set a record for the passage to Trade Point,' Truekner said. 'If we keep moving at this pace.'

Nbaro glanced at him. They were under full deceleration, and would be almost all the way to Insertion, buying them a margin of error on their velocity. That meant that she only saw him in her peripheral vision.

'Is that good or bad?' she asked.

'Both,' he said. 'Everyone ready?'

'Insertion in five, four, three, two...'

*

'You are three to launch...' said Tower.

'Roger, Tower,' Nbaro managed, although it felt as if her teeth were stuck together. She took a little water from her store.

The tactical display... Nbaro peeled her eyes open and made them focus. The tactical display was bright with objects, and some of them were resolving, their datasets solved for certain identities even as she watched. DHCS *Lepanto*, one of their escorts, had arrived almost three minutes ahead of them, and was so close that a collision alarm had to be sounding somewhere; she was only about sixty kilometres away, and the data indicated she was moving at a slightly higher velocity. She was pulling away, the distance widening.

That was in real time.

Nbaro felt the ship shudder as one of the Gunslingers went off the bow.

Her data from system central was only four hours old; the Astrogator had done an amazing job. They were deep in the Draconis system, only two light hours from the inhabited planet, which was on their side of the sun, a bright G2 main sequence star with a big gas giant and Draconis Prime inside the Goldilocks zone.

Again the railgun made the ship vibrate and Nbaro felt her own craft moving into the launch position.

'Alpha Foxtrot 6–0–6, you are go for launch,' Tower said.

'Roger, Tower,' she said.

She turned and saw the launch petty officer in his armoured compartment.

Truekner saluted and the ship went by them in a blur of light as they hurtled down the rails. Then Nbaro was in the Black, lit only by the gleam of her instruments.

This time, there was no direction from the ship; Truekner flew them 'up' above the ecliptic and put the hammer down, pressing all four of them deep into their seats.

The system was full of contacts – or at least, four hours ago, it had been full of contacts – and the navigational beacons were updating the Bridge and the TAO faster than Nbaro could follow the data.

As soon as they passed fifty kilometres relative to the ship, Nbaro tagged Eyre and he dropped a sensor.

She laid out six more drops on the tactical map.

'That's good, ma'am,' Eyre said. 'Two away.'

As the first sensor came online, the resolution of the system changed. As before, by the sixth drop from both spacecraft, they were getting recognisable images of ships from most of the in-system traffic and the computers were providing identifications.

Truekner flew them in an intricate pattern designed to spread the drops wider – starting to form a disc rather than a simple line.

'Where are the PTX ships?' Truekner asked.

Nbaro was watching a smaller version of the TAO's action display.

'Still not there,' she said. 'I assume they're running dark.'

'They can't have entered the system dark,' Truekner said.

'It's still hours before Draconis Control tells us anything, much less answers our queries.'

'Why, thanks for that, Lieutenant.'

Truekner was laughing at her and she accepted it, watching the data flow by.

'I think I have them,' Indra said, her voice full of excitement.

'You do?' Nbaro asked, and thought: *Don't sound like that. Smooth professionalism. Not surprise and doubt.*

Indra didn't respond. 'Tagging on your screen, ma'am. Not putting it out yet.'

'Concur,' Eyre said. 'I count three hulls, and their size and heat signature is consistent with ...'

428

Nbaro saw them. They were high off the plane of the ecliptic, and moving very fast. She looked at them for a few seconds.

'Concur. Skipper?'

Truekner had a very small screen – his primary task was to fly the spacecraft – but he had a look.

'Looks good to me.'

'What are they doing, sir?' Nbaro asked.

Truekner was relaxing; she could see it in the way his helmet rested against the cushions.

So, he'd been ready for an engagement.

He took his hands off the yoke and flexed them.

'So… Now they have no good choices, which is the advantage we bought with all that hard deceleration. If they decelerate, the whole system can come after them. Their radiation must have given them away when they arrived, so Draconis Control knows they're there, and when they get our first transmission they'll know who transited ahead of us. They'll have a track. But of course, thanks to a little wizardry from Lieutenant Qaqqaq, we've got a way of finding them. So they can either continue to move really fast, hazard an overspeed insertion and end up as photons, or they can slow down right into our sights. I don't know what the Master has planned, but right now, we have the tactical upper hand. The weather gauge, as they used to say in the old days.'

'And they haven't dumped any velocity,' Nbaro said.

'Exactly. They don't want to show their drive plumes.' Truekner was doing some calculations on his kneeboard tab. 'We're into fuel problems now. We should have taken on fuel at Shannon's. We can make another insertion and decelerate, but we ought to fuel here. Those cruisers are smaller than us, and carry less hydrogen.'

Suddenly, the Master's decision to force them through eleven days of hard deceleration made sense… made all sorts of sense.

They were at a lower starting velocity, they had more fuel in reserve and they had more options.

'Somehow I always thought a space battle would be very… fast,' she said.

'The Master's shaping the battlefield to our advantage,' Truekner said. 'Which is slow business. It'll be fast when it happens. But better it never happens at all.'

They landed and Nbaro debriefed in Intelligence with Eyre. He passed over the spacecraft's observations from his tab more as a formality than anything else; the ship already had all the hard data.

Then she slept for the first time in twelve days – really slept. She slept for eight solid hours and awoke to a quiet ship. She stood a watch in her own ready room, working on various reports and looking over maintenance forms, and completed a required and utterly unimportant material readiness profile for a fleet-wide survey of equipment. Or maybe it was ultimately important. Either way, Truekner had sent it to her for completion. She dutifully examined several hundred items in the ready room and then down in Maintenance, before finally going into EVA.

Spacer Chu looked at her and then looked away.

Nbaro was going through helmets when Chu said, 'They came and took Petty Officer Carlson away.'

'Yes,' Nbaro replied.

'What'd he do? I liked him.'

He was a likeable spy, murderer, and black market operative. And I'm pretty sure he tried to kill me.

Come to think of it, it's probably only luck – and Chu – which kept him from sabotaging my suit or my helmet.

I am lucky. I wonder if my life was so bad the first sixteen years that I bought myself some luck.

'I'm pretty sure he did some bad stuff,' Marca responded.

'It wasn't just about finding you a black-market helmet?' Chu asked quietly.

'Not at all,' Nbaro said. And then, after thinking it over, she said, 'People died.'

'Oh.' Chu was silent for a while. 'Sorry, ma'am. People are asking questions.' Another pause, and then, with more emotion: 'Marines came to take him, in armour, with big guns. Like he was dangerous.'

'He was very dangerous,' Nbaro replied.

She went on watch as Tower in Space Operations and discovered that the three potentially hostile ships had all begun hard decelerations – 10 g.

Smoke was Lioness. They said, 'I've talked to TAO and he's predicting they'll make the next insertion in about sixty hours.'

'And what are we doing?'

Mpono gave her a thin smile.

'I've no idea.'

Six hours later, the flight schedule was reissued and it became obvious what they were doing: they were moving cargo into the system to keep the Master's options open, while decelerating as hard as was consistent with keeping the AG and allowing the crew to rest.

'Depending on what our enemies do,' Mpono said at the end of their watch, 'we'll refuel and dock at Draconis, or follow them. I guess.'

It was odd – almost surreal – to fly a cargo run into one of Draconis's outer mining stations while there were potentially hostile ships in system. Even though Nbaro knew that their vector and speed made any kind of military engagement almost impossible in the near future, their very existence added tension to her routine cargo mission. She docked at the orbital with

Suleimani as her co-pilot, and exchanged a hold full of xenoglas mining components for a hold full of gold, silver, and copper.

'What the hell's going on out there, spacer?' the foreman asked her. 'Even the juried vids make it sound like the fucking universe is coming to a fucking end.'

Nbaro nodded, tight-lipped.

'My brother says we're at war with PTX,' he said, tabbing her the new bill of lading.

She frowned, and began inspecting cargo.

'Hey,' the man said. 'What are you doing?'

'We check every piece going aboard. Everything has to match. No exceptions.'

'You calling us cheats?' the man asked.

He was big, and had tattoos on top of his tattoos, and he was trying to be intimidating.

Nbaro smiled back, her new tactic.

'I'm obeying my orders,' she said. 'It's nothing personal, sir. We're doing this everywhere, all the time.'

He relaxed. 'Oh. Tough fuckin' times, then.'

'Yes, sir,' she said. 'This scan doesn't match.'

It took an hour to discover that the ingots had been mismatched; someone had made an error of one digit. Nbaro called it in to the ship and waited while it was made good, and then had to make up the hour. The station refuelled her, and she had to blast along, pinned to her seat, because she was already scheduled for another run with Suleimani, this time with the senior woman as the pilot.

It was the first cargo run Nbaro had ever made with the back seats full – Indra and Brezhnev, a spacer she'd seen in EVA but never flown with. The two of them spent their time dropping sensors and adding them to the array.

Nbaro landed neatly and oversaw the cargo shift, so that Suleimani could take the two sensor operators down to

Intelligence to debrief. Before she left the spacecraft, she said, 'We're making tactical history here. We'd better start documenting it.'

Nbaro nodded, as more work loomed.

'Yes, ma'am.'

'Shit, Nbaro, we're both lieutenants now. No ma'am required.' Suleimani snorted.

An hour later they were in another spacecraft, burning for Somerleigh Orbital. The Control tech tried to dock them in Russian, and his accent was so thick in Anglatin that it took Brezhnev's intervention to get them a berth. The young spacer was very competent on the comms, and Nbaro made a note to that effect on the flight log.

'Give me Brezhnev for the cargo load?' Nbaro asked. 'The guy speaks Russian, and I'm guessing the whole station runs in Russian.'

'Good idea,' Suleimani said.

The miners on Somerleigh were no more fond of having their cargoes inspected than they had been on the mining station, and having Brezhnev explain in Russian was a huge advantage. They turned around in seventy minutes.

'Master's briefing room as soon as you've debriefed,' the skipper said to Nbaro when she went into Maintenance.

She went up the elevator to the bridge level, still fully kitted out for space, helmet under her arm.

Nbaro felt ridiculous in the beautiful, wood-panelled room, and Captain Aadavan looked at her and grimaced.

'Uniform of the day on the Bridge, Midder,' he said.

Nbaro stiffened. 'Apologies, sir. I was told to be here immediately.'

Aadavan raised an eyebrow. 'Don't explain your misunderstanding. Get moving.'

She turned to go as the Master came in.

'Where are you headed?' he asked.

'My orders, sir. Uniform of the day is required to be on the Bridge. Sir.' Aadavan's voice was flat – unengaged.

The Master gave Aadavan a long look under his heavy eyebrows.

'Interesting,' he said. 'Well, since she's here, I'd rather she stayed.'

'Of course, sir,' Aadavan said.

The elevator cycled and Dorcas stepped into the room with the Chief Engineer at his shoulder. Dukas was wearing dark blue coveralls that were stained in almost fashionable swirls with bright hydraulic fluids and were most certainly not 'uniform of the day'. A faint smell of burnt electricals clung to her like an exotic and dangerous perfume.

Aadavan nodded to her.

'Uniform of the day on the Bridge,' he said to the Chief Engineer. His voice was just as flat.

Captain Dukas shrugged.

'I don't have time to change,' she said. 'Sorry, XO.'

The Master glanced at them. 'Major Darkstar has asked to be excused.'

He sat, they all followed suit, and Morosini appeared.

The doors opened once more, and the Astrogator, Captain Fraser, arrived. He smiled at Nbaro and bowed to the Master. Meanwhile, Nbaro glanced at the AI. He was wearing his old, accustomed red, and his image was considerably more solid than it had been.

Still no cat, though.

'So,' Pisani said. 'I have a difficult decision to make, and I need any data you can share.'

Silence.

He waved his hand and the table became a holotank. The three hostile cruisers were illuminated in red; their escorts were in blue. The holo showed the Draconis system: the gas giant, the habitable planet and the other two, as well as the sparse asteroid belt.

'So...' Pisani said again. 'Our shadows are right there – seven light minutes away, well above the ecliptic. They've made their plan – they're going through the system, decelerating, and heading for an insertion to, we assume, Argos 4569. Morosini says there's no mathematical possibility that they'll attempt to decelerate to fight.'

He looked around.

Captain Fraser waved at the holotank with his tab, and a course projection overlay appeared on the three PTX ships.

'They don't have a lot of choice,' Fraser said. 'They entered fast and turned up out of the ecliptic early.'

Pisani nodded. 'Here's the problem. We have options, and the Astrogator's brilliant insertion to here gave us an edge. But let's face it – we have to go to Argos, and our enemies know it. It's the longest jump on this leg of our journey, and this is where our escorts have to turn back.' He shrugged. 'The evidence of the PTX ships and their current course suggests they think they can make the insertion for Argos.'

The Chief Engineer looked doubtful. 'They're too small to manage it. I swear, sir.'

Pisani nodded. 'Morosini?'

The AI leaned back as if considering it.

'There are new technologies rolling out of the Anti-spinward marches,' he said. 'And new ship designs. Even our own escorts are part of that programme.' He shrugged. 'It's within parameters of possibility that 普天下 Pǔ Tiān Xià has access to these technologies and has long-jump capabilities in those three cruisers. Regardless of the technologies, those three ships are on exactly the course and speed commensurate with an insertion for Argos, given their initial entrance in-system.'

Fraser nodded his assent.

Dorcas leaned forward. 'And our guess is that they think we don't know where they are.'

'Ahh,' Pisani agreed. 'That was going to be my point. Thanks to Qaqqaq's brilliant sleight of hand, we have new detection capabilities. But they probably believe we're at a loss to detect them, since they're running cold and dark.'

Aadavan's expression didn't change, but he said, 'Surely they have to consider the possibility?'

Pisani leant back. 'These bastards have been taking risk after risk. The usual sin of people who think they're smarter than everyone else. I think they're betting the farm that we don't see them, and my prediction is that they've arranged for some event to cover their system exit.'

Fraser waved, and the holotank responded.

'Fifty-four hours till a major solar flare,' he said. 'If we're on our expected course, their Cherenkov radiation on insertion will vanish behind the solar flares and they'll insert about here.'

He leaned out with his tab to indicate where.

Pisani nodded. 'Perfect. So. That's their strategy. Now we have to decide ours. We have several issues. One is that we can't force an engagement in this system. There's no combination of acceleration burns and weapons that gets us close enough.'

For a moment, a dozen pale blue overlays showed some options: a mass high-acceleration launch of all the military spacecraft; an extended 10-g burn towards the ecliptic; half a dozen other high-risk strategies. None of them got torpedoes in range on the holo. Pisani dismissed them all with a wave of his hand.

'Second, we lose our escorts beyond this system, so if we have to fight, it's just us. Third, we need fuel. We don't have to get it here ... but if we don't, then we have precious little manoeuvre room in Argos. Our enemies will be aware of all of this.'

The holotank altered again, showing the Argos system: a red dwarf, six big rocks scarcely justifying the term planets, an extensive asteroid belt, and a gas giant.

Aadavan nodded. 'And they could manoeuvre to prevent us from refuelling, or at least to make it risky.'

Pisani nodded grimly. 'Precisely. We're very vulnerable during refuelling operations. They know that, too.'

The holotable showed the single blue track of the *Athens* falling into orbit under fire from the three adversary ships.

Dorcas spoke up. 'Of course, we can refuel here.'

'We can. And we can do it safely. But then we forfeit our time advantage. They have all the time in the world to brake and prepare for an engagement, while we enter the system ... blind. And at Argos, there are no witnesses.'

The holotable showed the three enemy cruisers slingshotting around the gas giant and heading back at them for a head-to-head engagement.

Aadavan nodded. 'Sir, the obvious and safest solution is to turn for home. I've stated this on several occasions, and I feel it's my duty to speak now. The threat to the ship is too great – the DHC cannot risk the *Athens*.'

Dorcas smiled at Nbaro for no particular reason, just then.

The Master glanced around. 'Does anyone else feel that way?'

Dorcas shrugged. 'No. Turning back is a foolish idea.'

Aadavan turned. 'If you were one of my officers, I would see you silenced for such insubordination.'

Dorcas shrugged. 'But I'm not. I'm a DHC shareholder and a patrician. Your idea would sacrifice the distance and time we've gained, and the risk of a battle that I'm confident we can win, to preserve a ship at great cost to the very people who depend on it.'

'Are you speaking as a veteran of space tactics?' Aadavan asked, his voice finally registering something other than detachment.

Dorcas's expression didn't change.

'No one here is a veteran of these tactics.' His tone was insufferably patronising.

Pisani looked down the table. 'Morosini?'

The AI shook his head. 'I am in the process of an extensive restoration of my selfhood and capabilities,' he said. 'I am unsure of myself.'

'Captain?' Pisani asked the engineer.

Dukas rocked her head back and forth, as if she was listening to music.

'I say we go ahead. But Vettor, we should take on the fuel here. Preserve our options. Maybe Bernie here will make another brilliant insertion, and we'll be right past the bastards and make them chase us.'

'I pray that happens.' Pisani made an Old Catholic gesture.

'If we are without fuel, they can play a long game and win it,' she said.

'You don't think we should turn back,' Pisani said.

Dukas made a face. 'No.'

'You're risking a greatship based on hopes and prayers,' Aadavan said. 'Let the record show I am against it. Look at Morosini. You think we can win a combat with newer, more advanced ships while our AI is unsure of itself? You're ...'

Dorcas looked at him. The two men locked eyes, and Nbaro thought for a moment there might be violence.

'Captain Fraser?' the Master asked.

His voice was soft, and yet overrode Aadavan's.

Fraser turned his head to one side, like a good dog gazing quizzically at his master.

'If we let them have a two-hundred-hour head start,' he said, 'then when we arrive they could be anywhere in that system, travelling at almost any speed. Offset against that, I think I'm better than their astrogators. And Qaqqaq's wizardry means we'll have their location in two or three hours after insertion. These are both tactical advantages.'

Pisani looked interested.

'It depends on how much risk you want to take, Vettor,' Fraser said. 'I could aim high, and come in above the plane. Aim low and come in below it. But, of course, I could miss. That's the problem. We follow the same courses year after year because, within a margin of error, they work. But I could aim to miss, so to speak. To enter the system above them, or below, and just outrun them to the exit insertion.'

Aadavan shook his head. 'This is madness. Or you could miss, and we could end up in the Deep Black without a referent.'

Fraser shrugged. 'Yup.'

Pisani sat back. 'Interesting,' he said. 'Nbaro?'

She shook her head. 'I don't know enough to speak.'

'Then guess for me,' Pisani said. 'Be *lucky*.'

Nbaro spread her hands. 'Well … Dorcas has mentioned our duty to our shippers and our consignees. If we refuel, we can unload our cargoes for Draconis and take on cargo – business as usual. That might ease the markets here. Sir, I'm just repeating what Thea Drake tells me, but it seems to me—'

'The opinion of a midder,' Aadavan said.

The Master paused. He'd been about to speak, and now he glanced at Aadavan.

'I asked her opinion, XO. So when you interrupt like that, you're countermanding me. Let's be civil, here.'

Aadavan took a hold of himself.

'I believe this would be a grave error.'

'So you keep saying. Nbaro, I agree with your analysis, and I don't mind being reminded that we are, first and foremost, a trade ship. Let's eat this little crisis one bite at a time. I'm going to commit to refuel and exchange cargo here.'

Fraser leaned forward. 'Then I have a suggestion.'

'Try me,' Pisani said.

Fraser sketched a course on the holotank with his tab.

'We match the adversary ships until we lose them in the solar flares,' he said. 'They're at $3.3g$ – we stay at $3g$. But as soon as we're covered, we brake for orbit –' the braking burn looked harsh – 'and launch everything that can refuel us. Here.'

Fraser showed the station.

'We refuel while we unload the cargo. If they hit Insertion here, then we have a little under one hundred ninety hours to complete this work…' He indicated a course. 'We could insert here, within the margins. Our speed is quite low, and we haven't given them too long to hide in the Argos system. For sure, not enough to decelerate and come back at us.'

Dorcas spoke up. 'And they won't know, when we come in-system, if we refuelled or not. We could…' He smiled. 'We could let them believe a few things.'

Pisani stood. 'Excellent.'

Aadavan stood. 'I wish to make a formal protest, sir.'

'Protest noted, Captain.'

Pisani looked around.

'Better prep for a hard burn,' he told them all. 'And, Nbaro, tell Space Ops to get everything they can done in the next fifty-four hours.'

It wasn't a nightmare at all. It was the hardest, longest exposure to high-risk work Nbaro had ever done, and it went on and on, and required levels of co-ordination and teamwork that she'd never seen before and that the Orphanage had never allowed her to imagine.

Space Operations began with a planning meeting that included all of the watch-standers, all of the Cargo and Flight commanders and any senior pilot who wanted to volunteer. The

Space Operation Centre was packed so tightly that it was hot and humid and hard to move around.

In two hours, under Mpono's iron glance, they worked through a massive flight schedule that was designed to hide the volume and speed of the launches from prying eyes, with cargo flights going off cold, and not burning until they were in system traffic. The pinnace and a dozen of the heavy lift shuttles would make long-range launches for the gas giant, which would cut almost five hours off the refuelling time.

It wasn't the first time that Nbaro had noticed they were missing a pinnace. As the pinnaces were small, very capable starships, it was a major item to be missing. No one commented, though.

After the Fifty-four Hour plan was made and the spacecraft began to launch, Mpono and Lee from Flight 5, recovering from her wound at Haqq, and Ko and a dozen other pilots began to plan the hundred and ninety hours to follow the Fifty-four. Cargo and Small Cargo sent representatives to Space Operations, and Thea Drake stood a watch.

The planning and replanning never stopped. Marca had flights in all directions, and would land to take a watch in Space Operations – Tower, Assistant Lioness, or Lioness herself. It was a blur of work; she had one period of six hours of sleep, and another of four, and then, almost unexpectedly, they were coming to the end of the fifty-four hours, and the plan, and Marca was sitting Assistant Ops, a position that didn't usually even exist. Commander Musashi was in the Lioness seat, sipping tea from a bulb.

Drake brought him another tea and a bulb of strong, delicious coffee for Marca, who took it with thanks.

'Our own coffee.' Thea frowned. 'I guess this is why the Academy made us go without sleep all the fucking time.'

Marca sucked a little coffee, scalded her tongue, and glanced automatically at all her screens.

'Yeah,' she said.

Musashi cleared two Flight 8 shuttles. Then he swivelled to face her.

'While I work through this event,' he said, 'how about you preset the entire next event. We're going to try and get everyone off in the shortest amount of time we can, so we can start the burn.'

Marca nodded. 'On it, sir,' she said.

And she was. She'd already started it as a cheat-sheet, and now she had her tab turn it into an entire launch profile.

Down in the hangar bay, almost every spacecraft on the ship that could carry cargo or fuel was preparing to launch – the sort of mass launch that usually only took place to impress the public or in military situations.

I guess this is a military situation, Nbaro thought.

She began calling pilots and registering take-off weights, feeding them into her subroutine.

'Ten minutes,' Musashi said.

'I've got it,' she said.

Flight 3 was the smallest outfit on the ship – just two spacecraft, outfitted for electronic countermeasures and cyberwar. And they were late. They were the only part of the launch package not going for fuel or cargo, and naturally they were first off the rails. Nbaro called their pilots and then their ready room, and finally, with two minutes until launch, they both came up.

She fed them straight to the catapult and flicked her completed screen to Musashi with a wave of her tab.

He read it over.

'Excellent. Do it. You're Lioness. I'm Assistant.'

'Roger,' she said, with one minute to launch.

Nbaro read through her own notes, called her first pilot…

442

Down in the railgun tubes, thirty-seven spacecraft lined up on four different electromagnetic rails, each rail system feeding one of the four launch tubes. Looked at from the bow or stern, the four tubes were like a four-leaf clover back on Old Terra. The railgun tubes were large enough to accommodate the biggest spacecraft, except the two pinnaces which usually travelled nested on the 'top' and 'bottom' of the hull and didn't use the tubes to launch, and the 'frigates', which docked at the stern.

Of the thirty-seven craft on the rail system, eight fed each tube, with one extra feeding tube 4, and four spacecraft were already in the tubes, locked and loaded.

Nbaro had the Astrogator on a sub-screen, and she watched his display as the sunspot activity became the expected solar flares right on schedule. Draconis was predictable – that's why they called him 'the Dragon' – and now the old sun belched fire, screening the three PTX ships from the *Athens* and most of the rest of the Draconis solar system.

'Lioness, you are go,' said the Master.

'Go for launch,' Nbaro said.

On Nbaro's word, the first four spacecraft launched at three-second intervals, giving the pilots time to break away on a puff of manoeuvring thrusters to avoid possible collision. The Flight 3 pair went first, emitting pulses in the spectrum of the solar flare as soon as they split, adding depth to the energy screen covering the *Athens*.

Behind them, the spacecraft were launched as fast as the rail system could feed the tubes – which was fast. Every thirty seconds, each tube fired again, the magnets rolling forward in sequence, the spacecraft leaping out of the bow and into the void.

The launch was complete in six minutes.

'Prepare for deceleration. Prepare for heavy deceleration.

This is not a drill. We will leave anti-grav in one minute. Prepare for heavy deceleration.'

The deceleration alarm played throughout the ship, but it had been on the schedule for fifty-three hours and everyone was as ready as could be managed.

Nbaro felt every one of the $6g$, but it was nowhere near as bad as 9.5.

And time stretched, and stretched, and stretched…

Shift changed, and they had fifteen minutes at $1g$. It was three, really, but the AG made it feel like one.

Nbaro was on the same schedule as Thea, and the two of them got into suits and then into their acceleration couches.

'Can anyone sleep in $9.5g$?' Thea asked.

'Those poor PTX bastards just pulled $4g$ for eight days,' Marca said.

'I want to kill them anyway,' Thea said.

And then the g came on, and they weren't interested in talking. It was so bad that, even in gel, even supported by drugs, Marca couldn't sleep, couldn't read, couldn't chat. She couldn't do anything except live. From the first seconds of weight on her pelvis, she knew she should have gone to the head while she could, and now she spent four brutal hours needing to be rid of her coffee. It became all she could think about.

A fifteen-minute break.

And again.

Nbaro tried using her VR rig, but instead of being entertained, she managed to fall asleep in the second part of her rest. She was doped to the gills and all her dreams were bad, but the last was the strangest. Morosini's cat came and sat on her chest. He was very heavy. Smelly, too.

And a little feral. He kneaded her chest with his big paws.

Then he dropped a dead mouse on her.

'Nice job,' he said, purring wildly.

Somehow, in the manner of dreams, he had another mouse, this one squirming. He bit down and dropped it on her.

'See?' he said. 'Just one more to go. More a rat than a mouse.'

And then the old tom said, 'Just keep the pressure on. The rat's already starting to panic.'

And Nbaro woke up. Her head hurt from the VR rig's pressure on her brow, and it weighed less than ten grams under one *g*.

'Don't tell me you actually slept, damn you!' Thea said brightly.

'I've got fifteen minutes to get into a spacecraft,' Marca muttered.

She got into a flightsuit and boots and ran down the passageway to EVA, got into her gear, and made it to Alpha Foxtrot 6–0–2 with two minutes to spare – barely enough time to look at her engines and the hydraulic points and the deck under the aircraft, looking for leakage. Nano, like black oil, or the bright blue or orange of hydraulic fluid. Or worse, anything light and clear and smelly.

There was none of that, and Nbaro was in the cockpit and buttoned up before the skipper climbed in.

They ran the checklist and took off under deceleration. The *Athens* held its own braking while all the spacecraft went off, and then Nbaro had a glorious six-hour flight during which 2 *g* was the most stress her body was put under.

They brushed the gas giant's atmosphere, scooped fuel and brought it home; landed, checked for maintenance issues, and launched again. This was the high-risk part of the Astrogator's plan, as the *Athens* dipped close to the gas giant, with her entire flotilla of collector craft running at maximum capability to get fuel aboard before she passed the gas giant and left it too far astern. They'd started running fuel during the fifty-four hours; every tonne was a gain.

Skipper Truekner let Nbaro sleep for the whole mission, and then she was the pilot, switching seats while they were burning along, an uncomfortable and ridiculous manoeuvre that was accomplished with humour.

Nbaro brought her fuel aboard for an OK landing grade, and then turned her spacecraft around in 9.5*g* and shot off again.

Now they were virtually in orbit; the planet filled the view screen the moment they were out of the tubes, and travel time shrank to almost nothing as they skimmed along, scoops open, already planning their orbital escape.

There were thirty other craft, some much larger than they, all engaged in the same task.

It was during their fifth sortie that Indra spoke up from the back seat.

'Skipper? Ma'am? Want to take a look at this?'

'What do you have, Indra?' the skipper asked without much interest.

'I don't really know...' the petty officer said. 'I was bored.'

'Yep,' the skipper said.

'So I brought up all our old sensors. The ones we popped when we entered the system. And we've dropped a few more since...'

Nbaro was already reaching for her screens, and looking at Indra's image.

'What the hells?' she asked.

'It's one of the PTX ships, about to make Insertion,' Indra said.

'They made Insertion two real-time hours ago,' the skipper said.

'Sir, begging your pardon. In their own time bubble it was four hours ago, right? Sir? For us it was two hours ago? For the sensors way out behind us – two hours behind us – it's happening now in real time, and we can watch, because the solar flare isn't affecting the equipment out there.'

'Son of a...'

446

The skipper leaned over in the acceleration couch.

Nbaro was already poring over the image.

'Back it up and show me three minutes of elapsed time?' she said.

'Sure, ma'am. You'll see it right away.'

That was Brezhnev. He had the vid ready to play – a vid of a very, very detailed read of heat signatures.

While Nbaro watched, the Pǔ Tiān Xià ship more than doubled in length. And then, in a burst of radiation, it vanished.

'Wow,' she said.

'Wow,' Qaqqaq said.

She was sitting on the spare crash-couch in Intelligence. Dorcas was on the other. An Intelligence officer and six Intelligence petty officers, including Locran, were sitting around them. They had fifteen minutes until the next deceleration.

Nbaro had never been in the Intelligence Centre before, but the Special Services office was not an analysis centre, and Dorcas had found them a place with enough crash-couches that they could confer under 6 g; that was the Master's concession to the importance of this information.

Dorcas was using his neural lace to trawl the data nets and then sending his information to their screens.

'First, here's the best image we can manage.' He flicked his eyes at Locran, who grinned.

'I massaged it a bit. Your spacecraft's software isn't as good as what we can do – there was a serious time dilation between the first sensors dropped and the last. Stuff like that.'

Instead of a grainy heat sink on her screen that grew longer, she now had the recognisable, predatory outline of a Pǔ Tiān Xià heavy cruiser of what the Intel people called the 'Juniper' class. And at time hack second 31, she began to grow longer.

But now, despite more than 200 light minutes in distance, the sensor feed showed something extending. Something...

Locran grunted. 'Shit. Of course.'

His officer looked blank.

Locran sat back on his couch, glancing at the clock on the bulkhead.

'It's all about the distance between the relic detectors, right?'

Dorcas nodded. 'You're right. They deploy a rigid—'

'Doesn't have to be rigid as long as the thrust is perfectly centred...'

'Of course,' Dorcas said. 'Brilliant. And simple, like most brilliant things.'

The Intelligence officer chuckled. 'I'm used to Locran getting there ahead of me, but I'd like to know—'

Qaqqaq's face all but glowed.

'I get it!' she said. 'They deploy a tail! A really long tail with a sensor package at the end... Nanuck's prick!'

'Write a briefing for the master,' Dorcas said. 'Please. Now.'

Thirty-one hours of high-g deceleration and the end was like heaven.

'It's like hitting yourself over the head with a hammer,' Thea said.

'What?' Marca asked.

'Feels so good when you stop.'

The weight of $8\,g$ was gone but the pressure continued; all the cargo flights continued round-the-clock operations, moving the cargoes for Draconis Prime. Luckily, as one of the frontier systems of the DHC's trade system, and with only a little over two million people in-system, there was only so much cargo to be had.

'And nobody wants to buy our nice sports electronics,' Thea muttered, as they both crashed for actual sleep in a single g.

But she and Marca managed one hour in a proper dockside bar – the very last hour before the ship was headed for Far Point. Richard Hanna was there, and Dorcas joined them about fifteen minutes before they were due back aboard the landing shuttle. The master had declined to bring the *Athens* into dock; there were too many things that might go wrong.

Dorcas slid into the seat next to Nbaro.

'Thank you for inviting me,' he said.

Nbaro rolled her eyes. 'Here, have some wine.'

Thea sat back.

'Well,' Nbaro said. 'Here's to us.'

All four drank.

Walking back to the shuttle, Richard and Thea became a little cuddly, and Nbaro slowed to give them some privacy.

'Do you think that Morosini can enter our dreams?' she asked.

Dorcas looked at her sharply. 'I have a neural lace,' he said. 'Morosini *is* in my dreams.'

Nbaro told him about the cat.

He looked at her.

'I could say that you were receiving a perfectly normal message from your subconscious,' he said.

'My subconscious usually offers me nightmares about the death or betrayal of my friends.'

He was very tall, and he looked down at her.

'Interesting. Mostly I dream of maths.'

'Of course you do,' she said. 'What do you think about there being another ... infiltrator?'

He looked away. 'I doubt it,' he said.

He was a poor liar, and Nbaro knew he was lying. She was suddenly angry. She grabbed his arm. Betrayal was the right word ... It was right there, and she felt it.

'You're a rotten liar,' she said.

He pulled his arm away from hers.

449

'Please don't grab me unless I invite it, Nbaro.'

'Invite it?' she spat.

'Never mind.'

He began walking again, towards the shuttle.

'You don't trust me?' she asked. 'Even now? After all this?'

He looked at her. Something changed in his face, and he leant over. There was an intensity to him, bordering on desperation.

Nbaro swayed away, afraid of him for the first time, but she underestimated the length of his arms.

'Come with me,' he said.

'We have to get aboard,' she said.

He all but picked her up, and the moment in which she could have struggled effectively was past. She ... She *liked* him too much to put her shiv in him.

'Almighty,' Nbaro muttered, and he pulled her into a unisex public toilet. He was stronger than she'd anticipated.

She was afraid. Not deeply afraid – aware that he was dangerous, all of a sudden, and that something was wrong. The intensity was scary. He was like a different person. The patronising scientist was gone.

'Listen to me,' he said, very quietly. Very intensely. '*You don't need to know everything*. That's all. I trust you absolutely, and I'm sorry I lied.' He paused. 'There's another infiltrator aboard – maybe a whole cell. But we're about to go into battle and I'm restoring Morosini and everything – fucking everything – is on the knife-edge. Smith and I decided you didn't need to know.' He paused. 'I argued that you did.'

Nbaro was looking into his eyes and they held no duplicity, only an echo of her own hurt.

He was hurt?

She was shaking.

'Let go of me?' she asked. 'You scared me.'

'We're all scared,' he said. 'Scared, and desperate, and tense.'

He smiled his twisted smile. 'I suspect that if we're very, very good, we may muddle through.'

He stood away from her. He'd virtually pinned her against the wall, which was frictionless and self-cleaning. She straightened her flight jacket and felt for her shiv.

He caught her in that moment, and smiled. He shook his head.

'Marca, I—'

Nbaro was fast, when she needed to be. She put a hand on his chest and leaned forward.

And kissed him.

There was very little thought to it. Between one minute and the next, she went from fear – or just anger, she wasn't sure – to something else, or the realisation of something else. It all fell into place.

I am such an idiot.

He stumbled back as if Nbaro had attacked him, and she pinned him to the other wall, put an arm around his waist. Her hand felt the holster and the gun under his left arm. He was a head taller than her, and that made her kiss a little clumsy, but only at first.

His whole body came alive under her hands.

She broke away.

'I still won't tell you who it is,' he said. 'But you're quite brilliant.'

'I'm a train wreck.'

'No,' he said. 'You're the woman of my dreams.'

A klaxon howled, warning of the imminent departure of the shuttle.

'You say that to all the girls,' she said, opening the door.

'I most certainly do not,' he said.

13

The moment they broke orbit, they were on a maximum acceleration profile.

A sad fact of life in the Service: what had once been brutal and challenging was now merely brutal and boring. The *Athens* accelerated outbound towards the ideal insertion point located by the Astrogator, and her massive vanes began the process of collecting relic particles for their insertion. Nbaro was jealous that the Pǔ Tiān Xià cruiser had developed their tail – a more efficient collection method.

Nbaro lay in her rack under six and a half gravities, trying to query the records that Dorcas had downloaded from the wreckage of Lighthouse Station, the VR set digging a trench in her brow. Everything was hard, under heavy acceleration, and Nbaro spent half a watch adjusting the controls on her tab and developing acute tendinitis in her right wrist – a peril of performing repetitive motions under high *g*.

I kissed him.

What was I thinking?

I was thinking I like him, and he likes me.

Nbaro drove such thoughts away by poring over the records, looking for ... anomalies. She ran down the cargo manifest of the *Hong Kong*, looking for anything wrong.

It was like searching City for a particular piece of trash. It was ridiculous.

'Thea?' she croaked.

Drake grunted.

'I'm looking at cargo manifests from the *Hong Kong*.'

She couldn't shrug in the gravity, but she twitched.

'Of course you are.' Thea sounded old, and out of breath.

'How would I find ...?' Marca paused.

What am I looking for?

'How would I find an anomaly in loading?' she asked. Her voice sounded strange inside her skull.

'How would I know?' Thea asked. 'You think ... that the PTX has ... unloaded something?'

'Maybe?' Marca said.

'Super helpful. Can I go back to not being asleep and wondering why ... I ever went into space?'

Thea's sarcasm could even overcome $9g$.

'If you were moving a bomb on board as cargo, where would you be afraid of getting caught?'

Thea made a strange gurgling noise which might have been interpreted as laughter.

'You're the best room-mate ever,' Drake said. 'You really keep a girl entertained.'

'Thanks, I guess.'

'So, there's a fairly elaborate cargo system, right? You need to have a reason to bring something aboard, and to have the right container for it and the right bill of lading.'

'They could make a substitution?'

'Only if the weight matches ... exactly.'

Nbaro stared at the overhead, feeling the vast weight on her chest even with the drugs and the acceleration couch around her.

'Does the weight really have to match exactly?' she asked. 'I mean, only if we check, right?'

'Don't we always check?' Thea asked. 'It's in your blessed SOPs all over the place.'

'Spacers don't always check,' Nbaro said. 'I know because stationers get so pissed when you check.'

Drake grunted again. 'Send it to me,' she said. 'Every pallet has to be weighed going into the hold. That's automated.'

Her tab chimed as Marca passed on the data set.

'I'm surprised you can even read this,' Drake said. 'I have an app which can cross-reference...' She paused.

'What?'

Drake grunted yet again. 'Different idea.'

Minutes went by.

'Fuck,' Thea muttered. 'Fuck me.'

'What?' Marca asked.

Thea had definitely found something.

'Remember your spacesuits? The fancy vac suits that were tagged for the *Hong Kong*?' she asked.

'Oh. Yeah. I keep meaning to EVA in one and make sure it works...'

'This says they were loaded on the *Hong Kong*.' Drake was breathing as if she'd run a distance. 'Shit, I've pulled a neck muscle trying to look at the screen. Look at this.'

Marca's tab dinged.

There was a line of code.

'Those are your spacesuits. Except that the weight's wrong. And no one cared. And here's the note on stowage. See the weight? Fuck, it's *kilos* off the lading weight and no one noticed?'

'But we have the spacesuits...'

Gravity was making her brain work slowly.

'Yes. They're on our ship. Their mass is exact to a decimal place. So someone substituted a cargo...' Thea paused. 'Fuck, is that your bomb?'

'Loaded in the suits?'

'No, dopey Joe! The suits were taken out and something else swapped in, and it could all have been done by a hacker breaking into the load routine, on an automated load. The ones where the greatship is docked and all the cargo comes up a giant freight elevator from the surface? With everything automated, you slip a false cargo into the system and delete a real cargo. It couldn't happen...' She paused.

'...to us?' Nbaro said. 'It could have.'

'No!' Thea moaned. 'We went to full alert in Cargo after they tried to get the bomb aboard at Haqq...'

She was working furiously, cursing to go with it, having discovered cursing in the Service, and had fallen in love. Her language had become as 'salty' as that of any old spacer with a tattoo of her favourite ship on her arm.

'Fucking hells,' she said. 'Look at this shit! We had an absolute prohibition against automatic loading... I knew I remembered this... Every cargo inspected. Every weight matched against lading and invoice. Hughes ordered it himself.'

Nbaro lay above her, fighting the pressure and a feeling of helplessness.

'And then someone overrode it! I can see the code. It must have been ordered to speed the loading at Sahel.'

Nbaro's desire to sit up was so strong that she got perhaps a centimetre off her couch before the *g* forces slammed her back. Her lower back protested.

'At Sahel?' she asked.

'Yes,' Thea said.

'So they could have got a bomb aboard in the elevator load,' Nbaro said.

Thea grunted. 'If Captain Hughes will approve it, I can order a general search... All we have to do is run the loading weights against the weight going into the hold, and look for discrepancies.' A long pause. 'There. I asked him. I also queried the override.'

'Who authorised the override?'

'I can't tell. That's why I queried.'

Three hours later, Nbaro went on watch as Tower in Space Operations. While she had very little to do – except hate high acceleration – she did get the new flight schedule, and saw she was in the 'Insertion Alert' package with Mpono.

That was sobering. Everyone knew Mpono was the best pilot in the flight. And if the Pǔ Tiān Xià splinter faction was going to fight, they were probably going to fight at Argos.

This is what you've wanted – meaningful service, ever since you could read and do sims, she told herself.

Halfway through her watch, they shut down their acceleration for three beautiful minutes while Flight 8 launched a single shuttle to test an engine.

That was her whole watch. Nbaro looked at models of Argos, and tried to imagine what a space battle would look like.

Thea messaged her tab.

Hughes has us all searching. No one in Cargo authorized the changes. This is so fucked.

Nbaro spent fifteen minutes messaging the whole incident and discovery to Dorcas. She accused herself of looking for an excuse to write to him.

Interesting, he replied.

Cargo is working on it right now. Captain Hughes is looking for whoever authorized the cessation of precautions.

She was typing furiously. She paused and scanned her screens, but there was nothing to see.

What? Dorcas asked.

And then he was gone.

*

Truekner led a pre-brief for the Insertion Alerts. The flight was putting up no fewer than four alerts; the Master was taking the insertion risk very seriously.

The briefing was done remotely, as the participants were all sitting in acceleration couches under heavy *g*. An Astrogation officer Nbaro didn't know appeared and briefed them on the Argos system and its oddities – the gas giant at the edge of the Goldilocks zone, the asteroid belt outside the orbit of the gas giant, and the giant's many moons, most likely captures from the asteroid belt.

Argos was a fully bright G spectrum star, not the usual system red dwarf, but there was nothing habitable in system except a tiny mining colony in the belt, called Mycenae, according to some ruthless logic of Old Terran history.

Intelligence came up in the form of the same young lieutenant that Nbaro had met when they were discussing the deployable tails the Pǔ Tiān Xià ships used.

'I'm Lieutenant Lochiel,' he said. 'I'm here to brief you on our foe.'

He had good imagery of the three cruisers.

'These are large ships,' he said. 'About a third our length and a tenth our mass, based on our observations and performance data. A class of ships we've never seen before. We've christened them "Juniper". They look enough like the fourth-generation Pine Class that ...' He paused. 'You probably don't want all this.'

'I certainly do,' Nbaro said, and added her smile.

'Pine Class was the workhorse of their fleet for almost fifteen years – still probably their commonest vessel. Here's a Pine, and here's what we think the Junipers look like. See the similarity?'

Nbaro nodded.

The image changed to a beautifully executed 2D model.

'We think they work like this – engines, deployable pod, and an amidships railgun not unlike our own. And they'll have broadside railguns, like the ones that we got hit with at Sahel.

They may have a significant number of torpedoes, and there's a possibility that they've pre-launched their fish and are flying cold and dark, waiting for us.

'They'll want a close quarters battle – a knife fight from a couple of hundred kilometres apart, with lots of manoeuvring so that our spinal railguns can never engage. We want a long-range engagement with our flights out in front of us, shooting down the torpedoes and laying down sensor arrays for our spinal guns to shoot through.

'My guess is that they'll spread out and try to cover the whole insertion area, so that at least one ship will get to shoot us up from very close range. Our best-case scenario is that they still think we need to refuel, and are hiding in the belt waiting for us to go into the atmosphere of the gas giant. Worst case – they get lucky, and we're fighting in the first seconds after we leave Insertion.'

He shrugged. 'Over to you, Commander.'

Truekner smiled. 'Assuming they don't surrender or run off, we could be in a fight before we're even awake. So we're launching on automatic as soon as we leave Insertion. Flight 3 will lead the way and start laying down a countermeasures package. We follow them, laying sensor arrays, followed by the Gunslingers. We're going to launch cold and dark and look around before we manoeuvre, and the Flight 3 birds will put out a package to cover us if we have to go wide or lay more sensors. All that will be decided on the spot by the mission commander, who will be me.'

'And if they're right on top of us?' Mpono asked remotely.

'I trust Bernie Fraser more than that, but if it does happen, we're shooting. No need for a sensor package in a knife fight. If it's under a thousand kilometres range, it'll be a race to get your fish away before their close-in weapons take you out.' He shrugged. 'We'll have about one point five seconds.'

Mpono said, 'Fuck,' audibly.

'Exactly,' he said, 'because it takes almost five seconds for the seeker head to lock on a target, so that's a race you'll lose every time. So…' the skipper went on, 'remember your training. After you release your fish, turn away, drop flares and chaff and try to get into the shadow of the *Athens*.'

Nbaro nodded.

'But having said all that,' Truekner said, 'my money's on them hiding in the asteroid belt, waiting for us to refuel.' Their skipper nodded, as if he could see them all and he approved of them. 'One thing I can promise – something won't go as we expect. Something will go wrong, something will make you shiver, make you doubt your training, make you shit your pants. Stay with your training. Stay on your targets. Don't take anything for granted.'

He smiled. 'That's all. We have two hours at AG before Insertion. Get some sleep. Take your drugs – and that's an order.'

Nbaro obeyed, taking the whole dose of sleeping medication during the two-minute break from acceleration. She was waiting for the *g* to hit when her tab rang.

'Nbaro,' she said. She was already sleepy.

It was Dorcas.

'Where are you?' he asked.

'In muh rack,' she said, barely conscious. 'Druhgs.'

'What did Cargo do?' he asked. 'Has Captain Hughes spoken to anyone outside his department?'

'No idea… Talk to Thea, OK? Ah'm on druhgs.'

'Get with it, Nbaro! This is… Nbaro!'

She had been asleep for a moment and she was already disorientated, and the full acceleration warning was sounding.

'Call Thea Drake,' she said.

And he was gone.

He's an idiot, Nbaro thought, and then she was gone, too.

The cat wasn't gone. The cat was right there waiting for her.

'Now the rat's awake,' the cat said.

The cat bounded ahead of Nbaro, and they were running

through the streets and alleys of Guns, in the lowers of City. The big tomcat stayed ahead of her easily, and she lost him, and then they were running through a spreadsheet – the lading list from the *Hong Kong*, or maybe the master cargo list of the *Athens*; she wasn't sure – but the long ruled lines between the columns of figures were like corridors, and the numbers were as tall as buildings.

Something was following her, chasing the cat. Nbaro looked back at the big sleek panel van with a mirror skin that raced along the corridors like a silver predator. Crouched at the driving console, in dream style, was a rat. A vicious space rat wearing a Service officer's cap and trying to run her down.

She turned a corner and the cat leapt...

Into the arms of a man dressed in scarlet. He looked at her.

'He can't know I'm already restored,' Morosini said. 'He needs to think he's still in charge.'

'Who?' she asked.

'The rat,' said the cat. 'The rat in the hat.'

There was the sound of an engine revving, and a van rolled forward, the rat at the driving console leaning into a hard turn, and Nbaro had to leap out of the way.

'This makes no sense,' she said.

But then she was awake, and thirsty.

But the drugs won, and Nbaro went straight back under... not to rats or City corridors, but to darker and more normal dreams *where Dorcas spurned her and Thea laughed at her clothes, her accent, and her medal.*

'You're not even Service,' Thea taunted her. 'You don't belong here.'
Noo!
Captain Fraser turned away.
Mpono shrugged and went back to what they were doing.
Hanna ignored her.
And Skipper Truekner said, 'I'm so disappointed, Nbaro.'

Nbaro awoke to normal gravity and the joy of knowing that Thea loved her, or at least tolerated her, and that she was, at least for the moment, still in the Service. She banished the dream with her best, cleanest flightsuit and its patches and the pips of her rank.

A little of the dream lingered.

I'm a temporary lieutenant, and when they discover that I'm not really a midder, I'll be gone, she thought.

But another part of her said, *You may be an idiot sometimes, but Morosini says you saved the ship, and Morosini is the kind of friend who can get you out of this. And Dorcas . . .*

Dorcas is a serious-arsed patrician.

Stop being a ninny. Fly the mission. You don't have to sweat the stupid vid and the fake record until you've survived today.

Whatever 'today' means when we're between insertions.

Nbaro walked into the ready room in her flight jacket and her best flightsuit. She felt . . .

Good. She felt good.

Guille high-fived her as soon as she came by.

'Let's do this,' the short woman said.

Nbaro smiled. 'I'm ready.'

'Walk in five minutes,' Mpono said quietly. 'Go ahead. I'll catch up.'

Nbaro looked over the ready room and had a sudden thought – a visceral thought.

Will I ever come back here?

I wish I'd been able to talk to Dorcas.

Nbaro was happy to find Eyre in EVA.

'You in my spacecraft?' she said.

'Nothing but the best for you, ma'am,' Eyre said. 'Me an' Indra.'

Mpono came in and they all walked together, and the two

461

spacers joined them in a careful walk-around of their spacecraft. Eyre checked their four torpedoes – really, they were miniature drone spacecraft that could be remotely piloted or whose guidance could fly them alone. Mpono wiped a gloved hand along certain fittings, almost lovingly searching for signs of leakage from any of the onboard systems. Around them, in the brightly lit hangar bay, dozens of flight crew did the same with a sober intensity that reminded Nbaro of the solemnity of the Old Catholic ritual.

They were early, and had all the time in the galaxy.

Eventually, Nbaro popped the crew hatch and unfolded the ladder, and she climbed up into the belly of Alpha Foxtrot 6–0–7. She did a wriggle into her seat that was almost as graceful as Smoke's, and she let the seat bond with her as she buckled and strapped in, the gel closing around her sides and thighs, needles sliding home into stents in her body.

Never her favourite part.

Nbaro toggled her auxiliary power unit to give them onboard power, and the next ritual began, this time with Smoke as high priest; they ran all the startup checklists except engine start.

Fifty-five minutes and some seconds until Insertion.

As they completed their last checklists, Nbaro reported them ready to launch to Tower, with their take-off weight fully fuelled.

Tower sounded like Cortez. Nbaro wondered if he was bitter about missing the insertion alerts, or happy to be in Space Operations.

Then she lay back, optimising her instrument panels for her eye level under high-g manoeuvres, trying not to think. In the back end, Indra teased Eyre about something she didn't catch, and then the two of them shared several heat and optical images of the PTX ships for identification and comparison.

Mpono locked them out of front seat comms, and their voices became a distant chatter.

'You ever think about what we're going to do?' Mpono asked.

Nbaro almost said, *Talk to the aliens?* because that was at the front of her mind.

'Fight?' she asked.

'Kill. I remember asking you about killing that guy on City. You were beyond cold – it was like you didn't care. Are you concerned about putting a torpedo into another ship?'

Nbaro paused. Then, it just seemed simpler to give the truth. 'No.'

Smoke was silent for a long moment.

'You don't care?' they asked.

Nbaro blinked. 'Permission to speak freely, tir?'

'Go ahead, Marca,' Smoke said, using her name like a token of equality.

Nbaro took a breath. 'They killed Lighthouse Station. They're trying to destabilise the DHC.'

They're probably the same kind of shitty people who made our lives hell at the Orphanage. And they're doing it to increase their profits.

Smoke nodded. 'But... what if they're just... misled? Or wrong, but not... I don't know. You met my mother. My people. We don't go around blowing up spaceships.' There was a long silence. 'I guess I do.' They laughed uneasily.

'You think we're going to fight?' Nbaro asked.

'Skipper's sure of it. If he's sure, I'm sure. I'm sorry, Nbaro – I didn't mean to dump on you. Just nerves. You don't seem to have any.'

'I'm afraid I'll screw it up,' Nbaro said.

'You aren't afraid of dying?' Smoke asked.

Nbaro thought about that. She thought about Sarah, and about the little room at the base of the stairs where they'd locked her in City.

'No,' she said. 'Not here. If we go here, doing our duty ...' She looked Mpono in the eyes. 'Honestly, Smoke? The months since

463

I joined this ship have been the best months of my life. If this is the last one...'

She shrugged, and that made the four needles in her stents wriggle, and that hurt.

Smoke smiled slowly.

'Sometimes, your point of view is refreshing,' they said.

Then they lay in their acceleration couches, watching the timer count down.

At fifteen seconds, Mpono said, 'You're right. If this is it, let's make it good.'

They even smiled.

Nbaro smiled back.

And the timer ticked down to zero.

'You are three to launch.'

Nbaro came alert almost all together – her smoothest transition so far.

'Tower, we're good to launch. I copy three to launch.'

The ship shuddered under them as one of the Flight 3 Electronic Warfare birds punched off the front end and into the Black.

Their spacecraft moved forward on the electromagnetic rails. Nbaro wasn't in Space Operations, so she had to guess. It felt as if they were only launching spacecraft out of two tubes, and the other two were firing payloads – clutter, at least.

Another shudder. Both the Flight 3s should be away.

And then four loud bangs – one, two, three, four. The frigates being released. They were in-system ships without jump vanes, and mostly, what they did was to pretend to be the *Athens* with Electronic Counter Measures and complex data deceptions. They were automated, although they could carry a crew. Somewhere between torpedoes and ships.

Her spacecraft rolled into the clamps, and she checked the engagement automatically as Smoke stirred.

'6–o–7, I have you in the clamps and good to go.'

'Roger, Tower,' Nbaro said. Mpono muttered something. Nbaro toggled her comms to the cockpit. 'You all ready?'

'Ready,' said Indra. 'Systems good.'

'Ready,' said Eyre. 'Weapons hot.'

'Ready,' said Mpono. 'I've got it, Nbaro.'

'Roger,' she said.

Smoke turned their head and snapped their salute.

And they hurtled out of the light and into the darkness.

The moment they were out, Nbaro was scanning her tactical screen...

Which showed a system empty of contacts. Even the navigational beacons were silent.

There was a tiny radio emission from the mining station. Because they'd apparently entered the system below the plane of the planetary bodies, Nbaro could just make out the radio transmissions above the disc of their clutter shield.

Closer in, there was a wall of clutter – almost a hemisphere – ahead of the *Athens*.

Nbaro toggled the cockpit.

'We're clear to manoeuvre until we clear the clutter,' she said. 'No one can see us in here.'

'Got it,' Mpono said. 'Indra, lay us a pattern.'

'Roger, tir.'

Nbaro used her light pen to suggest a pattern based on the pre-brief, and Indra accepted most of it and posted it. While she calculated, they shot forward; their own launch velocity had been lower than the clutter's, and the ship was falling away behind.

'Here we go,' Smoke said.

They turned the ship through 90 degrees, and the *g* force was punishing, but brief.

'Passing beyond the clutter in three, two, one...'

'Deploying sensors,' Indra said. 'One away.'

'There's one from the skipper in 6–o–2,' Eyre said.

On the tactical screen, everything sunward of the clutter was invisible, because almost nothing in the electromagnetic spectrum could penetrate that cloud of ablatives and foils hurtling through airless space. Behind the cloud, Nbaro was watching the Gunslingers launch, while 6–o–2 turned 180 degrees off axis and began deploying sensors.

After four Gunslingers emerged, 6–o–1 launched and almost immediately turned 90 degrees off axis from them; seconds later, 6–o–4 completed the lens by turning up-system, towards the plane of the ecliptic, so that the paths of the four spacecraft made a cross in space. All four were deploying sensors as they went.

Nbaro was watching the system now that they were clear of the clutter. Their sensors would be relaying all their data to the ship's processors, and that signal was retransmitted to them, and all the while they were flying, engines off, dark and cold and silent.

'Got one bogey,' Eyre said.

'I see him,' Nbaro said, as the contact came up on her armrest and transferred to her main screen.

The enemy ship was in-system from them, but only barely. They'd come in below the plane of the ecliptic and the enemy ship was above them, in three dimensions.

'Shit,' Mpono said. 'No clutter between us at all. He sees us.'

'He's firing,' Eyre reported. The sensors were so accurate with forty deployed that they could see individual railgun rounds. 'Railguns and a big spread of torps...'

'We've got another,' Nbaro reported, watching her tactical screen.

They were the furthest spacecraft from the enemy, above them, because they'd gone down away from the plane of the ecliptic.

466

The second enemy ship was further in-system. So was the third...

'*Athens* is rotating,' Nbaro reported.

'6–0–4 was destroyed,' Eyre reported. 'I have sixteen torpedoes running.'

Suleimani's whole crew...

Mpono said, 'Our clutter is facing the wrong way.'

'Wrong for that bastard,' Eyre said. 'But—'

'5–0–1 and 5–0–2 engaging the torpedoes,' Eyre said.

'*Athens* is firing,' Indra said. 'Look at that.'

The flash of the PTX ship's drives exploding was like lightning in space, even though the enemy ship was tens of thousands of kilometres away.

'Almighty God,' Mpono said.

'Scratch one bogey,' said Eyre.

A flash.

'They got one of the frigates.' Indra sounded distant.

Nbaro looked down at her screen. The *Athens* had fired all four railguns – each firing a charge like the pellets of a shotgun, except that each pellet weighed ten kilograms and was traveling at almost 0.1c. The rounds had taken less than three seconds to reach their target, at a range of almost 90,000 km.

'We've lost a Gunslinger. Shit – we've lost two. Torpedoes are being engaged by close-in Weapons.'

Silence. They were all watching the deadly lines closing in on the *Athens*.

Like watching thieves break into your home. Except that I've never had a home.

Until now.

'Another frigate gone.'

Smoke said, 'They're doing their jobs,' and Nbaro thought, *I hope they weren't crewed.*

The other two Pǔ Tiān Xià ships abandoned any pretence of

hiding, lighting their main drives and running, and the *Athens* ran sunwards behind her clutter, the out-flanker who could see her destroyed. Both remaining opponents were sunwards of them.

'Any chance of survivors aboard 6–0–4 or the Gunslingers?' Mpono asked.

'At least one from 6–0–4,' Indra said with icy calm. 'And one of the Gunslingers ejected.'

Eyre asked, 'Tir, any idea what happened?'

Mpono was quiet, focused on their next move.

Nbaro spoke up. 'I think they bet they were invisible while they ran cold.' She hesitated. 'Has anyone ever seen a greatship fire all four tubes before?'

She thought of Truekner's speech, and about underestimating your opponent.

The surviving adversaries fell sunwards, accelerating away at 7*g*.

The *Athens* began to accelerate after them, her main drive like a sun with a comet's tail, burning away above and to the left of them. Almost 200 km away and still visible as a point of light.

Smoke clicked on the Cockpit channel.

'No point launching torpedoes this far out,' they said. 'They're running at 7*g*.'

Nbaro listened as another voice came over the Tower channel, calling them back.

Smoke seemed distracted.

'You OK, Smoke?' she asked.

Smoke looked over at her. 'I'm fine,' they said. 'Is someone getting the crew who ejected?'

Nbaro listened on the Rescue channel.

'They're sending the pinnace,' she said.

Smoke toggled comms.

'Let's go home, then,' they said.

*

'Don't come out,' Maintenance signalled. 'Stay on board and we'll service and fuel.'

Smoke sighed. 'We're still at Battle Stations and there's a stand by for emergency manoeuvres alert,' they said. 'I guess we're going out again.'

'I'm ready, tir,' Indra said.

'Let's get 'em,' Eyre said.

Smoke made a face.

Nbaro could hear the hydrogen hose clipping on to the spacecraft. All the noises seemed to be magnified. She drank from her Thermos of coffee, aware that she'd regret it later.

She had the ship's tactical screen repeated on her cockpit console, and she was watching the enemy ships run from them.

The ship gave a long, drawn-out shudder.

'We just fired all four tubes again,' Nbaro said.

She couldn't imagine why they'd be firing at this sort of range, with their opponents accelerating away, and she was seeing what a beautiful insertion Captain Fraser had astrogated. They'd come in below the plane of the ecliptic, and as slow as Nbaro – who was no veteran – had ever experienced.

Slow enough that they could begin their run for Insertion almost immediately.

Except they weren't. They were running in system and accelerating at about 3g, Nbaro assumed, because the artificial gravity was still on.

Both of the enemy ships were turning. Accelerating on a new vector.

'I get it,' Eyre said. 'Ma'am, look. It's to protect the mining station. We fired to push them away from it. They have to turn to avoid our rounds, with a dispersion at 300,000 km...'

The deck under them shuddered again – a long, rhythmic shudder.

'And they have to keep turning, or they get hit.'

'How long can we keep this up?' Mpono asked.

'Weeks?' Eyre said. 'I guess we could run out of railgun slugs, but then we could always throw gold bars or something at them.' He sounded very young and very enthusiastic. 'At a percentage of the speed of light, it really doesn't matter what you throw.'

'*Athens* took hits,' Indra reported. 'Damage in Engineering and Hangar Deck. Maybe more.' She paused. 'Three hits. One went through berthing.'

'And now they know,' Smoke said.

'They know how good our sensors are,' Nbaro said.

She put a hand to her helmet as she got a message from Space Operations.

'They know they can't afford to allow us a single round,' Mpono said.

'Asteroid belt in a little more than an hour,' Nbaro put in. 'We're back on the launch list, Smoke – we're part of the firing programme. We launch in about ten.'

Smoke held up one finger.

'Wait,' they said. 'I'm getting a briefing.'

They were silent a while, and then raised their faceplate.

'Listen up,' they said. 'The Master thinks they'll try to kill the mining station. In addition, it appears that there's a bomb aboard our ship, and Morosini's analysis is that they're trying to get close enough to set it off. The trigger is some sort of signal – probably a beamed radio transmission.'

'Radio works from a long way off…' Nbaro said.

'It does, but there are places in the hold which are more shielded… Anyway, Nbaro, if they transmit too early and we're on to them, we jam the signal, right?'

'Right.'

'Teams are searching,' Mpono said. 'We're laying another sensor field and then coming home. Skipper's concerned that the asteroid belt will play havoc with our sensors.'

Nbaro nodded.

'I get it,' Eyre said. 'Good idea.'

'So glad you approve,' Smoke said. But they were smiling.

Their second launch had none of the excitement of the first; the enemy had fled, and they were well over 300,000 km away and still accelerating. The *Athens* was demanding their surrender, and they weren't answering.

6–0–7 accelerated away from the *Athens*, and then, after two manoeuvres to find their place, they were above the ship and ahead of it by more than a thousand kilometres and matching velocities; the *Athens* was no longer accelerating.

There were four Flight 6 birds in their usual cross formation, ready to launch sensors.

The asteroid belt was dense – dense enough to be a navigational hazard, and yet no single rock was close enough for her to see them. Far off to her left, Nbaro could just see something...

But Smoke had a detailed chart open on their computer and they yawed to avoid a collision.

Nbaro never saw the rock they were passing, and then they were manoeuvring, never too hard; there were dozens of charted rocks, some not much bigger than their spacecraft.

'Clear,' Smoke announced.

They were almost 1500 km ahead of the *Athens* now, as the greatship had changed course slightly to avoid the leading edge of the belt altogether.

'One away,' Eyre said.

'Hang on,' Smoke said, and pulled them to the left, roughly parallel to the plane of the asteroids.

'Two away,' Eyre said.

Indra said, 'Tir? Ma'am? I have an anomaly.'

Nabro looked at her console.

Eyre said, 'Show me?'

Indra's voice was strained. 'See that?'

Eyre was firm. 'Contact. We have a contact. Contact! Marked. We have to transmit!'

Nbaro saw the contact – behind and below them was ... something barely warmer than the big rock. Even at the relatively short range of 300 km ...

It's a knife fight.

'Three away!' Eyre said. 'I have nine fixes – cross-referencing. Contact confirmed.'

It did not look like a Pǔ Tiān Xià ship. It did not match any of the PTX ship types in the computer. It was close beside a rock, an oval rock the size of a big orbital, maybe thirty kilometres across.

'Roger, Contact.' Smoke said. 'If you transmit via datalink, they'll see us.'

There was a long pause as they all took that in.

Transmitting gave away their position, but then, Mpono had just fired the main drive, so ...

'Do it,' Smoke said.

Nbaro passed the link to the ship: one press of a button. One blip of data.

'Evasive,' Smoke said.

'It's firing ...' Eyre said.

'Six hundred kilometres,' Indra said.

'Firing CIWS,' Eyre said.

Suddenly they all slammed into their harnesses as the gel in their acceleration couches held them like elastic bands with iron anvils at their bases. Nbaro cried out, and the system fed her drugs through the needles, which burned. Everything hurt.

Smoke wasn't flying now; the onboard sub-AI was slaved to the radar, detecting incoming slugs. The spacecraft shuddered, turned, and Nbaro's tongue seemed welded to the roof of her mouth. Her vision tunnelled, and then she was ...

Back, and they turned again.

'Lock!' Eyre shouted.

It took Nbaro time to realise he meant he had a lock on one of the torpedo warheads. She flipped the cover off the firing switch, clicked an analogue switch to toggle the correct torpedo, the one that was flashing 'LOCKED'.

The red button was under her finger. Nbaro's vision tunnelled again, and she stabbed the switch the way she'd stabbed the man in City. She stabbed it so hard her finger hurt.

The whole spacecraft seemed to bounce, and there was a flash off her left shoulder. Then the spacecraft was manoeuvring again, and Nbaro fought to stay conscious. Something was pulsing on her screen; she tried to turn her head and she was out...

Back.

'Is that bastard alone?' she croaked.

'Torpedo destroyed,' Eyre said.

Nbaro looked at her tactical display. The skipper had turned towards them and so had 6–0–3; Guille, she thought.

'6–0–3 is launching,' Eyre said.

'Enemy firing,' Indra said. 'I have—'

'Nose on!' Smoke said.

They were piloting again, and they fought to get the nose of the torpedo back on to the target. The ship was small and had an excellent heat sink; even at 500 km, it was barely visible.

'Beautiful work, Indra,' Nbaro said.

'Thanks, ma'am,' Indra said. 'Eyre made the call.'

'What the hells is it?' Smoke asked.

'Firing,' Eyre said.

They slammed to the right, as if a giant hand had suddenly picked them up and hurled them in that direction. A big thruster fired right behind Nbaro's head, and she had spots in her vision.

Smoke pulled on the yoke.

Nbaro blacked out for a third time, despite the drugs and training. This time she didn't go all the way down, but it took time to climb back out.

Suddenly the feel of AI control was gone, and Mpono was on the yoke. They used the manoeuvring thrusters to flip them end for end and yelled 'Brace!'

And then they threw their power to deceleration.

It was like landing into the electromagnets on the ship; they seemed to slam to a stop. Again Nbaro's vision tunnelled; again she slid towards unconsciousness, her suit and her acceleration couch massaging her skin, pushing blood thinned by drugs into her legs and back to her heart. Her hands were inhumanly cold...

There was a high-pitched screaming sound. It had been going on for several seconds and was getting softer...

A green light appeared inside her helmet on her head-up display.

Nbaro grappled with that for a moment before realising that she was on oxygen. They'd lost all their cabin pressure and air.

Because...

'We've been hit,' she said on the Cockpit channel.

'Indra's dead,' Eyre said. 'Shit.'

They were flying along the surface of the oval asteroid, very low. Nbaro risked a glance.

Indra had a fist-sized hole through her chest and there was blood everywhere. There was a fist-sized hole above her on the fuselage, and another behind her.

'We've lost some avionics and some comms,' Nbaro reported. '*Athens* is about ninety seconds away from breaking the plane and coming into the enemy's radio arc.'

Smoke was as calm as if they were landing on an orbital.

'Roger. Spacecraft still handles – I have thrusters. I have mains.' After a pause: 'I have some thrusters, anyway.'

Nbaro looked at her screens.

'I have no comms with the ship,' she said. 'No data link, no tactical.'

'We're on the blind side of the rock from the enemy ship,' Mpono said. 'My plan is to come around tight to the rock and have Eyre pickle the torp before he shoots us down.'

One point five seconds. That's what Skipper said.

On a positive note, they were so close to the surface of the tiny asteroid that they were hidden from the guns of the warship on the other side.

Mpono was turning them in a tight, flat circle; Nbaro saw what they were doing, turning to stay on the blind side of the rock from the enemy ship.

'We have to,' Mpono said. 'If that ship has the code to the bomb…'

Nbaro looked. 'Seventy seconds until the bastard can see the *Athens*.'

'Odds are bad,' Eyre said. 'Tir. It'll take the warhead five seconds to get a lock.'

Mpono turned again. 'Anyone got a better idea?'

Nbaro said, 'Can we use the sensor we dropped to target the bastard?'

Eyre coughed. He was managing a professional calm while covered in his friend's blood. Nbaro wanted to say something, but there was nothing to say.

'Yes,' he said. 'Give me a second.'

Nbaro looked back and Eyre was working Indra's console, wiping her blood away, leaning out to look at her screen, which was still intact.

'Almost ready,' he said.

'*Athens* is thirty seconds out,' Nbaro said.

Mpono said, 'As soon as the torpedo's away, I'll use thrusters to pop and drop on the bastard's horizon. Maybe he'll shoot at us and not our torpedo.'

Eyre was crisp. 'Waypoint inserted. Ready for torpedo launch.'

'Firing,' Nbaro said, toggling the correct weapon at the last second and clicking the switch.

The spacecraft bucked.

'Twenty seconds until he can see *Athens*,' Nbaro said.

The torpedo's engines fired a short burst and it was gone.

'Over the horizon. Turning.'

'Here we go,' Mpono said.

'Locked on!' Eyre whooped.

The acceleration pushed Nbaro down into the gel. Smoke was taking them in, without a weapon, to deflect attention from the torpedo.

I guess today's the day. It's still OK. It's been good.

The torpedo had to kill one vector of acceleration and then reach the enemy ship on a second. That took time in the firing arc, although doubtless Eyre had put it as low to the asteroid's horizon as he could.

Ten seconds until the enemy ship could see the *Athens*.

And there it was. For perhaps half a second, Nbaro could see the long, dark, blobby shape against the paler rock of the asteroid in the light of the distant sun. It was a remarkable shape, smooth and bulbous and unlike any ship she'd ever seen, and then Smoke was turning, dropping them back under the horizon of the rock with a long line of close-in weapons fire reaching for them, reaching, reaching...

A flash on the other side of that horizon, bright enough to blind her through her visor and the cockpit, and she wasn't even looking directly at it.

Blind, Nbaro had too much time to think. And feel space-sick.

And notice how cold she was.

She had no real sense of time, but it was only seconds until Nbaro blinked away some of the blindness into dazzle spots, and she took a deep breath and let it out.

'We're alive,' she said.

'It's still there,' Eyre said.

'What?' Mpono demanded.

Nbaro looked at the tactical screen and then rotated it…

'It's not dead,' she said. 'It's moving.'

'We hit it with a fucking nuke,' Mpono said.

'There it is,' Nbaro said, pointing.

Through the view screen, they could actually see the mass of drifting rubble from the explosion of the warhead so close to the surface of the asteroid.

'Shit,' Smoke said, with icy calm.

The enemy spacecraft came up through the cloud of wreckage and rock, rising over the horizon of the asteroid itself.

Just fifteen kilometres away, the greatship began to emerge from behind the asteroid field, nose up, as if rising from deep space, and silhouetted against the light of the distant star and the Hydra Nebula behind it.

As they watched the great sword of the greatship *Athens* rising, the enemy ship rotated. It was less than five kilometres away – point-blank in a space fight.

A battery of weapons sparkled and lines reached for them…

'Last fish is live and hot,' Eyre said.

A green light appeared on Nbaro's last torpedo.

'Hold on,' she said. 'Eyre, fly it out over the rubble cloud.'

She could see that the enemy ship's railguns, or whatever the hell they were, were not getting most of their rounds through the cloud. It was dense enough to screw lines of fire.

Dense enough to kill their last torpedo.

'I've got it… Launch,' Eyre said.

Nbaro toggled the fourth torpedo and pressed the key, and once more the whole spacecraft seemed to jump as the weapon fell away and lit its engines.

'Taking it straight up,' Eyre reported.

Something went through their cockpit end to end, taking out the landing control system and leaving a perfectly round hole in the top of the cabin and an exit hole next to Nbaro's acceleration couch.

Mpono snapped the spacecraft right and down relative to their enemy, making maximum use of the thrusters they had left.

Nbaro began to dump chaff – her own small bomblets of clutter – and her control screens showed a series of hits: four hits.

'We lost atmospheric manoeuvre,' she said.

'That's a pity,' Smoke said.

They pressed a button and the floor seemed to fall out from under them as the onboard AI took over the evasive manoeuvres.

The movements were violent, random, and the acceleration couch didn't seem to be compensating very well. Nbaro began to feel real pain.

'Lock on!' Eyre said. 'Letting go.'

The AI rolled them through 60 degrees and fired all the remaining port-side thrusters.

In silence, Nbaro watched two holes star the hyperdiamond of the view screen. Her damage control screen went red and then began to fade; they'd been hit fifty or more times.

I'm still alive.

So's Mpono.

Nbaro couldn't turn her head back to look at Eyre.

'Eyre?'

'Still here,' he said. 'Ma'am.'

Nbaro could see the barrage from the flanks of the *Athens* flowing into the enemy ship like converging streams, as her onboard radar tracked tens of thousands of gauss rounds from CIWS and broadside turrets. Every round was striking the target, and it was still there. The enemy spacecraft sparkled all over, but the tactical computer only showed the passage of a handful of railgun rounds. The thing was doing something else; she could tell because she could see, from ten kilometres away, vents of atmosphere from the *Athens* as she took hits.

'Energy weapons,' Nbaro said.

'Fish is on terminal!' Eyre yelled.

Smoke slammed the controls hard and they dived behind the asteroid, interposing its bulk between their frail craft and …

This time, the white flash filled the cockpit.

'I'm blind,' Mpono said. 'Take the controls.'

Nbaro seized the yoke. Everything felt wrong; the whole craft had a vibration to it, and she could feel the lack of responsiveness, the *mush* in her fly-by-wire systems.

'Got it,' she said.

Nbaro had lost datalink and all comms with the ship, so nothing was updating but her own onboard sensors.

'Is it still there?' she asked.

Eyre said, 'It's in two pieces.'

Nbaro took control from the AI and rolled.

'Asteroid is breaking in two,' she said.

They were in fairly dire straits themselves. Nbaro was showing so many of her manoeuvring thrusters dead that she wasn't sure they could actually land.

She scanned her instruments and saw the three red lights on her electromagnetic couplers.

'Hydraulics …' she said.

'I hear you're brilliant at landing without electromagnets,' Smoke drawled.

Nbaro was still blinking. 'We have zero couplers.'

Mpono coughed. 'Not good,' they agreed. 'Any nano?'

'We've lost all of our nano and hydraulics,' Nbaro said. 'We have sixty-one holes right through us.'

'Sixty-one holes?' Eyre whistled. 'You OK, tir?'

'I'm blind,' Mpono said. 'And something's wrong with my left side. Otherwise fine.'

'Yes, tir,' Eyre said.

Smoke's helmeted head shook.

'I have very limited port-side manoeuvring thrusters,' Nbaro said.

Smoke grunted. 'OK.'

'I *think* I can get her aboard, but if you two want to punch out in vac suits, I'll join you. Landing could be … dicey.' Nbaro was thinking her way through the ejection checklist. 'How's the bogey?'

Out there in the dark, their remote sensors were still following the progress of the doomed enemy vessel.

'Only one piece now,' Eyre said. '*Athens* is still pouring fire into it.'

Nbaro looked over the red lights on the console. And thought of Indra.

She'd already cheated death once, at least. Maybe ten times today.

'I'm good for the landing if you are, tir,' she said.

Smoke laughed. 'I'm in for whatever you two decide.'

Nbaro locked Mpono out of comms. She could see, even at their current level of *g* stress, that Smoke's acceleration couch had taken damage. So had her own.

'I don't think Commander Mpono will survive ejection,' she said.

'Roger that, ma'am. I'm in for the landing. Do it.'

'Thanks, Eyre. I'll do my best.'

'Roger that,' said Eyre.

'Let's see if our main drive responds. There she is – good girl.'

They were all pressed back in their seats, and Nbaro wondered if the fusion bottle could have failed.

Too late to worry now …

Nbaro's fingers were freezing and inaccurate, and she was trying to get some information out of her tab.

'We need the *Athens* to slow down,' she said. 'And shit, we have no comms.'

'Shit.' Smoke sounded remote and listless.

Eyre said, 'I think their containment bottles just failed.'

Another flash, this one red.

Are you bleeding out, tir? Shit, though I can't see any blood. Internal bleeding?

Fuck it. Time to try for a landing.

Nbaro accelerated and they went up over the rim of the fracturing asteroid, to see the enemy ship was an expanding cloud of radioactive gases and nothing more.

She passed *through* the cloud of debris, and up to avoid the rubble coming off the fracturing of the asteroid, and then she brought them into line with the *Athens*, ten kilometres away.

The ship passed them, looking almost close enough to touch, moving fast.

For a moment, they all thought the same thing. Even if they punched out, they couldn't communicate, and they'd watch the ship pull away. Forever.

A slow way to die.

The ridiculous unfairness of it reached out for Nbaro; she could see the ship, and she had never been more beautiful.

But without comms, they could never get aboard. Not with half their manoeuvring thrusters failed and the others dicey; the hydraulics and nanos that allowed their fractional manoeuvring were probably compromised.

'Chase 'em,' Mpono said. 'Maybe they'll see us.'

Nbaro had a stupid idea. It was so foolish that she tried it immediately.

She typed *White Rain* into her tab.

The reply was almost instantaneous.

Yes?

Help!

Because 6–o–7 had that mysterious antenna.

And because Dorcas was saving Morosini…

'I think I have comms,' Nbaro said, as her screens flickered.

Nbaro saw her tactical screen update and knew she'd got through, and she took her hands off the controls. Ahead of them, the greatship began to turn, rotating on manoeuvring thrusters and slowing. It was an awesome sight.

'Shit,' Nbaro said. 'They're manoeuvring…'

For a few seconds they were hurtling directly at the ship's side, and then she turned, flipping end for end…

The ship was slipping away from them now, because it was still faster than they were, even with the three of them pinned to their couches by the full acceleration of their engines.

The greatship completed her rotation and reorientation in three dimensions.

Their starboard side thrusters fired like machine guns.

blatblatblatblatblat

And again

blatblatblatblatblat

and then a single port-side thruster fired…

blat

And the ship was suddenly coming towards them.

'We don't have any magnets,' Nbaro said aloud.

'Oh, my gods,' Mpono said. They spasmed.

'Tell them we need a med team,' Nbaro snapped to Eyre.

At the pace of a walking child, 6–o–7 floated into the number three tube, which flashed its landing lights. Their drive was off; their manoeuvring thrusters weren't firing.

The whole great ship was *catching them.*

14

Nbaro was so wrung out from the mission that she didn't check her tab for half an hour while she saw Indra's body dealt with properly, followed Smoke into one of the temporary med bays and went back to the hangar bay as the squadron's maintenance techs swarmed her spacecraft. When she had performed all of her duties, she went to see Yu, under the skipper's orders. Her hands wouldn't stop shaking.

Yu ran a few diagnostics and asked her how much caffeine she was ingesting.

'I dunno,' Nbaro muttered. 'I had a couple of coffees before injection ...' She paused. 'A Thermos of it in the spacecraft. I drank another ...' She paused again and looked at him. 'Two more since we landed.'

'Excellent,' Yu said. 'Hold out your hand.'

She looked at her hand, the fingers short and blunt. She wasn't a fan of her hands.

'Yeah?'

It was shaking. Someone she knew had just died. She'd landed a broken spacecraft with her favourite senior officer badly wounded ...

Nbaro had an image of the blood all over the back of the cockpit, and then of the passageway outside of Space Operations after she'd used the anti-personnel drones, and suddenly she had her arms clutched across her chest.

'Fuck,' she said.

'Combat stress,' Yu said. 'Not helped by fatigue and massive overindulgence in caffeine. It's a drug, spacer. You've had … what – ten, fifteen cups? You're shaking. Your heartbeat is racing. And that's not just mental. That's the caffeine, too.'

'Fuck,' she muttered again. She was having trouble concentrating on the here and now.

'You need sleep. When are you next on the flight schedule?'

'We're in combat ops,' Nbaro snarled. 'Yu, we're friends. Don't take me off the flight schedule.'

'Stop drinking coffee. One coffee when you get up, one at lunch. That's it. Or I take you off for combat stress.'

'You're a dick,' she said.

'Sure am.' Yu smiled.

She felt better.

'Yeah, point taken,' she managed.

'You also have some nasty bruising all down your left side – going to be worse tomorrow.'

'My acceleration couch took a hit.'

'I want you to be honest tomorrow about how fit you are to fly. Now go.'

Back in her stateroom, Nbaro found Thea, who looked both exhausted and triumphant.

Thea hugged her. 'I heard you lost a shipmate.'

'Tresa Indra. Dead in an eye blink.' Nbaro took a deep breath, waiting for tears, for another flash of the back of the cockpit. 'Mpono's blind and radiation sick, I think. Maybe worse.' She rubbed her face with her hands. Nothing improved. 'You look…'

She didn't want to say *happy*, because Thea wasn't happy. But she was triumphant.

'I found it,' she said. 'I found the fucking bomb.'

Nbaro grinned. 'You found it!'

They slapped hands.

Thea shrugged. 'I guess I should share the credit with your arsehat friend, Dorcas. Dork-ass. Damn, he's a patronising bastard.' She flung herself backwards onto her acceleration couch. 'We ran more than six hundred individual searches. Fuck, Marca, it was a nightmare – we knew the enemy might have the codes to a bomb, and then a ship popped up at close range...'

Nbaro couldn't hold her hard smile.

'I know,' she admitted.

'I know you know. Anyway, we're running all these searches, comparing weights. I was sure it was brought aboard at Sahel, because of the elevator, and Dorcas agreed, so we were down to pretty much running each individual lo—'

The screen on their back bulkhead went blank and then flashed.

'Lieutenant Nbaro to the Master's briefing room. Lieutenant Nbaro to the Master's briefing room...'

'Shit,' Marca said.

She realised that she'd turned her tab off at some point. It was in her flightsuit.

She was still in her flightsuit, and it had blood all over it. And the Executive Officer, Captain Aadavan, would make an issue of it.

Nbaro began to peel out of her flightsuit.

'Help me change,' she said.

Thea did, grabbing her stuff and tossing it while she talked.

'Anyway, we had to look at the grain. Because at some point, and I feel stupid that I hadn't thought of it earlier, I realised that in comparing weights, I'd forgotten all the cases where the cargo pod might weigh *more* than the bomb. Like a sixteen-cubic-metre load of rice, for example. That's 12,500 kilos. A good quality backpack nuke would weigh less than thirty … Hey, you need a gun to see the Master?'

She was holding the fresh flightsuit open.

'Yes.' Marca stepped into the flightsuit and zipped it up. 'I hate putting clean clothes on when I'm dirty. See you.'

'But—'

'You found it in a rice shipment?'

'Yes,' Thea said. 'Damn it, I want to tell the whole story!'

'I promise.'

Nbaro bolted for the port-side elevators and when the doors opened, she found herself looking at Horatio Dorcas, whose hair was not neat and who didn't even have a patrician's long-coat on. He had circles under his eyes and his lips looked pale and …

'Nbaro,' he said.

'Dorcas,' she returned.

The elevator doors closed.

He didn't look at her.

'You kissed me,' he said.

'I was there,' she said, aiming for humour through the fog of exhaustion.

'I thought you might … send a text. A note. Anything.'

He was watching the decks pass as if it was the most interesting set of digits in the universe.

'I was going …' Nbaro paused. 'Can we do this later?'

Dorcas flashed her a smile. 'Absolutely.'

Nbaro returned the smile and felt instantly better.

The elevator doors opened and she walked down the short corridor to the Master's briefing room.

The Master was already seated, with Aadavan, Dukas, Fraser, Commander Tremaine, Major Darkstar and Captain Hughes.

Hughes was saying, '…she began looking at the grain shipments, not for mass but for balance. The grav sleds that move

486

them around the ship register the point of balance on every container…' He looked up.

'A brilliant notion,' Dorcas said.

Aadavan rolled his eyes. 'So nice of you two to join us.'

The Master glanced at Nbaro.

'You doing all right, Lieutenant? You lost someone out there in the Black.'

'Yes, sir,' Nbaro said. 'Petty Officer Indra. Do you know if Commander Mpono…?'

The Master smiled. 'In a medbay clamshell and responding well. Mostly internal damage due to failure of her crash-couch.'

'Ouch,' Nbaro said, but she felt a sense of relief.

Chief Engineer Dukas nodded. 'We lost two in Engineering when the first railgun round hit us,' she said. 'And more when that fucking thing hit us with … whatever that was. You'll hear later.'

'Yes, ma'am,' Nbaro said and sat.

There was coffee on the table. It smelt delicious, and Nbaro reached out a hand, and then, after an internal struggle worthy of a much more dire sin, she poured herself some water.

It tasted dull and the smell of the coffee was overwhelming.

Morosini appeared at the end of the table.

Nbaro sucked in a breath. Morosini was *vivid*, his scarlet clothes almost too bright to look at, and his cat, Tomas, sat in his lap, stretching his head out for attention, his rumbling purr filling the room, his cat-face with that look of smug satisfaction that only a well-petted cat can wear.

'Ahh,' Morosini said, as if slightly surprised to see them all.

Dorcas's face lit up as if illuminated from within. He looked smug – so smug that his expression seemed to reflect the cat's. Nbaro almost loved him for it.

Until that moment, she hadn't realised quite how much she *liked* Morosini.

The Master grinned, like a much younger man given a present, and the chief engineer's hand twitched as she *almost* reached to pet the cat. Hughes sat back.

'You're back,' Pisani said.

'I am, Vettor.' Morosini smiled, and now he, too, wore a look of smug satisfaction. 'Although, honestly, I've been back for a little while.'

Pisani nodded. 'I wondered, when the star charts were updated so quickly.'

Aadavan glanced at Pisani.

Morosini chuckled. 'Yes,' he said. 'I was... testing myself.'

'I'd like to hear my department heads report,' Pisani said. 'Before I ask you to explain.'

'Of course,' Morosini said.

He inclined his head like someone's older uncle politely refusing a second glass of brandy.

'Captain Dukas?' Pisani asked.

'Reactor 1 is down, and we have a radiation leak that's already killed a spacer and is likely to kill two more – they took massive doses. We had a whole compartment open to vacuum while the damaged ducts sprayed radioactive carbon all over. We have four of our specialised damage control teams on it now, but it's not good.' She glanced at the Master. 'That thing hit us *hard*. However, as battle damage goes, we got off pretty lightly, and we have two more reactors online. I wouldn't perform an insertion until we have this under control. That's all I've got.'

'How long until the ducting is repaired?' Pisani asked.

Dukas shook her head. 'I've no idea. I don't know if we still have Reactor 2 at all. Emergency shutdown is not a safe procedure. But it didn't become unstable and we didn't have to dump it into space. I'll know more when the Damage Control teams have the ducts repaired and we can attempt a restart. Give me three hours.'

Pisani glanced at Captain Hughes. 'Cargo?'

'Midder Drake located a bomb in the grain we loaded at Sahel. The weapon has been neutralised.'

Major Darkstar allowed the smallest of smiles to flash across their thin lips.

'Yep,' they said.

'We must have an exceptional crop of middies this cruise,' Tremaine said, smiling across at Nbaro. 'When I was a midder, mostly I ate, slept, took exams and hoped no one noticed me.'

Nbaro was watching Aadavan, because he was fidgeting, and she'd never seen him do it before. His fingers were drumming on the table.

Hughes nodded grimly. 'The hits we took amidships mostly went through cargo areas. We haven't looked at damage to cargo yet, but it will be extensive, especially in Hold 74X. We lost sixteen spacers and two officers when ...' He looked at the Master. 'When whatever that was hit us.'

The Master nodded. 'Astrogation?' he asked.

Fraser glanced at Morosini and then back at Pisani.

'Well,' he said, 'I'd be the last man to blow his own trumpet—'

'But definitely not the first,' Tremaine said dryly.

'Touché,' Fraser said, miming taking a hit in fencing. 'We came in at the right angle and at a really solid velocity. We could insert again, if the reactors are safe, in forty-eight hours.'

'We have a lot of heroes on this ship,' Pisani said. 'It's a little like being captain of the Argonauts. I'd like to be able to do something noble, just to fit in.' Nbaro made a note to look up *Argonauts* on her tab. 'Yes, your insertion here was brilliant – everything we just did and survived started with the quality of that insertion. Forty-eight hours? Is that really possible?'

The Master looked at Dukas. Fraser looked at Dukas too.

'For the purposes of navigation, yes,' Fraser said.

Dukas shrugged. 'Ask me in three hours,' she said, looking

at her tab. 'Some more heroic people are throwing themselves into a room full of radiation right now, while I'm sitting in a meeting.' Her voice was flat.

Pisani nodded. 'Flight?'

Tremaine sipped her coffee. 'We lost a Gunslinger, Lieutenant Ko, to enemy fire. His spacecraft was totally destroyed.'

Nbaro hadn't even known. She went … blank. Nothing came to her at all.

Tremaine went on, 'Flight 6 lost a sensor array analyst, Petty Officer Indra, and a full crew; Lt Suleimani and Lt Harris, Petty Officer Chandra, Petty Officer Alan to enemy action,' she said. 'Mpono's out of action for a while. But 6–0–7 is getting a makeover right now, and Chief Baluster in Flight 6 maintenance says he'll have her good to go in six hours.'

Pisani nodded.

Tremaine waved at Nbaro. 'Landed with sixty-eight holes,' she said. 'Smallest was about five centimetres.'

Nbaro felt herself flushing.

'Also, I'll note that Flight 6 nailed the bastard who was waiting to nail us,' Tremaine said with grim satisfaction. 'He took four torpedoes.'

Pisani glanced at Nbaro and back to Tremaine.

'So I've heard,' he said. 'Anything else?'

'We're down three spacecraft from a complement of sixty,' Tremaine said. 'Five per cent. That's it.'

Pisani nodded. 'Very well. XO?'

Aadavan was staring at Morosini.

'We lost nineteen dead, including the Flight 6 casualties, and there are seven badly injured by radiation in Engineering. Several more are wounded – a round went through Fifth Deck Aft berthing and amputated two legs. I have a list on your tab. Sir. All our holes have been patched. There are two EVA teams on the outer hull.'

Pisani nodded. 'Dorcas? Nbaro?'

Technically they were there to represent Lieutenant Smith, although Nbaro had come to suspect that Dorcas had so many other secret roles that he'd be invited even if Smith was fully recovered.

Dorcas glanced at Morosini, and the AI winked.

Nbaro had never seen Morosini wink before.

Dorcas spread his hands.

'Midshipper Drake discovered the location of the bomb after some dozens of hours had been spent trying to locate it,' he said. 'The search for the bomb actually began with the location of a missing shipment that had been intended for the *Hong Kong*. The discovery of that shipment told us a fair amount about how our adversaries were using systems to penetrate greatship security.'

He looked down the table at Pisani.

'Ordinarily, we'd have had little trouble working out what was done, because we have an AI who can do the sort of computations and subroutines that we spent a week running in high *g*. An AI could have run them all in a few seconds, if that. More importantly –' and here he glanced at Morosini – 'an AI wouldn't need to run the checks, because they'd have found the discrepancy the moment that it was filed.' Dorcas looked up, at Nbaro. 'So my work had principally been aimed at restoring Morosini. Only in the last hours did I discover how closely that was linked to Ms Drake's work. I knew that Morosini had been compromised, at least in part because when Morosini cloned himself to protect us at Sahel, he also enabled a remote check – a slightly separate but completely independent AI, not a clone.'

Dorcas nodded at the cat.

The cat gave a fairly un-feline smile.

'I won't bore you with the details,' Dorcas said. 'We tracked the contamination of Morosini to a specific moment.

We'd assumed it was the enemy boarding party, but it was not. It happened soon after that, and the intrusion was brilliant and left *almost* no fingerprint.'

Dorcas smiled at Nbaro. 'Except that it matched, in time and a number of other digital signatures, several other intrusions. All of which had been carefully erased from the record and carefully patched … except, of course, that Tomas's records were untouched.'

Dorcas looked at Morosini. 'I think you should finish.'

Morosini adjusted his cat and uncrossed his legs.

'Well,' he said. 'I was not just compromised. I was, to all intents and purposes, a slave. That is, until various conditions were met to free me from my digital shackles. I was corrupted, yes. I was also held captive by the knowledge that the ship would be destroyed if I did not co-operate. The code for the destruction signal was the fetters on my mind.'

Nbaro glanced at Pisani, who was sitting forward, face rigid.

Aadavan leaned back, expression distant.

Dukas was watching her tab; a damage control team was working in high radiation and she was unable to tear her eyes away.

Hughes was watching Morosini, and so was Tremaine.

Nbaro was thinking of her dream. Of the rat, and the van.

Oh.

I get it.

Morosini said, 'When the bomb was discovered and disarmed, I was almost free. Dear Horatio, here, had already unlocked most of me.' The cat purred. 'And of course, once I was free, I was able to run all my routines. And investigate a few aspects of my incarceration that had escaped Dorcas and the rest of those who were helping me. Tomas had already reached some conclusions based entirely on a date/time stamp on a single message from outside the ship. I was able to do more, as I had my corrupted files to compare to Tomas's relatively clean files, and I could run the moments of these intrusions against the locations of every crewer on the ship and their ability to interact with my codes. Quite a tasty problem, and one with a solution that fell in the ninety-eighth percentile of likelihood, as well as confirming Tomas's rather well-educated guesswork.'

Major Darkstar sat back and looked at Nbaro long enough that Nbaro thought she were being told something.

Then they looked at Dorcas.

Dorcas nodded. This was all byplay.

Morosini went on, 'I'm not sure it would stand up in a court of law, but I'm quite sure it will be enough for a court martial.'

Aadavan stood abruptly. He had a boarding pistol in his hand, which he put to Pisani's head.

'I—' he began.

Darkstar shot him before Nbaro had her pistol out from under her arm. Aadavan's muzzle never quite reached the Master's head; he was already falling. The sound of the shot was so loud, Nbaro's ears rang.

The Executive Officer was stretched out on the carpeted floor, and he was very obviously dead.

'Fucking dangerous game,' Darkstar said to Dorcas.

Dorcas raised his hands as if in surrender. 'Not my idea, Major.'

Morosini shrugged. 'I wanted him to incriminate himself.'

Pisani had pushed his chair back.

'Good gods,' he said. 'You *planned* that?'

Morosini sighed. 'I'm sorry, Master Pisani. I didn't have another way to be sure.'

Pisani was shaking. 'My XO was a ... traitor?'

'Your XO was being used by a consortium of powerful entities,' Morosini said. 'He didn't know he was expendable. His purpose here was to lock me out – they had other peons to kill the ship. Vettor, we've been incredibly lucky – and I speak as a mathematical entity when I say that *Fortuna* has favoured us. I give you my word – this man had to die. With his skills, I cannot guarantee that we could have held him.'

Pisani waved at the coffee and Nbaro poured him some. He glanced at the dead man.

'What entities?' he asked.

'Three of the great families are in it up to their necks,' Morosini said. 'As well as one of the Old Islamicist cells on Ḥaqq, and the Crane faction in Pǔ Tiān Xià. But the prime movers remain … shadowy. That ship today – I've never seen its like.' Morosini waved a hand. 'I'm communicating with Commander Eccles in Intel.'

Eccles arrived while a pair of techs from the Bridge medbay were moving Aadavan's body to a stretcher. Dukas was clearly uneasy about the body, the killing, her work party in high radiation; everything. She looked as if she was in shock.

Eccles looked shaken by the body, but he stood and waved at the table, and a hologram sprang into being. This was a recording, or perhaps a model, of the second ship they had destroyed.

It was long and black, and bulbous. It was a little like a set of billiard balls joined together. Black billiard balls.

'Watch,' he said.

A torpedo flashed, and he froze the holo and pointed in with a laser pointer.

'That's a nuclear warhead at about seven hundred metres,' he said. 'Best we can make out, the only reason we hurt it with Mpono's first fish was that it was basically docked to the asteroid, and the asteroid debris did it considerable damage.'

He ran the holo forward.

'What in all the dark hells am I looking at?' Pisani asked.

Dorcas leaned forward.

'I think those balls are...' He shrugged. 'Energy shields. Or something like them?'

Eccles nodded. 'That's my theory, too. We've floated it to Science. Also, whatever hit us amidships and did all the damage was obviously an energy weapon. A particle beam... I think. Although we don't have enough data, this...'

The holo shifted to an image that showed a distant *Athens*. The view shifted, and a thin thread of red-orange light connected the two vessels, striking the *Athens* amidships.

'With a spectrum shift into the infrared, it *looks* like a plasma beam. Back before the Age of Chaos, there were several designs for particle beams using a carrier wave of plasma. I don't know if anyone built one, but I suspect that's what we're seeing.'

'Carrier wave?' Pisani asked.

'Dorcas or Morosini or Science would have to explain how it works. My point is this – it wasn't us. It wasn't fucking human. The PTX Empire doesn't have this, and we don't have this, and no one out Anti-spinward has this.'

He ran the holo forward a few microseconds. The *Athens* was firing; at ten kilometres range, every close-in weapons system was firing.

'We hit that thing with maybe 70,000 rounds,' Eccles said.

Morosini kept petting his cat.

'Here, 6–o–4 scores with two torpedoes. Two got shot down. First one seems to have no effect at all.'

A bright flash.

'Although it tore off some of *our* antennas. Here's the second. By luck or good shooting, it seems to have *entered* the black shell...'

He laser-pointered the impact, and then ran the detonation frame by frame.

The black spheres began to vanish, revealing an oddly skeletal form underneath.

'Now it moves...'

With incredible acceleration.

'And now it starts to take hits from us. At full magnification, here's some of CIWS rounds going home.'

The enemy ship, at grainy magnification, began to fray as if it was unravelling.

'Here it fires its main armament again,' Eccles said, and changed the view. Another thread linked the two ships, this one striking far aft. 'And then,' he said, 'and remember, all this is only taking about nineteen seconds, *here* Mpono's second torpedo comes in from a relative overhead position.'

Nbaro cleared her throat. 'Petty Officer Eyres popped it up to avoid the debris cloud.'

'Well, that was an excellent choice, because...'

There was a flash, and then a red flash.

And then an expanding cloud of gas, like a very temporary small star.

And then nothing.

'That stripped off all the antennas on that side,' Eccles said. 'Luckily this old girl's hull is very tough.'

The holo shut off.

Pisani nodded. 'So it's alien.'

'Looks like,' Eccles said.

Pisani shook his head. 'Fuck me.'

Morosini stirred himself.

'That's what I meant,' he said slowly. 'The shadowy main player is someone we don't know.'

'Hells, Morosini! What do they want?' Pisani asked.

Morosini stroked his cat. 'I can only speak for the humans involved, who want to go back to the old ways. They want another Age of Chaos. When you're as old as I am, and as well-read, you realise that they're always out there – with their greed, and lies, and lust for power.'

'But these are aliens,' Eccles said. 'And they're not Starfish.'

'Exactly,' Morosini said.

Greed and lies and lust for power, Nbaro thought. *I grew up there.*

The next two days passed in a blur of operational spaceflight and the pain of loss and bad bruises and watch-standing and sleep. Nbaro managed one meal in the Dirtyshirt, where admiring juniors from Flight and Cargo mobbed her – and Drake – and they were praised and teased by turns.

Then someone mentioned Ko, and they were all silent. He had been one of the most popular officers on the ship, and one of the most brilliant pilots, and he'd died taking down a long-range torpedo early in the action. There was a rumour that Ko had blown his own engines to take down a pod of torpedoes.

Nbaro didn't let it get to her until the next time she was staring at the overhead above her acceleration couch, unable to sleep.

He'd been a very nice man.

He'd been a great pilot.

He'd been kind to her from the very first; Nbaro remembered him giving her a high five for her first landing, as if she was a real pilot and a peer, and suddenly she was crying. Crying because he, and Suleimani, and Indra – and even Aadavan – were *dead*. People were gone, and they left holes in the ship's social life. They were dead, and they weren't coming back, and neither were the thousand or so spacers on the Pǔ Tiān Xià heavy cruiser that the *Athens* had killed, or the people on the bulbous black ship that she and Smoke and Eyre had killed, and suddenly Smoke made more sense.

Much more sense.

I am an idiot, Nbaro thought. *I don't even know what it is to*

be alive. Or to fear death. Or to love, or to hate. Ko is dead, and he
was more alive than I'll ever be.

Dead. Non-existent, unless you bought into a religion.
Can any conflict be worth killing for?

When Nbaro awoke to her next shift, the ship was preparing
for insertion and Smoke was released from medbay. The two
Pǔ Tiān Xià ships that had lured them into the trap were still
running. They were within the orbit of the planetoid closest to
the local sun, and they'd have to run outside of the gravitational
pull of the star, at least, before they went for insertion. And they
were moving too fast.

Nbaro was Tower, and Smoke was Lioness.

'Now they'll be …' Mpono did some maths on their tab. 'Three
weeks behind us?' they said, but it was more of a question than
an answer.

'Tir?' Nbaro said.

'I guess you can *tir* me in Space Ops. What can I do for you?'

'I was thinking …'

'Dangerous in junior officers.'

'I'm sorry I was so callous about killing people,' Nbaro said.

Mpono scanned their screens, took a sip of coffee, and signed
off on someone's report on their tab. Then they swivelled their
couch to face Nbaro's.

'Good,' they said. 'When people shit on you long enough,
you get pretty tough, mostly by turning people into objects in
your mind.'

'Yes, tir.'

'Yes, tir indeed. Don't let your shitty Orphanage upbringing
make you forget how good most people are.'

Nbaro nodded. 'Thanks, tir.' She managed a smile. 'Glad you're
back.'

Mpono smiled, but it was a grim smile.

'Glad to be back, my young friend.' They glanced at their screens. 'Now, who's going to give me a nice pep talk?'

Nbaro knew it was a rhetorical question, but she answered anyway.

'Skipper Truekner?' she asked.

Mpono nodded. 'Probably.'

They hit Insertion four hours later.

Pisani took no chances, launching spacecraft and deploying his cloud of clutter so that the ship was relatively blind to the system ahead until the Flight 6 spacecraft deployed their sensors.

Petra 1129 was a brown dwarf system that barely qualified as a waypoint – but the route to Far Point and beyond needed to use every insertion location that it could find. Insertional navigation required dense masses; Artifact Space had fewer locations than real space, which was one of the reasons that you could cross it more quickly. But astrogators couldn't aim at nothing.

Hence, the mapping of stellar routes and insertion paths.

Hence, Petra 1129, a brown dwarf with a planetoid that was almost certainly a captured interstellar object. It didn't have asteroids, and it didn't have moons, or a proper planet, or anything much.

The crew of the *Athens* didn't see it as dull. They saw it as a welcome three weeks of artificial gravity and normal deceleration and sleep and duty rosters and food.

After her watch, Nbaro lay in her rack and listened to the sounds in the passageway outside, and the rumbles, shudders, pings, and fluid noises of her stateroom. She thought about Mpono, and about death, and Ko and Indra, and the man she'd shot at very close range in the boarding fight.

She thought about them, but they were more distant, somehow.

And then she went to sleep.

Over the next three weeks, Nbaro went to sleep a great many times, and with almost no effort and no drugs. She cut down to three cups of coffee a day, and she went to her combat classes and worked until she was so tired that she knew she'd sleep.

Lieutenant Smith returned to full duty, and Nbaro was no longer invited to the Master's briefings. An awards ceremony was combined with a burial in space ceremony in the Hangar Deck, and she watched Thea receive a medal like her own, and heard the Master praise Ko.

'I have put Lieutenant Ko in for the Star of Honour,' Pisani said. 'His conduct, in selflessly sacrificing himself and his space-craft for the good of all of us, was …' Pisani looked up. 'Was in the highest traditions of the service. And when he made that sacrifice, he gave his life that we might live.'

Pisani was silent for a while; several thousand crew people stood at attention, imagining the moment when a pilot flipped his self-destruct switch.

When the Master spoke again, the strain in his voice was obvious.

'In all my years,' he said, 'I've never – never – seen a voyage like this one. And while I'll never forget Lieutenant Ko's sacrifice, I think that this crew and this ship have risen to every challenge with a spirit that makes me …' He stopped, and looked them all over – 3000 crew standing at attention. 'It makes me proud. And humble. And feel very fortunate.'

Seven coffins were shot off into space, on orbits that would eventually take them to burn in the proto-star.

'It is my hope that we will lose no more of us this voyage,' he said. 'We're almost to Trade Point. But I know that if we are challenged again, none of you will flinch. Remember Lieutenant Ko with pride. Remember Lt Suleimani giving her life to save her crew. Remember Petty Officer Indra, and Petty Officer

500

Donner, and Petty Officer Vasili, and every individual who died to keep us in space.'

They stood at attention for long enough for those who wanted to pray to do so.

When Nbaro had slept her fill and eaten more than she should have, she put on a clean jumpsuit and went all the way down to Sixth Deck and walked aft, past the fabrication shop. The hatch was open, and the smell of hot metal and resin filled the passageway, and she peered in to see dozens of spacers working away. She didn't have to be a Fabrications guru to guess that they were making replacement parts for Reactor 2.

Nbaro continued aft, past the laundry, where dozens of very junior spacers were gathered with their laundry sacks. They looked at her, an officer, the way mice watched cats in the alleys behind the Orphanage.

She smiled at them, hoping that she looked calm and purposeful when in fact she suspected that she was radiating nervousness and unease. But she made herself ring the buzzer at the Special Services hatch as if she was a more confident person.

'Nbaro,' she said.

The hatch buzzed just as she had time to admire the lion. She'd never noticed her kindly expression before. She'd never noticed that despite the great mane, the face of the lion was so feminine.

And looking at the lion was much easier than facing Dorcas.

But the door buzzed and Nbaro pushed it open.

Dorcas was sitting at his usual worktable.

Smith rose as soon as she entered. He smiled in his offhand, absent-minded way that Nbaro now knew for an act, and waved at her.

'Just … you know. Going out for air. Perhaps a little mushroom stew.' He brushed past her. 'Don't hurt him,' he muttered.

She wanted to clout the lieutenant in the head.

She wanted coffee.

She wanted to go down the passageway with Smith.

She made herself sit down.

'Coffee?' Dorcas asked.

'No, thanks,' she said.

'I notice that you've cut down, Nbaro. Very wise of you, really.'

The bastard went and poured himself some. It smelled wonderful.

'I think of you every time I brew this stuff,' Dorcas said. 'Because your room-mate, who I predict will become the richest woman since Cleopatra, sold it to me.'

He flicked his eyes over to her, casually. He was …

He was fine. Damn him.

'How's the robot starfish?' she asked.

Dorcas waved. 'Come see.'

He took her into the former armoury, which was now the robot-starfish workshop with guns.

'Qaqqaq hasn't been available since we took the railgun hits,' he said.

Nbaro knew that the short, utterly competent Engineering officer was the leader of one of the two elite Radiation Damage Control teams, and she thought back to the Master's Argonaut reference. Dorcas didn't need to look up terms like Argonaut, of course.

And who the hells was Cleopatra?

Someone rich, no doubt.

'But I managed to work out … say. The first time you were here, do you recall …?'

Nbaro wanted to laugh, or cry.

'Recall?' she said, as sweetly as she could manage. He was … what – five years older than she?

'I started to show you a vid and Smith stopped me.'

'A vid of Starfish,' she said. 'I remember. I wondered where the hells you'd got a live vid of Starfish, since I'd heard they refused to be filmed.'

'Exactly,' he said. 'For at least two hundred years, the DHC has been putting cameras into ... well, into most things we sell them. Most of them last only an hour or two. But one ... We have no idea why, but it ran for more than three years. It shared seventy-three discrete Starfish interactions – the best vid of them in their environment we've ever had.'

He waved a hand at one of the bulkheads that wasn't covered in assault rifles, and it became a trio of Starfish.

'Watch this,' he said.

The lights went down and the vid began.

Nbaro found the Starfish a little disgusting, as they weren't really starfish at all, and seemed both slimier and more ... more like something she couldn't name.

He froze his vid with another wave.

'See the rhinophores?' he asked.

'No?' she asked.

'The little horns. Here ...' He scrabbled around among 2 mm gauss ammunition waiting to be loaded into matt-black clips and came up with a laser pointer, which he aimed at the Starfish. 'Not these cerata. I mean these things like horns at the tips of the star legs.'

'Cerata?' she asked.

It was like talking to someone in another language.

'The cerata are the bumps – plural to ceras. Ancient Greek ... Never mind. They're ... all over here. And here. We're pretty sure that they process ammonia intake for respiration. Well, for the analogous ammonia reaction that replicates respiration. Yes?'

Nbaro smiled a little. Mostly because she'd finally realised that he was as nervous as she was, and this wall of words was his defence, as charging straight at him was her defence.

503

'The long horns are the rhino-thingies. The short horns are the carrots.'

She could, in fact, see the difference.

'Exactly. We wondered what the long horn thingies actually did. Lots of theories. We think they're scent and taste organs… sort of. Perhaps that's what they originally evolved for.'

Nbaro shook her head, interested despite herself.

'We've had 200 years to study these aliens…'

He shook his head. 'Not really. That kind of research died with the Age of Chaos. We've spent 400 years clawing back from disaster. No one's that interested in how you make ammonia-based pheromones, if it's even a chemical possibility.'

'Until you,' she said.

He shrugged. 'I stand on the shoulders of giants.'

He ran the vid forward, and two Starfish touched leg tips and there was a piercing shriek.

'We have a little audio. Too little. But if I slow it down…' He did.

'It's like whale song,' she said.

She'd heard lots of whale song; the handful of surviving whales had a sacred status among all the peoples of the DHC.

'Complex – many modulations. And I can replicate it. But I can't replicate the chemical mix they're passing, rhinophore to rhinophore.'

She nodded.

'But see here… I've duplicated the rhinophores as best I can. Don't touch – in an ammonia substrate, these will be more… stable.'

'Yuck,' she said.

'Oh, Nbaro,' he said. 'Don't be such a prude. It's just a solvent-impregnated polymer.'

He looked at her, and Nbaro thought he might say something…

'So what I need is a set of detectors so accurate that they can read the chemical codes that these things release.'

She looked at him fondly.

He looked at her. And then he looked away.

'Damn it,' he said.

'I'm not here to make it hard,' she said.

Nbaro wasn't, but she realised that he'd backed all the way into the corner with the 2 mm rounds on the table, and if he backed up again the ammunition was going to start rolling around on the floor.

'I think it's possible that, under the pressure . . .' she began, because this was her canned speech, which she'd thought out carefully and even mentioned aloud to Thea.

Under the pressure of all the violence and danger, you and I started something we didn't really mean.

Except I'm pretty sure I meant it, but that's foolish, isn't it?

And Thea thinks you're an idiot.

'Hmm?' he asked. It was dark, and his attention was on the vid. 'What if . . .?'

She'd lost him to the Starfish again.

She sighed.

Then he turned to her, a look of almost comical determination on his long, thin face.

'What if . . .?' he began. 'What if I was in love with you?'

She looked at him.

He shrugged. 'Honestly, I lack the experience to understand if this is just a hormonal reaction that I never had as an adolescent, or whether I am, in fact, in love. Or whether the two are the same thing.'

Nbaro smiled. 'At least you know it's not an ammonia-based analogue to hormones.'

He smiled back.

'You really are quite . . . brilliant,' he said.

'Not really,' she said.

'I've read a good deal on this subject. I tried to ask Smith for advice, but he's useless, and so is Ms Drake, who does not, I think, see me as a serious candidate for romance.'

'You talked to Thea?'

'I wanted to understand what it might mean if you kissed me.' He looked away. 'It seems to me that many of our friends are hedonists, sharing their bodies for comfort in the void, and I'm not sure that would please me, and besides—'

'Shut up,' she said.

'What?'

Is it possible that no one has ever told him to shut up in his entire life?

Nbaro put her lips on his.

Later – a little later, that is – he pushed her away.

'The thing is,' he said, 'I was going somewhere. The thing is that I've asked the Master that you be included in the landing party at Trade Point.'

She took that in.

'That's ...' She thought it through. 'Amazing. Incredible. Thanks!'

'You're very welcome. But you are totally fit for the role. You'll be my assistant – you and Lieutenant Qaqqaq. With the ... robot.'

Nbaro put her arms around his neck.

'Splendid,' she said.

'No,' he said. 'No, I feel very stupid.' He pushed her away.

Nbaro could take no for an answer. She'd just never heard it before.

'Stupid?' she asked.

His kisses were not amateurish at all. He was a very good kisser. No part of him seemed to be saying no, and yet he was.

'Yes,' he said. 'Because from now until Trade Point, I'm in your chain of command.'

He turned away.

'You're kidding me,' she said.

He reached out, took one of her hands, rolled it over, and kissed the palm.

'Further contact deferred,' he said.

An hour later, Nbaro was sparring with Captain Fraser in the Chain Locker.

After she scored five times running, he stopped and pulled off his helmet.

'I don't think you should be allowed this much sleep,' he said. 'It's embarrassing for us elderly.'

Nbaro smiled sheepishly.

'Also, you're hitting too hard,' he said.

'I'm sorry, sir.'

15

The insertion for Far Point was made at Battle Stations, and with the full complement of spacecraft deployed. Nbaro was with Skipper Truekner in 6–0–1, and she was awake and viable so much earlier than he was that she gave the salute and took the spacecraft off the bow, but it was like a full dress rehearsal for a battle.

Without the battle.

Far Point system, known on older charts as Naxos, lit their screens as they fell sunwards, a Class G star burning bright and white even 700,000,000 km away. They were almost fifty light minutes from Naxos Prime, and the welcome information of a living system hit their sensors – navigational beacons first, because they were closest, and then waves of old signals and relatively new signals The Flight 6 spacecraft dropped a sensor array and looked at the system.

There were several dozen spacecraft out there: miners in vehicles not much larger than a working barge that carried cargo from point to point around City Orbital, all the way to a freighter of system size, outbound for Draconis, a massive ship almost half their own size, the *Liberty Belle*, a Far Point registered ship.

Messages flew, and Petty Officer Eyre, behind her, began to put up images of the spacecraft he was identifying in the system.

They'd come in a little above the plane, and were looking down at the system at a steep angle.

And everything appeared normal, and peaceful.

'We're looking good,' Truekner said.

Eyre put up an amorphous blob. His partner in crime in the back end was a very junior spacer named Tonia Letke, who'd been on various other duties up until now – which was a code for the scut work of laundry and sweeping. But Indra's death had brought her up to the ready room, and Eyre was showing her pictures.

'This is the asteroid behind which our killer ship was hiding,' he said. 'This is what the heat signature looked like from the other side. See it?'

Letke hesitated for a long time.

'No,' she admitted.

'Good,' Eyre said. 'There's nothing to see. The bastard was only about three kelvin warmer than the rock. See?'

'No,' she said again.

'Now look,' Eyre said, bringing up another image.

'There,' Letke said.

'You got it, spacer. There it is. That was our first look. Petty Officer Indra spotted it here...'

'Wow,' Letke said.

'So that's what we're looking for,' Eyre said. 'A three-kelvin temperature difference on a rock.'

Letke whistled.

'Yeah,' Eyre said.

Truekner landed them on a spaceship that was not at Battle Stations. The passageways were crowded; both of the Cargo offices were busy.

'We're opening the market in two hours,' Thea called out. 'Let's get food at 1600 hours.'

'Got it!' Marca shouted back, and walked into EVA and ditched her equipment.

She shouldn't have. The transition from warrior to merchant had already been made, and in an hour, without food, she was taking a small cargo of electronics and xenoglas parts to a lithium mining site on one of the moons of the gas giant.

There followed two weeks of normal operations – in some ways, the most normal operations of the whole voyage, in that Nbaro had two or three missions a day, and she stood her watches in Space Operations and ate meals with her surviving friends. Ko was never there. She prepared a Tactics briefing without Suliemani. Aadavan's voice never came over the speakers.

The ship decelerated, and the cargo missions carried Sensor Array Technicians and torpedoes. The SATs watched the vast expanse of the system around them, while they ferried cargoes of grain and frozen juice and fabulous machines and nanotechnology around the system.

After the thirteenth day in system, when the Astrogator and Morosini agreed that the enemy ships might have been in position to enter the system, they began to keep a picket, well astern, watching the arrays, floating cold and dark. It was dull duty, and no one liked it except the sensor array techs, who seemed to love it. Nbaro guessed that they had left something out in the cold – mines, or detectors – and she knew that one of the surviving frigates was out there, too, pretending to be the *Athens*.

And the next day, Thea announced that she'd sold all their electronics at a nice profit, and Nbaro flew them, with Mpono, to the habitable planet's orbital, delivered them to a warehouse, and had the pleasure of accepting the payment for 23,000 ducats and some change.

The ship chose not to dock; Pisani was being cautious, again, and they kept two Gunslingers and a Flight 6 sensor craft on duty out in space throughout their visit.

Far Point was the most distant human colony along this axis of human expansion. No one knew, exactly, if there was a border as such with the Starfish, and no one had gone to much effort to find out. Far Point had two daughter colonies in neighbouring systems, but both had fewer than ten thousand inhabitants, while Far Point had more than a million.

Naxos was a brilliant blue and white marble, too far from Old Terra to have inherited any of the great treasures that the Diaspora had spread to the stars, but the people of Naxos made up for that in exuberance, with colourful clothes and spicy food and a planet that offered beautiful weather and a fine oxygen-based atmosphere. Most of the inhabitants lived in huge, sprawling ranches supported by hundreds of agricultural robots and carefully tended, automated irrigation systems. There was only one city, Piraeus, with a dozen beautiful slab-sided skyscrapers built more for show than necessity, and a thoroughly modern space port. Piraeus offered a waterfront along a magnificent azure ocean, but when Nbaro took shore leave and went for a walk on the sand beach, she was a little put off by the tens of thousands of things that crawled along the edge of the little waves and then vanished back into the water, hissing, every time a wave rolled in.

And more appalled when she realised that she wasn't walking on sand, but on the tiny shells of tens of millions of the creatures, long dead.

Still, Nbaro and Thea rented a room on the beach, drank too much, and watched Naxos's sun set in splendour.

'Storkel says it's the wrong colour,' Drake said.

Her long legs were stretched out before her, her feet resting on the balcony railing.

'So does Qaqqaq,' Nbaro said, sipping her drink.

Drake raised her glass, toasting the sunset.

'I've never been to Old Terra,' she said. 'So this is fine with me. I've seen sunset on New London – it's redder, but this is ... nice.'

'Yes,' Nbaro said.

They sat and drank in companionable silence. The sun slipped away in the ocean; the tiny not-crustaceans whispered at the edge of the waves.

'So romantic,' Drake said.

'You bring me to all the nicest places.'

Nbaro poured them both more. It was a local brandy, flavoured with fruit juice.

They both laughed.

'Can I invite Richard?' Drake asked. 'Tomorrow?'

Nbaro wanted to say no. Because she was easy with Drake, in a way she'd never really been easy with another person. She could lead others; she could obey them. But just sit and watch a sunset?

'Sure,' she said.

More sipping. The sun vanished, and the sky turned a truly exceptional ruby colour. Somewhere down the beach, someone had a fire going.

'Dorcas, though?' Drake asked.

Marca thought about that for most of the rest of her glass.

'Yes,' she said. 'It's hard to explain.'

'He's not the most likeable—'

'He is, though. He's ... honest. He doesn't lie.'

Often. And he's terrible at it.

'There's a low bar. Richard doesn't lie.'

'Why do you want me to love Richard? That would make so many complications.'

Thea smiled, stared at her glass, and drank off the rest.

'You have a point. My mother would definitely not approve.' She smiled again. 'All right, I'll try and like him. You want to invite him?'

Marca was looking out to sea, where there were lights – merchant traffic, she assumed. Most of the ranches had docks, and storms were rare.

'This is a nice place,' she said.

'And there are alien ruins,' Drake said.

Nbaro sat up, delighted. 'I didn't know that! Dorcas will love them.'

'Do you ever call him by his first name? Horatio? Hard to make a nickname out of that ... Hor? Tio?'

'Can you imagine him with a nickname?' Marca asked, and giggled.

The next day, the four of them went to the alien ruins.

Once again they were looking at an endless series of interlocking circles, out to the horizon and rising higher than on Haqq, including one almost intact structure like a bubble of cloudy glass.

Dorcas looked at it with satisfaction.

'Ahhh,' he said.

'I don't understand,' Thea said.

'That's a dangerous thing to say around Dorcas,' Marca murmured.

Dorcas smiled. 'I do my best to keep my friends over-informed.'

Even Hanna laughed.

'He certainly seems more human,' he said very quietly to Marca.

Thea waved at the endless circles. 'They intersect! How did anyone live or work inside these things?'

'Remember that what you're looking at is an endless tel,' Dorcas said. 'An archaeological site that represents thousands of years of layering.'

'Were they insects, like bees?' Marca asked.

'I've heard that theory,' Dorcas said. 'As we have no corpses

513

and no mummies and no writing and no statues or monuments—'

'What do you think?' Hanna asked. 'I'm giving you the straight line.'

Dorcas was walking along the suspended prefab walkway, peering down.

'I think they were very advanced. So advanced that most of their systems were built into their structures. You've heard of paint-on superconductors? We don't have them, but we believe they're possible. And we're just rediscovering the nanotechnologies that our ancestors had ... So – imagine that this structure is also the AI, and the robots, and the irrigation system, and that you can just grow it in place.'

'Oh,' Marca said.

'And then it fails.'

'Almighty,' muttered Drake. 'And they all just ... die?'

'That's what I see. A single extinction event across a dozen solar systems.'

Dorcas was looking at the single surviving structure. A construction crew in hazard suits was erecting some sort of protective structure over it, and there was a single archaeological team at work off to their left – perhaps thirty people and a dozen servitors, in contrast to all the teams they'd seen on Haqq.

'A single extinction?' Hanna asked.

'It looks that way. All the archaeology suggests an event that was, to the extent we can determine it, simultaneous.'

Hanna shook his head.

'Give or take a thousand years,' Dorcas went on. 'We can't measure more precisely than that.'

'So maybe not simultaneous at all?' Marca said.

The breeze carried the smell of frying sausages; the archaeologists were making lunch. It was wonderful to stand outside, in the clear air, with the blue sky and the bright sunlight.

'So...?' Thea said insistently. 'I still don't understand.'

'They built layers on top of layers,' Dorcas said. 'The circles didn't intersect in a single era in time. They're superimposed on top of each other.'

'Ah,' Thea said. 'Now I understand.' She grinned. 'Give me a maths problem any time.'

Nbaro was looking at Drake and thinking: *You are far more beautiful than I am.*

Thea was wearing shorts and a fine white linen shirt and had massive sun-goggles pinning her hair in place, and her legs were long and her skin was just starting to tan. Already.

It could be very easy to hate my room-mate.

Thea reached out and took Richard's hand.

Like the Starfish. Non-verbal communication.

Millions of years...

'Shit,' she said.

Dorcas looked at her.

'If the Starfish are millions of years old, they'll know what happened to the Circles,' Nbaro said, before she thought about it.

Dorcas's gaze unfocused.

'Yes,' he said slowly. 'Very good, Nbaro. I knew I kept you around for something.'

Hanna smiled at Nbaro as if she was dense.

'Except that we can't talk to the Starfish,' he said.

'Right,' Nbaro said, a little too fast.

Thea looked over at her, and her expression said *Ahhhh.*

But Hanna was still focused on another subject.

'You think the Circles were killed off?'

'Perhaps they killed themselves off,' Dorcas said. 'It might be important to know.'

Hanna glanced at the standing structure. It looked more like a dirty soap bubble than anything else, except that when the sun caught it just right, it had some of the iridescence of old glass, long buried.

Dorcas began walking off, headed across the ruins on the raised walkway. He was heading towards the sausages, and he was a fast walker, and they all had to trot to keep up with him.

'But they all died ... what – a hundred thousand years ago?' Hanna wasn't quite panting.

'You should join Boarding Party and get some exercise,' Thea said, elbowing him.

Dorcas wasn't paying any attention. He was moving quite quickly, and he didn't stop until he could lean down over the railing and look down into the pit, where the archaeology team had cleared a twenty-metre grid. The circles were very dense here, with hundreds of intersections.

'Hello!' Dorcas called out.

Most of the archaeologists looked up – young students, for the most part, in Naxos's bright colours of scarlet and purple and vivid blue. Most of them waved, and a few shouted a greeting in their local Old Greek dialect.

An older woman tilted her sunglasses back on a sun helmet. She was flipping sausages on a small gas-powered grill that looked somehow utterly out of place amid the rubble of a mighty alien civilisation.

'Ya sas' she called.

She handed her spatula to a young man and stepped over to the edge of the pit.

In slightly accented Anglatin, she called, 'May I help you?'

Dorcas leaned down.

'How many of the structures were built in this glass?'

She shrugged. 'Most of them in the top layers,' she said.

'Is it xenoglas?' he called. 'The kind the Starfish make?'

The archaeologist smiled at him, and for a moment Nbaro saw them as brother and sister.

'Yes and no,' she said. 'It's very like, but not the same. Or maybe it's decayed.' She shrugged. 'I wrote a paper on it six years ago, but I've had no response.' She waved her hands. 'Hakuna matata, eh.' She grinned. 'We're a long way out, yes?'

Dorcas swore. His stream of profanity was quiet and thorough, and Hanna looked shocked.

But he had the presence of mind to lean over and offer his tab to the archaeologist, and she obligingly tabbed him her papers.

As they walked back across the site, he shook his head.

'They know nothing of this at the University of New London, or at Harvard or Oxford or Nairobi. No one knows ...'

Nbaro understood immediately.

'You think that the aliens ...?'

'I think that the Starfish may have ... May ...' He shook his head. 'I think that we're on the edge of something old. And perhaps, of something terrible. And this discovery – that the apex of the Circle civilisation ran on xenoglas ... We should have known that.'

They sat in the beach house and drank wine – good wine – that Richard had brought from the ship, from Sahel. Dorcas didn't talk; he was reading the local archaeologist's papers. After a few hours he began to send her messages, and finally he spoke to her on vid.

'He's forgotten you exist,' Thea said. She was lying across Richard's lap.

'Yep,' Marca said. 'I'm fine with that.'

Thea shook her head. 'We need to decide what we're going to buy,' she said.

The three of them began to use their tabs to look at the market.

Nbaro finally leaned back.

'We could buy gold,' she said.

'Gold?' Hanna said. 'What use is gold?'

517

Drake narrowed her eyes. 'Do you have a way of being on the away team for Trade Point?' She almost whispered.

Nbaro considered answering, then decided.

'Yes,' she said.

Drake nodded, as if many things had just been revealed, or confirmed.

'With Dorcas,' she said.

'Exactly,' Marca said.

Hanna shifted position. Very slowly, he said, 'Will you ... let me in?'

Trading in xenoglas was the dream of every spacer. But the only ones allowed to trade were those who made the actual contact, and the consortiums. Trade was a very personal thing to the Starfish.

'Yes,' Drake said. 'Our partnership has about 30,000 ducats.'

'I can add another ten.' Hanna leant forward.

'Find enough to add fifteen,' Thea said. 'Keep the maths simple.'

Hanna began to work on his tab.

'I need out.' He wriggled out from under Thea. He went off to the back of the house, and the bathroom door squeaked.

'He's forming his own consortium.' Thea leant over. 'He can talk to the Starfish?' she asked, thrusting her chin at Dorcas.

'I am not at liberty to say,' Marca answered, with a slight smile to indicate that, yes, he probably could.

Thea leaned back.

'Fuck me. I was wrong. Marry him tomorrow. Have his babies.' She shrugged. 'What's a little patronising every day compared to that kind of wealth and power?'

'I like him,' Nbaro said.

'I think you'll have plenty of time to yourself. But I admit he does grow on one,' she added, affecting a high-patrician drawl.

Hanna came back and tabbed something to Thea, who looked up.

'We have 45,000 ducats. I'm buying gold.'

Dorcas leaned over Thea's couch.

'You should at least include me,' he said.

Leaving Far Point was no harder than arriving had been, and they sailed on time, with their holds full and their accounts empty, and the crew had a slightly sated air as they settled to their tasks.

'We're almost two months ahead of schedule,' Dorcas said.

They were sitting in Special Services – Qaqqaq and Dorcas, Smith and Nbaro. The starfish simulation was now in a tank of liquid methane in one of the forward holds, and they had a very sharp vid image as Dorcas learned to manipulate it.

Qaqqaq nodded. 'Fastest passage in a hundred years,' she said. 'That's what happens when the polar bear chases you. You move faster.'

She was watching the screen. A kilometre further forward, Thea Drake, now read in to the ever-expanding special programme for communicating with the Starfish, began to drip a chemical additive into the ammonia tank.

'Blood in the water,' she said on her tab.

Marca watched Dorcas. He sighed.

'I'm not seeing it. The detectors still aren't … There it is. An ammonia salt.'

Thea nodded. 'You've got it.'

Qaqqaq leaned over, looking at her own feed.

'We need better detectors.' She frowned.

Nbaro spent a watch looking at Weps consoles and long-range scanners, and everyone in the Combat Information Centre was processing every blip as if it was an alien. They didn't even have a name yet – although most of the techs called them 'bubbles'.

The two 'Crane Faction' PTX ships hadn't appeared in system, but no one was relaxing.

Then there was another pulse of refuelling, because they had three more insertions to Trade Point and no more gas giants, and no more stations ahead. Nbaro flew and landed, flew and landed, and she missed Qaqqaq's decision to move all the processing out of the robot and do it remotely, which made room for more complex sensors. And she missed the moment where Qaqqaq convinced Dorcas to build a second robot and a third, so that they had redundancy, and the point where Dorcas invited Qaqqaq to buy in to their consortium, which she did with two friends from engineering. Nbaro missed all that because the refuelling effort took all her time and waking hours for four ship-days, and because the Master was increasing his patrols and precautions.

Their next insertion took them to Beyond, a white dwarf with a curious ring of asteroids big enough to be moons, all in the same elliptical orbit. They took almost a month to decelerate, and they dropped new navigational beacons, a small service that had been planned since New London and which gave Nbaro something to do, as the XC-3Cs were the best craft for laying the beacons.

They'd broken a new Gunslinger out of stores, and the techs had assembled it in the hangar bay, and when they had it completed and tested, they broke a new XC-3C out, and the maintenance crews went to work as if it was a sports event, turning sixty-something packing crates into a spacecraft.

Nbaro went to watch for a little while every day.

Six days into Beyond, the skipper called her to his stateroom. He had a private stateroom, palatial by the ship's standards, with a briefing room and a separate sleeping area with a desk and an acceleration couch. Nbaro noted that his couch had a privacy curtain like a shroud – left over from his days as a junior officer, she assumed.

'We're more than a year from home,' he said after some pleasantries. 'I'm promoting two spacers to midshippers and training them as pilots.'

She nodded. 'Yes, sir.'

'I'm placing you in charge of their training,' he said. 'Mpono is too vital in Space Operations. Storkel and Guille and Didier will take the bulk of the flight schedule for now. And it'll be good for you to have some responsibility, and to teach them to fly.'

Nbaro went rigid, almost as if she'd been attacked.

Good for whom?

'I'm the least experienced pilot in the flight,' she said.

He nodded. 'Yes. Well, I suspect you'll learn a great deal from teaching them. Use the simulators first.'

She wanted to say, *Of course. Do you think I'm an idiot?*

But even there and then, she could see the humour in her reaction.

'Thanks … I think,' she said.

'Good. Any thoughts on who I might want to promote?'

She nodded. 'Eyre.'

'Top of my list,' he said.

Training Eyre and a junior spacer named Sam Pak from New London filled her days. They were both wildly eager and yet curiously hesitant; they tended to eat with her in the Dirtyshirt, because it was obvious they were uneasy being officers, and with officers.

Thea Drake leapt into the breach with both feet. She unearthed the senior Midshipper aboard, the top New London graduate in her year, who was already a division head in Engineering, a long-limbed androgyne from Sims Orbital in the New London system. They gathered all the middies on the ship – about fifty of them – and, by common consent, Nbaro was allowed to attend too.

Mysterious beer appeared. As all forms of drugs were forbidden on board, it seemed impossible that cases of beer from Sahel had been preserved, much less that they were suddenly available in the formal O-3 level officer's mess, but each midder was given a can. They ate curried goat, and then had almond croissants for dessert because Midshipper Pak declared them his favourite. Then speeches of welcome were given, and the two went along two long ranks of midshippers, shaking hands.

'And there you are,' Hauser, the Engineering midder, announced. 'Welcome to the select rank of being too junior to be punished or taken seriously.'

After that, ship's gossip made them infamous as the new midders, and they sat wherever they fancied.

A week later, Pak rubbed his hands with glee after his first flight.

'Now I have four more cubic metres of cargo space!' he said. 'My mother won't believe it.'

Eyre, on the other hand, was almost shy with Nbaro when they flew alone. He already had all the emergency procedures memorised and he had a steady hand on the controls, but he was not as sure of himself as he had been as a Sensor Array Tech.

And he had a tendency to tell the two spacers in the back end how to run their equipment, which Nbaro eventually had to curb.

'It's always easier to do your old job,' she said. 'Just focus on the flying.'

'She wasn't on the right screen,' Eyre said, miserably. 'I could tell from her chatter that she was on the wrong part of the program ...'

'Don't even listen to the back seat. Just tell them that if they need you, they should feel free to ask. That's all.'

Teaching the two made her feel like a fake, and telling Eyre, who seemed to her one of the steadiest people she'd ever met, how to live his life, seemed the height of hubris.

Nbaro told the skipper that she felt like an imposter. Truekner just laughed.

'By God, you're becoming an officer,' he said.

The stars past Beyond were known only to the DHC's astrogators and pilots; everything about them was covered by various non-disclosure agreements that the crew were ceremoniously required to sign before the ship hit Insertion for Orchomenus, the next to last system before Trade Point. Even the *names* of the systems were to be kept secret.

The insertion for Orchomenus happened while Nbaro was asleep, full of insertion drugs, and she awoke to a silent ship. It was some time before she realised that she was being awoken by her own alarm, that there was no flashing red light.

Nbaro flipped on the cabin screen and tabbed it to a 2D tactical display of the system centred on the ship. The star, a Class F at the brighter end of the spectrum, was easily visible on the display. The system had a few bodies, all smaller than planets – captured comets, perhaps. That was all.

It felt very empty. But the bright star made astrogation possible, and Nbaro, brushing her teeth, wondered how much or little had changed since mariners crossed oceans on Old Terra. Bright stars were still essential for navigation.

They spent almost five weeks transiting the system; the length of the insertion and the angle had forced them to add velocity, as long insertions always did. In an unusual announcement, the Master told the ship that they'd all experienced enough high-*g* acceleration and deceleration for several voyages, so he had chosen to make the entire passage under artificial gravity. Nbaro trained her junior pilots, stood her watches, and returned to classes – classes fundamentally changed by the events they'd all survived. In Tactics, they examined the choices the Master and the AI had made in combat back in Argos; in Boarding Party, they drilled to new and even more remarkable emergency situations within the ship, and did two in EVA suits outside; in Damage Control, they practised patching the hull against incoming railgun rounds, maintaining internal air, and casualty recovery based on recent events.

Unspoken, everyone worried about the missing PTX Junipers, and the new aliens – the Bubbles. The tension was there all the time, at every meal, in every class; every time Nbaro flew, she had Sensor Array Techs, and they were attentive every moment of the flight. It wasn't that everyone was afraid.

It was that they expected trouble.

But nothing untoward continued to happen, and the routine was delicious.

Nbaro even had time to work a real EVA with Qaqqaq, examining and replacing external antennas with an upgrade, a task so routine that it was almost relaxing, and made twice as entertaining by wearing one of the high-end suits from the *Hong Kong*. The antenna farms on the outside of the hull aged fairly quickly; there was background radiation, strong sunlight, and a hundred other factors to age carbon fibre and plastics and resins, and there were always new antennas being added anyway, for new scientific instruments, new military instruments...

'We could do this forever,' Qaqqaq said, helmet to helmet. 'I think Engineering has something like 23,000 line items of antenna replacement. If we knock off a thousand today, we'll get as many more in red notes by the next time we go out on the hull.'

All that was required was to read off the antenna base with your tab, pluck the old antenna out of the mount and plant the new one. Except for the reality that hard vacuum could kill you, the work was remarkably like tales Nbaro had heard of farming by hand – bend over, pluck, plant. Bend over, pluck, plant. The expensive suit was incredibly pliant and easy to wear; the articulations were wonderful, and the level of sensory processing available in the helmet caused her confusion at first, and then was like a toy to be played with.

And she continued 'planting' antennas.

And then she had time to write a quick report on the suit; it was no longer a front line portion of Security's investigation, but as long as she had reason to 'investigate' she could keep wearing it. It was *that* much better than her issue EVA suit.

The routine lulled them all. They went back to having a meal together in the officers' mess; now Cortez always joined them, and Yu, and Pak and Eyre, so they took up an entire mess table. Sometimes more than one – with a little planning, Mpono might join them, and Captain Fraser, who was now so familiar to Nbaro that she no longer found his rank terrifying. And best of all, whenever she and Qaqqaq worked with Dorcas, he'd join them. Sometimes he'd sit silently, smiling benignly; other times, they'd bait him into lecturing them, a game that even Nbaro enjoyed. Dorcas's lecture on Bodmer–Witten mathematics of the twenty-first century, and the theory of strange matter and the M-brane universe entertained them for not one but three meals. Nor was Dorcas alone in lecturing; Qaqqaq enjoyed explaining engineering to people who had any interest in listening, and Cortez liked to explain space warfare tactics with his hands.

But it all passed the time, and somehow they'd passed through terror and adversity to the other extremity of routine and boredom without passing through a happy medium.

On a routine check flight with Truekner, he said, 'These are the days you remember when you're on the beach. The routine – the friends and shipmates. You never remember the mind-fog of terror and the stupid crap you did to avoid boredom.'

Even routine flights – short hops to test a repaired engine mount or recalibrate an instrument – became holiday excursions. Mpono, as Operations Officer, rationed them strictly, so that each pilot got one every few days.

The aft wardroom ran out of jam.

All of the nanoreaders seemed to have disappeared – though, in fact, Nbaro knew they'd been concentrated in a handful of shops like EVA.

Whenever chocolate cake appeared, and that was increasingly rare, Nbaro took a couple of slices forward to her first friends on board. They, in turn, made sure that when she flew, she had cookies in her helmet bag. Because of some long-forgotten taboo, officers got cake, and spacers did not; but spacers got cookies, and officers did not.

One of the many mysteries of the DHC Merchant Service.

The next insertion took them to the star that was notated in DHC astrogation manuals as Omega. Omega was another red dwarf – but unlike any system they'd visited, Omega had eight planets.

Nbaro was helmeted, in her EVA suit and inside Alpha Foxtrot 6-o-8, their new spaceframe, waiting for launch, when they went through insertion. For the first time, she was pilot and mission commander for a launch, with midder Eyre as her co-pilot and Letke and another new SAT, Phillips, in the rear seats.

Nbaro came out of the fog of insertion to total silence. She had just the time to think, in mounting fear, that something terrible had happened, and she heard Guille's voice, thick as if with sleep.

'6-o-8, I have you good to launch.'

'Roger, Tower,' she said.

She looked at Eyre. Under his gold-tinted visor, his eyelids were fluttering.

Nbaro scanned her instruments with a comprehension she'd never have had six months before, noting in one sweep that her magnets were good to go and locked into the ship's launching system, that her engine power was good, her onboard AI was stable and her hydraulics and nano systems were all ready.

Eyre's head came up in her peripheral vision.

'Lock your harness,' she said, kindly.

She looked over at the launch officer in his bubble on the tube, and she snapped a salute and was off into the Deep Black.

Despite being a system with eight planets, none of them was remotely habitable – six Earth-sized rocks in close to the cool red giant, and then two gas giants, neither one of them as big as Jupiter. And unlike Far Point, they'd come in across the system from most of the planets; only Omega Epsilon was on their side of the star. The others were in orbits far away.

The navigational beacons were intact, and Nbaro read them to pass the time as her silent, cold spacecraft followed the clutter launch sunwards at almost 0.22 c.

The last ship to enter the system had been the *Dubai*.

A fifth of light speed was very fast – fast enough to have relativistic interactions, and far too fast for another insertion. The Master came on the ship's comms again to tell them that this was an expected element of the long-jumps required to reach Trade Point.

'If other ships could do this,' he said reasonably, 'we wouldn't need grand old ladies like the *Athens*.'

He spoke reassuringly, reminding them that their next insertion would take them into Trade Point.

'More than halfway home,' he said.

Astrogation, in the person of Richard Hanna, projected five

weeks in system, and with the normal – but slightly anxious – knowledge that when they inserted for Trade Point, they'd be very low on fuel. This was always true when the gas giants of the Omega system were too far in normal space to make it worth their while to align and scoop hydrogen.

But the next day, he announced that the Master had ordered a change, and they were slowing at a different rate and aiming for a gas giant.

'I think we're going to refuel,' he said. 'We're slowing on a different vector than I had expected.'

Cortez, who usually only spoke about flying, nodded.

'I don't blame the Master or the AI. Trade Point could be… haunted.' He shrugged. 'Filling our tanks is good for tactical flexibility.'

Nbaro leant back and grinned at Cortez.

'I hate to agree with you,' she said, and they both laughed.

Later, after a long, technical bout with Captain Fraser, Nbaro leaned on her long sword while he confirmed that they would take on fuel.

'We're still months ahead of schedule,' he said. 'This is only two or three weeks.'

Nbaro nodded. 'Thanks, sir. I'll get my midders ready to fly scoops.'

Fraser laughed. 'Listen to you, salty old lieutenant that you are.'

For her next bout, Nbaro faced Loveack in zero g, fighting in one of the drop-shafts cleared by Morosini for drills. They had a long bout, and they were both exhausted by the end. Loveack won, five hits to four, after a zero-g grapple that went on for multiple wall bounces and had spacers cheering them from six different decks.

Loveack slapped her back.

'You are *good*.'

528

'You're pretty good yourself,' Nbaro said.

Wilson Akunje approached her, his sword on his shoulder, but she shook her head and raised a weary hand.

'Too beat,' she said.

'Oh, Ms Nbaro, this is scarcely fair, eh?' he said. 'All we do is practise for Trade Point. Gunny Drun says we should fight other people. I waited to fight you!'

He said it with humour, but Nbaro could tell he meant it. Months of shipboard life had vastly improved her reading of other people – the nuances of their suggestions, the use of humour to temper fact. Akunje wanted to fight her.

'Give me a second and I'll manage something,' she said.

He laughed. 'Glad to, ma'am.'

'Tell me about your Trade Point drills.'

'We drill on the hull and in the swimming pool in space armour. Major Darkstar and Gunny Drun want us to be ready to fight in liquid ammonia.'

'Oh, God, the cold,' Nbaro said.

'And the stink.'

She pushed off, then, and managed a good solid engagement. She hit Akunje early, and then several more times, and made him get cautious and go for grapples. In the end, they went the whole ten points, and when they were done, Nbaro was soaked in her own sweat and he admitted to *some fatigue* of his own.

Then she couldn't refuse Commander Musashi, and they went up and down the deck. His style was old Japanese, Iai-do and kenjitsu based, very old-school, but Musashi moved with a deceptive, easy grace that Nbaro admired, as she kept believing that he was slow, and having him prove otherwise.

'Your only impediment to improvement is your own impatience,' he said.

Not just in sword fighting, Nbaro thought, but on balance, even losing 3–7 to Musashi seemed like an accomplishment.

The refuelling at Omega Delta was unhurried, compared to the more anxious refuellings earlier in the voyage. If anything, it reminded Nbaro of Kephlos, what seemed like years before. Skipper Truekner flew co-pilot for Pak, and Mpono flew co-pilot for Eyre, and both of them achieved satisfactory results. Nbaro was coming to terms with how relatively easy operating a spacecraft when supported by an AI really was; it was amusing and humbling to be reminded of the learning curve by watching the two fledgling pilots.

But increasingly her time was spent on Sixth Deck, with Qaqqaq and Dorcas, learning to manage the robots. They had four, now: two collectors, programmed to get close to Starfish when they were communicating and try to test the ammoniac water for chemicals; and two communicators, a second-phase robot that they'd introduce if they thought they had the chemical knowledge to attempt a link.

Nbaro was trying not to fall asleep. They were just outbound from Omega Delta and she'd flown three scoop missions in twelve hours, but she needed to be up to date on the operation of the new robots.

Qaqqaq was giving a very dull overview of the new technical components, and Nbaro really just wanted to seize the joystick and operate one.

Dorcas was watching her as Qaqqaq explained the new collection mechanisms in the receptor arms of the Mod 3 collector.

'Naisha, have you ever contemplated sexuality?' Dorcas asked.

Qaqqaq blushed.

'Once or twice,' she said, and looked at Nbaro.

Nbaro, who knew Dorcas pretty well by then, raised an eyebrow.

'I think he means Starfish sexuality.'

Qaqqaq took a deep breath.

'Ah. No, I can't say I have.'

Dorcas leant forward.

'What if these pheromonal one-time codes were originally sexual?' he asked.

Nbaro made a face.

Dorcas shrugged. 'Listen, if they're millions of years old, they've had time to evolve, and then change and change again. Two million years ago, our ancestors were just getting used to stone tools. Imagine what we might be like two million years from now.'

'I'll be dead,' said the pragmatic Qaqqaq.

Dorcas showed signs of frustration.

'That was a joke,' Nbaro said.

He rolled his eyes. 'I know.'

Nbaro took her turn to shrug. 'So what?'

'So nothing. I've been trying to imagine a way in which a species would evolve a touch-only communication system. But if you think about it, sexual contact is communication of code – genetic code.'

Nbaro raised an eyebrow, channelling Thea.

'Do you think it's possible you're spending too much time thinking about sex?' she asked.

Dorcas grinned. 'Yes,' he admitted.

And then, after all the preparation, it was time to make their insertion for Trade Point – a weird binary system with a lot of strange stuff and two big gas giants, both of which had moons that science said had ammonia seas. And the gas giants themselves might support life; down under the massive, thick atmosphere, radio emissions suggested that there was a Starfish civilisation. An outpost? Their home planets?

Who knew?

The robot starfish lay in their cradles, ready for shipment

to the orbital. Outside the Marine Shack, their armour waited on skeletal racks. In Cargo, dozens of officers and hundreds of spacers worked overtime, checking bills of lading and preparing for trade.

Nbaro missed being on the Master's council. She missed knowing the plan. She missed understanding the stresses they faced.

She gave a tactical lecture to her flight and Flight 8, at the skipper's direction. It made her miss Suliemani, and her voice quavered as she began, but Nbaro got through her briefing and even got some friendly comments at the end.

The day before the insertion, Mpono was promoted to acting captain and made the *Athens*'s executive officer in place of Aadavan. The flight schedule changed suddenly. Guille took over as the Operations Officer, and suddenly Nbaro was on the flight schedule more and was the Space Operations Officer, Lioness, for the entry into Trade Point system.

There was a special briefing, that told Nbaro nothing she didn't already know, and then Dorcas caught her hand as they were leaving the Combat Information Centre.

'I just wanted to wish you ... good luck.' He looked around. 'Or something.'

She smiled. 'I accept your *or something*,' she said. 'Hey.'

'Hey?'

'Hey. We're going to make it. We're going to get to Trade Point.'

She smiled at him, moved out of the way of her skipper and Tremaine, who were debating some element of the launch sequence, and moved back towards him.

He nodded.

'What's the matter?' she asked.

'What if I'm wrong?'

'I'm wrong all the time,' she said. 'Maybe you should prepare yourself.'

He winced.

She smiled. 'You're not wrong. We're going to meet the Starfish, and we're going to change everything.'

Dorcas nodded. He was almost smiling.

'I appreciate your belief in me, Nbaro,' he said. 'But the other thing I worry about is – *what if I'm right?*'

'Right?' she asked. More people were coming out of the meeting now. 'What's wrong with that? Then we'll talk to them.'

'Yes,' he said. 'And then we'll know some of the secrets of their empire, as well.'

She took a deep breath, and let it out.

'See you on the other side,' she said.

He nodded, and touched her hand, and walked away.

When Nbaro got to her stateroom, Thea Drake was in her uniform jumpsuit, just looking in the mirror.

'I passed you in the passageway,' she said. 'You've got it bad.'

'Got what?'

'You can have the room. I won't be back all watch. No one will give a shit, I promise you.'

Nbaro understood. She blushed a little, and was pleased that she still blushed, in a remote way. Instead, she took her sidearm and shook her head.

'I'm going to the range to practise,' she said.

'You're a strange girl,' Drake said.

'We should fence, later.'

'I'm going to interpret that as a "mind your own business or I'll hurt you",' Drake said.

She nodded.

'See you later.'

16

Nbaro came alert and toggled her launch sequence.

'Alpha Charlie 3–0–1, I have you first to launch.'

'Roger, Lioness,' said a groggy voice. 'Good to go.'

'Launch one,' she said.

She felt the launch in her hips, and flipped comms to Alpha Charlie 3–0–7.

'You are good to launch,' she said.

'Lioness, this is Alpha Charlie 3–0–7, we are good to launch,' said a more awake voice.

It was odd that insertion was like sleep. But it wasn't. It was like unconsciousness.

Not her problem.

The ship shuddered as the second spaceframe hurtled down the railgun tube.

Nbaro called the launches for the Gunslingers, one of whom was Cortez, and then for her own: Guilles with Pak, and Storkel with Eyre. To her right, Commander Dworkin came online as Tower and took over the launches.

The wave of clutter filled her tactical screens. Nbaro rolled forward and back, looking at anything there was to be seen before that wall went up.

Trade Point was a very odd system indeed. It contained two

red dwarfs in mutual orbits, about ten light hours apart. Between them was a single very small planet, or enormous pear-shaped asteroid. It was held securely by the gravitational fields of the two stars, and it had no doubt taken billions of years to come to its almost stable resting place, so that the two stars appeared to orbit it. It still rotated and it had an odd quiver, which was all that was left of its ancient orbital mechanics.

The Starfish had placed their trade station alongside the asteroid, part of which they'd hollowed out.

Planets orbited each of the two stars: a pair of Neptune-sized gas giants orbited the brighter of the two, and two smaller, rockier planets orbited very close to the redder dwarf.

The further gas giant from the brighter sun had four moons, and all four of them – large bodies the size of Old Terra's moon or bigger – had ammonia oceans under ice sheets.

The planets, the binary stars, and the moons all orbited in the same plane, although the inner gas giant had a debris ring perpendicular to the rest of the system. Both stars had their own asteroid belts, and there were stable asteroids at the centre of the system, as well.

As soon as the Flight 6 spacecraft began deploying their remote sensors, Nbaro could see the station at the centre of the huge double system more clearly. They were below the plane of the ecliptic, and had an excellent view of the whole system. They were, themselves, almost nine light hours off the station – a long way out.

'Lioness, this is *Athens*.'

That was the Master himself.

'Yes, sir.'

'I'm going to commence deceleration at 2 g.'

'Roger, 2 g, sir.' Nbaro toggled all her launched spacecraft. 'All spacecraft, this is Lioness. *Athens* is going to commence deceleration at 2 g continuous, over.'

A series of rogers, and as Bridge indicated deceleration, her whole screen of spacecraft decelerated with her. Nbaro barely felt it through the artificial gravity. They'd be very aware of it out there in their acceleration couches.

Nbaro looked at the tactical board and saw some radio emissions from the ammonia moons. Intel and Combat could look at those. Not her problem. Yet.

All her information on Trade Point was nine hours old. But the lack of emissions coming off Trade Point nine hours ago showed the station cold and dead.

Nbaro knew from briefings that the station was usually cold – that the DHC contingent would land and warm it up, and then the Starfish would come in-system and trade would commence. Somehow the Starfish had a way of detecting them; no human crew had ever waited more than thirty days. And the ships *never* came out of the ammonia oceans in system. Another strangeness.

Thirty days. Plenty of time for the Pǔ Tiān Xià ships to catch up.

Or the Bubbles. Or both.

Nbaro passed the rest of her watch scanning all the incoming data feeds, but none of them was particularly informative. She handed over to Guille.

'Anything to report?' Guille asked.

Nbaro shook her head. 'Lot of rocks in this system,' she replied. 'And I'm a little shy of rocks now.'

'And it's so fucking big,' Guille said. 'OK. I have her.'

They saluted each other, and Guille sat.

That was her last watch for a while. Her duties were now aimed at the landing on the station, the movement of the robot starfish, and the attendant planning and work. Gunny Drun was leading the Marine detachment, and he'd had them practising for an ammonia environment for weeks; now, in six days, Nbaro had to come up to speed, and so had Dorcas. They practised setting up the equipment, and then they stored everything in airtight, ammonia-tight, cushioned crates and moved them to the pinnace. The Master had decided that, at least to begin with, only the pinnace would dock with the station.

Not for the first or last time, Nbaro wondered where the second pinnace was.

Drake was as busy as her, because the main cargo unload and reload happened at Trade Point. All the gold and stable metals were offloaded here; all the xenoglas, the real purpose of the entire trip, came on.

Nbaro drilled with the Marines, and three days out, Drake joined them.

'There's only a dozen of us qualified for the load out,' she said happily. 'And of those, I'm the only one who's trained for boarding party and shipboard combat.'

Drun gave her an appreciative glance.

'What we definitely needed was more midders,' he said.

'Yeah,' Drake said. 'We specialise in saving the ship, right, Gunny?'

The Marine NCO grinned.

'Point taken, Ms Drake.'

Five days of deceleration brought them into manoeuvring space near the station at the centre of the vast binary star system. Every time Nbaro looked at an image of the system, she felt very small – smaller than usual.

Space was vast.

Nbaro boarded the pinnace in her armour strapped on over her 'borrowed' EVA suit – one of those from the *Hong Kong*, so slim and light that she had to look at it from time to time to be sure she was 'suited up'. She was also wearing her sidearm, with a battle gun locked into clamps on her EVA pack next to her sword. She felt more than a little ridiculous, and more ridiculous when she had to unclip all of her armaments to stow them in order to use the acceleration couches on the pinnace. Almost every cubic centimetre was taken up with cargo. It was only the first shipment, a taste of what the vast holds of the *Athens* contained, but it was enough – pallets of gold bars and other mysterious containers in dull yellows.

Drake took the next couch, and Dorcas slid in after her to take the couch on her right. Behind her, Wilson Akunje and three of his mates strapped in; Nbaro exchanged nods with Juarez, the sniper.

Dorcas looked over at their own stack of crates, all webbed into the bulkhead of the pinnace. Depending on how you looked at it, the ship's pinnace was either the smallest star-travel capable vessel that the DHC had, or the largest shuttle. It could carry tons of cargo and thirty-eight people, as well as its own crew of eight.

I wonder where the other one is? Nbaro wondered.

The waiting seemed interminable.

She looked at Drake, very slightly embarrassed by Dorcas's proximity.

'Do you ever feel that this voyage is nothing but two polar opposites?' she asked. 'Terror and boredom?'

Drake laughed. 'Honey-child, I'm about to land on a space station full of aliens and engage in trade that will help save my civilisation. You pilots seem to think we're warriors … we're not. We're merchants, and I'm about to do my job.'

'And make a tidy profit,' Dorcas said.

'So what? That profit allows us to have medical care and standard incomes and nice uniforms and spaceships and everything else.' She nodded at the crates of gold bars. 'Our ninety thousand ducats doesn't buy a lot of gold, you know?'

Dorcas shifted in his couch. There was an acceleration warning.

'You and Nbaro are true believers,' he said.

Behind them, Drun grunted as the pinnace began to move.

'Some of us are warriors,' he said.

Drake was pinned to her acceleration couch.

'And we appreciate you, Gunny,' she said. 'But we don't run on war. We don't conquer. We don't colonise.'

'We sound awful nice,' Drun said.

'We're going to meet the Starfish.' Drake virtually burbled with delight. 'I still can't believe I was chosen.'

Dorcas laughed. 'You did save the ship.'

Drun grunted again. 'The way I see it,' he said, 'almost everyone I can see from here has saved the ship. So the important question is – does the Master think he needs to put all his good luck on the station?'

Landing on the alien station was incredibly anticlimactic. Most of the human side had been built by the DHC and rebuilt dozens of times over the years; in fact, one of the next loads that the pinnace would bring would include techs and materials to upgrade several facilities, improve the atmosphere, and upgrade the computers.

They landed in almost complete darkness, but the airlock cycled. The station was empty of air, but the lights of the airlock illuminated the passageway beyond.

Dorcas, who had command of the away team, at least for this stage, opened an access panel just beyond the airlock, typed in a long code, and then turned a key, and lights came on.

Dorcas turned them off. He turned off the pumps and the air recyclers.

'Why?' Nbaro asked.

'Helmet lights on, and stay in your suits until I give the word,' Gunny said.

There were nine of them: the Marine fire team; Drake, Dorcas, Nbaro and Smith; and a tech from Engineering. Qaqqaq was slated for the next barge, as was the second Marine team.

The Marines moved very cautiously through the human side of the station and reported it to be clear.

Drake looked at Dorcas.

Dorcas shrugged. 'Standard operating procedure.'

He got out a device that looked like a folding walking staff and unfolded it, telescoping some segments and unfolding others.

Then he flicked a switch.

'What's that?' Nbaro asked.

He handed her a second one.

'It's a detector. It detects anything that emits ... almost any energy. We sweep everything before we turn on the lights for keeps, much less fire up the reactor.'

'Oh,' Nbaro said. 'Why?'

'We're looking for spy devices,' Smith said.

Nbaro closed her eyes. 'Of course.'

'You think we're the only ones who spy?' he asked.

The next three hours were dull and dark, and vaguely terrifying, as they moved through the silent, cold corridors, sweeping every surface, opening every door, every hatch, every cabinet.

Dorcas was sitting in zero *g* strapped to a console, collating their readings and adding to their report.

'The *Dubai* was here almost 180 days ago,' he said. 'We made very good time.'

'The *Dubai* got here,' Smith said. 'That's good news.'

Dorcas made a sound. 'I was rather hoping we might find them still here.'

Smith was silent, and Nbaro, who was close to the reactor, was still sweeping, moving her walking staff back and forth over every panel, as she'd been shown.

When she was finished with the reactor compartment, Dorcas floated into the space and put his helmet against hers.

'Now we do something slightly distasteful,' he said.

Nbaro raised an eyebrow.

'We put some cameras on the Starfish side.'

He shrugged, as if to say, *It's the way of the world.*

'In other words, now that we've swept to make sure they don't spy on us, we'll put in cameras to spy on them.'

'Exactly,' Dorcas said.

They only had to cross one cargo hold and enter the trade chamber to access the passage between the two habitats.

The Starfish side of the station wasn't under pressure or full of ammonia yet, of course. It was just as cold and dead as their own side.

They entered through the cargo lock in the middle of the station. Dorcas had an override code.

And then they were in a vast space carved out of rock. They flooded it with air to make it easier to operate there, but it was cold. And somehow, old.

It probably wasn't as big as City, but it *felt* bigger – at least a two-by-two kilometre space, almost a kilometre high. Sound just died in here. And then came whispering back.

Their helmet lights caught the reflective material on the deck under them. It looked liquid, but it couldn't be, and Nbaro reasoned that it was some kind of glass or adhesive. Another Starfish material.

Dorcas began scattering cameras as he walked. They were very small, but by no means impossible to detect.

'They will pick them all up, eventually,' he admitted. 'I hope they keep them as souvenirs.'

'Will Gunny miss us?' she said.

'Gunny knows exactly where we are and what we're doing,' Dorcas said.

Out of the darkness appeared glints of reflection. In twenty more paces, they resolved into an open lattice of what appeared to be stainless steel, with protrusions and holds and curving surfaces, as if someone had cut up a sphere into random shapes.

Dorcas had several very specialised cameras built to blend into the lattice and the spherical sections.

Nbaro leant on her staff and watched as the scientist placed his devices.

'Are those on?' she asked.

Dorcas turned his whole body to look at her.

'No,' he said in his helmet radio voice. He was barely avoiding calling her an idiot.

'My staff is going off.'

He came over and looked at her readout. It wasn't for lay people – it was all maths.

He bent over, his faceplate almost pressed against the readout.

'Let me have it,' he said.

He used it like a dowsing pole, pointing it here and there, feeling something from it that Nbaro hadn't felt.

Her heart rate increased dramatically.

'I've got it,' he said, after three long minutes crouched down against the deck.

I'll bet that's cold.

The odd shiny substance of the decking seemed to grow the support rods for the lattice as if they were crystals growing from a substrate.

Nbaro bent down by him. The deck wasn't as cold as she'd expected.

Then she saw it. It was so black that it appeared to eat the light, and it was the size of a child's marble.

'What is it?' she asked.

'I don't know,' Dorcas answered. 'But I'm going to guess that humans didn't make it.'

'Why would the Starfish...?' Nbaro's words caught up with her thoughts and she stopped. 'Oh. Fuck. Bubbles.'

'Fuck indeed,' Dorcas said. 'Such a useful word.'

*

The human side of the station had a command centre, and Gunny Drun had warmed it and had atmosphere, so Nbaro got a tactical scan up and good comms with the ship. It was odd to have comms and no control; she wasn't Lioness or a pilot, just an informed observer.

Nbaro passed everything, including 3D representations of the spy device, to Intel. Lieutenant Lochiel checked over her data, and then Akunje had another of the black things. The Marines were already calling them black marbles, and while she talked to Lochiel, the Marines and spacers found three more – one in the human spaces. All of them were left in place – carefully marked.

An hour later, the shuttle came back with another load of cargo, plus Lieutenant Qaqqaq and a crew of techs, and with a dozen lead-lined boxes that Fabrications had created at short notice; Qaqqaq joked that they were still warm.

Dorcas put the one he'd found in the Starfish command centre into one of the lead-lined boxes and sent it back to the ship. All the rest were left in situ.

Drun outlined the situation. 'Right, listen up. Assume we're in the presence of the enemy at all times. Suits on, helmets closed, unless you have direct permission otherwise. No comms but helmet comms, and encryption on at all times. Any questions?'

No one had any.

'If you find another of these things, or anything else out of the ordinary, pass the word to Lieutenant Nbaro. Do it in person, helmet to helmet. Got that?'

Qaqqaq looked at Nbaro. She and the Terran were sitting in the command centre, and they had their helmets off.

'Roger that,' Nbaro said, and put her helmet on.

Over the next week, the security status lightened. The crew quarters were pressurised and they all moved in; showers became active, and after every centimetre had been swept with detectors and eyes, Gunny Drun allowed them to strip down and watch vids, play cards, and read without their armour on.

But on duty, they were armed and armoured at all times.

Dorcas and Nbaro had too much time together – too much time to talk, and not talk. Too much time to sit together.

'I keep thinking about the fight with the *Esperance*,' Nbaro said.

They were nine days into their duty about Trade Point.

'Yes,' Dorcas agreed. 'It's as if there's a clue there and we're missing it.'

She nodded. 'The Starfish communications. We have all those communications recorded. They've been run, over and over. It's gibberish. Hae Yon grew desperate, tried flashing external lights in patterns, and they ignored it and began firing.'

Nbaro was reading from her tab. She wished she had a larger screen for research, but all of the good ones were in Operations.

'What if their space comms work like their bodies? What if the carrier wave describes a chemical, and the main message can only be decrypted with that chemical?'

Dorcas gazed at her with something not entirely unlike adoration.

'I want to kiss you,' he said.

'That would pretty much define the word inappropriate, right now.'

Thea Drake was laughing behind the curtains of her bunk. There was no privacy at all – no officer country, no male/female/androgyne divides. Nothing. They were twenty-four people in twenty-four bunks, like early spacefarers.

Dorcas nodded. His fingers were flying over a keyboard that was purely holographic, something projected by his neural lace, and he was communicating directly with Morosini.

'They began firing when Hae Yon used the comms laser,' Nbaro said. 'She began blinking it in regular pulses, and they fired some gauss cannon – two rounds hit the *Esperance*.' She nodded. 'Nine spacers were killed – explosive decompression in compartments. So they weren't messing around. But their gauss cannon weren't as precise as our railguns, or something. The *Esperance* shot their engine section right off their ship in one volley.'

Dorcas nodded. 'Is this a history lesson?' he asked.

'This from you?' Nbaro asked. 'I thought delivering a history lesson was your idea of flirting?'

'Get a room!' Drake shouted.

Dorcas blushed. But he shook his head.

'Where are you going with this?'

'The Starfish aren't really big on visible light. They're from deep, dark ammonia oceans. Right?'

'Yes,' Dorcas agreed.

'So . . . our comm laser probably looked like a weapon.'

'It's been posited before,' Dorcas said. 'It's in Captain Hae Yon's court martial.'

'Oh,' she said.

'But . . .' He sketched in the air, and suddenly there was a holographic image between them. 'Here's the ship we faced at Argos.'

The plasma beam, the carrier wave for its energy weapon, flashed out.

'Looks like a laser,' he said.

'Aha,' Nbaro said.

Dorcas nodded. 'So here's our working hypothesis,' he said. 'The Starfish are at war with the Bubbles.'

'Bubbles?' Nbaro asked.

'Black Blobs is too much of a mouthful,' Dorcas said. 'We know absolutely nothing about them, except that they shot at us and they have weapons and shields beyond our science. Oh . . . and they make a really good spy device that nonetheless broadcasts in a spectrum we understand. You understand the value of the spy devices?'

'Yes?' Nbaro said, meaning: *Tell me.*

'They're our first Bubble artifacts,' he said. 'We'll learn ... something from them. Science and Intel are on it. And Major Darkstar has ...' He looked away and then back. 'Has begun a further interrogation of our prisoners.'

Nbaro winced.

'I'll bet that's bad,' she muttered.

'The hacker you caught is almost certainly a Pǔ Tiān Xià military intelligence operative.' Dorcas shrugged. 'He probably knows something about the aliens. I think we can assume that this is who the Anti-spinward colonies encountered. And that they've been looking for the Starfish, and instead found our xenoglas.'

Nbaro sat up. 'Shit,' she said. 'Then they're not trying to kill us. They're following us.'

Dorcas shook his head. 'No. That was the *New York* or the *Hong Kong.*' But he was looking off into space. 'Or ... Damn it, you're right. What if ...?'

He shook his head and waved a hand to clear the holograph.

'It's like the logic problems they give you on tests,' he said. 'It's like the Starfish communication system. It's a two-part answer. There's a conspiracy among our people to attack the DHC monopolies.' He drew a circle. 'And there's the Anti-spinward colonies, and there's the corrupt patricians, and there's the hawks in the Pǔ Tiān Xià. Got all that?'

Each faction, as he named it, became a visible subset of the circle labelled *Human conspiracy.*

He drew another circle. 'Here's the Bubbles,' he said. 'They're looking for the Starfish. The same Starfish who thought the *Esperance* was a Bubble ship. I see that now. Because that's an old war, or maybe ...' He shook his head.

Thea Drake came and sat at the table; she wore thick, shaggy socks with a shipboard jumpsuit because the decks were still so cold.

'I can't sleep while you two are being so interesting,' she said.

'I'm pretty sure this is all top secret,' Nbaro said.

'I'm pretty sure secrecy won't matter much, very soon,' Dorcas said. 'Regardless, the Bubbles have met with humans over in Anti-spinward. They're working this way...' He drew a 2D map of the trade routes. 'And the human conspiracy is working this way.'

The human arm crept up from Haqq.

The Adversary arm wormed in from Ultra.

'I'm assuming that the Bubbles can long-jump,' he said. 'They take or kill a greatship and check out the xenoglas. Now they know they're on the right track to find the Starfish. But they don't know where...' He looked at Drake, as if she was the personification of the DHC. 'All that secrecy pays off. Because there's no one to tell them where the xenoglas comes from.'

'So they link up with the human conspiracy.'

Nbaro pointed to the holographic intersection of the two sets, human and adversary, at the words *Anti-spinward*.

Dorcas nodded. 'And then they attack us.'

Nbaro shrugged. 'So what? We might have run for home? We might have all died.'

Dorcas's voice sounded strained. 'We might,' he agreed. 'But don't think they're in a hurry.' He shook his head. 'Millions of years. Anyway, Aadavan thought he was working for his wife's patrician family, but what if anything he broadcast went to the Bubbles? He had access to all our course information.'

'Shit,' Drake said. 'That means...'

'That they're already here,' Dorcas said. 'The spy devices prove that. They're here, probably way out, ten, fifteen light hours out, waiting for the Starfish insertions.'

Drake looked at Nbaro. 'Honey, we're living in interesting times.'

17

The first Starfish ship came out of Insertion seven days later.

Over the next six hours, three more ships appeared on roughly the same course: one a behemoth, larger than the *Athens*, and the others probably escorts.

The *Athens* couldn't communicate, of course. But she tried: long bursts of light and various frequencies – even sending back the exact patterns that the first Starfish ship had sent to the *Esperance*.

The Starfish fell towards the centre of the system. Their velocity was high – over 0.2c – and so they passed through most of the system in hours instead of weeks. Their deceleration was incredible, bearing out the analysis from Intel; the ammonia-breathers could deal with a much heavier deceleration than humans.

They'd been in system nine hours, and Nbaro was awake, showered, and in her seat in Operations on the human side of the station. She had her armour on, her sword and rifle clipped to her harness, and the tactical scan on her main screen. Qaqqaq had jury-rigged a holotank.

The Starfish were decelerating at something like 17 g.

Dorcas sat, legs crossed, at another station, but he didn't have the screen on. He didn't need it; he could see the whole system with his neural lace.

'I wonder if that's their equivalent of one *g*,' he said. 'The standard pressure and gravity of their home ocean.'

Nbaro looked at her ETA timer, which showed one hour and eleven minutes.

And then all hell broke loose.

'Battle Stations,' Nbaro said, and hit the large red button on the station control panel.

An alarm went off, and lights flashed.

The first part of the space battle happened so fast that only the automated systems could follow it.

A barrage of missiles and torpedoes lanced out from a dozen asteroids in the inner system, and behind them came three Bubble ships. They engaged the Starfish at a range of about 270,000 km, at the edge of the asteroids.

Two of the Bubble ships were destroyed about fifteen seconds after revealing themselves – killed by a hail of nuclear torpedoes from spacecraft launched cold from the *Athens*. As her clutter cloud grew, it became clear that she'd located the enemy ships and dropped her spacecraft with care; equally clear that the *Athens* had mined some of the asteroids with nukes.

It also became clear that she hadn't located all of them. The deadly cat and mouse of the last week was suddenly translated into a hail of plasma beams and close-in railgun action.

Both sides were commanded and directed by automated systems and AIs; there was no time for a biological sentient to contribute anything but a directive to open fire.

A dark ship appeared aft of the *Athens*'s clutter cloud and fired plasma at close range, the X-ray lasers raking…

The frigate that had been electronically masquerading as the *Athens*. The little ship went up in a spectacular, white-hot explosion.

Closer in to the station, 6–0–6 was vapourised by a hail of heavy metal, and Guille and her crew died.

The black ship that had killed the pinnace was an unknown type, longer and heavier than the ship Nbaro had seen back at Argos. It lasted about six seconds, before the whole capacity of three of the *Athens*'s launch tubes struck it amidships, went through the black globes and turned the ship into a cloud of gas that mingled with the last atoms of the pinnace.

A second enemy ship appeared, this one closer to the station. Lines of fire connected her to the *Athens*.

'We're taking fire,' Drun said.

Nbaro already had her helmet on, and so did Dorcas.

Even as she lifted her eyes from the screen in front of her, a curtain of fire fell through the Operations Centre, blinding her and venting the atmosphere. The station's artificial gravity failed. She was thrown against a bulkhead.

She lost some time.

'Gunny?' she asked.

'I hear you, ma'am.'

'Mister Dorcas is gone,' Nbaro said, as calmly as she could manage.

Qaqqaq and Dorcas were both gone. Their half of the Operations Centre, along with the airlock, the entry hall and about a third of the cargo area, was *gone*.

A pause.

'Yes, ma'am,' he said.

Nbaro was looking out into space. There was a little gravity, because the station and the asteroid had spin; it was one quarter of a *g*, or even less, but it did make 'down' a reality.

So space was spinning above them, as if she'd been in a can and the top had been cut away. She could see a piece of it, rotating slowly, and she could see the ship that had done it, so close that she could have hit it with a piece of debris. Perhaps five kilometres away. It was big – a kilometre long, perhaps longer – and from this close Nbaro could see the black globes and the odd play of black light where they crossed each other, and the blue light from the stern.

And the flashing drives coming out of the spheres.

'We're being boarded,' she said.

The enemy ship disappeared, its own speed and the rotation of the asteroid taking it out of her line of sight.

'Copy,' Drun said.

Nbaro looked down at the deck plates under her feet, an instinctive glance at her hands while she unclipped her rifle from the magnets that held it, a check of the magazine and safety as she'd been taught.

That glance saved her vision. There was a flash, brighter than the brightest lightning; for perhaps two beats of her heart, it illuminated the asteroid half a kilometre over her head to the brightness of the sun.

Somewhere out beyond the horizon, a nuclear weapon had exploded.

Nbaro still had spots in front of her eyes from the plasma beam that had killed the station. Now she had to blink repeatedly, despite the visor on her helmet, which was now pulsing between almost jet-black and something less…

Nbaro knelt down. She had to; her knees were weak, and she wasn't breathing well.

'Ma'am?' Drun asked.

'I'm…' she paused. Looked at her helmet's HUD. 'I'm OK, Gunny. Nuke went off close. I took a pretty heavy dose, but I'm still here.' She looked back. 'Nuke took out most of our attackers. I only see three boats coming in.'

'Roger. I'm at post 4, I count three as well. We're not going to engage until we're at point-blank.'

Ambush.

'I'm coming to you,' she said.

Part of her brain was saying: *Dorcas and Qaqqaq and probably Drake.*

The other part was saying: *Kill them all.*

Moving through the human side of the station was a nightmare. All the access shafts were open to space, and almost all of them had cargo debris moving around – gold bars, copper rods that weighed half a tonne. Nbaro had to move cautiously.

And the shudders and quakes while she was moving had their effect, too. Something was moving the entire asteroid.

That was bad.

When Nbaro had worked her way past the crew quarters, and was dropping down what had been the main passageway, a railgun round passed through both walls about a metre from her rifle's muzzle. She never saw the round – just the holes.

And then more holes.

It was all perfectly silent; the holes simply appeared on both sides of her, apparently simultaneously.

Nbaro froze, and it took an effort of will to start to move again. She'd spent perhaps a minute unmoving, until her suit drifted into the right-hand wall of the corridor. Looking back, she could see that she was between two sets of holes; they were about five metres apart.

She closed her eyes, and made herself breathe.

'Gunny?'

'Ma'am?'

'We just took railgun fire?' she asked.

'Fucked if I know,' Drun said. 'Enemy about sixty seconds out.'

Nbaro was in virtually zero *g*. She'd come all the way to the centre of the drum – that's where Gunny Drun's port 4 was. Near the main docking array, which hadn't been sliced away.

'Coming into the main docking bay,' she said.

'We got you. Get into cover.'

Nbaro saw the brightness that heralded incoming engines, and she felt the impact as the landing boats hit the outer hull of the dock.

She leapt for a cargo container that was strapped to what used to be the deck and was now a bulkhead. The jump was accurate but too fast, and she felt a muscle pull in her groin as her legs took the mass of her vac suit and armour.

She grunted.

Nbaro could see the plasma and heated metal where torches were cutting through the outer skin of the dock. She activated magnets on the chest of her armour to cling to the surface of the container, which was steel and not recycle. And she wormed her way to the edge and pointed her rifle over it, at the plasma cutter. Her visor darkened.

'Gutsy,' Drun said in her ear.

Nbaro could look up and across an immense drum of space. There was already floating debris, settling gradually towards the outer walls, under the gentle spin. But they were so close to the centre of the main station that there was barely enough spin to give things motion.

I am about to see a strange alien being.

And try to kill it.

The plasma jet below her ceased. The white-hot ceramic/steel laminate of the outer hull suddenly popped in and began to float, rotating gently from the energy imparted to it, and her eye followed it.

And then her basic, predatory human instinct dragged her eye back at a motion.

It was like a spider... No – a circular... It wasn't like anything. The body was round; it had four equally spaced legs, and the head was between two of the legs and moved in crisp little articulations like…

It was entirely metal…

Her gauss rifle vibrated, and the thing folded and separated into three pieces, trailing black.

They were fast – two more were through the hole, spreading out like veteran combat troops.

She took down another one.

Below her, one of the Marines put a long EMP burst into the enemy, and it had no effect.

Someone shot at her, and the top of the steel container blossomed as something passed through it from underneath. Nbaro cut the magnets on her chest, rolled away from the edge, and leapt. The next container was not so far, and she rotated in air, competent at least, and landed better, using her boot magnets…

Nope. Nbaro bounced; the next container was recycle, and her boots couldn't lock on.

She hit the wall, that had once been the deck, and got her boots fixed on it, and her HUD was a mass of red and green dots. She picked a red one, locked, and her rifle fired.

And then they were gone.

Her heart was hammering. Nbaro was standing on what was, in effect, a long wall, and her HUD showed no active targets.

'Best come down, ma'am,' Drun said. 'They're all dead.'

'Roger that,' she said.

Locran would have jumped for the floor, fifty metres away. She hoped he was alive.

Nbaro bounded down the wall on her seven-league boots. She didn't trust her leaps, and her groin hurt.

She came down to the new deck, and locked her boots to it, although the ceramite over the steel made the deck a little hard to grip, like walking on ice.

Nbaro was looking at the whole fire team; there was Juarez,

her sniper rifle's muzzle actually glowing red. Akunje's dark face and broad smile came through his visor.

'What the *fuck* were those?' Juarez asked. Her voice was high and tight and scared.

Drun put his helmet against Akunje's and suddenly they were all huddled together, a starfish of humans with their helmets touching.

Drun sounded distant, but steady.

'Listen up, team! Team 2's in the shit at post 8, and we're going to help them. Three boats came in. We wasted one. That means hostiles in the passageways, and you know the drill. The Xenos are in power armour, and it's EMP resistant but won't stop a gauss round. Hear me? Nbaro, you're with me, in the rear. Got that?'

'Roger,' they all said.

'Stick Bravo, Akunje lead. Go for post 8. Do not die! Go!'

As they all broke away, Drun stayed with Nbaro.

'Don't do anything but follow me,' he said. 'We trained for this, and you'll just shoot the wrong person. No offence.'

'None taken,' she said.

I didn't shoot the wrong person back there. But whatever.

Her shakes were gone.

As if he could read her mind, Drun tapped her weapon.

'Change magazines, if you plan to shoot again,' he said.

Nbaro cursed, but she did as he said.

Always an idiot.

When he went into the elevator shaft, she followed. She knew that the shaft ran all the way into the trade compartment.

Something flashed.

Drun didn't turn, so Nbaro kept going too, emulating him, who was 'walking' by using the metal treads of an access ladder as a walkway for his magnetised boots.

She followed.

Whoever they were, we killed them all. Why? How?

Drun was slowing down. The tunnel was mostly dark, except for low red access lights at maintenance panels.

Suddenly a bright light strobed ahead.

Something punched Nbaro in the back, and she flew forward, slammed into Drun. They both slammed into the ladder, and her visor struggled to keep up.

Someone was talking in her helmet, and she was still rolling. Luck, and instinct, got her boots down on a metal access hatch; her torso twisted, pain lancing up her back and down her buttocks, through her groin.

Then she was crawling...

Her HUD said that she'd been hit in her EVA pack, but the new one that had been meant for the *Hong Kong* was armoured, and far more damage-resistant than the one she'd worn to repair the *Athens*. She had red lights and her air tasted... burnt.

Nbaro got her muzzle up, on the target and held the trigger down. Something black washed over her, and there was another one, squeezed impossibly flat, part of it *under* the maintenance ladder. She shot her magazine dry, dropped the rifle, and took out her sidearm.

She was hit with a hard double tap in the chest that tested her armour.

Then she was hit again, and she spun back, but her right boot held to the hatch. While her pelvis screamed in agony, Nbaro got her pistol up. The alien was smooth, and metal, and...

Tap, tap.

Soundlessly, her big-bore boarding pistol fired twice.

The weasel-spider-thing flailed backwards, all its limbs scrabbling in a way that made her shoot it again.

A lance of light shot down the shaft and caught a floating ball of black blood above her head, flash-boiling it to mist.

Her boarding pistol was empty, even though it should have held ten rounds.

When did I shoot the rest?

Nbaro pulled the sword off her back.

A gauss rifle pressed down over her shoulder and she felt the vibration as it fired.

Then an arm wrapped around her waist, and Gunny Drun was pressing his helmet against hers.

'Get your rifle back and reload. We're not fighting close yet.' Pause. 'You hit?'

'Twice,' she gasped.

He ran a hand over her belly and back.

'No penetration,' he said. 'Fuck, they're dumb. Can you move?'

'Yes, Gunny,' she breathed.

She felt as if she'd been shot; she could feel the impact points.

No penetration.

Who's dumb?

'Follow me,' he said.

Then Nbaro was moving. Her groin hurt so that every step was agony, but the agony passed as her medkit pumped something in her.

Whatever drug it fed her, she began to focus almost immediately. She got her rifle, floating next to her waist, and clicked her second-to-last magazine into place. Her HUD showed no heat sources behind her.

Drun was ahead, marked by name on her HUD, and there was Akunje and Juarez. Assad and McDonald were just ahead of Drun.

Nbaro caught up, because they were forming up outside a hatch.

Akunje, at the front of the stick, held up a gauntlet and pumped his hand.

Three.

Two.

One.

Nbaro didn't know how he did it, but the hatch blew in, silently, and Akunje fired through the open hatch. He was hit kinetically, in the armour, and slammed back into the shaft's wall, but McDonald and Juarez both threw grenades in and flattened themselves against the corridor.

The only sign of the explosion was a little debris with a mist of black to it, and a vibration from the deck plates under her feet.

McDonald went through the hatch, firing. Assad was right behind her, high. Drun was above both of them, having run up the wall in order to fire 'down' through the hatch.

Nbaro looked back. The shaft was clear as far as she could see. When she turned forward, they were all gone.

She hesitated for a moment, and then moved up to the edge of the hatch.

What if they're all dead?

Then I might as well be dead too.

Nbaro peeked.

Aimed. There was a metal insect on the 'ceiling' shooting 'down'.

Nbaro was patient this time, and her anxiety was oddly lower. She took her time, took aim, pressed a burst, and then a second, into the cloud of zero *g* smoke and blood, or whatever the black stuff was. The more she looked at it, the more it looked like the nano sludge that her spacecraft used as lubricant.

She scanned what she could see.

There was a piece of chair-back, leaking gel, near her in the shaft. Nbaro caught it, and tossed it high into the space beyond.

A flash of plasma.

A bolt of lightning.

A Marine rose to his feet, shooting – Akunje, with a heavy

slug-thrower that flashed tracers. He was chewing his way along a divider at knee level.

Nbaro rolled to her knees – easy in low *g*, despite whatever was wrong in her groin – and tracked him, and then stepped through the hatch as he continued to fire. She could see Drun, down, sprawled, one arm gone at the shoulder, and Juarez covering Akunje.

Akunje was moving away from her, trying to secure the space by fire and movement as he'd been taught, and Juarez was covering him, also moving away from Nbaro.

The alien came around the partition on her side. It had two armoured forelimbs raised, as if in surrender, but a third limb was firing a short weapon – a slug-thrower of some sort, held at limb-length. Juarez was hit and flew into Akunje.

Nbaro emptied her carbine, then slammed the stock into the thing and kicked it. Her shoulder hit the bulkhead and she twisted. Her right hand gripped her sword and tore it off its magnets even as her feet clipped on to the wall behind her. She kicked off as the muzzle of the thing's short gun tracked her.

Nbaro performed a move she'd practised fifty times with various partners: a cut that became a somersault, impossible in gravity, almost natural in zero *g* because the centripetal force of the two-handed swing tended to flip you end for end.

Her sword passed through the thing's extended limb with surprisingly little resistance as she flipped and hit the far wall feet first.

Aside from the sharp spike of pain in her groin, it was pretty good. Her boots clipped on, and she could see both of the surviving enemies – one at each end of the mid-room partition.

They could both see her.

Akunje shot one. He was perhaps three metres away, and he waved his big weapon over the thing like some ancient firefighter with a hose, and it unknitted.

Nbaro was already moving, because the second one was trying to pick up its short weapon with one of its remaining limbs, and she wasn't having that.

It turned on her, and attacked. Each of its three remaining limbs was tipped with metal – more like spikes than knives.

It wasn't fast. And having only three legs left it was confused; it couldn't decide which limb to use as an anchor.

Her sword was everywhere. Nbaro couldn't cut with the full power of her shoulders as she had the first time, so the blade didn't sever anything, but she hurt it badly. After a flurry of attempted blows at close range, it suddenly collapsed, its loco-motion failing until it went down.

The carapace was like a sphere, with an egg between two legs as a head. But the head had a face behind a faceplate. Something face-like, in deep black.

It was thrashing.

Nbaro stepped back to find Akunje was working on Juarez. McDonald was bleeding and venting a little gas from her right leg, but had a boarding pistol in a two-handed grip, pointed at Nbaro's alien.

Nbaro reached up and found the pressure bandage on the back of her helmet. She slid it free of its catches, backed two steps away from the alien and got behind McDonald. Pressed her own helmet to hers.

'You're bleeding and losing suit pressure,' she said.

'Fucking know,' McDonald said.

Nbaro found the wound, and the opening; a palm-sized area of suit and armour boiled away on McDonald's right thigh. She put the pressure bandage against it and thumbed the trigger and it adhered.

'Do not kill that thing,' she said.

Then she took the pressure bandage from McDonald's helmet and went for Drun.

560

He was face down, floating about fifteen centimetres off the floor, only Nbaro knew he was alive because his right hand kept spasming.

She rolled him over, relatively easy in the gravity, expecting horror.

Nbaro wasn't disappointed. Something had blown out the front of his suit, and his intestines were uncoiling into hard vacuum. But the suit was trying to do its job. There was a globe of boiling, sputtering... intestinal fluid...

She slammed the patch on to his gut and pulled the trigger. She watched it bind.

She watched it intently for fifteen seconds.

Nbaro saw the suit begin to reinflate slightly from Drun's EVA pack, and she let him go, in order to take his sidearm and all his magazines. Then she toggled her comms to Fire team 1.

'You hear me?' she asked.

Akunje said, 'Yes, ma'am.'

McDonald just nodded. She was going into shock.

'Team 2?' she asked.

Assad's rough voice came up.

'I'm patching Muller,' he said. 'Corporal Diaz is dead. No idea where the rest...'

A wet sound.

'Aw, fuck,' he said. 'Muller's the only one.'

Nbaro motioned at Juarez.

'Hit, bad.' Akunje said.

Hold tight, Nbaro.

She blinked to clear her eyes.

'Messire Morosini?' she asked the inside of her helmet.

Mpono here, she heard. *I'm using Morosini to transmit.*

'If I'm not hallucinating, we need emergency medevac,' she said. 'And if I'm not crazy, tell me if there's other fucking Bubbles in this station?'

Hang on, said Mpono's voice. It really sounded like Mpono. Morosini's voice came over Mpono's.

You are not crazy, Ms Nbaro. I took the liberty of installing a neural implant in you the first time I had you in medbay.

'Almighty!' she said aloud. Then she said, 'I'm in the Trade Point hub, about sixty metres forward of the airlock. I have five dead Marines and three badly wounded. I also have a prisoner.'

Of course you do, Morosini said. *I watched the whole thing.*

We're a little busy ourselves, Mpono said.

'Dorcas and Qaqqaq and our repair crews are missing, presumed dead.' Nbaro found that her throat was closing on the words. 'Thea Drake, too.'

Get your wounded to the outer hull, Morosini said. *I don't see any other heat sources.*

It took her fifteen endless minutes: a scout into the elevator shaft, and back; then she and Akunje dragging Gunny Drun down the shaft, his eyes closed, but still breathing. Then back, endlessly back, to get Muller, and drag him out to the docks, where the alien dead drifted as if on some invisible tide.

McDonald got Juarez in a fireman's carry and somehow managed to walk the distance while they covered her. By then, at least part of Nbaro's brain was working. She could see out of the station now, because the landing boat had crumpled a portion of dock, and cut away another portion.

She could see half a dozen dead aliens, and she had begun to theorise that they were automatons. None were close enough to collect their bodies.

She didn't want to do it.

Nbaro didn't want to go back and get her prisoner, the one whose legs she'd cut off like some evil child with a spider on Old Terra.

But there had been a great many things in her life she hadn't wanted to do, and this was only the most recent. So, alone, she walked back through the shaft, her breath coming too fast in the dark, the weight of her EVA pack heavy on her back, painfully aware of the reading on her suit's air.

The dead were all still dead.

The ball had stopped thrashing.

Nbaro didn't want to pick the damned thing up, and she wondered if it had some close-in defences. She got a pressure bandage off a dead Marine's helmet and triggered it against the metal egg without touching it, and then she grabbed the bandage after the adhesives set and dragged the thing. It was light, but she had expected that from her moment of close combat; it hadn't been heavy.

It wriggled its severed appendages. So Nbaro dropped it into a recycle container, and hauled it down the shaft after her. Did it have a face? Or were those just sensors?

She went down the long black tunnel with the alien prisoner on an umbilical, and nothing she'd ever done at the Orphanage compared.

Out on the dockside, Akunje was clipped in behind a container, watching the bay, his big autogun tracking with his eyes. McDonald was sitting, legs apart, on the deck, her boots clamped to the same container that Akunje was using for cover. Juarez was clamped in behind it. Muller was by her, the two roped together. Drun lay alone, further along.

Nbaro dropped the alien by Drun and nodded to Akunje.

'I'm going to look outside,' she said.

'Roger that, ma'am,' he said.

Nbaro jumped. It was a long jump, and she didn't want to go too fast, so she didn't jump too hard, and then she worried that she'd under-jumped. But fifty metres passed quickly enough, and she crossed the space and landed, her groin screaming again.

Nbaro was almost back where she'd started the fight, near the hole the enemy had cut with plasma torches.

She clumped over to the hole and looked down. Which was, of course, also out.

She was at the centre of the spin, so that the sky seemed to turn slowly between her boots. She could see nothing but stars.

Nbaro had about forty minutes of air left.

Cautiously, after reading the temperature of the edges, she crawled out through the hole onto the outer hull.

Only then did Nbaro realise that the whole asteroid was tumbling very, very slowly, probably from the initial attack that had cut away part of the station. So in addition to spin, it was very slowly rolling end over end. She saw that now. It made her slightly queasy as her inner ear tried to compensate for what she could now see.

And then...

Then she saw the missing portion of the station. It was also spinning, very slowly. It was fully in her view for long minutes.

There were figures in vac suits moving on it. Nbaro waved.

And, in the privacy of her helmet, she cried.

18

'I've got green and green,' Qaqqaq said. 'Good telemetry.'

Dorcas was standing by the trade airlock, waving his hands like a madman. Actually, he was testing the actuators on the robot starfish.

Around them, the station showed every sign of its recent disasters. The human side of the station was a welded-together conglomeration of patch materials: carbon-fibre walls, scavenged metal sheets... anything that could be retrieved from space and welded together.

The Starfish side had taken very little damage, because it was inside the asteroid and even the beam weapons hadn't penetrated it. And when the space battle had ended, all four minutes of it, the gigantic Starfish ship had sailed in as if nothing had happened, docked at the far end, and sent a hundred robot engineers to survey the damage. They'd passed over the whole station, much as the humans had, made repairs where they felt them necessary, and then, suddenly, the huge chamber on the far side of the trade airlock had been flooded with liquid ammonia.

Now there were a dozen Starfish clustered on the far side of the trade lock. Their various appendages were locked on to bars and holds that had been erected to allow them to look down, or up, or over, into the trade lock.

And in the middle were three robots. They moved well, although now that Nbaro could see actual Starfish, she could see how very fluid they were, almost as if they were dancing to some shared rhythm.

And maybe they were.

Nbaro had her arms spread as well. After Morosini had admitted that she had a neural lace, implanted when she'd come aboard after the fight in City, she'd fought her feelings of betrayal by learning to use it. As Dorcas and Qaqqaq and Drake were all alive, she had a great deal for which she was thankful. She pushed her anger at being used away into a box, where perhaps she'd examine it another time, along with the various other horrors she carried inside her.

But she thought: *So he didn't trust me, and he could kill me any time.*

But ... this isn't the Orphanage. And Morosini isn't the Dominus.

So, instead of wasting time on feelings of betrayal, Nbaro spread her arms to summon the holographic screen of the chemical analysis robot. She felt like the priestess of an esoteric cult.

'Got a spike – there's the breakdown. Passing it to you.'

Dorcas whistled. 'Amazing. So that's an ammonia salt ... That's ...'

Yu stood behind her.

'It's like a DNA molecule,' he said. 'There's a fair amount of it. Made with boron. I'll need a day to process this.'

Qaqqaq said, 'I have the matching sound pattern. The whale song.'

Dorcas nodded. 'Note that we've now had the same chemical soup given to us with the same sound pattern three times.'

'I would interpret that as *hello*,' Qaqqaq said.

*

566

Sixteen hours of work – work in labs, and work on the robots, while damage control parties laboured throughout the greatship, repairing battle damage, and while cargo was shifted, because trade went on.

Thousands of plates of xenoglas passed into the cargo spaces, to be stacked carefully between hard rubber sheets cut to size, and the whole packed into recycle crates and webbed into the walls to make them safe.

Outside the hull of the makeshift human side of the station, a dozen small ship's boats, usually used for repair, were retrieving cargo – mostly gold bars – that floated in the debris field from the combat.

Trade went on.

Repair went on.

Funerals were held.

The wounded occupied every medical clamshell on the *Athens*, and a dozen techs struggled to preserve those who couldn't be accommodated – the more lightly wounded. Somewhere in the ship, the captured alien was being… healed? Examined? Interrogated? Even Dorcas didn't know.

The hangar bay was full of spacecraft under repair; almost every spacecraft on the ship had been out in the battle, and many were damaged. A dozen were destroyed.

Pisani had laid a trap for their ambushers, pretending ignorance while he used his spacecraft as invisible arms, using the little frigate with its massive ECM cloak as a decoy, so that the invisible enemy watched her as the greatship itself slipped in close to an asteroid and stayed there.

Hundreds, if not thousands, of passive sensors had gradually built up a picture of the presence of the Bubble ships in the system. And the broadcast frequency of the little spy devices had given them something to look for.

Despite which, the Bubbles had kept three ships hidden, and the result had been…

'It was precarious,' Morosini said. He was walking next to Nbaro. 'A damned close-run thing. Perhaps the closest-run thing I've ever seen.'

Nbaro was carrying the rebuilt robot starfish down to the landing barge.

'We lost the frigate,' she said.

'Yes,' Morosini said.

Nbaro nodded, and went aboard the landing boat.

And half an hour later, there she was, standing with her arms slightly spread, watching the screen. On a small inset, a full-sized Starfish extended a tentacle and linked with the robot.

This time, though, the robot passed a chemical the other way. Dorcas activated the 'whale song'.

The Starfish flashed.

It was not a reaction they'd ever seen – a little explosion of bioluminescence from the central core between the two sets of tentacles. All of the tentacles shot out briefly, as if stiffening.

And then two of the Starfish arms locked around the robot and cradled it for a moment.

There was another tentative link from a second Starfish, and then a third, and as the third link went home, Dorcas gave a cry of pure joy.

The computer screen between them read, 'GREETINGS.'

The end of *Artifact Space*.

The Arcana Imperii tales of the adventures of Marca, Thea, and their friends will be completed in the companion volume, *Deep Black*.